AN UNWELCOME GUEST

AT THE CASTLE gates, the keeper of the castle—one of Huntly's sons—stood with hands on hips, flanked by guards armed with swords.

"What sort of welcome is this for your sovereign queen?" I called out.

"No welcome at all, madam!" came the reply. "On the orders of my father, George Gordon, earl of Huntly and master of this castle, entry is denied."

His reply stunned me. This was treason. I was not about to tolerate defiance of my royal authority.

I called upon my guards to withdraw, heard them muttering, and glanced up to see the archers on the battlements

My decision came swiftly.

"Storm the castle," I ordered the men. "Seize the young Gordon who has refused to open the gates to his queen and sovereign and hang him from the battlements."

The captain looked surprised. "Hang him, my lady?"

It was harsh, but I knew that I had to establish my authority quickly and without wavering. "Hang him," I repeated.

We watched from a low rise as the men stormed the castle. It was over quickly.

"There is still time to change your mind," Seton whispered. "About young Gordon."

"I will not change it," I said, but I hid my trembling hands.

OTHER BOOKS BY CAROLYN MEYER

A YOUNG ROYALS BOOK

THE WILD QUEEN

The Days and Nights of
MARY, QUEEN OF SCOTS

Carolyn Meyer

HOUGHTON MIFFLIN HARCOURT
Boston New York

The Library of Congress has cataloged the hardcover edition as follows:
Meyer, Carolyn, 1935–
The wild queen / by Carolyn Meyer.
p. cm.
Summary: Convicted of plotting against her cousin Queen Elizabeth I
of England and awaiting execution in 1587, Mary Stuart,
queen of Scotland, recounts her life story, including becoming a
widow at age eighteen and her brutal campaign to regain
her sovereignty after being stripped of her throne.
1. Mary, Queen of Scots, 1542–1587—Juvenile fiction. [1. Mary, Queen
of Scots, 1542–1587—Fiction. 2. Kings, queens, rulers, etc.—Fiction. 3.
Scotland—History—Mary Stuart, 1542–1567—Fiction.] I. Title.
PZ7.M5685Whs 2012
[Fic]—dc23
2011027318

ISBN: 978-0-15-206188-3 hardcover
ISBN: 978-0-544-02219-5 paperback

Manufactured in the United States of America
DOC 10 9 8 7 6 5 4 3 2 1
4500411547

For Susan Wien Groene

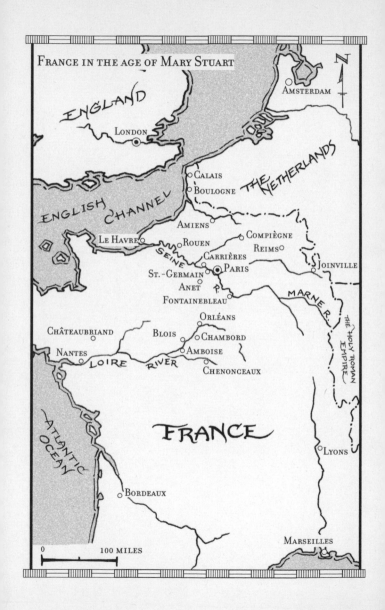

FRANCE IN THE AGE OF MARY STUART

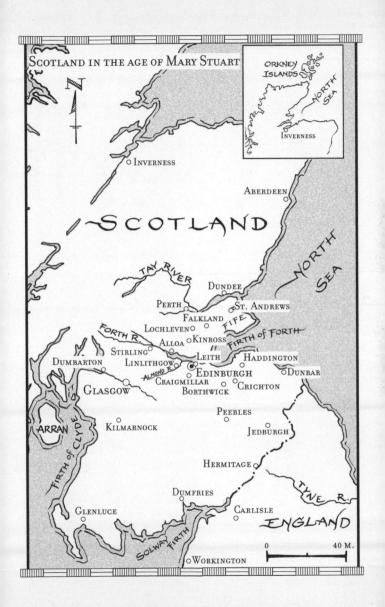

SCOTLAND IN THE AGE OF MARY STUART

ORKNEY ISLANDS

NORTH SEA

INVERNESS

INVERNESS

ABERDEEN

SCOTLAND

NORTH SEA

TAY RIVER

DUNDEE

PERTH

ST. ANDREWS

FALKLAND

LOCHLEVEN

FIFE

FORTH R.

ALLOA KINROSS

FIRTH OF FORTH

STIRLING

LEITH

HADDINGTON

DUMBARTON

LINLITHGOW

ALMOND R.

EDINBURGH

DUNBAR

CRAIGMILLAR

CRICHTON

GLASGOW

BORTHWICK

ARRAN

KILMARNOCK

PEEBLES

FIRTH OF CLYDE

JEDBURGH

HERMITAGE

TYNE R.

DUMFRIES

GLENLUCE

CARLISLE

ENGLAND

SOLWAY FIRTH

WORKINGTON

0   40 M.

I

At the Center of Disastrous Events

THE MIDNIGHT HOUR being well past, the day is now Wednesday, the eighth of February, 1587. The sound of hammering in the great hall of Fotheringhay Castle has not ceased. In a few hours the most important day of my life will dawn. I have written letters to those I love. My red petticoats and my black gown lie ready. My women, dressed in black, sit with me, and I ask one of them to read aloud the story of the good thief crucified beside our Lord.

When she has finished, the women are weeping. "It is true that the thief was a great sinner," I remind them, "but not so great as I have been."

I lie down and close my eyes, though I have no wish to sleep. Outside the door of my dreary chambers, the guards tramp back and forth, back and forth, stationed there lest I try to escape. They need not worry. My body remains here, but my thoughts have already flown away, back to my earliest beginnings and all that has followed.

CHAPTER I

Farewell, Scotland

I WAS THE CAUSE OF MY FATHER'S DEATH.

My father, King James V of Scotland, drew his last downhearted breath and died when I was just six days old. "He had not been ill," my mother explained to me years later, "but was deeply saddened by his defeat at the hands of the terrible English."

Henry VIII, king of "the terrible English," was determined to take over Scotland. In the bloody battles between the two countries that shared a border, the outnumbered Scots always got the worst of it. After my father's humiliating loss at his last battle, he took to his bed.

My father had badly wanted a son who could be the next king. When he married my mother, a French duchess, he already had three illegitimate sons, but by law a bastard could not inherit the Scottish throne. My mother bore him two more sons; both infants died. I was my father's last hope, and when the news reached him of the birth of a lass—a girl—that bitter disappointment was more than he could endure. Had I been a boy, he would still be alive. I have no doubt of that.

From my earliest days I have too often found myself at the center of disastrous events. That was the first. My birth killed my father, and I became queen of Scotland.

I was playing with my friends when the guard rushed in from the watchtower and announced to the queen, "My lady, the ships flying the colors of France are moving up the firth," and my mother burst into tears.

"Mither?" I jumped up from my game and ran to her. I touched her cheek. "Maman?" I asked, changing to French, my mother's language.

She dabbed at her eyes and tried to smile. "Shall we go see the ships, Marie?" Her voice trembled. She took my hand, calling to my friends, "Come, dear little Maries!" All four of my friends were named Mary, as I was, but my mother called us by the French version of the name—even Mary Fleming, who was pure Scots. To everyone, they were the Four Maries. Trailed by governesses who always seemed to move too slowly, we dashed eagerly out of the castle and peered down over the stone parapet to see for ourselves these foreign ships far below us. A strong north wind, chilly even in July, whipped our skirts and petticoats and blew our long hair into our faces.

"Look," my mother said, "the king of France has sent

his own royal galley for you. This shows how much he honors you."

"*Me?*" I gazed up at my mother, puzzled. It was the summer of 1548, a few months before my sixth birthday, and there was much I did not yet understand.

Maman sighed deeply and pulled me close. "The time has come to explain it to you, *ma chère* Marie."

At the age of nine months I was carried in a great procession to the royal chapel at Stirling Castle and crowned Mary Stuart, queen of Scotland, in a solemn ceremony. I remembered none of it, of course, but the event was described to me so often—how I reached out and tried to grasp the scepter; how I did not stop wailing throughout the ceremony—that in a few years I came to believe I actually *could* remember it all.

I was barely a year old when the Scottish Parliament signed an agreement with England declaring that when I reached the age of ten I would marry Prince Edward, the son of King Henry VIII. I was pledged to marry the "auld enemy"! That promise was not enough to satisfy King Henry. He demanded that I come to live in England until my marriage—for my safekeeping, he said. My mother refused to allow it. Fearing that King Henry would have me kidnapped, my mother moved me from Linlithgow Castle, where I was born, to Stirling Castle, far north of the border and better fortified against an English attack. But still my mother did not feel easy. We moved again, to an even more remote castle.

While we were there, news came from England that Henry VIII had died. Nine-year-old Edward was the new king. I was four.

"I am certain it is safe now," said my mother. "We can go home to Stirling."

But she was wrong. The English continued their attacks along the border. They mowed down ten thousand Scots in the Battle of Pinkie Cleugh and began the march to Stirling. In the dead of night my mother and I were bundled onto a litter and carried to an Augustinian priory on a quiet lake far from the smoke and noise of battle. Within a few days the Four Maries and their mothers joined us on the island of Inchmahome. I would have happily stayed on that pretty island, unaware of the bloody fighting that still raged, chasing butterflies, gathering eggs from the hens' nests, and devouring the rich buns the monks baked for us every morning.

My mother now made a decision that would determine the course of my life: Instead of marrying Edward, the new king of England, I would marry the future king of France. But the future had its beginning in the present. "Until you are old enough for marriage, you will live at the French court and learn their language and their ways," said my mother. "Someday the king's son, the little dauphin, will become king, and you will be queen of France."

"What is the laddie called?" I asked—my first question.

"His name is François de Valois. He is four years old, a little younger than you."

"You are coming too, are you not, Maman?" I asked.

"*Non,* Marie," she said. "I must stay here. But your nurse and your governess will go with you, and Lord Erskine and Lord Livingston as your guardians, and the Four Maries, and your three Stuart half brothers, and many others who know and love you. When you arrive in France you will have your grandparents and your uncles to look after you, and the king of France and his children will welcome you into their family. You will not be lonely, Marie—I promise."

"Then you will come later," I insisted stubbornly.

"*Oui,* my darling child," she said, smiling. "Later."

Her smile was a lie. I sensed the tears behind it, ready to pour again at any moment. I knew without asking that once I left Scotland, my life would change. I could not possibly imagine how much.

<hr />

To prepare for my departure for France, we moved again, this time to Dumbarton Castle, in the far west of Scotland. The ancient fortress was built high on a rocky mound where winds howled and rains lashed, and no English soldier would dare scale the steep rock face that jutted straight up from the water and overlooked the Firth of Clyde, where the river joined the sea. To avoid the English ships, the French fleet had taken a long and dangerous route to reach me, sailing around the northern end of Scotland before heading southward to Dumbarton.

I hated to see my mother weep, but on the day those French ships appeared in the firth, I was too filled with excitement to be overly concerned. The king of France had sent his ships to fetch me! I was going to marry the king's son, and one day I would be the queen of France! I loved the sound of that: *queen of France.* Even my mother did not have such a splendid title. While my father was alive, she had been titled the queen consort of Scots. Now she was known as the queen mother, meaning that her husband, the king, was dead and she was in charge of things in the kingdom until I, her child, was old enough to rule as queen of Scots.

My own little court was made up of the Four Maries, my father's three bastard sons, and a number of others. My nurse, Janeen Sinclair, would accompany me, as would my governess, Lady Janet Fleming, Mary Fleming's mother. Mary Livingston, the daughter of Lord Livingston, one of my guardians, was in my party as well. Mary Seton and Mary Beaton were the other two Maries, and Seton's younger brother Robbie was coming too.

The Marie dearest to me was Mary Fleming. Because of her reddish curls and mischievous smile, we called her La Flamin. A little older than I and "irrepressible," in my mother's opinion, La Flamin made it her duty to keep me informed of what was really going on. It did not occur to me that she might have been inventing some of her stories, or at least embellishing them a little. Her father had been killed at the Battle of Pinkie Cleugh.

"You and I had the same grandfather, you know," she told me proudly. "King James the Fourth."

"I do know that," I said, not wanting her to think I was

ignorant, but in fact I was not sure I *did* know. "He was killed in battle too," I said, eager to show off my knowledge of Scots history. "Fighting against the English at Flodden Field."

"He was married to Queen Margaret, so he couldn't marry my grandmother," added Mary Fleming with a deep sigh. "And so my mother is a bastard."

"Pity," I said, nodding sympathetically. Queen Margaret was *my* grandmother. It was indeed unfortunate that a person born out of wedlock could not inherit titles and property—like my three older Stuart half brothers. "But you and I are still cousins, are we not?"

"Aye, of course! But I am pure Scots on both sides of my family," she boasted, tossing those red curls. "The other Maries have Scottish fathers and French mothers, like you. When Marie of Guise came to Scotland to marry your father, the others came with her as her ladies in waiting."

"I know that too," I said.

"And did you know that your father had another wife, before your mother?"

Sometimes I had to pretend I knew more than I did; this time I did not. "Her name was Madeleine," I said, "and she was the daughter of the previous king of France. She was sixteen when she came here to marry my father, and within forty days she was dead of a fever, poor thing. They blamed it on the Scottish air."

"The air in France is said to be much more pleasant," said La Flamin helpfully.

"My mother's first husband, the duke of Longueville,

died as well, when she was expecting her second child. Poor Mither! That baby died when he was only four months old. But her older boy still lives in France. I suppose I will meet him when I go there."

"That must have been so sad!" Mary Fleming said, her brow furrowed sorrowfully. "And then your mother, the duchess, received a proposal of marriage." She leaned toward me eagerly and took my hand in both of hers. "My mother told me about it. Do you know who her suitor was?"

"My father? The king of Scotland?" I hoped I was right. I did not like La Flamin knowing more than I did about my own family, even if she was my dearest friend.

"No!" she cried. "You are wrong! He was a king, it is true, but not of Scotland!" Mary Fleming was bursting with her triumph in our storytelling. "It was Henry the Eighth of England!"

"That horrible man wanted to marry Mither?" I was so shocked by that bit of information that I flung Mary's hand away. Why had my mother never told me this?

"Aye, but she refused him! My mother knew all about it!" La Flamin struck a pose that she considered queenly. "This is what Marie of Guise said: 'I may be a big woman, but I have a very little neck.' King Henry had had his second wife, Anne Boleyn, beheaded, you see, and before the swordsman cut off her head, Queen Anne said, 'I will be easy to kill, for my neck is little.' Your mother had heard that story, and she was not about to have *her* head cut off."

"Then I thank a gracious God that she refused him and

I did not have Henry the Eighth for a father!" I exclaimed. "How horrible to have one's head cut off!"

My friend agreed that it was horrible. "But still you had him for a great-uncle, you know. King Henry married three more times before he died. Six wives all told!" she went on, sure of my interest. "He divorced two of his wives and had two beheaded. One died—that was Edward's mother—and one outlived him. I would never have married that dreadful man—would you?"

I shuddered at the thought. "Or his son either," I added. "A wicked lot, the English."

My cousin clearly enjoyed shocking me with her grisly tale. I shivered at my mother's good fortune in escaping the clutches of the evil King Henry. I did not stop to wonder then how she must have felt when she left France for Scotland, a country she had never seen, to marry a man she had never met, leaving behind her little son without knowing when she would be with him again.

CHAPTER 2

Storms at Sea

FOR TWO DAYS after the arrival of the French ships, a small army of servants bustled around my apartments at Dumbarton, packing my possessions in brass-bound leather trunks under the watchful eye of my mother's friend Lady Seton. Some trunks were filled with gowns of silk and velvet trimmed with lace and gold braid and embroidered with sparkling jewels. Others were stuffed with dainty gloves and little slippers and underthings. I amused myself by counting the trunks as the servants struggled to carry them down the steep, narrow steps to the royal galley tied up at the pier. I could not yet count past twenty, and there were still more to come.

My mother fretted that my finery would not be fine enough for the French court. "The French have a different idea of fashion," she said, sighing as she watched the trunks being carried off. "But your grandmother will see that you are given many new clothes when you arrive." Then, as happened often during those last few days, tears began to slide down her soft cheeks. "Oh, my sweet Marie, you will have so much to learn!" she cried, brushing away the tears. She took me on her lap and kissed me, murmuring endearments in French, which I understood well enough, though I always replied in Scots. "You must learn to speak French, *ma chère*," she said softly, pushing strands of hair away from my face. "No one in France understands the Scots language."

"Then I shall speak Scots with the Four Maries," I declared.

"What a stubborn child you are," she said fondly. "Besides that, you are accustomed to being the sole object of all our attention. Now you will join a family—the dauphin and his two sisters—and you must remember that you are no longer the most important person in the room."

"But I am the queen of Scotland!" I exclaimed, surprised and a little put off by what I had just been told.

"Yes, dear child, you are the queen of Scotland, but you are going to live in the French court. The dauphin outranks you. Fortunately, you are young, and I have no doubt you will learn quickly."

While the French ships were being provisioned for the journey, my mother arranged farewell banquets in my honor and invited the Scottish lords and ladies and the landowning lairds. Royal banquets were usually merry affairs, but young as I was, I sensed the sadness rippling like an underground stream beneath the music and dancing and feasting. Though everyone rejoiced that I was going off to marry the future king of France, I would be living far, far away, and I had no idea when I would see Scotland—or my dear mother—again. I tried not to think about that.

The day came to say goodbye: the twenty-ninth of July in the year 1548. My mother and I clung to one another and felt our hearts breaking, though I had been taught that as a queen, I must not give way to displays of emotion. "Your subjects do not wish to see your nose dripping and your eyes red with weeping," my mother had told me over and over. "It is your duty as queen to appear calm and steadfast, no matter what you may feel."

On the occasion of my leave-taking, I tried to follow her instructions but failed entirely. The French ambassador, sent by the king to escort me on my journey, attempted— without success—to lure me away from my mother. "Go, dearest child," my mother said at last, her voice thick with tears. "I shall remain on the parapet and watch you from here."

Finally my guardian Lord Erskine swept me up in his arms and began the long descent down the steep steps cut into the rock to the waiting ships below. I insisted that he put me down at once. "I am the queen," I lectured him, "and I do not wish to be carried like an infant. I shall walk to the ship myself."

From somewhere below me on the rough path, Lady Fleming complained that her shoes were being ruined, that they were not made for climbing mountains, and I called down to her, "Lady Fleming, we are not *climbing* a mountain, we are *going down!*" That only made her more irritable.

Musicians played lighthearted tunes, but once my companions and I were taken aboard the ships, they turned to something slow and serious. A priest gave a final blessing to the passengers, the crew, and the royal ship itself, and every one of us prayed for a safe journey. Dozens of galley prisoners chained below deck bent to the oars and rowed the royal ship away from the shore, and the crowd that had gathered high above us on the parapet cheered, their shouts carried on the wind. My mother waved her handkerchief. As the ship moved through the Firth of Clyde, my companions and I stood on the deck and watched until Dumbarton Castle, looming remote and forbidding on its great rock, was far behind us. We could no longer make out the tiny figures on the parapet, though I was sure I could still see my mother's handkerchief fluttering bravely. Then that, too, disappeared.

When my friends were done sniffling and wiping their noses over the sadness of leaving their families behind, we set out to explore the ship. I found my quarters and thought them too small, and I protested that I should be given a much bigger cabin. Then my half brother James, who was seventeen and on his way to France to continue his religious studies and who had traveled there once before, explained, "We are truly going to sea, dear Mary, and this is how seafarers live. Even queens must travel this way." So I decided that my tiny cabin was, indeed, quite large enough after all.

As a child, I was always full of energy and high spirits, and besides, my dearest friends were with me, and I was sure we would have nothing but happy times during our voyage. Neither I nor any of the Four Maries had been to sea, and so we had no idea of what lay ahead of us. At that hour we were very pleased with this grand new adventure, but our enjoyment was not to last.

We passed the Isle of Arran, its rugged mountains shrouded in mist, and were about to enter the open sea. But Captain Villegagnon observed the sky rapidly filling with black clouds and ordered the ships to heave to just as a great ocean storm roared down on us. The royal galley pitched and rolled in the angry waves, and a gale blew so hard across the deck that I could scarcely stand upright. Hours stretched into days, and still the storm punished us. My three half brothers organized games of handy-dandy and hide-fox-and-all-after to amuse the children. But eventually they as well as the rest of the passengers, young and old, grew sick and listless; they could not bear the sight of food and spent their time clutching the rails of the galley. Day after day passed in misery while the captain waited for the storm to wear itself out and the benevolent west winds to rise and carry us on.

"When will the winds be right?" I asked the captain, and he explained wearily that it was all in God's hands.

Lady Fleming was not willing to wait for God and made a great fuss to the captain, demanding to be put ashore. "It is utter nonsense to have us all imprisoned on this wretched ship and going nowhere!" she complained. "I shall die if I cannot go ashore and recover myself."

But Captain Villegagnon refused to yield to her. "You are not going to shore but to France," he said curtly. "If that does not please you, madame, you have my permission to drown."

Lady Fleming let out a sharp little cry and closed herself in her cabin and did not come out again for at least half a day; her usually rosy complexion seemed quite green when she eventually reappeared.

On the tenth day the clouds broke. The captain ordered the sails raised and the prisoners on the oars to row. The royal galley began to plow through the still towering waves, heading westward into the Irish Sea, passing by the Isle of Man and then going south along the coast of Wales. My friends never ceased to be plagued with seasickness and whimpered piteously. I was not afflicted and could not understand why they were so distressed.

Within a day the storm had caught up with us. Once more the royal galley bobbed like a cork on the white-tipped waves, and the rudder was smashed. While the men struggled to repair it, the ship began to roll from side to side so violently that objects slid back and forth across the deck. I had a favorite doll I called Wee Mary—I could not think of any other name for her—and she was swept overboard as I watched helplessly. For the first time since we'd sailed from Dumbarton I was truly upset, and I sobbed until Lady Fleming promised to find me another, though I knew no new doll would be nearly as pretty as Wee Mary.

My oldest brother, James, was bent over the captain's chart table, studying our course and reporting on the progress of our voyage to anyone who cared to listen. The French fleet rounded Cornwall and entered the English Channel, still with no relief from the battering sea. Then, just as everyone had begun to think that we might never arrive, that we were doomed to endure calamity after calamity, land was sighted.

"France! France!" rejoiced the passengers, though it was said weakly by those suffering from a delicate stomach. We had been on the open sea for eighteen days, twice as long as expected.

Nearly every citizen of the little fishing village where we landed turned out to welcome the king's galley. The deck had heaved beneath us for so long that our legs wobbled as we left the ship and came ashore. *"Vive la petite reine écossaise!"* someone shouted. "Long live the little Scottish queen!" Others joined in. The cheering crowd accompanied us in a joyful procession to a nearby town, where the local lord received me at the gates with great ceremony. I understood hardly a word of what he said—it was all in French—but I believe it included "welcome" and "safe arrival." I said, *"Merci"*—thank you—and smiled.

But then: trouble. As our mounted guards crossed the drawbridge, it collapsed, carrying men and horses into the moat below, where some surely drowned and others were crushed beneath their mounts. Cries of "Treachery!" went up from the Scots, causing the French lord to shout insults back at them.

Lady Fleming rushed to assure herself that I was unhurt. "It was just an unfortunate accident," she said soothingly, for I was badly frightened and had begun to weep. "No one meant us any harm."

Lord Livingston was not convinced. "Perfidious French!" my guardian muttered darkly. "I have never trusted them, and I do not trust them now!"

Once calm had been restored and our safety guaranteed, we entered the town by a different gate and found our way to the church. A Te Deum was sung in thanksgiving for my safe arrival. All seemed peaceful again, but I still felt shaken. I had thought everything would go perfectly, and it had not. For the first time since I left Scotland, I wished desperately that my mother were there to comfort me and reassure me that all would indeed be well.

CHAPTER 3

Grand-Mère Antoinette

AFTER SEVERAL DAYS OF REST—I was not in the least tired, but the others seemed exhausted—we resumed our journey by land. We were bound for the palace of Saint-Germain-en-Laye, where the children of the king and queen were presently residing. "No doubt to escape the heat of Paris," Mary Seton explained. "My mother told me that Paris is very hot in summer. Much hotter than Scotland."

With leather trunks piled on wooden carts, the ladies carried in litters, and the gentlemen mounted on horseback, we traveled first to Nantes, a city at the mouth of the River Loire. It was quite a long procession, several hundred people, and it attracted a lot of attention. In every village through which we passed, I was received with great ceremony and whatever festivities had been arranged. As a mark of respect for me, the doors of the local prison were thrown open by order of the king and the prisoners released.

"Robbers too?" I asked Lord Livingston, who nodded. "And murderers?"

"Aye, and every kind of villain. It is the custom of the French, I am told. We Scots are more likely to hang a blackguard than let him walk away a free man."

Each night we stopped at a convent or at a château, the French word for "palace," I learned. In Nantes we boarded a luxurious riverboat—*bateau de rivière*—that moved smoothly upriver, passing densely wooded forests, handsome châteaux, and neat little villages. If all of France was as beautiful as this lovely river valley, so different from the ruggedness of my homeland, I would surely be proud to be its queen.

"How delightful to be on a pretty boat on such a pretty river with no huge waves trying to drown us!" remarked Lady Fleming, who had quickly recovered herself and was again in bright spirits. All agreed that traveling by *bateau de rivière* was much superior to being blown about at sea, and we cheerfully returned to the singing and dancing and games we enjoyed. There seemed to be no rush to reach Saint-Germain.

But our pleasure came to a quick end when, one by one, the gentlemen in my company began to fall desperately ill. The first was Lord Erskine, followed within hours by Lord Livingston. Both of my guardians were much too ill to go ashore, and though physicians came aboard the riverboat to bleed the patients, they suffered greatly, raving from fevers and shivering, though the day was hot. No one knew the cause of the illness. Poor Mary Livingston sat by her father's bedside hour after hour while he hovered between life and death. All those on board prayed for his recovery. We also prayed that we might be spared the same unhappy fate.

Not all prayers were answered. Next Mary Seton's younger brother Robbie was stricken. After one feverish day and night he was dead. Mary Seton was inconsolable. Little Robbie's body was carried to a nearby church, Mass was sung for the peace of his young soul, and he was buried in a grave far from home. We shed tears for Robbie, a bonnie lad everyone had dearly cherished. This was the closest I had ever been to the death of someone I loved, and I was deeply shaken by the experience.

Downcast, we continued our journey, praying that no one else would be taken from us. For some reason, all the women and girls in my party were spared, but my two guardians as well as several other men still languished. Perhaps it was God's mercy that saved us. Or perhaps, as my nurse, Sinclair, suggested, it was because we are the hardier sex.

Despite these early trials, I eagerly looked forward to our arrival in Tours, where I was to meet my grandmother Antoinette, duchess of Guise, and my grandfather Claude, duke of Joinville. As the boat nosed close to the dock, Mary Fleming was first to see them. "Look," she said, pointing, "I think those old people are your grandparents. Shall we wave to them?"

I knew at once that the stately female figure, elegantly

dressed and attended by liveried servants, was my grandmother. Beside her, my grandfather stood straight as a ship's
mast. I hesitated, not sure what was the proper thing to do,
but La Flamin was already leaning over the rail and waving,
first one hand, then the other, then both, to attract their
attention.

Musicians played, and servants helped my grandparents
to board the riverboat. My grandmother took a long moment to look over the group eagerly waiting to greet them,
including me and the Four Maries. *Why is she frowning?* I
wondered, but as I stepped forward, my grandmother's
frown melted into a smile. She swept me into her embrace
while my grandfather beamed.

Both grandparents spoke to me rapidly in French, and I
judged from the tone of their voices as well as their expressions and gestures that they were very happy to see me, but
I understood only a bit of what they actually said. "*Bonjour,*
Grand-Mère. *Bonjour,* Grand-Père," I murmured and repeated the greeting I had practiced: *"Je suis très heureuse de vous
voir."* I hoped it meant "I am very happy to see you," though
I was not sure if I had gotten it right.

"Non, non, non!" Grand-Mère frowned again. She carefully
repeated my words, but somehow they sounded different
on her lips. Grand-Père gently tugged her sleeve, gesturing
that she must proceed slowly.

Grand-Mère turned her attention to the Four Maries,
who were hovering nearby, staring wide-eyed at my regal
grandparents. Grand-Mère's frown deepened. She spoke to
each girl as she was presented. Only Mary Fleming stepped

forward boldly and made a deep *révérence,* bending her knees and bowing her head; I cannot think how she learned it, as it was not then the custom in Scotland.

The other three Maries anxiously turned their eyes toward me. I did not know what to say, but Grand-Père came to the rescue, gallantly bowing to each of my friends and greeting her by name. "*Bonjour,* Mademoiselle Marie!" They rewarded him with grateful smiles.

Once my grandparents' entourage and their baggage had been brought aboard, our river journey continued on to Orléans. Grand-Mère devoted herself to my wardrobe, my language, and my habits. She decreed that I must forgo my usual breakfast of oat porridge with fresh cream, which had been prepared for me every morning of my life by Sinclair, and ordered that I have hot milk and a delicate pastry instead. We spent hours going through my leather trunks, my servants unpacking them one by one while my grandmother critically inspected each item.

"Those things that you will be allowed to keep are to be put here," she said, pointing to a small table on her right, "and the rest, which will be given away, over here." A much larger table on the left was for the discards. Some gowns were not even deemed fit to try on. "*À gauche!*" she would announce haughtily. "To the left!"

Most of the gowns that were sent to the left were not poorly made; they were merely not equal to the standards of fashion she had for an almost-six-year-old queen. Most of my shoes she judged sturdy but too clumsy, and away they went.

"You are already growing tall, *ma chère* Marie. Your uncles, like your dear *maman,* are all very tall. Like your *grand-père,*" she added, nodding toward my grandfather, who beamed proudly as he watched the proceedings. "The child is a Guise, that much is plain to see," Grand-Mère liked to point out to anyone who would listen.

She loved to compare me to my mother, how my auburn hair was like my mother's, my complexion delicate and white like hers. My face was well formed, she decided, adding thoughtfully, "but your chin *is* a trifle long. Perhaps I should not tell you this, *ma chère* Marie, for I do not want it to turn your head, but I believe you will someday be a great beauty—perhaps even greater than your *maman.* And that is saying a good deal."

During my first weeks in France I understood scarcely anything Grand-Mère said and relied mostly on her eloquent gestures. But I did have what my tutors called a good ear, and soon I was picking up much of what was said, though I was much slower in learning to speak it.

It was obvious that my grandmother was not favorably impressed by the Four Maries. She shocked me by speaking of them as *les petites sauvages*—"the little savages." "They are ill-looking and certainly not even as clean as they might be," she complained to Grand-Père, who waved away her complaints.

"They are children," he replied. "And they are beautiful, all of them."

Grand-Père must have sensed that I was troubled, for he did his best to comfort me with gestures and simple words. I believed he was trying to convey to me that my grandmother had strong opinions, and I must not let it bother me.

❧

When the riverboat reached the city of Orléans, our trunks were again loaded onto wooden carts for the last part of the journey. There were not as many trunks, I noticed (we were counting them again, and I enjoyed showing off to my friends that I could now do it in French: *un, deux, trois, quatre* . . .). The silk and velvet gowns that my grandmother had decided were not suitable would be delivered to a convent where one of my Guise aunts was the abbess. Grand-Mère promised that the nuns would salvage what they could and make them into altar hangings, and the plain woolen dresses I wore for every day would be distributed to the deserving poor. Not many of my gowns had survived Grand-Mère's critical eye.

Only one outfit became a source of real disagreement between us: the furs and leathers that made up the traditional dress of the Lowland Scots. I stubbornly refused to part with them.

"Surely you do not want to keep them, Marie," said Grand-Mère with a little grimace.

"*Oui!*" I cried. "*Je vous en prie!* I beg you!" I had learned enough French to plead with her.

She sniffed, pointed to her nose, made a face, and turned away. The costume did have a gamy odor, I realized, but I adored this outfit. I took my pleas to Grand-Père, explain-

ing that even if I never wore it again, it was my most important possession.

Grand-Père listened sympathetically. *"Je comprends, ma
petite,"* he said. "I will speak to her."

At last Grand-Mère gave in. She ordered the furs and
leather packed in a separate trunk, and I watched closely
until I was certain that the trunk with my Scottish costume
would indeed be going with me and not to an orphanage—
or worse.

"Do not worry, *ma chère,"* my grandmother said as the
last of the trunks were tied to the baggage carts. "You will
have everything waiting for you when you reach your
new home."

My new home! If I had been a little older, I might have
felt uneasy, perhaps even fearful of what this could mean.
But I was not yet six years old, I was the queen of Scots, and
everywhere I went, I was greeted with cheering crowds
and music and adoring children presenting gifts. It was the
kind of welcome I had come to expect, and I delighted in it.

CHAPTER 4

Madame de Poitiers

I HAD LEFT Scotland in summer, traveled for two months by royal galley, litter, and riverboat, and finally in autumn arrived at Carrières-sur-Seine, a huge old fortress that reminded me of the castles in my homeland. Bands played, flags fluttered, and I was welcomed with pomp and ceremony. Lord Livingston, now somewhat recovered from his illness, explained that I would be staying here while one of the other châteaux was being prepared, the cleaning that always preceded the arrival of the royal family.

The welcoming ceremonies, so enchanting at first, had grown quite tiresome. I was impatient to meet the family of which I would become a part—King Henri II and Queen Catherine; their son, François; and his sisters. However, at Carrières I was not presented to the queen, as I had expected to be, but to Diane de Poitiers, duchess of Valentinois, a handsome older woman who seemed to be in charge of everything. *Who is she?* I wondered.

"I am a great friend of King Henri," the duchess said, as though she had guessed my question. She spoke to me in slow, careful French that I was able to understand, at least in a general kind of way. "The king is in Italy and regrets that he cannot be here to greet you. He has asked me to see that you are made welcome and comfortable."

The duchess then presented Princesse Élisabeth, who made a graceful *révérence*. I judged her to be at least two years younger than I. And then I met the dauphin, François, the boy I would someday marry.

Prodded by Madame de Poitiers, the dauphin stepped forward. I knew that he was more than a year younger than I—he would not be five years old until January; my mother had told me that much—but I had not expected him to be quite so small. He was thin and pale, and his eyes were listless and dull. My three older Stuart half brothers were all big, strapping lads, but I did not think that this little fellow would ever grow to be so large and muscular. His nurse was continually wiping his dripping nose.

The dauphin bowed deeply and stammered a little speech of welcome in a high-pitched voice. I felt sorry for him. But when he smiled at me, his eyes suddenly came to life, and his whole face changed. I believed his words were heartfelt, and his smile seemed true and genuine. I attempted to respond to him in French, resorting to Scots when the French words failed me. The dauphin seemed pleased by my efforts, crude as they must have sounded to his ear.

"W-w-we shall soon become good friends, I am sure," said François.

I understood that perfectly and would have been happy to try to converse with him, but Madame de Poitiers instructed his nurse to lead him away. Another nurse appeared, carrying a plump and smiling baby. This was Princesse Claude.

Only then did I notice the rather plain woman who had been sitting quietly nearby while the royal children were being presented. Princesse Claude reached out her chubby arms to this woman, who kissed the infant and returned her to the nurse.

"I am Queen Catherine," said the woman as she rose to leave. "You are welcome here, Queen Marie," she said, and walked away without waiting for my slow response. I had no experience in acknowledging queens. Everyone had always acknowledged *me*.

"Madame Marie," said the duchess after the queen had gone, "it is my duty to inform you of the rules of precedence, as ordered by His Majesty King Henri." François, as dauphin, would take precedence over me, while I, a crowned queen, would take precedence over François's younger sisters, the two princesses, Élisabeth and Claude. These were rules that I had never actually had to think about—who was first to enter a room, who was seated first, who was served first at a banquet, who left first. Except for the first six days of my life, I had always been a queen, and so I was always first. I had never thought of the arrangement being any other way. Now I understood what my mother meant when she had warned me that I would no longer be the most important person in the room.

"It is the king's desire that you share lodgings with Princesse Élisabeth," continued Madame de Poitiers.

Share lodgings? I had never shared lodgings with anyone. I was surprised but said nothing. Perhaps someday this young girl and I would become great friends.

That was only the beginning of the changes to which I now found myself subjected. The hardest was the departure of the Four Maries. During the first weeks in France, my friends went everywhere that I did, and their company helped me adjust to all the strangeness of my new circumstances. Then quite suddenly they were gone, sent to a convent to learn French and be schooled in the ways of the French court. I burst into tears when I found out—tears that distressed little Élisabeth but left Madame de Poitiers unmoved.

"It is feared that you will not learn to speak French well if your friends remain here and you are continually tempted to converse with them in your native tongue."

The duchess left me to deal with my misery alone.

I had barely learned my way around the château at Carrières-sur-Seine when the entire court moved to Saint-Germain-en-Laye. "Papa's favorite château," Élisabeth told me. During the move—it was not far, and within half a day we were settling in—I discovered that I had been separated not only from the Four Maries but from nearly all the Scots who had accompanied me. Lord-Keeper Livingston, as my guardian was titled, stayed on, but now that Lord Erskine had recovered from his severe illness, he and most of the other gentlemen in my suite were on their way back to Scotland. My half brothers Robert and John Stuart went with them, though James stayed in France to study. We went to see them off, and Lady Fleming remarked that unlike the French, our men went about gripping the hilts of their swords. "Our loyal Scots are always on guard, as though they expect to be attacked at any time. Doubtless, they are relieved to go home to Scotland."

Fortunately, Lady Fleming remained with me as my governess, and Sinclair stayed on as my nurse.

Sinclair seemed to have as much trouble as I did deciphering this distinctly new way of life. I missed the oat porridge that she had always fixed for my breakfast, and she curled her lip at the broth she was given in the servants' hall.

"Aye, they want to get rid of me too," she complained. We were whispering in Scots, though I had been warned by Madame de Poitiers that Sinclair too would be sent away if we persisted. "These French hate the sound of our auld tongue. I heard one of their fancy gentlemen say that he could scarce believe such ugly sounds could come from such a pretty little mouth like yours."

Sinclair was mending one of her thick woolen stockings, and she bit the thread angrily. "Seems to me like these folks want to drain every drop of Scots blood from you and replace it with French," grumbled my nurse, who never ran out of complaints. She yearned for "just a crumb of oatcake and a tasty bite of salmon from our own fresh rivers," she said every time it came to mind, which was often. "And ne'er mind that you're first and foremost the queen of the Scots and will someday come back to your own country to rule your own people, God be willing."

"I am to be queen of France, Sinclair, and I shall rule Scotland from Paris. But," I added wistfully, for I often felt homesick, "no doubt I shall be able to visit whenever I please."

⚜

I missed the Four Maries, but I did not have time to dwell on their absence. Soon after I arrived at Saint-Germain, my grandparents brought my half brother François, duke of Longueville, for a visit. He was the son my mother had had to leave behind when she left France for Scotland to marry my father. The duke, who had inherited his father's title, was now fourteen, tall and auburn-haired. I thought him quite handsome.

"You are so like our mother!" he exclaimed at our first meeting, though how he knew that I cannot say, as he had been just three years old when he had last seen her.

"And so are you!" I replied.

Our grandmother smiled and nodded. "You are all Guises," she said, dabbing at the tears that sprang to her eyes.

François wanted to hear everything I could think to tell him about our mother, and he asked me many questions that I tried hard to answer.

"Did she sing to you?" he asked. "Before you went to sleep at night?"

"She did! Mither has a lovely voice. I can sing the tune but not the words. *Lu lu la, lu lu lala lu,*" I sang.

"I remember, I remember!" he cried, and began to weep softly. *"Venez rêves, venez à mon enfant."*

Before he left that day, my brother kissed my hand and told me I was as beautiful as his memory of our mother and he was sure we would spend many happy hours together from that day on.

I now belonged to the royal nursery. The king had decided that I must be educated with the royal children, including the dauphin. That seemed a surprise to many—especially Lord and Lady Humières, who supervised the nursery (though it was Madame de Poitiers who told them, and everyone else, what to do, claiming she had received her authority from the king). It fell to Lord and Lady Humières to make certain that, from the time I opened my eyes in the morning until the moment I closed them at night, I heard nothing but French. They were pleased when I was able to reply in complete French sentences.

I was delighted with my new "sister" Princesse Élisabeth, probably because she seemed delighted with *me*. The infant Princesse Claude was still at least a year or two away from joining in our conversations and little games. The dauphin, François, was closest to me in age, so naturally I spent a great deal of time with him. He became the one who answered my many questions.

"Who is Madame de Poitiers?" I asked one day when we

were not attending to our lessons, and Lord and Lady Humières had left us a little time to ourselves. "Why is she with us so much more than your mother, the queen?"

"She is my father's mistress," he replied with a shrug. "She wants to make sure we are properly trained in the ways of the court."

I nodded, having only a vague idea of what a mistress was. Later I overheard Sinclair muttering to Lady Fleming on this very subject. Neither my nurse nor my governess liked Madame de Poitiers. In truth, they could not abide her.

"It is beyond understanding that the queen puts up with that woman," said Lady Fleming. "The king must be in her thrall."

"I've heard all about it in the kitchens," said my nurse with a snort; she always enjoyed a bit of gossip with her meal of bread and sausage. "King Henri has been Madame de Poitiers's lover since he was a young lad and she old enough to be his *mither*," Sinclair said disapprovingly. "And poor Catherine de Médicis, coming here from Italy to marry him when she was a lass of fourteen and him not wanting much to do with her in the way of husband and wife. Married eight years and not a single bairn! At last God showed His mercy to that good woman, and she brought forth the little dauphin, someday to be the husband of our own darling Mary!"

"Now the queen is about to give the king a fourth child," Lady Fleming pointed out. "Another for Madame de Poitiers to rule."

"Aye, and how hard it must surely be on Queen Catherine, her rival running the royal nursery with an iron fist like she does. Nobody can do anything regarding the queen's children without Madame's say-so."

"I wonder if it is so when the king is here," mused Lady Fleming. "He is expected in the next week or two, I hear. I look forward to meeting him, as I am sure you do as well."

"Not much," said Sinclair sourly. "But we shall see what we shall see."

CHAPTER 5

The Dauphin

"*JOYEUX ANNIVERSAIRE,* Madame Marie," Madame de Poitiers caroled cheerily.

It was the eighth of December, my sixth birthday as well as the Feast of the Immaculate Conception of the Virgin Mary. The duchess had arranged for a special celebration for me.

After Mass in the royal chapel, the king's children and the children of the court gathered in the nursery. My French half brother, François de Longueville, came, accompanied by my grandparents. Servants carried in platters of cakes and pastries. Minstrels entertained us with shawm, recorder, sackbut, and hurdy-gurdy. Jugglers and acrobats performed. Queen Catherine, heavy with child, was on hand, observing quietly.

Madame de Poitiers had chosen this as the perfect occasion for me to have my first dance in public with the dauphin. "Soon you will be expected to dance together at the wedding of your uncle François, duke of Aumale, to the duchess Anne d'Este," she said. "Great royalty as well as the highest nobility from all over Europe will be watching." She must have seen how this unnerved me, but she smiled and added, "I am confident that you will perform faultlessly, Madame Marie."

For several weeks, the dancing master had been instructing the dauphin and me on the pavane, a simple dance with long gliding steps and a few *révérences* and bows. But Madame de Poitiers wanted us to dance the much more complicated courante.

"Queen Catherine brought the courante to the French court from the Italian court of the Medicis," Madame de Poitiers told me. "It will be sure to please her."

The steps of the courante were not difficult—two single steps and a double to the left, a little skip followed by the same steps to the right—but there were gestures and poses meant to accompany each step. "The gestures are the signs of love," our dancing master explained. We were supposed to pretend that François was courting me; I was to refuse his advances until at last I feigned acceptance and we danced off together. We had practiced this for days, but we had not yet learned the gestures to the dancing master's satisfaction. Now, with the queen herself and members of the court all watching intently, we were expected to perform it.

I had dreaded this. It was not how I wished to celebrate my birthday. I looked to Lady Fleming for a way out. My governess, who had been supervising my dancing practice, glared at Madame de Poitiers—no one could fail to see the look of disdain that passed between them—but she did not argue with her. "You can do it, Marie," said Lady Fleming. "It will be a good rehearsal."

At a sign from Madame de Poitiers, the musicians began to play. I did not recognize the tune. Surely it was not the same as the music played at our practice—this was so much faster! Poor little François looked frightened half to death. "Be brave," I whispered to him as we took our places. He proceeded to stumble about clumsily while I urgently whispered instructions: "Whenever I turn my back, you must kneel and pretend to implore me."

"Implore you?" he asked, bewildered.

"Beg me!" I ordered. It would have been so much easier if our roles were reversed!

But he either backed away when he was supposed to step forward or knelt at the wrong time. With his every misstep, the duchess's frown deepened. Lady Fleming forced an encouraging smile.

When the music stopped at last, the dauphin had tears in his eyes; he forgot that he was supposed to bow to me, rushed to his mother for comfort, and buried his face in Queen Catherine's lap, leaving me to make my *révérence* to an invisible partner.

"More practice is in order. The king returns tomorrow," Madame de Poitiers announced sternly. "His Majesty will not be pleased."

Little François sobbed harder as the duchess led him away without a word of protest from his mother. I glanced at my governess.

Lady Fleming shrugged and raised her eyebrows. "*Joyeux anniversaire*, Madame Marie," she said. Then she added in a whisper, "You did beautifully, Marie. Have no worries about the dauphin."

But, of course, I did.

II

As Though We Had Known Each Other All Our Lives

LIFE IN THE FRENCH COURT was unlike anything I had known in Scotland. Though I was schooled in the language and manners of my new country, the most important lessons were not taught but learned by observing. I saw that one might have a great title and still have very little power, and that the reverse was also true. Young as I was, I discovered that power was important to me, and I felt sure that someday I would know how to use it. I did not consider that I might also lose it.

CHAPTER 6

King Henri II

THE KING'S PORTRAIT hung in the great hall at Saint-Germain, brought from Carrières-sur-Seine when the court moved, and so I already knew what he looked like. King Henri II was tall and slender and had a long, narrow face with a neatly trimmed brown beard and sad eyes. The king knew what I looked like too: soon after my arrival in France he had ordered drawings to be made of his children, including me, and he had had them sent to him while he was traveling in Italy.

We awaited his arrival with growing excitement.

Late one afternoon the king and his gentlemen, all mounted on handsome horses in rich trappings of bright silk and gold, rode into the courtyard heralded by trumpeters. We hurried out to welcome him.

King Henri dismounted and strode toward the great hall, looking exactly like his portrait. He first greeted his son, the dauphin, and then turned to me. "Ah, *ma petite reine,*

Marie!" he cried, holding out his arms to me, just as my dear grandfather had done, and I eagerly accepted his warm embrace.

Minutes later, in the great hall, the dauphin and his two sisters and I crowded around the king, the two girls on his lap and François at his feet, all of them chattering at once. Claude reached up to stroke her father's silky beard. I stood near his shoulder, speaking only when he spoke to me. Queen Catherine looked on fondly, but I noticed that the king had offered the queen only the most casual greeting. Later, when his children had climbed down from his knees, he made a courtly bow to Lady Fleming, who blushed rosily, and then left the hall in the company of Diane de Poitiers. We did not see the king or the duchess again until dinner the next day.

❧

Not long after the king returned from his journey, my uncle François, my mother's brother, married Anne d'Este, the daughter of an Italian duke and the granddaughter of Louis XII, an earlier king of France. I had attended weddings before, but Lady Fleming assured me this one would be different from any other.

"It will be the grandest affair you have ever seen!" she said. "I hear that King Henri has spared no expense for this wedding. Diplomats from all over the Continent will be among the guests. And you will have an important part in it, Marie."

"Dancing with the dauphin?" I asked, dreading the answer.

"Aye, Marie. Remember, the whole world will be watching."

I had not forgotten.

Since my birthday celebration, Madame de Poitiers had insisted that the dauphin and I practice every morning and again in the afternoon. My grandmother had ordered me a new gown with embroidered sleeves and rows of glittering gems stitched to the hem. I was given several more gowns to wear at other events before and after the wedding. I loved the gowns and tried to put the dancing test out of my mind.

I took an immediate liking to my uncle's seventeen-year-old bride, but my grandmother was somewhat critical of her. "I would have hoped for someone more beautiful. Have you noticed her chin?" said Grand-Mère. "She *does* look healthy enough, and her dowry *is* quite large. She will no doubt provide us with the necessary sons." My grandmother added, sighing, "Perhaps in time she will become more graceful."

Everywhere I went during the three-day celebration, King Henri made it a point to present me as "my daughter the queen of Scotland." I overheard him telling everyone that from the day the little dauphin and I had met "the two got on together as though they had known each other all their lives."

It was true. The dauphin, though a year and a month younger than I, had attached himself to me like a limpet. He seemed to prefer my companionship to anyone else's, running after me and calling, "W-w-wait for m-m-me,

M-M-Marie!" When I let him catch up, his pleased smile was my reward.

We were not yet formally betrothed. The wedding—which I knew would surely be even grander than my uncle's to Anne d'Este—was still far off. But as the future queen of France, I was well aware of the attention I attracted wherever I went. And now, at the dazzling wedding feast, by the light of hundreds of candles, the moment had come for me and my future husband to dance together before not just our family but—as Lady Fleming reminded me—*the whole world.*

The musicians played an introduction as the dauphin and I took our places on the polished stone floor; the wedding guests—with the smiling bride and groom seated above them—stood aside to give us plenty of room. My shoes felt too tight. Had my feet grown since they were made for me? And my gown was weighed down by the embroidery and lace and jewels. Poor François looked more than frightened—he looked terrified.

"It worked perfectly when we practiced yesterday in front of Lady Fleming," I whispered. "It will work perfectly now."

"All r-r-right," he stammered.

"Remember to smile, François, no matter what happens!"

I suspect we looked rather odd, for I was half a head taller than the dauphin. But the difference in our sizes did not matter, and it did not matter that our steps were not perfect, because the wedding guests were delighted simply to see us together in a make-believe courtship. When the dance ended, we were expected to kiss tenderly, but because I was so much taller, I had to bend my knees so that the little dauphin was not forced to stretch up on his tiptoes to reach my lips.

It must have gone off well enough, for my future father-in-law, the king, was beaming, Queen Catherine was nodding indulgently, and Madame de Poitiers was smiling triumphantly while the assembled crowd applauded and murmured their approval.

The French court celebrated Christmas Eve with a special Mass in the royal chapel, followed by a great banquet the next day. On January 6, the Feast of the Epiphany, gifts were exchanged. With Lady Fleming's help I had painstakingly stitched small bookmarks in silk thread on velvet for all the members of the royal family, as well as for Diane de Poitiers.

Later in January we observed the dauphin's fifth birthday. It was a happy occasion, with plenty of sweets to eat and jugglers to enjoy, and no one forced François to dance.

I loved dancing as much as François disliked it, but we did have some common interests and occasionally set off together in what we called "little adventures." A favorite exploit involved stealing into the larder when we thought we were unobserved and helping ourselves to cream-filled puffs of pastry or the fruit tarts glazed with jam that were the dauphin's particular favorites. On the day before a feast or royal banquet, the pastry kitchen was crowded and noisy, and we knew that it was best not to go there. But on the day *after* the feast we were guaranteed a delightful supply of leftover confections, and we could eat all we wanted. We were united by our fondness for sweets as well as a taste for petty thievery.

On the second of February, the French court celebrated the Feast of the Purification of the Virgin and the Presentation of the Infant Jesus. During the banquet that followed Mass in the royal chapel, the queen quietly withdrew. The next day she gave birth to her fourth child, a boy. The king was delighted to have a second son and named him Louis. Almost as soon as he was born, Madame de Poitiers whisked the wee bairn away to the royal nursery, to be cared for under her watchful eye.

By the king's order, I shared my studies with Princesse Élisabeth, as well as a few children of the nobility. François, as dauphin, had to be tutored alone—a shame, I thought, for he was an intelligent lad and would have been a fine addition to my classes.

Each week Lady Fleming helped me write a letter to my mother. After six months in France I spoke French almost as easily as I did Scots and wrote it well enough too. I dutifully described to my mother the interesting things I had learned and the people I had met. When the mail arrived from Scotland, I almost always received a letter from my mother. I looked forward to those letters and wept if there was none, but they also reminded me painfully that I had not seen her for months. I had settled into my new life, as I knew she wished me to, but my longing for her never left me. Though I was always the center of attention at royal events and was surrounded by people who seemed to care about me, I missed Maman deeply.

I also missed the Four Maries, who were still being kept at the convent in Poissy. "When will I see them again?" I asked Lady Fleming repeatedly.

"Soon, Marie, soon." She always sighed.

Lately my governess had seemed distracted. I thought her distraction and her deep sighs were because she yearned for her daughter, La Flamin, at least as much as I did.

But as it turned out, I was wrong.

CHAPTER 7

Fontainebleau

THE ENTIRE FRENCH COURT was moving to Fontainebleau. For a week, servants swarmed through the apartments packing furniture, plates, and cups into crates, and clothing and linens into trunks. They had done it many times before.

"King Henri likes to move," grumbled the woman charged with seeing to my belongings. "Once there, it is fine enough, but getting there is no pleasure." She stood with her hands braced on her wide hips. "The journey itself cannot end too soon for these old bones. You will see that for yourself, Madame Marie." She went back to her duties, muttering under her breath.

Soon after sunrise on the Monday of Holy Week, a long procession of people and mule carts wound its way out of Saint-Germain. At the head of the procession rode the messengers, who would be the first to arrive at the village where we would stop well before dark. Next came the cooks, the bakers and pastry makers, and the boys who turned the roasting spits, followed by dozens of stewards in charge of setting up the banquet tables and serving the meal. The noblemen, their wives and children, and their household servants made up the rest of the procession that stretched farther than I could see.

In this great river of people, Élisabeth and I rode together in a litter cushioned with velvet pillows. I now understood the old servant's complaints. The pillows were not nearly thick enough to protect us from the jostling of the mules carrying the litter. By the time we stopped for the first night, the excitement had worn off and we were tired.

Sinclair was traveling with the servants and did not try to hide her feelings about them when we retired to rooms prepared for us at the convent where we were to spend the night. "Those Frenchwomen look down their fine noses at me," she complained, her eyes red rimmed—from weariness or weeping, I was not sure. "They call me 'the auld Scot' and mock me when I speak our natural tongue. They jeer at me for not saying their French words the way they should be said, by their lights, and they point and laugh at me for the clumsy way I use a fork, the likes of which I had never seen before I set foot on this godforsaken land!"

But her misery reached a peak on the second night of the journey when she was forced to share a flea-infested bed with one of the wardrobe mistresses.

Unlike Sinclair, Lady Fleming seemed serenely content, going about with a pleased little half smile. The Four Maries had been released at last from the convent outside Paris where they had studied French and been instructed in the customs of the French court. Lady Fleming would soon be reunited with her daughter. That, I thought, must be the source of her pleasure.

Early in the evening of the third day we stopped in a small village just outside the royal forest. The weather had turned damp and cold, and tents were set up for the evening meal. Later, while musicians played for the king and his court, the servants hurried on ahead to begin unpacking, which would take them most of the night. At midmorning the next day—Holy Thursday—the procession arrived at Porte d'Orée, the south gate leading to the château of Fontainebleau.

I shall never forget my first view of the château—the enormous size of it and the awesome beauty. "Oh, I do wish my *mither* could see this!" I exclaimed, lapsing into the Scots tongue as I still sometimes did when I was thinking of her. I could no longer remember much about the castles and royal palaces of Scotland except for Dumbarton, my last home before leaving my country for my new life. I did realize that compared to this glorious château, Scottish palaces were quite small and, it must be said, rather dreary.

Lady Fleming nodded agreeably. "The queen mother would like this place well enough, I am sure," my governess acknowledged. "But I fancy she saw it many times before she left France to marry King James. She grew up not far from here. When she first came to Scotland, she often talked of her home at Joinville. You are likely to see it too before many days have passed."

I watched her drift away, still in her dreamy state. I had known Lady Fleming all my life, for she was one of my mother's closest friends. Everyone admired her shapely figure, her thick blond hair, and her eyes the color of Scottish bluebells. She was indeed beautiful, I thought, but not as beautiful as my *mither*.

❧❧❧

Easter fell late in 1549—the twenty-first of April—and from then on the days were nearly always warm and pleasant. At Fontainebleau I again shared a large apartment with my good sister-friend Princesse Élisabeth. It seemed that one could easily become lost in this vast château, but Élisabeth knew it well and delighted in being my guide. Soon the two of us were roaming through the many corridors and grand halls, venturing out into the gardens, and stopping by a pool teeming with carp that clambered greedily over one another for the bread we tossed them. The dauphin had been unwell since his birthday in January, but now he was feeling stronger and sometimes came out to join us.

The Four Maries had arrived in time for the Easter celebration. Peals of laughter rang out as my friends rushed to embrace me. We were happy to see one another after our long separation, and without thinking we were soon prattling happily in Scots. I saw Élisabeth staring at us. "I cannot understand you when you talk like that, Marie," she complained, pouting a little.

I knew I had made a mistake. The Four Maries had barely appeared, and already we had broken an important rule. "I will not forget again," I told her, apologizing, and changed quickly to French. But it was too late. The next day Madame de Poitiers sent for me.

"Madame Marie," she began. "You are to speak only French. You do understand that, do you not?"

"*Oui,* Madame de Poitiers," I said.

"Then you must promise me you will not speak your former language with the Four Maries."

My *former* language? Was it not still my language? *"Je vous promets,"* I said. I stared at my shoes, knowing it would be a hard promise to keep now that my friends were with me again.

❧

We now spoke French among ourselves with ease. None of my four friends called herself Mary anymore; we were all Maries.

When I lived in Scotland with my mother, I had spent my days with the Four Maries for my companions. No one cared how we passed our time, and we ran about freely wherever we wished. But life at the French court was different. I was constantly surrounded by swarms of people. I was either at court with the king and queen and their children, the dauphin in particular, or visiting, or being visited by, my mother's family, and I loved them all. I often saw my grandparents, as well as uncles and aunts. My uncle François, recently married to Anne d'Este, was a soldier. A long scar on his cheek gotten when he fought bravely in battle against the English had earned him the name Le Balafré—

"the Scarred One." Despite the scar, or maybe because of it, I thought him very dashing and handsome. His brother Charles was a churchman, cardinal of Lorraine. He was handsome too, but not as dashing.

Twice each month I journeyed to Joinville to visit my grandparents at their château, a huge medieval fort on the River Marne only a day's ride from Fontainebleau. My brother François, duke of Longueville, was usually at Joinville when I arrived on Saturday evening. I was happy to see him, and he always had some little surprise for me. He loved to draw, and the gift was often a sketch of a bird or a flower that had caught his eye. "It reminded me of you and of our mother," he explained each time, "and so I had to draw it."

On Sunday after we had all heard Mass together in the chapel at the old château, we walked a short distance to the Château du Grand Jardin, a banqueting house surrounded by beautiful gardens that my grandfather had built as a place to entertain his guests. The Guise family gathered here for a fine meal, followed by dancing. My brother François and Grand-Père were my favorite partners. "You dance exquisitely, *ma petite* Marie!" my grandfather said, and his praise always delighted me. Sometimes Grand-Mère invited mimes to entertain us or itinerant troupes of actors to perform.

But most important was the lively conversation among my Guise aunts and uncles and grandparents. My uncles asked me a great many questions about life with the royal family and seized eagerly upon whatever court gossip I could report. I always did my best to please them, but Grand-Père usually brought the questioning to an end.

"Enough, gentlemen! Our lovely little queen is tired of such talk. Marie, I propose a visit to Grand-Mère's apartments for a chat with her pretty birds—would that please you, *ma chère*?"

Of course it would, and off we went together, my small hand in his large one.

I was a keen observer and a curious child, though I was still too young to understand the meaning of most of what I saw and heard at court. I also knew instinctively that I must not ask direct questions about what interested me but must wait to be told. I still had many unanswered questions— about Madame de Poitiers, for instance. I noticed that she always dressed in black and white and that King Henri was very close to her and spent nearly every afternoon with her. She had a daughter who was about the same age as the king and queen. "The duchess's daughter is in charge of the palace servants," I heard Lady Fleming say, "and the duchess is in charge of the king."

What does that mean? I wondered but did not ask. How could a duchess be in charge of a king? That would surely make her very powerful! When I repeated Lady Fleming's remark to my uncles François and Charles, they laughed heartily. Grand-Mère changed the subject quickly, asking about the Four Maries. I knew by her tone and her expression that she still did not approve of them, but she no longer referred to them as *les petites sauvages,* at least not within my hearing. But I received no explanation of what I had heard.

After three or four days with my Guise relatives, I returned to Fontainebleau. When summer came and the king ordered the court to move back to Saint-Germain, I continued to make the trip to Joinville, but now I traveled by riverboat. It had been a year since the king's royal galley arrived in Dumbarton and my friends and I had embarked on the journey to France. But the anniversary of my departure from Scotland passed without notice. I was by now thoroughly and completely at home in France.

CHAPTER 8

Death in the Family

KING HENRI WAS the most important man in all of France—I never doubted that. But I was unsure who was the most important woman: Queen Catherine or Diane de Poitiers? I understood why the king spent so much time with Madame de Poitiers, who was lively and amusing, and so little time with his wife, who seemed dull and unfriendly compared to the duchess. The queen had the superior title, yet I had heard members of her own court refer to her behind her back as "the merchant's daughter." What did they mean?

I asked my grandmother, who explained it this way: "Though it is true that Queen Catherine lacks royal blood, her family, the Médicis, were not simple grocers, as some jealous courtiers would have you believe. Hers was a family of great prestige and enormous wealth and influence in Italy. The Médicis built a fortune through trade in spices and cloth and an even greater fortune in banking. The queen's great-grandfather Lorenzo the Magnificent ruled the city of Florence like a prince. Her parents died when she was very young. Everyone called her Duchessina—'Little Duchess.' Her uncle became pope and arranged for her marriage to Henri, who was then duke of Orléans. Catherine de Médicis came with an enormous dowry, and old King François was happy to have her marry his second son. When the first son died, Catherine found herself queen of France. Poor girl—it was not easy for her here. Years passed before she produced her first child, your future husband, François. Before that finally happened, there had been talk of sending her back to Italy."

This story made me feel more sympathy for the queen, but I was more curious than ever about the duchess. "What about Madame de Poitiers?" I asked.

Grand-Mère sniffed disapprovingly, almost as she did when she spoke of the Four Maries. "Henri became infatuated with her when he was just a boy, even though she was old enough to be his mother. They are still very close, the queen tolerates it, and that is all I wish to say about it." I had more questions, but Grand-Mère was not in a mood to answer them. "Now you have the queen's story. You can make up your mind about her yourself. She will no doubt be your good friend if you do not cross her."

"Just one more question, *s'il vous plaît!* Why does Madame de Poitiers always wear black and white?"

Grand-Mère smoothed the skirts of her gown. "Because it pleases her," she said. "The reason she does everything."

✦

One day Queen Catherine surprised me by saying, "Should you wish to develop your needlework skills, Madame Marie, I would be pleased to help you."

I was not certain I wanted the queen's help or instruction—she seemed so remote and cold—but, remembering Grand-Mère's advice, I thought it was better to accept than to refuse.

My mother had not been much interested in needlework, preferring to spend her time with music. I remembered her sweet voice and the harp and lute she played so beautifully. And how she loved to dance! She and Lady Fleming and her other ladies often spent whole evenings dancing in her royal apartments. Needlework, when my mother did take it out, usually lay forgotten in her lap. It had fallen to Sinclair to teach me the few simple embroidery stitches I knew.

But stitchery, not dancing, was Queen Catherine's passion, and she devoted many hours to it. I shyly showed her a piece of linen embroidered with a lopsided bird perched on a crooked branch bearing two withered-looking leaves. "You have chosen pretty colors for your bird, Madame Marie," she said, examining my work. "But we shall have to begin at the beginning with the most basic stitches so that you learn them correctly. I have no doubt that with practice you will soon master them."

She showed me the running stitch, several in-and-out

stitches in a row. That was one I already knew, and I quickly produced a sample I considered perfect.

"Very nice," she said. "Now let us see if you can improve them. You must make the stitches quite small and even, each one exactly the same size as the one next to it."

How annoying! I thought. I did not like to be corrected, but I said nothing and did as she had asked.

When I had mastered that to her satisfaction, I moved on to the backstitch, and then to the chain stitch, the split stitch, the tent stitch, the satin stitch, the herringbone. After I was introduced to each one, I practiced it over and over, until I did at last improve. Queen Catherine was always patient, as quick to praise as to correct. During those long and sometimes tedious hours I became better acquainted with her. I began to enjoy her company and look forward to our time together.

While I worked on my embroidery, I listened to the conversation of the queen and her ladies, thinking I might learn something interesting to report when I next saw my uncles and grandparents. But the talk was dull, and my mind drifted off. When I was finally dismissed, I made a hurried *révérence* and rushed away.

The dauphin often hovered outside his mother's chambers waiting for me to emerge.

"Ah, dear friend!" François would pipe, taking my hand, and we would wander to the tennis court to watch his father play or to the lists to cheer when King Henri, mounted on horseback, charged against his opponent and knocked him off balance or sent him sprawling.

François confided that his biggest dream was to participate in a real tournament with his father. "How exciting that w-w-would be!" he exclaimed.

He insisted on demonstrating his skill for me. His servant helped him into his specially made suit of armor—a gift from my uncle François, the Scarred One—and seated him on his pony. Carrying a lance, the dauphin urged the pony to gallop at full speed at a series of rings suspended by cords from a wooden arm. He managed to pick off the rings one by one with the point of his lance, and then he trotted over to where I sat waiting, saluted me, and proudly presented me with the rings.

Occasionally I persuaded the Four Maries to accompany me to the lists, and Princesse Élisabeth as well. But my friends were quickly bored. "It would be so much more exciting if we could actually do it, not just sit here and watch," said Beaton. "Do you suppose they would let us try?"

The rest of us turned to stare at her, stunned by her suggestion. Beaton, the most athletic of us, had been riding since her father set her on a horse when she was barely old enough to walk. Not yet seven, she was fearless.

"They will not let girls do it," said La Flamin, always the most daring, the one who produced the wildest schemes, "but we could disguise ourselves as boys and creep into the royal stables and borrow horses."

"Who would saddle them for us?" Seton asked uncertainly.

"I know how to saddle a horse," Beaton declared. "I can

show you how, or I can do it for you. We could use the dauphin's ponies." She turned to me. "Do you think he would mind, Marie?"

"Of course not," I assured her, though I had no idea what he would think.

"We would need armor," Livingston reminded us. "And lances."

We never put our scheme into action. But we did spend many hours discussing it and promising one another that someday we would actually find a way to do it.

The weeks and months slipped by in an untroubled stream, each day much like the one before it. I studied diligently with my tutors. My stitchery improved to the satisfaction of Queen Catherine. I enjoyed my life as part of the royal family, paid regular visits to my Guise relatives, spent as much time as possible with the Four Maries, and accepted the dauphin's unflagging devotion.

In the summer of 1549 King Henri decided to go to war against England with the aim of winning back the town of Boulogne, a French town that had been in English hands for many years. Accompanied by my uncle François, the king rode off at the head of an army to do battle against his old enemy while the rest of the court retired to the hunting lodge at Compiègne. Then in October the royal family experienced a great loss: eight-month-old Louis suddenly sickened and died. The queen was overcome with grief.

The king rushed back from his battles to mourn with her. He appeared even more melancholy than usual. A heavy cloud of sadness hung over the court.

"Maman and Papa pray for another son," Princesse Élisabeth whispered.

Having only one son was a serious problem for the royal family. What if something happened to François? By French law, neither of the princesses could inherit the throne. A few weeks later their prayers were at least partly answered when the queen learned she was again expecting a child. But what if it was another daughter? Would King Henri grieve as my father did and lose his will to live?

I was the cause of my father's death. That knowledge had begun to haunt me. By Scottish law, a woman could inherit the throne and rule Scotland, but that did not mean she should. At least my father did not believe so.

The court moved to Blois in the Loire Valley, and everyone's spirits lifted. The Four Maries were particularly enchanted by the spiral staircase in this beautiful château, and La Flamin devised challenges of hopping up and down the stone steps until Madame de Poitiers ordered us to stop. In December I observed my seventh birthday. Christmas came and went, and when gifts were exchanged on the sixth of January, the Feast of the Epiphany and the Day of the Three Kings, I presented elaborately embroidered handkerchiefs as gifts and received much praise for my skill. The next occasion for celebration was the sixth birthday of the dauphin. When spring came we moved again to Fontainebleau, where Élisabeth turned five and had to be prevented from eating herself sick at the banquet in her honor.

One day, after I had completed my morning lessons, Madame de Poitiers came to my quarters. This was unusual. She took both of my hands in hers—that, too, was unusual. "Madame Marie," she said solemnly, "I bring you most unhappy news. Your grandfather died just three days ago."

My dear *grand-père,* dead? I threw myself weeping into the duchess's arms.

"You are too young to attend the funeral, Marie," she told me. "It is your grandmother's wish that you be represented by a friend of your uncle's."

Who had decided I was too young? Surely not my mother. The news would not yet have reached Scotland. Realizing that she did not yet know of her father's death made me sob all the harder. I longed to share my grief with my grandmother, my uncles, my brother François. The royal family offered their condolences. Their kindness did little to console me. I put on a black mourning gown. But still I was not allowed to attend the funeral.

Maybe it had nothing to do with my age. I overheard talk among the servants that my grandfather had not died a natural death, that he had been murdered. But no matter whom I asked—"Is it true?"—I received only evasions. The exception was Sinclair, who reported what her sources at the servants' supper table had said.

"Poison, is what I've heard," she said. "But no one knows for certain, or else no one is saying. Seems to me the old duke should not have had a single enemy. These French are not at one another's throats, like they are in Scotland. Still, the old gentleman always looked healthy enough to me."

A month later I was taken to Joinville by my uncle Charles. It seemed unbearably bleak without my dear grandfather. My brother the duke of Longueville had come down from his château in Amiens, and we wept together. Grand-Mère remained steadfastly dry-eyed. She showed me the letter she had received from my mother. *I have lost the best father a daughter could hope to have,* Maman had written. How sad, I thought, to be so far away when a loved one dies.

Before I returned to Fontainebleau, I had a few moments alone with my brother. "Have you heard that Grand-Père was poisoned?" I asked quietly. "It is a rumor at court, but nobody tells me anything."

He frowned. "I have heard that too, but I don't know the truth of it. Grand-Mère doesn't speak of it."

"We could ask our uncles," I suggested, and my brother agreed that we might.

But then I had an even better idea. When Anne d'Este arrived with our uncle François, duke of Aumale, and greeted me with a warm embrace, I whispered, "Madame, may I speak with you in private?"

"*Oui,* Madame Marie," she said, following me into a curtained alcove. "How can I help you?"

"Just answer a question, *s'il vous plaît,*" I said. "Is it true that my grandfather was poisoned? And if so, by whom?"

Anne d'Este shook her head. "Often when a man in a powerful position dies unexpectedly, rumors spread that he was poisoned. Sometimes the rumors turn out to be true. But my husband does not believe this to be the case, and your grandfather's physician has confirmed it. The duke died a peaceful death, and for that we can be grateful."

I was relieved, but I felt my lip begin to tremble, and I knew that tears would shortly follow. "I miss him," I murmured.

Anne d'Este knelt down and put her arms around me. "I am sure you do. We all do. But be assured that your grandmother and your uncles are here to care for you and to look out for your best interests."

I leaned against the lady's shoulder and wept until she produced a handkerchief and wiped away my tears so they would not stain her gown. My uncle her husband, the new duke of Guise, peered behind the velvet curtain and came to lay his hand on my arm. For the moment, at least, I felt comforted.

CHAPTER 9

Scandal

THE COURT CONTINUED in its usual routine, moving from one château to another. Each was my favorite for as long as we stayed there—the beautiful gardens at Fontainebleau, the elegant staircase at Blois, the four hundred ornate rooms at Chambord. Queen Catherine loved bright colors and had had the rooms of each château decorated in vibrant reds and blues and greens with lavish gold trim on the ceilings. The furniture, which always moved with us, was richly carved and painted and gilded, and the carpets had been woven in Venice. Everyone, from the highest noble to the lowliest page, dressed in vivid colors—everyone except Madame de Poitiers.

Our animals traveled with us too. Two horses were my favorites: a pretty little black pony named Bravane and a frisky sorrel, Madame la Réale, that occasionally tossed me into the mud. I had become a fearless rider, thanks to my friend Marie Livingston. The other Maries called her Lusty, because of her outspoken opinions. She convinced me to wear breeches under my skirts and to ride astride.

"As we would if we were in Scotland," she argued. "And with breeches you need not be concerned about your modesty when you fly off."

I had my own falcon for hunting—I called her Caramel—and she quickly learned that mine was the gloved fist to which she must return. The dauphin persuaded the chief falconer to give him a bird as well. For weeks we discussed its name, with François changing his mind several times.

"Why not name him Chocolat?" I suggested. "We both love sweets, so that would be a good idea. Do you not agree?"

"*Oui,* Marie, you are r-r-right!" cried the dauphin, who nearly always accepted my suggestions. But François seemed fearful of his hawk's sharp talons and usually stepped back and let the falconer's apprentice take Chocolat on his glove.

The four big curly-haired dogs that accompanied the king on royal hunts rode to each château in kennels built on wooden carts, and every lady in the court carried one or two lapdogs with her in her cushioned litter. Lady Fleming's little spaniel was a particular favorite, with his long silky fur and big ears. She named him Papillon, the French word for "butterfly." My own Biscuit, a white ball of fluff with two black button eyes and a black button nose, followed me everywhere. Princesse Élisabeth had one also, and now little Princesse Claude, who was nearly three, insisted that she must have one just like ours.

We were playing with our dogs, attempting to teach them to sit up and beg, when a messenger delivered a letter from my mother. I was always delighted to receive a letter from Maman, and I broke the seal assuming this would bring an Easter greeting. But the news was much more exciting: my mother was coming to France for a long visit!

I tossed a treat to Biscuit and rushed off to write Grand-Mère with the wonderful news, knowing that she would be as happy as I was, or at least as happy as she could be in her widowed state. I had become skillful with quill and ink, and my pen scratched quickly across the page with no mistakes or unseemly blots:

I have been very glad to be able to send these present lines for the purpose of telling you the joyful news I have received from the Queen my Mother, who has promised me that she will be here very soon to see you and me, which is to me the greatest happiness which I could wish for in this world. All I am thinking about now is to do my whole duty in all things and to study and to be very good.

I showed the letter to my tutor Monsieur Amyot, whose eyebrows looked as prickly as hedgehogs. He praised it and brought me the wax and my gold seal to finish it, and then he summoned a messenger to carry it off at once to Join-ville. My mother had not said exactly when she expected to come, but from that day on I waited with growing impatience for her arrival.

❧⚜❧

At the end of May the court moved again to Saint-Germain. A month later Queen Catherine gave birth for the fifth time. The king was with her when their third son, named Charles-Maximilien, came into the world. For once, Madame de Poitiers was not there to attend the birth. "Queen Catherine must be pleased about that," Sinclair remarked.

We had all heard why Madame de Poitiers was not present: Away on a visit to the Loire Valley, she had fallen from her horse and broken her leg. The king had sent a royal litter to take her to her château at Anet, where she now rested while her leg mended.

"How pleasant it is not to have Madame de Poitiers here," said Marie Fleming bluntly. "I do not like her much."

I disagreed with La Flamin's and Sinclair's opinion of Madame de Poitiers. The duchess always treated me with great kindness. Sometimes she invited the king's children, including me, to visit her at Château d'Anet, the ancient castle she was having restored. I always enjoyed my time with her there.

Meanwhile, a scandal was in the making. There had been rumors for some time that Lady Fleming had a lover. My governess's rooms adjoined mine, and when the rumors reached my uncles, they asked me pointed questions.

"Has your governess been receiving visits from a gentleman?" Uncle François asked.

"Baron de Montmorency, the king's constable, for example?" suggested Uncle Charles.

"*Non,* I have not seen the baron," I replied, adding innocently, "but King Henri visits Lady Fleming quite often, to discuss my education."

The uncles looked at each other, smiled, and thanked

me. I later learned that they had immediately carried my thoughtless remark straight to Diane de Poitiers. Even with her broken leg, the duchess rushed from Anet to Saint-Germain. That same night, after I finished my prayers and was preparing for bed, Sinclair discovered Madame de Poitiers sitting outside Lady Fleming's door.

"Who is she waiting for?" Sinclair wondered aloud, extinguishing all the candles but one. Soon Sinclair was snoring loudly, and I fell asleep quickly after her.

We awoke sometime later at the sound of a door being slammed. We heard voices, first the startled exclamation of King Henri followed by Madame de Poitiers's shrill cry. "Good sir, what were you doing in there?" the duchess demanded loud enough for everyone to hear. Sinclair tiptoed to our door and knelt at the keyhole so as not to miss a word.

"You and that woman, Lady Fleming! Sir, you have betrayed the entire Guise family; your wife, the queen; and your son the dauphin! And the dauphin's future wife, Queen Marie, who is so unfortunate as to have that disgraceful woman as her governess! I have nothing more to say to you on the subject, good sir, for I love you as sincerely today as I always have."

There followed a stunned silence, and then the king's mumbled reply.

"The king insists there was nothing evil going on," Sinclair reported to me in a whisper.

Diane de Poitiers's voice rang out clearly. "You have dishonored the innocent child sleeping behind that door!" she cried. I supposed that I was the innocent child to whom she referred. "The niece of the Guise family is being brought up by a woman who is nothing better than a whore!"

Sinclair gasped. "Now that is going a bit too far," she said, shaking her head.

The duchess's shouting and the king's mumbling went on for a while longer, and then all became quiet again. "I wonder what Queen Catherine will have to say about this episode," said my nurse, settling onto her pallet near my bed. "Seems that King Henri has *two* mistresses. I'll wager the queen will get a bit of pleasure from learning that her rival has a rival of her own."

Sinclair was soon snoring peacefully again, but I lay awake thinking of my friend Marie Fleming. No doubt La Flamin would quickly be hearing about her mother's transgressions. But then I, too, fell asleep. It would be some time before I learned the rest of the story.

CHAPTER 10

Maman's Arrival

THE MONTHS CREPT BY with unbearable slowness as I waited for my mother. In my impatience I exasperated the duchess and my governess and everyone else within hearing with my constant questions. When will the queen my mother leave Scotland? How long will the journey take? When do you think she will arrive? Will she come here immediately after she leaves the ship?

Near the end of August Madame de Poitiers announced brightly, "You have not much longer to wait, Madame Marie. The king has dispatched six French galleys to Scotland to fetch the queen mother."

Have the king's galleys arrived in Scotland? How long will they stay? When will they return?

My brother François, duke of Longueville, would be sent to meet her, but I would not. I received this news with tears of bitter disappointment. "Why may I not go too?" I asked Madame de Poitiers, who replied in a soothing manner,

"The king believes it is better this way. Your mother will likely be very tired after her sea voyage. When she has rested and recovered, she will be all the more ready to greet you."

I had no more success persuading Queen Catherine, though she did seem sympathetic. "Dear child, if it were up to me, you would be the very first to throw your arms around your beloved mother and receive her grateful kisses. But the king believes it is the son's duty and privilege to greet his mother first. Then it is the daughter's turn."

"But I am a queen, and my brother is only a duke!" I protested. "I should take precedence."

Queen Catherine gave me a long, searching look. "Sometimes," she said, "precedence is everything, and sometimes it means nothing at all. Be patient, Marie. You will soon see your mother, and you will forget this little delay."

I agreed, though reluctantly, for I saw no reason why a son should be more important than a daughter, especially when the daughter was a queen.

During the long days of waiting, Monsieur Amyot hovered over me as I prepared, memorized, and rehearsed a formal address welcoming my mother. After two years in France, this would be my first public speech. In flowery language, I was to inquire about the state of the church in Scotland. Next, I was to turn to the Scottish nobles in her retinue and exhort them to be loyal to our country and grateful to the king of France for the protection he offered me and my realm. When I had finished, I was to step aside and allow the queen mother to reply.

We learned that the French fleet carrying my mother

and her entourage had encountered foul weather. Then, after a harrowing journey of twelve days, the French galleys sailed into the harbor of Havre de Grace on the north coast. It was the nineteenth of September. Six days later my mother and her court, accompanied by my brother François, rode into Rouen.

At my first sight of my mother, every word of my fine speech flew out of my head. I heard my tutor nervously prompting me, but I remained dumb. My mother smiled encouragingly. At last I found my voice and had managed to stammer only the first two or three phrases when my mother uttered a loud cry, reached out, and pulled me to her bosom. Half suffocating in the brocades and velvets of her gown, I heard the shuffling of the startled dignitaries nearby. After a time, we regained our composure and I finished my ridiculous speech. I cared about none of this! I simply wanted it to be over! When the ceremonies finally did come to an end, we rushed into each other's arms and wiped away our happy tears.

Everyone said I had played my role to perfection. *Only two years ago the child did not speak a word of French that anyone could understand.* My mother's pride in me was evident. She could not let me out of her sight.

The king had taken care to arrange every kind of fête and pageant to honor my mother. We watched from a gilded pavilion built on the banks of the Seine and decorated in brilliant blue silk. Dozens of colorful banners fluttered from gilded poles. Horses pranced by, wearing headdresses that transformed them into unicorns. Men in slave dress pushed wheeled platforms carrying tableaux portraying King Henri as a Roman emperor surrounded by his children. Costumed actors fought make-believe battles. Giant papier-mâché elephants thrilled the children, who believed they were real.

The crowds seemed immensely entertained by the pageantry. Out on the River Seine a mock sea battle was set to take place when disaster struck. Without warning, a barrel of gunpowder exploded on the deck of a ship. The ship sank, drowning members of the crew. I was painfully reminded of the collapse of the drawbridge when I first arrived in France. I had wept then at the loss of life, and I wept now.

Many of those who witnessed the spectacle did not realize it was a terrible accident, and they cheered and applauded wildly and cried out for more. The organizers arranged another sea battle for the next day, and the same awful accident occurred—another keg of gunpowder, another explosion, another ship down, more lives lost. King Henri ordered a stop to the sea battles, and Maman hurried me away from a scene that upset me dreadfully. I could not rid myself of the feeling that I was in some way responsible for the terrible things that happened, though Maman tried to assure me I was not.

Once the fêtes were over, my mother, my brother, and I traveled to Joinville to visit my grandmother. It was the first time Grand-Mère had seen her daughter since Maman left

France, eleven years earlier, to marry my father. It would have been a brilliant homecoming and reunion if Grand-Père had been alive, but as he was not, there was far more sorrow than joy.

Grand-Mère appeared thin and pale, almost ghostly, in her mourning clothes. She received us solemnly, embracing my mother and greeting my brother and me with dry kisses. She seemed an entirely different person from the lively woman who had so loved to entertain friends and family at the Château du Grand Jardin. During our visit we never went to the banqueting house my grandfather had built, or even strolled in the once beautiful gardens that now lay neglected. Instead, we sat quietly in Grand-Mère's gloomy apartments, where black cloth on the windows blotted out every glimmer of sunlight. The little dogs that had once greeted me with joyful barks had been banished. The cages of exotic birds were gone.

"I have considered withdrawing to pass my last days in a convent, away from this cruel world and its wicked ways," Grand-Mère told us.

"What have you decided, dearest Maman?" my mother asked. She was distressed to find her mother in such dark despair.

"That I am needed here, to oversee the welfare of my family," my grandmother said. I wondered whose welfare she meant.

We accompanied Grand-Mère through a dimly lit gallery to offer prayers in her private chapel. The only sound was the whisper of skirts and our hushed footsteps on the stone floor. We passed an empty coffin with an ornately carved lid and a lighted candle at each end. The sight startled me. "Whose coffin is that, Grand-Mère?" my brother asked, his voice echoing in the gallery.

"Mine," she said. "I pass it every morning on my way to hear Mass, and several times each day when I come to pray, and I am reminded of the transitory nature of our lives here on earth."

I loved my grandmother, but I was relieved when this doleful visit ended. Promising one another to meet again soon, my brother left for Amiens and my mother and I rejoined the French court at Blois, the château with the wonderful staircase. We would spend the winter in the Loire Valley. My mother's brothers, my Guise uncles—François, who had inherited the title duke of Guise when my grandfather died, and Charles, the cardinal of Lorraine—soon joined us.

My mother and my uncles often retired to the privacy of a small library in the suite of rooms my mother had been given for her stay. Surrounded by leather-bound books, they discussed certain matters that were not of interest to me. But once, as I came to beg my mother to settle an argument with one of my friends, I heard her declare firmly, "I will not rest until Arran is out of the picture and I am the sole regent for our little queen!"

She was talking about me, *la petite reine*. Naturally, I stopped to listen. A Scottish nobleman, the earl of Arran, had been named regent by the Scottish Parliament to rule Scotland until I came of age, with my mother serving as co-regent. My mother did not wish to share this duty with him or anyone else, that much I understood. She and my uncles decided that I should be declared fully of age at eleven plus one day, four years earlier than the usual age of fifteen. "Then I will serve as queen regent," my mother said, "and Arran will be *out!*"

Such matters were far beyond my comprehension, but I liked the idea of being declared of age when I was eleven— even if I did not know just what that involved. I turned and left quietly.

On another occasion, when the discussion seemed more interesting, I did not leave. My mother and her brothers were discussing what should be done about Lady Fleming. I hid myself behind a heavy drapery and listened.

"Lady Fleming is creating a scandal," said my uncle Charles. "She is having an affair with the king, and she is not even discreet about it! Madame de Poitiers is furious."

"Queen Catherine is angry as well, but not nearly so angry as the duchess," Uncle François remarked. "I think she rather enjoys Diane's humiliation. The queen has had to sit by quietly all these years while the king openly acknowledged Madame de Poitiers as his mistress. Now they have a common enemy—Lady Fleming."

"There is more to the story," my mother told her brothers. "I have learned from Sinclair, who has an unerring ear for court gossip as it is being discussed among the servants, that Lady Fleming is expecting a child."

Expecting a child? I strained to hear better, nearly falling out of my hiding place. *Does La Flamin know?*

"How very interesting!" my uncle François exclaimed, and I could imagine him stroking his silky beard as he spoke. "King Henri himself confided to me just days ago that the queen his wife is also with child."

A chair scraped across the floor. Someone might leave the reading room at any moment and find me there. Not wanting to be caught eavesdropping, I scurried away—and nearly collided with La Flamin, who had come looking for me.

"Let us ask the cooks to make us some sweets!" she proposed.

I was happy to agree. *Poor girl,* I thought as we ran off together, hand in hand, to the kitchens. *She probably has no notion of the trouble her mother is in.*

CHAPTER II

Frittered Pears

AS MARIE FLEMING and I hurried away from my mother's rooms, the other Maries caught up with us. We were soon joined by the dauphin, François, and Princesse Élisabeth, and our little group made its way, laughing and talking noisily, down the elegant staircase. All of us loved to spend time in the royal kitchens, where we no doubt made nuisances of ourselves but were tolerated by the cooks. Matteo Panterelli, the Italian pastry chef brought to the French court by Queen Catherine, always welcomed us. Even when he was busy preparing for a banquet, he never turned us away. Chef Matteo said we reminded him of his grandchildren back in Florence—he called it Firenze—where he hoped to return someday. I was fond of Matteo, but not of his assistant, Lucas, a dour man who said little but was clearly annoyed by our presence.

Chef Matteo wiped his hands on an apron covering most of a great belly and led us to the table he kept set up for us, out of the way of the other cooks and their apprentices and helpers. "What shall we make today, my lady Queen Marie? My lord the dauphin? Gracious ladies?" Matteo asked jovially. His round head was wreathed in a halo of fluffy white hair. "Are you yearning for frittered pears?"

My favorite dish was frittered pears, and Matteo often helped us make them. Afraid we might harm ourselves using knives, Matteo peeled the fruit and cut out the core and the seeds. I sliced the pears, and Beaton dipped each slice in a batter mixed by La Flamin under Matteo's watchful eye. Seton and I presided over the skillet of melted butter in which the battered pieces were fried to a golden brown.

But on the day that I heard my mother and my uncles discussing the scandal of Lady Fleming, I asked instead for pâte à Panterelli, the pastry puffs that were his specialty. I knew they were La Flamin's favorite.

Matteo allowed us to mix water, butter, flour, and eggs together to make a stiff paste. He showed us how to mold the paste with spoons so that the blobs formed the most enchanting shapes as they baked—swans, for example. The results seemed almost magical. Princesse Claude, who insisted on joining us though she was only three, always made a great mess. Princesse Élisabeth could not bear to have her hands sticky. La Flamin wanted to try anything new, and the other Maries followed her lead. The dauphin, meanwhile, waited to be served, as a king would do. When our pastry swans emerged from the oven, puffed and golden and somewhat lopsided, Matteo helped us fill them with sweetened custard. "Shall we save them for later?" Seton suggested, but of course we did not. We ate every one of them immediately.

Delicious as our pastry swans were, frittered pears remained my favorite—until they were nearly my undoing.

This is what happened. In March of 1551 during the spring of my mother's visit, the court left Blois and moved to nearby Amboise on the opposite side of the river. Overlooking the Loire and surrounded by Italian gardens, Amboise was a favorite of Queen Catherine's. We arrived the week before Easter, and the king ordered a grand feast to mark the end of the long Lenten fast.

After Mass in the cathedral on Easter Day, as we made our way in a formal procession back to the château, we heard loud noises and became aware of a sudden disturbance. The captain of the Garde Écossaise, the Scots Guard, specially appointed to protect the king and the royal family, appeared and whispered to King Henri. I saw them both glance at me before the captain saluted the king and left, and then the procession continued on to the banquet hall. I was curious—*Why did they look at me?*—but there were so many people gathered that I soon forgot about it.

The royal family, my Guise uncles, my mother, and my brother the duke of Longueville were present. Grand-Mère had ended her formal period of mourning and come out of seclusion for the first time since Grand-Père's death. Diane de Poitiers absorbed the king's full attention, and Queen Catherine pretended not to notice. The great hall of Amboise was crowded with French noblemen and their wives as well as the Scots courtiers who had accompanied my mother to France and now followed her as she moved from château to château. Everyone of importance was there, with one exception that I could not fail to notice: Lady Fleming. It was not like my governess to miss a big event like the Easter feast. La Flamin and the other Maries had been assigned to sit in a distant part of the hall, and I would not have a chance to speak to my friends until later. I wondered if La Flamin now knew what I knew: that her mother was expecting a child.

King Henri gave the signal for my uncle Charles, the cardinal, to bless the feast, first in Latin and then in French. A dozen trumpeters blew a fanfare, and a parade of servants in brilliant blue and red livery entered carrying silver platters piled high with every kind of festive dish, one course after another of roasted meats, grilled birds, baked fish stuffed with herbs, and vegetables I had never tasted before I came to France, such as one called broccoli, which looked like a miniature tree and had been brought from Italy by Catherine de Médicis. Queen Catherine had told me a few days earlier as we sat at our needlework that she had ordered frittered pears to be included on the menu, especially for me.

I was always a hearty eater, but on that day I forced myself to eat sparingly as I eagerly awaited the frittered pears that had been denied me since the beginning of Lent six weeks earlier. An array of tarts and pastries and other sweets appeared—oranges from the Holy Land, preserved figs, apricots in syrup—but no frittered pears. I was disappointed but said nothing. Later, after the banquet had ended, my mother, pale and shaken, explained the reason.

"Someone wished to do you harm and poisoned your frittered pears," she said, still tearful. "The plot was discovered in time, thanks be to a merciful God. The chief conspirator has fled, and his fellow conspirator is in irons. But for your safety you will remain deprived of your favorite dish until the villain has been caught and punished."

Someone wished to poison me? I was shocked. Why would someone try to murder me? I was only eight years old. I had many questions, but my mother offered only vague answers. "It really had nothing to do with you," she said, trying to ease my fear. "Someone with a bitter grudge against the royal family of Scotland believed that the best way to harm us all was to harm you. He changed his name, joined the Scots Guard, and came to France. Then he befriended one of the cooks, who knew your favorite dishes."

"Not Chef Matteo!" I gasped. "Matteo would never try to harm me!"

"No, not Monsieur Panterelli. It was someone else in the kitchens. Monsieur Panterelli somehow uncovered the plot and accused him."

I thought of Matteo's assistant, the dour-faced Lucas. I would not soon forget the way he glared at me. "Where are they now?" I asked. "The cook and the guardsman?"

"The man in the kitchens has been caught, and the guardsman who escaped will soon be caught as well," she assured me.

"What will happen to them?" I asked, not wishing to be put off. I was not worried, but I was indeed curious.

"They will be punished," she said. "There is no further danger. You must not worry." She would say no more.

Later I learned that the guardsman had been seized as he fled to Scotland; he was brought back to France, where he was tortured, hanged, and quartered. Lucas may have suffered a similar fate, for I did not see him again in the kitchens. I could not easily put the incident out of mind. Would there be others who wished to harm me? But those worries did not hinder me from begging Matteo for frittered pears.

When the court departed from Amboise late in the spring and moved to Fontainebleau, I found out why I had not seen Lady Fleming since before Easter.

"The king sent her away," La Flamin told me between sobs. "Everyone knows she is expecting a child. The king is the father, and he made her leave."

I scarcely knew what to say. Everyone at court was talking about Lady Fleming. Queen Catherine and Madame de Poitiers had banded together and insisted that the Scottish woman not continue to embarrass the court. I took La Flamin's hand and told her sympathetically, "It will be difficult for you to be without your mother. But you must console yourself that when this is over, she will be back with you and all will be well again."

Marie Fleming looked at me, her lip trembling. "All will

not be well again, Madame Marie. My mother humiliates me."

Now I truly did not know what to say. I shook my head and ran off to find Sinclair, my source of all court gossip.

"Lady Fleming likes to put on airs," my nurse reported smugly. "And she has not the sense of a cat. Went about boasting that it's the king's child swelling her belly, and her a grandmother herself! You knew that, didn't you? That she has grown sons back in Scotland who've presented her with children of their own?"

I nodded as though I knew all about it. Maybe I had at one time, but I had been gone from my old home for so long that I had forgotten much of whatever I had once known.

Sinclair prattled on about Lady Fleming. "With my own two good ears I heard her say, plain as I'm telling it to you now, 'I have done all that I can, and God be thanked, I am with child by the king, for which I count myself both honored and happy.' Her exact words, I heard them from her own lips, said not just to me but to anyone willing to listen."

Sinclair helped herself to a bit of bread and spread on a thick layer of fruit conserve. "Where has Lady Fleming gone?" I asked impatiently. "And what will I do now for a governess?" I had not loved her, not the way I did Sinclair, for as governess Lady Fleming had too often seemed preoccupied with her own comfort and not sufficiently concerned with mine. But I had known her since I was born, she was my mother's friend and familiar to me, and now that she had disappeared, I missed her. And I understood why La Flamin felt humiliated.

"Gone to a convent herself, most likely," said Sinclair with pursed lips. "Madame de Poitiers is not likely to want her back at court, and the king will do whatever the duchess says, just as he always does, poor fool." Sinclair could not understand why I liked the duchess as much as I did. "As to a new governess," sniffed Sinclair, "you'll likely find out soon enough."

CHAPTER 12

Heartbreak

FOR THE NEXT FEW MONTHS my mother traveled all over France, accompanied by her Scottish court. I was often with her. In June, both courts moved to Châteaubriand, a royal palace near Nantes. The English ambassador arrived in France with the purpose of reminding King Henri once more that Edward VI, who had succeeded his horrible father, Henry VIII, as king of England, desired me as his bride. King Henri refused, explaining to the ambassador, as he had done many times in the past, that I was to marry the dauphin. Then one jolly evening King Henri and the English ambassador arrived at a solution, agreeing that Princesse Élisabeth would make an even better match for fifteen-year-old King Edward. This seemed to please everyone. Even Princesse Élisabeth liked the arrangement, though it would not have mattered if she had not.

A series of fêtes was organized to celebrate the future union. During the day the noblemen engaged in archery, tennis, and wrestling in the open fields while the ladies looked on, wretchedly uncomfortable in the formal court dress that the occasion required. The feasting was put off until midnight, and we dined by moonlight at banquet tables set up under the trees with the benefit of a cooling breeze. On some nights torches were lit, and the men went hunting for red deer, the party going on into the small hours of the morning.

Rumors of an outbreak of plague in the region of Nantes brought an end to the celebration, and people fled to other parts of the country. When it seemed safe to do so, Maman resumed her progresses, but she had begun to speak about returning to Scotland. Such talk never failed to distress me.

I pleaded with her not to leave. "Dearest Maman," I begged, "stay with me here! You belong in France, do you not?" I was sure I would eventually be able to persuade her if I just kept at it long enough and strongly enough. She put me off with a smile and soft words, but as the bright greens of summer were fading, she silenced me firmly.

"*Ma chère* Marie," she said, "let me explain something to you. You are the crowned queen of Scotland, and one day you will return to rule the country in which you were born. Until that day comes, it is my duty to protect your interests there, to keep peace among the jealous clans, and to prevent the English on our border from resorting to harsh measures, as they have done in the past. I would prefer to remain here with you, my son François, my mother and brothers and other relatives. Everything I know and love and cherish is here in France, but my duty is in Scotland.

And *your* duty, my dear child, is to savor every moment we have together for as long as I am here, and to carry on bravely when I am gone."

This was not what I wanted to hear. For a moment I wondered if I might not order my mother to stay. I was the queen, was I not? I took precedence over her, did I not? But in the end I understood, and I stopped pleading and tried to do as she asked.

In September, as summer drew to a close and the long days grew shorter, I accompanied my mother to Amiens, where my brother lived in the château he had inherited from his father, the first duke of Longueville. My mother had lived there during her first marriage, and François had been born there. Her visit to her old home and to François was to be my mother's last before she boarded a galley in Rouen for the voyage back to Scotland.

François was not yet sixteen, but he welcomed us with great style. There were banquets at which my mother's Scottish courtiers were served the simple fare they pre-ferred, meat and fish without the delicate sauces favored by Queen Catherine. No strange vegetables made an ap-pearance.

We passed the evenings with music. My mother danced exquisitely. She played the lute and sang the songs she had sung to each of us when we were small children. François was kind and affectionate to me, exclaiming that I was growing fast and would no doubt someday be as tall as my mother. "And surely as beautiful," he added, making me blush. When the weather was fine, the three of us rode out into the countryside to enjoy a picnic served in a pretty grove of trees near the River Somme. It was as though we three had lived together all our lives.

One day, as we dined by the river, the weather changed suddenly and dramatically. Dark clouds swept in and covered the sun like a blanket, the air turned cool, and a cold rain began to fall. Our servants scrambled to gather up the remains of our meal, and we rushed back to the château, but not before we were all thoroughly drenched and chilled.

My mother and I changed quickly from our wet garments into dry clothes and were soon cozily warming ourselves by a fire. While we waited for François to join us, I showed my mother the needlepoint I had begun working as a gift for him under Queen Catherine's attentive gaze. I pointed out his coat of arms, a yellow shield with a red chevron and a blue fish, traced onto a piece of canvas for me by the king's official embroiderer.

"I hope to finish it for his birthday," I confided.

"François's birthday is the thirtieth of October," Maman reminded me. "And you still have a great part of it to do."

"I know," I said. "I work on it as often as I can." I hurried to put it away before my brother arrived and spoiled my surprise.

But an hour passed, and part of another, and still François did not join us. Puzzled, my mother sent a servant to inquire. The servant returned and reported, "Monsieur the duke is unwell, madame," he said. "He has taken to his bed with a fever."

"Unwell?" My mother was on her feet in a moment and hurrying out of the chamber. When I rose to follow her, she said sharply, "Wait here, Marie, I beg you."

I obeyed, but my mother did not return. I sat alone, working on my brother's gift without fear of discovery. It grew late. Servants lit candles and drew the draperies. At last my brother's steward came to tell me that I was to have my supper with several members of the Scottish court.

"Where is my lady mother?" I asked, unhappy at being deserted. "And my brother?"

"Your mother is with the duke your brother," he said.

"Is my brother ill?"

The steward hesitated. "*Oui,* Madame Marie, he is ill. Very ill. His physician is attending him."

"I wish to see him," I said.

"Your lady mother has given express instructions that you may not see him. She fears that you might then fall ill, as he has."

I nodded, pretending to agree, and accompanied the steward to the small dining hall where some of the Scottish court had gathered. They all rose respectfully. I signaled them to be seated. The meal began. The Scots quickly forgot about me and began talking among themselves in the language that had been mine until I was forced to learn French. I understood them, but the words no longer came easily to my lips.

As soon as the meal was finished, I ran from the hall. Whether my mother wanted me to or not, I was determined to find her and my brother. And because no one was paying any attention to me, I succeeded.

François, pale as death, lay in his bedchamber surrounded by somber physicians and priests. My mother knelt beside the bed holding his hand. I pushed past the small crowd and went to kneel beside my mother. "Why are you here, Marie?" Maman demanded in a hoarse whisper. "I gave orders that you were not to come."

"I know," I said simply. "But I am here."

François groaned and moved his head. A surgeon held a basin and watched my brother's blood flow into it from his arm. Tears rolled down my mother's cheeks, and she wiped at them impatiently. "He is dying," she said in a voice roughened by sorrow and weeping.

For three days and nights my mother did not leave my brother's bedside. Too despairing to protest, she permitted me to stay with her through the long hours of his suffering. Food was brought to us. I ate with scarcely diminished appetite, as usual, but my mother swallowed hardly a mouthful. She dozed for a few minutes at a time on a pallet made up for her, but she was fiercely adamant that I must sleep in my own bed in my rooms in a separate wing of the old castle. She promised to send for me if there was any change in my brother's condition.

But she did not. On the morning of the fourth day my mother met me at the door of his chamber. She was very calm. "I have borne four sons," she said, "and I have lost four. Your brother awoke during the night and cried out. I rushed to him. He died in my arms."

My brother's body was removed and a funeral arranged. Again, as with my grandfather's funeral, I was not permitted to attend in person but was represented by a proxy—one of the old Scottish gentlemen took my place. I did not understand why I was being kept away. Was I somehow the cause of the death of everyone my mother loved? Was I being punished? And if I was being punished, what was my sin? The idea came to me during this particularly somber time that perhaps being a queen of not one country but two carried with it a special curse.

My uncle Charles celebrated the funeral Mass. Maman, who had been out of mourning for my grandfather for just six months, again went into deepest mourning. She and I, as well as every member of the French court, dressed in black cloaks with hoods and long full sleeves.

While we grieved, news reached us that Queen Catherine had given birth to her sixth child, Edouard-Alexandre, on the eighteenth of September, 1551. Just a few days earlier, Lady Fleming had sent word from the convent that she had given birth to a boy, and the king had acknowledged the infant as his son, naming him Henri d'Angoulême. Now there would be two new *enfants* in the royal nursery—Queen Catherine's and Lady Fleming's—under the critical eye of Madame de Poitiers. La Flamin did not wish to speak of it, and my mother was too deeply enveloped in her grief to pay any attention to this.

Even with all that had happened, I tried to savor every moment of our last weeks together as my mother had requested, but I found little joy in it. Inevitably, the day arrived when my mother and her entourage boarded the king's galley, and I watched her sail away.

For days I wept, mourning her departure as though she too had died.

III

A French Girl, Through and Through

HOW INNOCENT I WAS! The seeds of all that is now happening to me were sown during those early years. The dangers I faced were not just from a single disgruntled Scot who tried to poison me but from the people closest to me, people I loved and trusted. But I was young and naive, blinded by the grandeur of my position, and I did not recognize the threat.

CHAPTER 13

Madame de Parois

As soon as Lady Fleming had recovered from childbirth, she was sent back to Scotland in disgrace. La Flamin wept to see her go—she had forgiven her mother's transgressions, though it was surely difficult to have her mother the subject of gossip and crude jokes.

I was unhappy also after Lady Fleming was gone, for now I had to deal with my new governess. Madame de Parois was a virtuous woman who proved to have no humor, little sense, and a thoroughly nasty disposition. She had no discernible bosom or waist, her lips were thin and unsmiling, she wore a perpetual frown, and her voice was as harsh as a crow's.

"You can see why the queen and Madame de Poitiers chose her," remarked La Flamin. "Madame de Parois is so ill-looking and unpleasant that no one could possibly be jealous of her."

It was cruel of La Flamin to say such a thing, but I did not disagree.

My uncle Charles, who had recommended her, assured my mother that the lady was devout and would see to it that I was regular in my prayers. I thought that a poor reason for hiring her. I did not need anyone to monitor my devotion or oversee my prayers. I wanted a governess who would order new gowns when I needed them and make sure that my living arrangements were suitable to my rank as queen. Now almost nine years old, I truly believed I was more adult than child, though Madame de Parois seemed to take pleasure in reminding me that I was *not* an adult and should not expect to be treated as one. We were at odds with each other from the start. The situation did not improve.

A little more than a year after the arrival of Madame de Parois, when François was nine, King Henri decided that the dauphin should be given his own apartments and a staff of servants. Queen Catherine insisted that Princesse Élisabeth and Princesse Claude, who were still very young, did not need their own households but would stay with her in the queen's dressing room.

I learned of these changes in a conversation with Anne d'Este, my uncle's wife, who was always very kind to me and, above all, honest. We were sitting together in the large enclosed court where King Henri played tennis nearly every day. She had her children with her, Henri and Catherine, named for the king and queen. Her infant daughter greeted me with chortles and waves of her tiny fists. Her little son grinned up at me impishly and clutched my skirts.

I adored them both and thought that someday in the far distant future, the dauphin and I would produce enough chubby little ones like them to fill the royal nursery.

The king was a commanding figure, dressed all in white from his fine white cap to his white shoes. An excellent tennis player, he was quick on his feet and powerful in his return of the ball. His opponent that day was Anne's husband, François, and though my uncle played well, the king played better. We did not see the end of the match, for the infant set up such a fuss that we had to carry her out, leaving Queen Catherine and other members of the court to watch the inevitable outcome of the game.

"Your uncles were shocked to learn Queen Catherine's decision to keep the princesses in her quarters," Anne said while we walked back and forth to quiet her howling daughter. "They are quite displeased. What, they ask, is to become of the queen of Scots? Your uncles do not believe that you, the eldest of the royal children as well as a crowned queen, should ever have to accept less than the privileges the dauphin enjoys."

"What will happen now?" I asked, and took little Catherine from her mother. She immediately ceased her noise and smiled at me.

"We shall see," Anne replied. "The main issue is money. I am sure you know that."

There had been many discussions about money, that much I did know. It was often assumed, incorrectly I believe, that young persons did not understand the tensions and issues around them. In fact we overheard much more than the adults realized, discussed it with our friends, and came to conclusions that might have been inaccurate but were likely somewhere near the truth.

Madame de Parois, in particular, misjudged me. She boasted to my mother that she kept me ignorant of the financial problems, but she was wrong. I was to have my own household, my own servants, and as many horses and dogs as I wished. But the moves of the court were always costly. Three pack mules were needed just to carry my bed from one château to the next, dozens more to carry the rest of my furnishings—wall hangings and books, even the plates and cups and spoons needed for dining, as well as trunks filled with gowns, furs, shoes, gloves, stockings, and underthings, and the three large coffers with my jewels. Who should pay for moving them? Were my expenses the responsibility of Scotland and my mother or of France and King Henri?

It was not just moving expenses. I loved pretty clothes and had a fondness for luxurious touches. I wanted to be well dressed, and I understood that a splendid wardrobe was my due. If the French princesses had a special kind of silk to line their dresses, then I wished to have the same. I attended numerous events where as a crowned queen I had to dress the part, in gowns made of cloth of gold or silver tissue. Besides, I was growing. My skirts were becoming too short, my bodices too tight. And I could scarcely be expected to attend a fashionable wedding in a gown that had been seen at least twice before.

"I wish to have my monogram stitched onto my dresses," I told Madame de Parois. "Anne d'Este has her cipher on her gowns, and so do all the fashionable ladies of the court. I must be as well turned out as any of them!"

"The monogram is an extravagance and unaffordable," Madame de Parois replied stiffly.

"My rank demands it," I insisted.

"There is not enough money to buy the gowns you believe your rank demands," my governess informed me. "Your wardrobe and other expenses are more than the Scottish government can afford and the French are willing to pay."

So much for her claim that she kept me ignorant of financial problems. Still, I did not react well to being told I could not have something that seemed to me an absolute necessity and quite within reason.

I took my complaint to my uncle Charles, the cardinal, who was known for his luxurious taste. Like his brother François, he was tall and slender, with heavy-lidded blue eyes, thick brows, a well-tended mustache, and a perfumed beard. He dressed in the red robes of a cardinal only on official occasions. For his private visits with me he wore the finest silks and a beautifully embroidered velvet doublet.

"Surely, *mon cher oncle,* you understand how important it is for your niece to keep up appearances in the French court!" I argued with my most persuasive smile. Anne d'Este had shown me that a gracious manner achieved more than frowns and foot stamping, and I did my best to imitate her elegant style.

The cardinal laid aside the leather-bound volume he had

been reading and regarded me carefully. "You do understand, do you not, Marie, that funds are not unlimited, though we may wish otherwise? When only a certain sum of money is available, then economies must be made in one place in order to satisfy needs and desires in another."

"I do understand, Uncle," I said, congratulating myself for having this very grown-up conversation. "What economies do you propose?"

"I have been thinking this over for some time, Marie, and after due consideration, I recommend that you accompany the court on fewer journeys. Stay longer at the châteaux you most enjoy, such as Fontainebleau, omit the few that are less interesting—Compiègne, for example—and rejoin the court a month later. This makes a great deal of sense, I am sure you agree, and it will save a great deal of money."

Uncle Charles leaned back, made a steeple of his fingers, and waited, a satisfied smile on his lips. He no doubt expected me to give my assent immediately. But I did not.

"Surely you cannot be serious!" I cried, gravely disappointed—even horrified—by his suggestion. "I would be separated from the dauphin, whom I shall one day marry, and the other royal children, whom I love as my own sisters and brothers! I would no longer be in the company of Queen Catherine, or Madame de Poitiers, or King Henri, my own dearest family!"

The first tears had begun to trickle down my cheeks.

The cardinal appeared startled by this vehement response. "My dear Marie," he said soothingly, "it seems to me a small enough sacrifice. You would still have the company of your old friends the Four Maries. I was not suggesting that you be abandoned."

He was maddeningly calm. Could he not understand how much this mattered to me? I took a deep breath. "It is not a small sacrifice!" I shouted, forgetting the lesson of Anne d'Este.

The cardinal's lips formed a thin, disapproving line. "Very well," he said after a long pause, during which I had begun to weep in earnest. "Your journeys will not be curtailed. We shall have to find other economies, and you are no more likely to approve of them. But be assured, my dear niece, that in the end you have no choice in the matter."

He picked up his book again and began to read, and I understood that I had been dismissed.

❧

I continued to move from one château to the next with the court, but I soon realized there were fewer servants moving with me to tend to my needs. Several who had received no wages for some time simply quit. My hairdresser stopped coming. Fortunately, my friend Seton had always enjoyed frouncing my hair, and she readily took up the responsibility, fixing my hair in a different style every day. While she crimped and curled, we chattered about important matters—fashions we desired (I was still determined to have my embroidered monograms); delectable treats we might persuade Chef Matteo to prepare in the royal kitchens (gâteau de crème, the cream cake that was a favorite); people we loved (Anne d'Este, among others); and people we loathed (Madame de Parois, without question).

Madame de Parois became more and more discontented and ill-tempered. She got into a terrible argument with one of my senior ladies in waiting, and I stood open-mouthed as they flung harsh words at each other. In the end, the lady stormed off and handed in her resignation. I hoped that Madame de Parois would also resign, but she did not, and our arguments grew more heated.

It was in my nature as well as my upbringing to be generous to others, and so when I believed a gown was no longer suitable because I had outgrown it or the fashion had changed or I had been seen in it too many times, I sent it to my mother's younger sister, the one who was the abbess of a convent—the same convent to which Grand-Mère had given my unsuitable gowns when I first arrived in France. The good nuns would take the dresses apart and salvage what they could of the luxurious fabrics to make altar hangings for their convent chapels and vestments for the priests. At my mother's suggestion, I frequently gave gowns made of less expensive fabrics to friends or servants. But I did not give any to Madame de Parois.

My governess objected. "What, are you afraid to give me any of your castoffs lest you make me rich? That is laughable! Anyone can see that you intend to keep me as poor as a beggar!"

What can be said to such a jealous and spiteful person? I felt as though she had slapped me. I was about to utter some cruel words, but I thought of my mother and said only, "Madame, I am sorry for you."

Then I told my mistress of the wardrobe that if she saw the governess taking away any of my things without my explicit consent, she should inform me quietly. "If I want to give one of my gowns to the abbess or to any other worthy person, that is my right. Madame de Parois has nothing to say about it."

That was not the end of our battles. Parois insisted she had the authority to tell me what I could and could not wear. I was fond of jewels, like many girls of my age, and I could indulge my fondness because I had so many—several chests of costly necklaces, rings, bracelets, and earrings. One day I decided to put on a pearl necklace with a large sapphire that went nicely with the blue velvet gown I was wearing. As Magdalène, my maidservant, was clasping it around my neck, Madame de Parois noticed and frowned. No one could frown as deeply as my governess.

"Do not wear that necklace, Marie," she said. "*Je vous en prie*—I beg you."

Magdalène began to remove it, but I stopped her. "Do continue, Magdalène. I want to wear it."

"It is not appropriate for you to wear that necklace to your lessons," insisted my governess. My maidservant hesitated, looking from one to the other, unsure whom to obey.

"It is my necklace," I said, "and I shall wear it if I wish."

I refused to surrender in this battle of wills, and so did my governess. "It is my responsibility to you, your mother, and the royal family of France to see that you are appropriately attired," she barked, her jaw tightly clenched. "And I am instructing you that the necklace is not appropriate. Kindly remove it at once."

In a temper I seized a handful of rings and bracelets and defiantly began to put on all of them. Tears were streaming down the cheeks of poor frightened Magdalène, who had no idea what she should do.

"You leave me no choice but to report your willfulness and your disobedience to your lady mother!" The furious woman was seething with righteous anger.

"*Comme vous voulez, madame!*" I told her in a saucy singsong. "Do as you like!"

"You are becoming a wild thing!" she cried passionately. "Your behavior and your speech are unseemly!"

"A wild thing, you say? Then I say, Good! I shall be as wild as you think I am. A wild queen!"

To make my point, I wore the necklace and more than enough rings every day for a week. Meanwhile, Madame de Parois, true to her word, wrote to my mother. I knew this might not end well, and I also wrote to my mother, trying to win her support.

Please, dearest Madame my mother, I wrote beseechingly, *pay as little attention as you possibly can to the reports sent to you by my lady governess, Madame de Parois, on the issue of my wardrobe, over which I know that she has full authority, though it would seem such authority is no longer warranted, as I am now of an age where I may be trusted to make decisions on my own behalf on my manner of dress.*

I was not sure my mother would agree that at almost eleven I could be trusted in such matters, and I was sick with worry that my governess's complaints would cause my mother a great deal of displeasure. Nothing in my life could distress me more than knowing the dearest person on earth, my mother, would love me less because of this thoroughly unpleasant person. What if Madame de Parois reported the conversation in which I had vowed to be a wild queen?

As a result I fell seriously ill—and I was certain my illness *was* a result of the worry—and I even believed for a time that I might die. And if I did not die, I was convinced that I would not fully recover my health and spirits so long as Madame de Parois was my governess.

In the end I did recover, and Parois remained stubbornly in place. But I could not tolerate the miserable situation much longer.

CHAPTER 14

A Miserable Situation

FOR THE NEXT TWO YEARS Madame de Parois clung to her position as my governess and continued to find ways to make trouble—some minor and some quite serious.

Queen Catherine, my kind friend and companion during hours spent together over our needlework, suddenly turned cold. I was no longer invited to her apartments. She ignored me. I had no idea why. Had I done something to offend her? I could not imagine what.

Court gossip made its way down to the servants' dining hall, where my faithful Sinclair learned the actual facts and related them to me. Madame de Parois had been spreading a false rumor about me. She claimed I was overheard speaking ill of Queen Catherine to her rival Diane de Poitiers. The rumor reached the queen, who believed what she was told about my behavior.

It was true that I had become fond of Madame de Poitiers, especially after her kindness to me when my mother left for Scotland at the end of her yearlong visit. To take my mind off my sadness, the duchess had several times invited me to Château d'Anet.

The old square towers of the château had been torn down and replaced by dramatic black and white columns. The intertwined initials *H,* for Henri, and *D,* for Diane, and her cipher, three interlaced crescent moons, were to be found everywhere. At the entrance to the château an enormous clock with a hunting scene stood atop the massive gate. Every time the minute hand reached the twelve, a pack of bronze hounds holding a large bronze stag at bay leaped toward the quarry; the stag turned to flee, stopping first to strike the hour with its raised hoof before bounding away from the dogs. I never tired of that marvelous clock and begged to be present as each hour approached.

Anet became a place of enchantment for me, and I was delighted that Madame de Poitiers welcomed me as her guest. But I should have known that Queen Catherine would not be pleased when her young companion of the needle and embroidery silk deserted her for her rival's magnificent retreat, especially when I learned that Anet had been a gift to the duchess from the king. Naturally, Madame de Parois knew of my excursions from Saint-Germain to Anet—I could go nowhere without her knowledge—and on one of her frequent trips to Paris, my governess launched the rumor that "the little Scottish queen" had become an intimate friend of the king's mistress. To add spice to her story, Parois claimed that Madame de Poitiers and I passed our time remarking on the queen's shortcomings—her aging looks, her dreary gowns, even the way she spoke French with an Italian accent. Worst of all, Madame de Parois went about saying that I often referred to Queen Catherine as "the merchant's daughter," which I had not, though I had overheard courtiers who disdained the queen speak of her in that way.

"That's the talk among the servants, my lady," said Sinclair. "They hear their mistresses gossiping about the gossipers and add a bit to it. You are paying the price for your governess's wicked tongue, you who have never said an unkind word about Queen Catherine. Sadly, the queen believes what she has been told."

Sinclair was not fond of Madame de Poitiers, but she heartily disliked Parois. "A person cannot help but feel an ache in her heart for Queen Catherine at having the king's haughty mistress parade in front of her every hour of the day and night. But Madame de Parois is a shrew and a mischief-maker, and I have long wished her gone."

The situation caused me great distress, but there was little I could do to mend it. I did complain to my uncles and to my grandmother about my governess's behavior. But it was not easy to remove such a woman from her perch, to which she clung with all her might.

During the year when my body was changing from a child's to a woman's, I was also growing quite tall, and by the time I observed my thirteenth birthday, in December of 1555, I had reached nearly six feet in height. Nothing escaped the critical eye and sharp tongue of Madame de Parois.

"A queen does not go about with her shoulders hunched. Your posture must be impeccable, and you are becoming stooped. Stand up straight, Madame Marie!" she commanded. "Shoulders back! Chin up!"

Commands and lectures failed to correct the problem. Every morning Madame de Parois appeared in my chamber with a book or some other object that I was to balance on top of my head while I walked rigid as a statue up and down the gallery several times, trying not to let the object fall. If it did, I had to start over. This exercise was repeated again later in the day. My governess developed a habit of clicking her tongue whenever she caught me slumping. I could be sitting with my tutors or walking in the gardens with the Four Maries or dining with the dauphin, and I would hear a distinct *tch-tch,* the signal from the dreaded governess that my posture was not perfect.

I must confess, however, that her method was successful. As much as I detested those exercises and hated the click of her tongue, in time I outgrew the slumping, and my posture became truly regal.

The tension with Madame de Parois did not resolve itself until at last she left for Paris permanently, claiming that her health no longer permitted her to stay on as my governess. I, too, fell ill rather often and for long periods, and I blamed these bouts of sickness on Parois. But now that I was thirteen, the family finally agreed that I no longer needed a governess and was entitled to my own establishment. From then on two of my uncles—François the soldier and Charles the cardinal—would oversee my education with advice from Grand-Mère, all of whom I loved deeply and whose guidance I would respect and cherish. I enjoyed my increasing independence and looked forward to the day when no one would have any say over me and I would be in charge of my own life.

Having a household of my own was expensive. I already had a wardrobe mistress and two or three maidservants, but now I required men and women to look after my horses and dogs and organize transport during the court's moves from one château to another, as well as a steward to be in charge of everything.

Most important, to my mind, was a chef to oversee a small kitchen staff. I wanted nothing so much as having Monsieur Matteo on hand to make frittered pears every single night if I wished, but the problems Madame de Parois had created between me and Queen Catherine meant that I did not dare to lure away the queen's favorite. Then Anne d'Este told me that Monsieur Matteo's nephew Giorgio had recently arrived from Italy. She brought the young cook to my apartments, and Giorgio immediately agreed to become my chef.

As soon as a kitchen staff was in place, I invited my uncle Charles to supper. He oversaw my finances, though I had the freedom to spend money as I wished—giving it to favored servants, to musicians and actors, to the three old men who cared for the royal bears, to anyone who particularly pleased me. I wanted to show Charles my gratitude. I felt very much a grown-up queen when I summoned Giorgio to plan the menu.

"We shall have frittered pears," I said.

Giorgio acknowledged my order with a bow and asked, "Will there be anything else, Madame Marie?"

I had not thought beyond the pears. When I hesitated, Giorgio said smoothly, "May I suggest canard à l'orange— duck in an orange sauce. It will go nicely with the pears, madame."

I agreed that it would. Besides, the duck would give me a chance to show off the silver forks I had ordered. I wanted my table to be just as elegant as Queen Catherine's.

Uncle Charles was fond of excellent food and fine wine, and I was proud to be able to offer him both. The canard à l'orange impressed him. So did the peas and other vegetables Giorgio had persuaded me to serve, and we both enjoyed the frittered pears. We discussed the tutors who would be continuing my education, as well as many other matters, and when I knelt to receive my uncle's blessing before he left, I felt that I was truly becoming a woman who could make up her own mind.

In 1553, Queen Catherine had given birth to another daughter, Marguerite, whom we all called Margot. Less than two years later another son, Hercule, was born. Then in June of

1556, the queen barely survived the difficult birth of twin girls, Victoire and Jeanne, who died almost as soon as they were born. The queen had borne ten children. Seven were still living. Princesse Élisabeth was the second oldest, after the dauphin, François.

England's sixteen-year-old King Edward VI had died during the summer of 1553, putting an end to King Henri's plans for Princesse Élisabeth to marry him when she came of age. King Henri began to consider other prospective bridegrooms. Though we were both very young, Élisabeth and I often discussed our eventual marriages. My future was entirely settled: I would marry her brother François when the king determined we were old enough. But at the age of eleven, Élisabeth did not yet know her future.

"Papa and Maman discuss it often, but I am not supposed to know about it," Élisabeth confided to me. "I think they want me to marry a Spanish prince, Philip, provided he does not marry someone else first." She sighed. "I doubt I shall meet him before the wedding. Not like you, Marie, growing up here with my brother and seeing him almost every day. You have even learned to speak French, and beautifully too."

I saw that her lip was trembling and her blue eyes were swimming with tears. We understood well that neither of us had any say in the choice of a husband. That decision was entirely up to our parents, who were most concerned about making alliances that would benefit our countries. "You will learn to speak Spanish just as easily," I said, trying to reassure my dear friend. But Élisabeth had begun to weep.

"Philip is so old!" She sobbed. "He is twenty-eight—almost eighteen years older than I am—and he has already been married once. He has a son my age. His wife died." She dabbed at her eyes. "What if I loathe him?"

"You will not loathe him," I said as though I knew what I was talking about, but I was thinking, *What if she does loathe him?* "I shall come to visit you in Spain if you marry Philip," I promised, wondering if I could really do that. "And I am sure your father will arrange for you to visit France. But nothing is decided yet, and there may be other prospective bridegrooms that you will find easier to like."

"Do you think so?" she asked plaintively.

"Of course!" I seized her hand. "Now let us find Giorgio and ask him to make us something delicious."

CHAPTER 15

Lessons in Ruling

THE LONGER I LIVED in France, the less I could remember about being a Scot. I spoke French as well as the dauphin and his sisters. I never spoke my native Scots, not even to Sinclair, who had come to understand French well enough, though she was often ridiculed for her strong Scots accent, her rolled *r*'s and bitten-off final consonants. "It sounds as though you are choking," she had been told.

My Four Maries, who were now officially my ladies in waiting, spoke nothing but French, even when we were alone.

Long ago I had abandoned wrapping myself in the traditional Scottish furs and leathers that I had once worn so proudly, partly because I had grown too tall for them, but mostly because I had come to love French fashion.

I had become a French girl, through and through.

But I was also learning to become a French *queen,* and for this role I was in training every day of my life. My uncle

Charles, who traveled with the court and was constantly in the company of King Henri, easily persuaded the king that I must receive the best possible education. I had demonstrated that I could learn English and enough Spanish and Italian to carry on a polite conversation. I had mastered the grammar of Latin and could read, write, and speak it well.

Every day I was required to compose an essay on a different theme, all assigned by Monsieur Amyot and addressed to people I knew. I wrote an essay to everyone I could think of—not only to François and Élisabeth, but to the king and queen and my Guise uncles and aunts, my grandmother, and any cousins I thought deserved my words of wisdom. I labored over these assignments, but they were only for practice and were not sent.

It was the study of geography that captured my imagination. "Did you know," I asked my four friends, "that France lies farther south than Scotland, and that is why it is warmer here?" I showed them a copy of a manuscript written hundreds of years earlier by Ptolemy, a Greek astronomer and geographer. "And did you know that Scotland receives more sunlight in summer than France does?"

"Hmmm," they murmured, plainly not much interested.

My uncles had other priorities for my education. "You must have a thorough understanding of history," said Charles, the cardinal. "The examples of history will demonstrate how to govern well and will aid you in your understanding of politics."

"It is most important that you learn to present your ideas persuasively. To do that you must speak eloquently," added

François, the soldier. "The arts of speaking well and ruling well are like the strong hand in the well-fitting glove."

I looked from one to the other, happy as always to be in the company of two uncles who loved me so well.

Charles wore a satisfied smile. "I must say, *ma chère nièce,* that you have quite enchanted our king. He has told me how much he enjoys chatting with you, sometimes for an hour at a time."

I knew this was true. From my first months in the royal nursery, King Henri had always seemed to take pleasure in my company. Now that I was older and in my own establishment, he came by often to question me closely about my studies and to ask my opinion on certain texts I had been reading. He decided that the dauphin and I should take some of our lessons together, and Monsieur Danès was hired to instruct us in Greek. I enjoyed the lessons, but François was an intolerably lazy student.

"Monsieur Danès told me that his own teacher Budé was so brilliant he taught himself Greek perfectly in a little more than a month," the dauphin grumbled. "But I dislike it, and no matter how Monsieur Danès tries to teach me, I cannot learn." François showed me a manuscript written by Budé, bound in leather and stamped in gold. "He presented this to my grandfather King François. I cannot make a thing out of it."

"It *is* beautiful," I said, turning the pages carefully and reading bits of it aloud.

"Well, then, you keep it," said the dauphin sourly and

waved it away. "I just want to get rid of the thing." Abruptly his mood brightened. "You are a much better student than I am, Marie," he said. "I think the old king would have loved for you to have it."

François was nearly twelve, his skin so pale I could make out the blue threads of veins beneath. He was still small; I stood a full head taller. We often shared little jokes at the expense of our tutors, laughing at Amyot's unruly eyebrows' looking like twin nests and speculating what manner of bird might have assembled them. We had cruel things to say about the bedraggled feather in Monsieur Danès's cap and the way the velvet had rubbed off the elbows of his coat. When the craving for sweets struck us, we found ways to coax one of the chefs to prepare them for us. My mother had sent me several ponies from the Shetland Isles of Scotland, as well as a litter of terrier pups, and I gave François first pick of both. He was my champion in all things, as I was his. He had become my dearest brother.

At the age of thirteen I was required to compose a discourse in Latin to declaim before the king and queen and the entire French court. Monsieur Amyot suggested that I speak about the responsibilities a ruler had to the church, but I had a different idea.

"I wish to speak on the importance of educating girls," I said. Monsieur Amyot's eyebrows twitched. "I have heard it said," I continued before he could interrupt, "that some courtiers feel that girls do not need an education, that it is bad for us and interferes with our proper conduct as women. I want to contest those ideas and prove them wrong."

The eyebrows quivered excitedly. "As you wish, Madame Marie," he said. "Then let us get to work."

It was much harder than I expected. I had all kinds of ideas and opinions, especially on the subject of the rights, or lack thereof, of Frenchwomen to inherit property and titles. I had been shocked to learn that a woman could not by law become the ruling queen of France.

"But suppose the dauphin and I marry and have only daughters? Could not the eldest princess inherit the throne?"

"*Non,* Madame Marie. According to ancient Salic law, she could not."

"This is not true in Scotland," I reminded my tutor. "I am the queen of Scotland, and I shall someday rule the Scots. An education is important for all women, not just queens."

"A woman may inherit the throne in Scotland, and in England too," Monsieur Amyot conceded. "But not in France."

I retreated reluctantly from my most outspoken opinions, and finally, after several rewritings, I had a thesis that won Monsieur Amyot's approval. My tutor in public speaking made sure I knew which words to emphasize. Orating in Latin, I practiced my delivery before my audience of three—two tutors and the dauphin, François, who felt obliged to try to distract me.

I was ready to appear before the most important members of the French court as well as my family. They gathered on a rainy afternoon in the Louvre, a beautiful palace built by the king to replace an old fortress. I was not nervous because I had practiced and I knew the material thoroughly. I enjoyed being the center of attention, and I had a lovely new gown. But François was sweating and even paler than usual. The dauphin did the worrying for both of us.

"Please go sit beside Élisabeth," I said firmly. "You make me nervous as well. When I finish, we will find some bread and marmalade and have a feast."

All went well, as I expected, and I received all manner of praise. I was told that my ideas were "well founded, well thought out, and spoken admirably." I would not have been satisfied with anything less. It did trouble me that it was unlikely I would ever have an opportunity to express my most serious ideas to the French people. My subjects in Scotland were far away, but I hoped the day would come when I could address them as their queen.

❦

That summer Diane de Poitiers invited me to Château d'Anet. I was accompanied by three of my Four Maries—La Flamin refused to go. She hated the woman responsible for sending her mother back to Scotland.

"Madame de Poitiers spoke of my mother's lack of dignity in flaunting her condition," La Flamin complained. "As though the duchess herself has not shown a complete lack of dignity in her years as the king's mistress."

We left her sulking at Saint-Germain, and I easily persuaded Princesse Élisabeth to accompany us instead. Élisabeth was in a much better mood because she was no longer pledged to marry Philip II of Spain; he had married the newly crowned queen of England, Mary Tudor. Mary had become queen after the death of her half brother Edward VI.

"Queen Mary is ten years older than Philip!" Élisabeth exclaimed. "And he is already twenty-nine!" Then she added, "Maybe I shall never have to marry anyone, and I can live with you and François after you are married. Would that not be splendid, Marie?"

"It would indeed!" I agreed. I did not add that it was highly unlikely. Élisabeth was much too valuable to France's position in the world for her father to allow her to remain unmarried.

It was an easy journey down the Seine by *bateau de rivière* to Anet. Madame de Poitiers greeted our group and escorted us to the château. She was an excellent equestrienne and proposed that we all ride out to a little pavilion in her park. But the skies were becoming dark and threatening, and the other Maries and Élisabeth eagerly accepted her suggestion that they stay behind. Madame de Poitiers and I would take our chances.

We had ridden a distance from the château when a sudden downpour sent us hurrying to take shelter in a small pavilion in a willow copse. The pavilion was exquisitely furnished, everything in black and white. I wanted to ask the duchess if she owned clothes in other colors, dresses that perhaps she wore when she was alone. But before I could think of a way to pose my question politely, Madame de Poitiers began inquiring about my studies, which I described, though she surely knew the answers already. Then she asked about my friendship with the dauphin—"your intended," she called François.

"The queen has me to thank for her large family," she added confidentially. "It was simply that she and her husband needed a bit of instruction, which I was pleased to provide."

I nodded, not sure how to respond. I knew—kitchen gossip, by way of Sinclair—that for years everyone had believed young Catherine de Médicis was barren. The birth of François proved them wrong.

Madame de Poitiers paused and arranged her black riding skirts. "Someday it will be up to you to produce the future kings and queens of France," she continued. "But of course that is not solely your responsibility. I have already introduced conversations with the dauphin concerning his responsibilities as well. When the time draws closer for your wedding, you and I will have conversations that will be of help to you." She took my hand in hers and looked at me earnestly. "You are fortunate to have a friend like me who can speak with you honestly and plainly," said the duchess.

"I once asked Madame de Parois a few questions," I blurted out. "She was not forthcoming."

"I suppose not," she replied and quickly changed the subject. "Now look—the rain has stopped." She rose and prepared to leave the pavilion. "Come, my dear Marie—it is almost time for the great clock to strike, and I know how much you enjoy that!"

CHAPTER 16

Preparation for Marriage

DURING MY THIRTEENTH YEAR, and then my fourteenth, my studies occupied most of my hours. Still, I found time for music. I practiced the lute and the harp, the clavichord and the virginals. My music teacher assured me that my singing voice was quite pleasant, though it is possible that some of the praise was mere flattery. I loved to dance and nearly always took part in the ballet, a form of dance that Queen Catherine had enjoyed watching in her childhood in Italy and introduced to the French court. But above all else I adored poetry.

I fairly worshiped Pierre de Ronsard, known in France as the prince of poets. A gaunt-faced man with close-cropped hair and a trim little beard, Monsieur Ronsard had traveled to Scotland with the court of my father's first wife, Madeleine of France. After Madeleine died, Monsieur Ronsard left Scotland and roamed the world before returning to settle in France. His was not like the classical poetry

I was assigned to study; it was written in the simple, natural words of the people. I had read the work of the Italian poet Dante. Ronsard's poetry was like that: elegant, pure, the language of the heart.

I read his poetry and listened to it read and sung, and I began to write poetry myself. For several carefree years I danced and sang, made music and wrote poems, rode horses and followed the hunt and enjoyed the company of my dogs and my family and my friends. My education was nearly complete. It was a wonderful life, and it never occurred to me that it would not go on forever.

In December of 1557, my fifteenth birthday was observed with feasting and music. There was an even greater celebration when the dauphin, François, turned fourteen a month later, just days after my uncle François thrilled the whole nation by wresting the port city of Calais away from the English, who had ruled it for more than two hundred years.

My uncle was now a national hero, praised as a military genius and lauded throughout France for his valor. No one had believed the French would ever see the last vestiges of the English removed from their country. Now the nation was giddy with joy, and in the midst of this buoyant mood King Henri decided that the time was right for the betrothal and the wedding of the dauphin, François de Valois, to Marie Stuart, queen of Scots. Diane de Poitiers brought me the news.

"Most of the forty days of Lent will be spent in prepara- . tions for the event," said the duchess. "I shall oversee the planning and the details. You may be assured that everything will be of the utmost elegance and to your complete liking."

My Four Maries were in ecstasies over the coming events. Princesse Élisabeth was delighted. But most excited of all was the dauphin, François.

"It is happening, Marie!" my future husband squealed joyously. "We are to be m-m-married very soon, and then we shall be together all the time! I shall never be apart from you, and you shall have my whole heart forever," he added solemnly, bringing my hand to his lips and covering it with kisses.

François was clearly devoted to me. We were best friends, as close as brother and sister. But in the swirl of excitement surrounding our coming wedding, I could not imagine how these feelings of kinship were to change into what I vaguely understood were the feelings of passion that existed between a husband and wife. Madame de Poitiers had promised she would speak to me on the subject. Oddly, it was Queen Catherine who spoke to me about it first.

She dismissed her ladies in waiting, something she had rarely done in my presence. "*Ma chère* Marie," she began when we were alone, "I want to talk to you honestly, an older woman to a young, inexperienced one. You are about to marry my son, as has been arranged and understood since you were both tiny children. Your living here among us for nearly ten years has allowed you to become acquainted with us in a way that is frankly unusual for a royal bride. I did not meet my husband until the night before our wedding, not an easy thing for a young girl, and I know that one day I will see my own sweet daughters in that same situation." She smiled faintly, staring off into the distance. "This does not mean it cannot end well for them, of course. I fell in love with Henri from the beginning."

That, I thought, *is an untruth, or at the very least an exaggeration.* But I murmured, *"Oui, madame ma reine,"* and kept my eyes on my embroidery, waiting for whatever the queen was about to say.

"I am very well satisfied you will make an excellent consort for my son. But you know that I am always concerned about his delicate health. He is very brave and follows his father into the jousting lists as though he were a grown man of robust health. But he is not. Far from it!" She hesitated, watching me intently. "I fear that he has not yet reached manhood. Do you understand me, Marie?"

"Oui, madame, je comprends," I replied. "I understand."

I did not need to be told that François was still physically a child. La Flamin, the most knowledgeable of the Four Maries, having had older brothers in her household in Scotland, had stated it bluntly: "He is still just a boy, Marie. The dauphin has not started his growth—he is more than a head shorter than you. His voice is as sweet as a babe's, and at fourteen it should be breaking. No soft fuzz on his cheeks, or anywhere else, I wager," she said, causing me to blush and turn away. "But," my friend continued, "that does not mean he will not have all he needs in the next six months or so."

His mother was telling me much the same thing. I had become a woman, but the dauphin, whom I was soon to marry, was not yet a man.

"I believe there is no rush to marry," said Queen Catherine, looking directly at me. I longed to look away, to avoid her steady gaze, but her eyes held mine. "However, my husband, the king, has been persuaded by your Guise uncles that the time is right to go forward with the marriage. It will do no good for me to oppose it, though I have expressed my opinion strongly to the king. Nor do you have any say in the matter, Marie. I have heard that Madame de Poitiers also opposes the immediacy of the wedding, preferring to delay it for a while longer. But she too seems powerless to change the king's mind."

I thought I detected a twitch of satisfaction in the queen's mouth when she stated that her rival, too, had limits to the amount of power she could exert once the king had made up his mind. Now I was more curious than ever to learn what Diane de Poitiers would say to me.

Secrecy surrounded the plans for the wedding, which was to be one of the grandest events ever to take place in Paris. Madame de Poitiers assumed responsibility for directing it all—from the viewing stands to be erected outside the Cathedral of Notre Dame in Paris, to the musicians who must learn music for all the parts of the celebration, to the cooks who would prepare the wedding feasts, and not forgetting the glove makers and embroiderers and seamstresses who would be creating the finery for everyone participating in the ceremony. And my wedding gown!

There was one issue on which I had made up my mind to stand firm, no matter what forces might be brought to bear against me. I had learned, to my dismay, that white was the traditional color of mourning for French queens and so was never worn at weddings. I was determined that white was going to be the color of my wedding gown, even if it meant defying convention. I knew what I wanted, and I saw no reason why I should not have my way.

"The color of the lily," I said firmly. "That is what I shall have."

There was surprise at my choice, maybe even some shock, but no argument. I think they understood that if I was old enough to marry, I was old enough to make certain decisions. This was one of them.

<hr />

Early in April, while the court was still in residence at Fontainebleau, two of my uncles invited me to dine with them in their private apartments. This was unusual. I had entertained each of them in my quarters—my uncle François and his lovely wife, Anne d'Este, on several occasions, and at other times the cardinal. I took pride in providing excellent food and drink. I had never been invited to dine with just the two brothers of my mother, and I felt this must be a meeting of grave importance. I expected that they would have advice of various kinds to offer me, and I looked forward to hearing it. It was a step toward my future as queen of France, my role when my husband someday became king.

"We wish to go over the nuptial contract that is being put in place for your protection," said Uncle François.

I nodded agreeably. "I will do whatever you think is appropriate."

He smiled and patted my hand. I dearly loved this uncle, who was like a father to me and was now hailed as a hero wherever he went. I would have done whatever he asked.

"In fact, there are two nuptial contracts. The first"—he handed me a document—"is quite straightforward, prepared by the commissioners in the Scottish Parliament, with the approval of our sister the queen mother, all of them acting in your best interests."

Yes, I thought, *my mother will have made sure everything is exactly as it should be.* I signed my name.

"There is a second contract we wish you to sign, Marie," said my uncle the cardinal. "But you must say nothing about this to anyone. Not anyone! Do I have your word?"

I raised my hand and promised.

"*Bien,*" said Uncle Charles. "Good. By the terms of this treaty, you agree that should you die without having produced children by François de Valois, the kingdom of Scotland and any rights you might have to the crown of England will be given over to the king of France, and all revenues will be paid to the king of France until the sum of a million gold crowns is reached."

The papers lay on the table in front of me, several pages densely written in French. There was the place I was to sign. The sharpened quill and block of ink lay ready. I tried to read through them, to understand exactly what they authorized. I read French very well, but I found these documents hard to comprehend. The letters swam before my eyes. My uncles hovered over me. "I am to promise that Scotland will be turned over to the king of France if I die without heirs?"

"In that extremely unlikely circumstance," my uncles agreed.

"And a million gold crowns as well?" I did understand that this was an enormous sum.

"*S'il vous plaît,* Marie," said my soldier uncle, "remember that France has protected Scotland from the English for years and will continue to do so. The death of Henry the Eighth did little to stop the raids at the border between England and Scotland. During his brief rule, Edward the Sixth did not stop them, and Queen Mary Tudor has done no better. It is only right and proper that in the unlikely event that you fail to produce heirs, the king of France should be compensated for his efforts and his great expense on behalf of Scotland. And of course, King Henri will continue to be Scotland's protector. For that you are grateful, I am sure."

"*Oui,* grateful, of course," I murmured. There seemed to be much more to it, and perhaps I did not grasp it all. But in the end I decided that I must trust my Guise uncles, as I always had, these two who had faithfully stood by my side and would surely continue to do so.

I picked up the pen and signed my name in large, even letters: *Marie Stuart.*

We were not yet finished. "Just one more document, *ma chère nièce,*" said the cardinal. Uncle François stepped out of the apartment, and while he was gone I thought I might look more carefully at the document I was about to sign and perhaps learn under what conditions Scotland would leave French hands and be returned to the Scots, but the cardinal distracted me with questions and comments about the coming wedding celebration. I had no chance to examine this third document before my uncle reappeared, this time in the company of my future husband. Both of us were to sign this paper, which stated that the previous two documents were valid and would remain valid no matter what promises I had made in the past or what contracts I might sign in the future. I did not fully realize then, nor did I for some time after, that I had signed away Scotland forever and made it a gift to France if I should die without leaving a living child.

The dauphin and I signed. My uncles looked pleased and—I think now—relieved.

The doors of the small room where we had met were opened wide. Musicians appeared seemingly out of nowhere, and a supper had been laid out. Anne d'Este and other specially invited friends of the Guise family, including a jubilant King Henri, joined us for a celebration. It was the first of many.

That was the fourth of April. A few days later the court moved to Paris, where on April 19, 1558, François de Valois and I would plight our troth in the great hall of the Palais du Louvre, where I had given my Latin oration. The wedding would take place five days after the betrothal. There still remained so much to think about and so much to be done—gowns fitted, headdresses created, a trousseau prepared—that I forgot all about the documents I had signed and the promises I had made in them.

CHAPTER 17

The Wedding

KING HENRI STOOD in the great hall of the Palais du Louvre and announced to the entire French court that the dauphin and I would marry at the Cathedral of Notre Dame on the coming Sunday, the twenty-fourth of April. Applause and cheers greeted the announcement. No one was surprised that we would be married—it had been expected ever since I had arrived in France, nine and a half years earlier—but that the marriage would take place just five days hence came as a shock. I could guess what the ladies and gentlemen were thinking: that there was no time to order new gowns and doublets for the greatest social occasion of the decade.

When the crowd had quieted, my uncle Charles, dressed in brilliant red robes and wearing his cardinal's hat, called for me and the dauphin to step forward. Poor little François looked even smaller and paler and frailer than usual. He had grown very little in the past couple of years, and he was still quite thin. His dripping nose was red from constant wiping. His eyes were watery. One shoulder was noticeably higher than the other. His hair was thin and limp. There was nothing robust about him.

The cardinal joined our hands and blessed us, and we exchanged jeweled rings and pledged ourselves to marry.

"The dauphin looks sickly," remarked Marie Fleming afterward. We had persuaded Chef Matteo to give us a generous sample of the iced fruit creams he was preparing for the banquet to be served later that day—"Whatever pleases our lovely bride!"—and we carried bowls of the delicacy to my little boudoir to enjoy our treat. La Flamin spoke her mind plainly, without bothering to soften her words. "Do you really think he will be able to perform his marital duty?"

I had been wondering the same thing. Madame de Poitiers had promised to speak to me frankly on this delicate subject, but she had not yet done so. I wished she would, but I decided not to mention this to La Flamin, given her dislike of the duchess. I shrugged off the question, saying, "Time will tell. Now let us see if Chef Matteo will allow us more of this delicious cream!"

<hr />

The next day, in the midst of the feasting and entertainments that were planned between the betrothal and the wedding, Madame de Poitiers appeared in my apartments at the Palais du Louvre, dismissed the servants, shut the doors, and sat down beside me.

"Queen Catherine and I are in agreement that the dauphin is not ready for conjugal relations," she said, getting straight to the reason for her visit. "King Henri, however, disagrees. The king desires that the marriage be consummated immediately, though I have warned him that this is extremely unlikely. And the king has the right to witness the event and to demand the customary proof—"

"Witness the event? The customary proof? I did not know that," I confessed. Embarrassed and frankly horrified, I felt the blood rush to my cheeks.

"You are to be forgiven for not knowing, Madame Marie. But now you must listen carefully, and I will tell you precisely how you and the dauphin are to behave on your wedding night. He will receive similar instructions from me, so there can be no misunderstanding. I will place a tiny vial of sheep's blood beneath your pillow. Before morning you must remember to spill a few drops of blood on the sheets as proof of the loss of your virginity. This harmless deceit will suffice until your new husband reaches manhood. Do you understand what I have said, Marie?"

I nodded, but Madame de Poitiers was not through. I listened in shocked silence as the duchess described how we must perform if the king insisted upon witnessing the consummation. It sounded extremely undignified, but I knew that her advice on such matters had made possible the large family that Queen Catherine and King Henri had produced. And so I paid close attention.

When she had finished her instructions, she favored me with one of her dazzling smiles. "For now, *ma chère* Marie, put it all out of your mind. This will surely be the happiest day of your life."

I was completely unsuccessful at putting the matter out of my mind.

Five days was not much time, but it followed a month of secret preparation that had been going on night and day. An army of messengers delivered the invitations. All the seamstresses and jewelers and goldsmiths in Paris, who had been working around the clock, looked worn and haggard. I endured a final fitting of my wedding gown. I was assured that everything would be ready in time.

The day before the ceremony I moved with my attendants into a specially prepared suite in the palace of the archbishop of Paris. The Four Maries were with me, all of them bubbling with excitement. King Henri had determined that the marriage of the dauphin would be the grandest event in all of Europe and named my uncle François as the master of ceremonies, but it was Madame de Poitiers, behind the scenes, who orchestrated everything. The only one who seemed detached was, curiously, Queen Catherine. I thought I understood why: she believed her little dauphin was too young to marry. But I knew that I could make the boy happy, and I was sure she would soon change her mind.

Long before the sun rose over Paris on my wedding day, I awakened, recited my prayers, and, still in my dressing gown, sat down to write to my mother. I was deeply disappointed that she could not be with me on this important day of my life, but there had not been enough time to arrange for such a long and difficult journey. Often when I wrote to my mother, I was in too much of a hurry to take proper care to write in the elegant cursive style I had been taught. But on this day, a Sunday before dawn under a clear sky full of stars, I formed each word carefully. *I must tell you, dearest Maman, that I am most assuredly one of the happiest women in the world.* I signed the letter and sprinkled sand on the page to dry the ink just as Sinclair arrived with a bowl of oat porridge and a pitcher of cream.

When she saw that I was about to turn it down, my nurse shook a warning finger at me. "You'll need every bit of strength today, my lovely girl," she said. I noticed that she was teary-eyed and sniffling. To please her, I took the bowl and ate every spoonful.

On a dressmaker's mannequin, my wedding gown waited, shimmering white satin embroidered with hundreds of pearls and diamonds. Since my betrothal I had been walking around in a copy of this gown, getting used to the weight of the satin and lace and jewels and learning to maneuver the long, sweeping train that would be carried in procession by two of the dauphin's young cousins.

My maidservants arrived to help me dress, and the Four Maries settled in to keep me company during this long process.

"You will truly be the white lily of France." Seton sighed when all but the train was in place.

"Everyone will be talking!" cried La Flamin. "And you will love every minute of it!"

It was true. I was perfectly aware that a white wedding gown was a break with tradition. I was also aware that white was the ideal foil for my auburn hair.

The royal hairdresser arrived, but I dismissed him, saying, "Madame Seton will see to it, thank you." He bowed and left, but I knew he was not pleased to be deprived of a chance to boast to his friends.

Seton stayed with me, and the other Maries waited until the last possible moment to leave for their own quarters. I had given them each an expensive new gown for the occasion, though I could imagine how Parois would have reacted to such an extravagant gesture. Seton draped a loose dressing gown over the wedding dress and began to brush my hair to a satiny sheen. Madame de Poitiers arrived and clasped a circlet of precious jewels around my neck.

"A gift from the king," she said, stepping back to admire the effect. "But where is your hairdresser?" she asked. "He will need to see that your hair is properly done and takes into account the golden crown."

"Seton is doing my hair," I said. I did not tell her that I planned to wear my hair loose, another break with tradition, not pinned up to accommodate a crown. "It will be fine, madame, I promise you."

Madame de Poitiers hesitated, glancing at Seton, who was smiling uncertainly. "Very well, Madame Marie," she said at last, and she left me and Seton suppressing unseemly trills of laughter.

The minutes ticked by until the gold clock on my dressing table chimed nine times. At this hour musicians would be entertaining the crowds gathering outside the cathedral. In another hour the bridal procession would begin. I wondered what François was thinking. Was he nervous? Ill, perhaps? But I did not have long to worry about this, for my uncle's steward arrived to escort me to the hall where the royal family, the princes of the blood—relatives of the king—and the highest members of the nobility were assembled for the procession from the archbishop's palace to the cathedral.

"*Un moment, s'il vous plaît,*" I said, and the steward withdrew.

I removed the dressing gown and took a long moment to study my reflection in the polished silver of the mirror. What I saw pleased me. I had been praised for my beauty since my childhood. It was gratifying to have courtiers and ladies in waiting and servants tell me that I was beautiful, but one was always a bit doubtful of their sincerity. Like my mother's side of the family, the Guises, I was tall and slender with a neat waist and delicate breasts. I was blessed with my father's coloring—rich auburn hair, eyes the color of amber, a flawless complexion as pale as porcelain—which set off my even features. My ears were larger than I would have liked, but overall the effect was good. On my wedding day, in my wedding finery, I did indeed believe that I was beautiful.

Oui, I thought. *Je suis prête.* I am ready.

The spring sun bathed the city in a golden light. The sound of music and the cheers of the crowd made a merry cacophony. A clock in a nearby church tower struck the hour, and immediately throughout all of Paris a tumult of bells began to ring. The great procession moved slowly toward the cathedral, a hundred gentlemen of the household followed by a swarm of noblemen. Somewhere in the crowd I spotted my bridegroom, François, a slight figure in a luminous suit of cloth of gold.

I was ready to experience every delight, savor every moment of this marvelous day. In spite of the weight of my magnificent gown, I felt as if I were floating. The crown of gold set with dozens of gems rested heavily on my head, but I knew I had made the right choice in wearing my hair loose. King Henri smiled broadly as he offered me his left hand, and I placed my right hand lightly upon it. As I had practiced with one of the king's footmen, we walked at a slow, steady pace through the wide archway leading from the archbishop's palace to the doors of the cathedral, giving the crowds time to get their fill of gawking. My uncle François had made sure that the noblemen and their wives did not block the common people's view. The roar of the jubilant crowd was deafening, and I had no doubt that the cheers were mostly for me.

At a signal from my uncle, the pages in their brilliant silks began tossing fistfuls of gold and silver coins to the crowd, shouting, "Largesse! Largesse!" In the wild scramble, people were caught in the crush, their hats lost and their clothes torn. (Unfortunately, some were injured. The results of the distribution of largesse were nearly always the same: the people expected it, royalty tried to meet the demand, and greed overcame civility and created mayhem. I did not witness this but heard of it afterward.)

The archbishop of Paris waited on a specially designed stage in front of the cathedral. My soon-to-be husband arrived with his brothers Charles and Edouard. François looked sickly, and I wondered if the fêtes leading up to the wedding had made him ill. *Perhaps he is just uneasy,* I thought. For my part, I was not in the least nervous, and I gave him my most reassuring smile.

The bishop greeted King Henri and the rest of the bridal party and made a speech. I heard scarcely a word of it. The king removed a ring from his finger and placed it on a satin pillow held by a page. The archbishop of Rouen blessed the ring, and François, trembling so much that he nearly dropped it, slipped it on my finger. The same archbishop led us through our vows, pronounced us man and wife, and blessed us.

We were married. It was that simple.

CHAPTER 18

Celebration

THE PAGEANTRY of a royal wedding had only just begun. My husband and I entered the cathedral to hear Mass and, kneeling side by side on golden cushions, receive the bread and wine of the sacrament. After the archbishop pronounced the benediction, we stepped out once more into the bright spring sunshine. I took François's hand—it was cold and damp—and that simple gesture elicited great cries of joy from the delirious crowd.

My uncle François seemed to be everywhere at once. "Take your time," he told us. "The crowd wants to see you, and they are entitled to that. This is a great occasion for the people of France."

We promenaded this way and that on the huge outdoor stage, each of us smiling and waving first one arm and then the other, acknowledging the cheers. But one familiar figure in that sea of joyous celebrants caught my attention: a tall, auburn-haired young man with his arms folded across his chest glaring at me, unsmiling.

"There is my brother James Stuart," I remarked to the dauphin. "I wonder why he looks so sour."

I leaned toward my father's oldest son and blew him a kiss. But his scowl merely deepened. I had seen little of James since he had accompanied me to France, nearly ten years earlier. He had spent time pursuing his studies but seldom came to court. I thought he had returned to Scotland. But here he was, making sure that I saw him and witnessed his displeasure.

My uncle signaled that we had done our official duty and should now make our way, at the same slow and stately pace, back to the archbishop's palace for the first of two banquets. This banquet was for the royal family, including relatives and the princes of the blood, and the highest nobility. Trumpets and sackbuts played fanfares. Servants carrying golden platters presented a parade of Queen Catherine's favorites, as well as some of mine: frittered pears and frangipane, a custard tart made with ground almonds.

Halfway through the feast, my neck began to ache from the weight of the gold crown. I signaled to a page standing rigidly behind my chair. "Tell the king that my crown is causing me great discomfort. Ask him what I should do."

The page made his way down the table to King Henri's page and repeated my message. In a moment he returned.

"Madame, one of the king's gentlemen has been appointed to hold your crown above your head for as long as shall be required."

The Chevalier de Saint-Crispin appeared at my elbow. "With your permission, madame," he said and gently lifted the crown from my head and held it up. What a relief! I finished my meal with the crown hovering just inches above my brow.

Then the dancing began.

Who would dance with whom, in what order, and in what style had all been arranged in advance. According to custom, I danced first with King Henri; my new husband's partner was his mother. Though the dauphin, at the insistence of Diane de Poitiers, had made an effort to learn the court dances, he plainly did not enjoy it any more than he had the first time we danced together, and went through the motions as though he were carved from wood. I, on the other hand, was in my glory. The king, who was as tall as I, made an excellent partner. My steps were graceful and sure. My shimmering white gown sparkled with jewels. My train had been removed, revealing interlacing bands of cloth of gold. My auburn hair rippled on my shoulders. I knew that every eye was upon me, and I reveled in it.

The dauphin-king (as a result of our marriage, François now held the title of king of Scotland) and I were now expected to dance together. We must have made a strange couple, as I towered over him. It surely looked as though I were dancing with a much younger brother. Nevertheless, I whispered encouragement, François smiled up at me gratefully, and we did well enough to be rewarded by the applause of our friends and family.

Late in the afternoon the whole court left the archbishop's palace and moved to the palace of the Parlement of Paris. The ladies rode in litters draped with cloth of gold—I shared a litter with the queen—and the dauphin and his gentlemen followed on horseback, their mounts trapped to the ground in red velvet. It was my uncle's idea to take a long, circuitous route through Paris, twice crossing the bridges over the Seine, giving the people every opportunity to see the royal family, the nobility, and most of all their dauphin and his dauphine in our gorgeous finery. Queen Catherine sat back, saying little, letting me receive the adulation of the crowd. At the time I gave scarcely a thought to my new mother-in-law and what she was thinking. Perhaps she was used to staying in the background. Even on her son's wedding day, she was again overshadowed by the elegant, confident black and white presence of Madame de Poitiers.

I did not mention to Queen Catherine that twice more in the course of the procession I caught sight of my half brother James Stuart, his glowering mien unchanged. He had been invited to the festivities but had declined. Why, then, was he making such a point of showing me his displeasure? The first time I saw him, I had greeted him warmly. The second time I acknowledged him with a wave.

The third time, feeling deeply annoyed, I pretended not to see him.

⊶⊷

The second banquet, followed by another ball, would be attended by visiting ambassadors representing our neighboring countries, as well as many local dignitaries. At the queen's insistence—"You will thank me for it later, my dear"—I withdrew for an hour, slept deeply, changed out of my white gown into an emerald-green silk, and returned to greet my guests, completely refreshed.

There was more dancing and more entertainment. The poet Pierre Ronsard read several excellent verses composed to celebrate the occasion, but the main event of the evening involved the mechanical devices that the king so much enjoyed. Six pairs of make-believe horses constructed of cloth and wood circled the hall, each pair drawing a coach carrying a group of musicians. A half dozen ships with silvery sails filled with wind from hidden bellows crossed an artificial sea of painted canvas. Somehow the sea was made to heave up and down like waves as the ships sailed around the hall, each with a "captain" aboard. King Henri commanded the first ship and ordered his vessel to stop in front of me. Four sturdy "sailors" then lifted me aboard to the seat of state. No one could have failed to be impressed by this display—and that, I understood, was the purpose of all the revels that took place that night, would go on throughout the next day at the Palais du Louvre, and would continue after that for three more days of tournaments and jousting.

Just before midnight Diane de Poitiers appeared at my elbow.

"Are you ready, Marie? The king expects you and your husband to withdraw now, before midnight strikes. You will be escorted separately to your bridal chamber and undressed. The archbishop will bless the marital bed, and everyone will leave—all but the king, who may or may not remain to witness the consummation. Do you remember the instructions I have given you?"

I nodded. I had managed for this one day to push out of my mind every thought of what was about to happen. But I could no longer avoid it. My throat was dry, raw from a day of talking and laughing. I was also suddenly nervous.

"The dauphin has been given corresponding instructions. You will sleep on the right side of the bed. Beneath the pillow is the vial of blood I promised you. Remember to use it."

"Oui, je comprends," I said.

There was no time to worry. Several of my older ladies in waiting were advancing toward me, and I knew that what was to follow was my first official duty as the future queen of France. If only I could now withdraw with my Four Maries, who had been hovering near me all day, always just at the edge of the celebrations. How nice it would be if the five of us could go off together and sip cups of the warm and soothing posset of eggs and milk that Sinclair used to make for me and gossip about the events of the day.

That would not happen. I caught the eye of La Flamin, who smiled and made the good-luck signal we had once worked out—left hand briefly touching right eyebrow. I returned the signal and left the ball in the company of my senior ladies.

In the crowded dressing room the ladies competently removed my jewels, my green silk gown, my slippers, and my underthings, and then replaced them with a delicately embroidered shift trimmed with the finest lace. They led me from the dressing room to the bridal chamber, in the center of which stood a massive bed piled high with feather mattresses and draped in rich silk brocade. An animated crowd was gathering in the chamber, the king among them, as well as both of my Guise uncles. *Are they going to stay too?* I wondered.

I climbed the three steps and lay down between smooth white sheets. My husband climbed into the bed from the opposite side. I slid my hand beneath a mound of pillows, felt for the promised glass vial, and found it. I tried to smile encouragingly at François. He looked utterly miserable—exhausted and ill and doubtless more frightened than I.

The archbishop quieted the crowd, stepped to the foot of the bed, and blessed us. Pages drew the curtains around the bed. We heard people leaving, laughing boisterously and talking loudly—they had been drinking most of the day and all of the night. The chamber fell silent. Not a sound. I listened carefully, but I did not hear the great door close.

"Is your father, the king, still here?" I whispered.

"I do not know," the dauphin replied.

"Then we had better do as the duchess instructed," I said. "He may be there listening."

We began our little performance. François bounced up and down on the bed beside me, making grunting noises and pausing long enough to whisper in my ear, "Remember to cry out joyfully, Marie."

I did so, feeling ridiculous. François joined in. The effort amused us both so much that it was all we could do to keep from laughing out loud. I found the glass vial, uncorked it, and poured a few drops of sheep's blood on the snow-white sheets. In the morning the sheets would be inspected for proof that the bride had come to the bed a virgin and that the marriage had been consummated.

We thought we heard the great door creak quietly and the latch click in place.

"Now we can sleep," said my husband. "I am very tired. Are you?"

I answered that I was. François curled up close to me, like a child, and flung his arm affectionately around my neck. "I love you, *ma plus chère* Marie," he said, sighing.

"And I love you, *mon cher* François," I replied, and I stroked his thin hair until he fell asleep.

Far away in Scotland there were no doubt fireworks, bonfires, processions, dancing in the streets in honor of the wedding of Mary, queen of Scots. The great cannon at Edinburgh Castle would even be fired. I lay awake for a while longer, thinking of my mother, how she would have loved this day, how proud she would have been.

When at last I slept, I believed the world was nearly perfect and that my place in it was secure.

CHAPTER 19

Year of Changes

SERVANTS AWAKENED US early the next morning. King Henri expected us to be present at the first of a series of tournaments at his favorite Parisian palace, Hôtel des Tournelles. I was drowsy and would have liked to linger there for a while longer, but my new husband fairly leaped from the bed where we had spent our first night together.

"I am to joust with the other men," he announced. "And I shall carry your colors, my dearest Marie." His menservants rushed to help him dress, while my ladies and I gathered ourselves at a more leisurely pace.

This was the first of three days of jousting, during which I received an unexpected and not entirely welcome visit from my brother James, whose dark presence had been the only blemish on my wedding day. I had seen almost nothing of him since he had traveled with me ten years earlier on the king's galley from Scotland to France. I was a five-year-old child on that long voyage, and he was sixteen, a young man on his way to Paris to study. He had been destined then for a career in the church, and during this visit he informed me that he had been named prior of St. Andrews in Scotland.

"To be truthful, sister, I have little calling as a churchman. This was our father's plan for me, but I have not done well." It appeared that he did not intend to explain his peculiar behavior among the adoring crowds on my wedding day, and I chose not to mention it.

"What is it you wish to do, James?" I asked.

"Why, to live the life of a gentleman," he replied, as though that should have been obvious. "And to do my duty as a proud Scot. Therefore, I am asking you, as queen of the country in which you no longer live, to grant me the earldom of Moray."

Unsure how to respond, I decided to put him off until I could ask my mother's advice. "I will consider your request, dear brother," I said. "You will receive my answer once you have returned to Scotland."

As soon as he had been escorted out the door, I wrote to my mother and sent off my coded letter by special courier. Her advice was to refuse him, since granting the earldom would cause trouble with other lords in the north of Scotland, particularly George Gordon, Lord Huntly, and so I did refuse, hoping to hear no more from him. It was obvious from his manner that my brother could barely tolerate me. I had done nothing to offend him, but I could guess at the cause: jealousy. No doubt he wished to be more than an earl; he thought he deserved to be the next king of Scotland.

The wedding festivities were still in progress but were now marred by a grievous accident. One of François's good friends was severely wounded and lost an eye in a joust. Even this unfortunate event did not diminish the pleasure enjoyed by the court, though neither François nor I could brush it off so easily. I prayed that it was not an ill omen.

After the wedding, the court returned to Fontainebleau, moved to Saint-Germain for the summer, stopped in Compiègne for autumn hunting, and moved on to Blois in the Loire Valley as the weather turned cool. The dauphin and I now had adjoining apartments, and he often came to talk late in the evening and stayed to sleep in my bed. I played the lute and sang for my husband, but we did not dance together unless some court event required it. I discovered that he was a keen chess player. We had chessboards set up in several different halls, and we sometimes paused on our way from one hall to another to ponder the next move.

François liked to think over his moves. I made mine quickly. "Recklessly," he said. "You must not make your decisions so hastily."

"But I usually win," I reminded him.

In the complicated world of royalty, there were always a number of moves in play on the chessboard that was Europe. Developments in one country always affected the situation in another. Seven months after my marriage to François, we learned of the death of Queen Mary of England. She died childless, and on November 17, 1558, Mary's half sister, Elizabeth Tudor, became queen. I sat down to write my congratulations to Elizabeth on the occasion of her accession to the throne of England, addressing her as "my dear sister," the custom among royalty, though we were not truly sisters but first cousins once removed. Elizabeth's father, the hated Henry VIII, was the brother of my father's mother.

I was quite unprepared for what the crowning of Elizabeth would mean to me.

"You have a legitimate claim to the throne of England!" my uncles pointed out to me, barely able to conceal their delight.

"Elizabeth is illegitimate," Uncle Charles added, unable to stop himself from gloating. "Henry's marriage to her mother—his second wife, Anne Boleyn—was not recognized by the pope. Henry himself dissolved his marriage to his first wife, Catherine of Aragon, mother of the late Queen Mary. What's more, Elizabeth is Protestant and will surely lead the country away from the true church. *Ma chère* Marie, you are quite clearly the legitimate ruler of England!"

I knew that Henry had not been allowed to divorce his first wife to marry the second, but until now I had not realized what this could mean to me. The idea was thrilling: I could very possibly be queen of not only Scotland but England and Ireland as well, and, in due time, France. So sure were my uncles and my father-in-law of my right to the English throne that King Henri ordered my coat of arms changed to include the English crown. The heraldic arms of England were now to be quartered with the arms of Scotland and France.

"A direct challenge to the English queen," my uncles announced triumphantly.

They ordered the coat of arms of England to be boldly displayed with the arms of France and Scotland on every plate, every chest, every piece of furniture that belonged to my husband. This new coat of arms was also stitched on the livery worn by my servants. When I was on my way to Mass or anywhere else, the ushers who walked ahead of me were instructed to cry, "Make way for the queen of England!"

Then my uncle the cardinal journeyed to Rome to meet with Pope Paul IV and to present the case that I, Marie Stuart, was the true and rightful heir to the throne of England.

He returned with a report that disappointed us all. The pope had refused to declare Elizabeth Tudor illegitimate, putting an end to the dream that I would become queen of England, Ireland, and Scotland. The pope was afraid to go against the wishes of powerful King Philip II of Spain, who wished to stay on good terms with Elizabeth. It was rumored that he had proposed marriage to her when her half sister, Mary, his wife, was scarcely in her tomb. Elizabeth had refused him. It was only after her refusal that Philip had proposed to marry our own dear Princesse Élisabeth.

Then King Henri too began to believe that it was a mistake to challenge Elizabeth of England. He even seemed to lose some of his great affection for my heroic uncle François, who had won Calais back from the English. When Le

Balafré asked to be made grand master of the king's household as a reward for his brave leadership, the king refused! My uncle's pride was hurt. Then the French signed a treaty with England, heaping praise on Queen Elizabeth. I had to make a speech saying how much the treaty pleased me.

That was a lie. It did not please me, but no one cared in the least what I thought.

Meanwhile, word got back to Elizabeth that I believed I had a better claim to the throne of England than she did. And that angered her.

No one was pleased.

CHAPTER 20

Death of a King

IT WAS A TIME for royal weddings. In January of 1559, Princesse Claude, not yet twelve years old, married sixteen-year-old Charles, duke of Lorraine. For a time it appeared that Élisabeth would marry Carlos, the son of King Philip II of Spain, but those plans were abandoned. Instead, my dear sister-friend found herself pledged to be married by proxy to Carlos's father, as had originally been proposed. She was frightened half to death of the life that lay ahead of her.

I was with Élisabeth throughout the preparations for her wedding. I tried hard to distract her, assuring her that her husband would be considerate of her, though I had no idea if this was true. Élisabeth was fourteen; Philip was thirty-two. "He is old," I reasoned. "He will surely make few demands on you."

I remembered the talk that Madame de Poitiers had given me before my marriage, and I hoped she would do the same for Élisabeth. And what of poor little Claude, who had not yet become a woman at the time of her marriage? The duke of Lorraine was a few years older but presumably inexperienced. What could one say to that poor child?

I felt myself fortunate that my dear little François was still a boy, not yet a man; we were the best of friends, closer even than brother and sister, but not yet husband and wife.

The royal family gathered in Paris for the wedding of Princesse Élisabeth to King Philip II on the twenty-first of June at the Cathedral of Notre Dame, with the duke of Alba standing as proxy for the Spanish king. Élisabeth's gown was a rich yellow satin adorned with pearls and yellow gems, and though she did not share my desire to be unconventional, the princess appeared to delight in being the center of attention.

"My mother says I do not have to leave France until late in the autumn," she told me, "and the journey to Spain will be a long one. There will be another wedding ceremony in Guadalajara, in Spain, and my husband, Philip, will be present." She colored a little, turning a pretty pink when she spoke of "my husband," which she did often. She asked again, "You will come to visit me, will you not, Marie? Promise you will not forget me!"

I gave my word that I would visit if I could, but in any case I would never forget her.

<hr>

A few days later, in celebration of his daughter's marriage and his own sister Marguerite's betrothal to the duke of

Savoy, the king and his court moved to the Hôtel des Tournelles to indulge in the king's favorite passion, jousting. No one could fail to notice that King Henri wore black and white in honor of Madame de Poitiers.

Late in the afternoon of the third day the king insisted on a rematch with the captain of the king's guards, though he had already broken three lances against the captain and two other opponents. Madame de Poitiers and Queen Catherine tried to persuade him that he had bested the captain fairly and no rematch was necessary. But, the king reminded them, the captain was ahead on points.

"I shall break one more lance, in celebration of the marriage of my eldest daughter!" the king insisted stubbornly and called for his white stallion, Le Malheureux—"the Unhappy One."

The captain reluctantly obeyed the king's command to mount, and the two men took up their lances. The crowd—gentlemen on one side, ladies on the other—settled back to watch what all hoped would be the last event of the day. The two combatants rode to opposite ends of the list, lowered the visors on their helmets, and prepared to charge at each other at full gallop.

We heard the sharp metallic clash as the captain's lance struck the king's armor and a loud crack as the lance broke. The king fell, blood gushing through his visor. The captain, leaping from his horse, was the first to reach him. For a moment the people in the viewing stands were too stunned to move. Madame de Poitiers and Queen Catherine rushed to him. The duchess dropped to her knees by his side, weeping. The queen gave an agonized cry and collapsed in a swoon. So did several of her ladies. François, pale with fear, hung back, clinging to my hand, crying, "What happened? What happened?"

A large sliver of wood had passed through a slit in the king's visor and pierced his eye. My uncle François took control, ordering the king to be carried to his bedroom and dispatching messengers to summon physicians and surgeons.

I attended the queen, who recovered herself quickly. My husband, trembling, looked to me for guidance. "Assist me with the queen, your mother," I told him, and the two of us raised her to her feet. In our path stood Diane de Poitiers, her black and white gown splattered with the king's blood. I saw the look that passed between the king's wife and the king's mistress; the duchess held her breath for a moment and then released it in a sigh. Madame de Poitiers bowed slightly and stepped aside.

Over the next ten days the queen and the dauphin and I never left King Henri's bedside. The finest surgeons in Paris examined him and brought the terrible news that the sliver of wood had entered his brain. Though they worked day and night to save him, and we prayed hour after hour for his life to be spared, the king was doomed. Ten days after being dealt the fatal blow, King Henri II received the last sacrament. He died on July 10, 1559.

François was declared king. I was now the queen of France.

CHAPTER 21

Coronation

FRANÇOIS AND I tried to collect our thoughts. Both of us were shattered. François could barely speak and escaped into sleep for long hours. Though exhausted from weeping, I could not sleep. We were not prepared for his sudden, awful death. We had both assumed—if we had thought about it at all—that the king, a strong and vital man of forty, would live for many years. Neither of us knew how to rule a kingdom. We would have much to learn.

Queen Catherine ordered the walls and floors of her apartments covered with black silk with just two candles burning on a black-draped altar. In the days after King Henri's death I did all I could to be of help to her, standing by her side and speaking with the important visitors who came to offer condolences.

My father-in-law and I had enjoyed a warm and cordial relationship. From my earliest days in the French court we had passed many pleasant hours together in conversation. I would miss him deeply. My feelings about my mother-in-law were much more complicated.

I would now take Catherine's place as queen consort, while she assumed the title of queen mother. She acknowledged this change in our relative status by sending me the crown jewels, adding a few beautiful pieces of her own to the dazzling collection. When I thanked her but protested at her generosity, she managed a sad smile. "They suit you better than me," she said. "I have little use for them now. I shall spend the rest of my life in mourning."

One of her first acts as the king's widow was to summon her great rival, Madame de Poitiers. Everyone was curious to see what Queen Catherine would do. She could order Diane to be imprisoned, or even executed, if she chose. I was not present for the scene that took place in private between the two women, so I do not know exactly what was said, though Sinclair repeated the gossip from her usual sources.

"Queen Catherine kept her kneeling for some time, like she was thinking it over. It must have been a delicious moment for the queen, and a very uneasy one for the duchess! Then Madame de Poitiers begged permission to speak, and the queen granted it, but the servant who was present was hard-pressed to hear what the duchess had to say, her voice was so quiet. 'I am most heartily sorry for any wrongs that I may have committed against your royal person, and I most humbly beg my lady queen's forgiveness.'"

"What did the queen say to that?" I asked.

"She accused the duchess of being an evil influence on

the king and told her she deserved severe punishment but would receive clemency," Sinclair reported with obvious satisfaction. "First, the queen ordered her to turn over all the jewels King Henri had given her. Then she ordered her to give up the château of Chenonceaux. It's one the queen always wanted, they say, but the king had given it to Diane. Now Catherine can have it."

"That was all? No more was said?"

"Oh, yes! Here's the best: 'Finally, madame, you are banished from this court from this day forward. We no longer wish to endure the sight of you.' And then the duchess was dismissed."

A sudden accident, an unexpected death, and the most powerful woman in the French court was now completely helpless, fortunate to escape with her life. Madame de Poitiers had been kind to me, and I valued her friendship. The swiftness of her fall stunned me, but I knew that I could not show her any sympathy without giving offense to the queen mother.

"Maman wishes me to write the duchess a letter," my husband told me when we had a few moments together. "I am to tell Madame de Poitiers that because of the evil influence she held over my father, she deserves to be punished severely, even with death, but that as king I intend to show her mercy."

"I thought you were fond of Madame de Poitiers," I said.

François shrugged. "I was. But she did make Maman unhappy. Maman wishes me to do it, and so I will."

"Of course," I agreed and turned away, wondering if as king he would always do as Maman wished.

There was one more significant change: My uncle the duke of Guise took over the elegant apartments that had formerly belonged to Diane de Poitiers. His look of triumph was undisguised.

The funeral for the king took place in mid-August at Notre Dame, the cathedral where, only a few weeks earlier, we had celebrated the marriage of Princesse Élisabeth with such joy. From there, the king's body was carried in a solemn procession to the Basilica of Saint-Denis, the final resting place of the kings of France. With my uncle Charles presiding, and my other Guise uncles playing major roles, the body of the dead king was entombed.

A month later, in September of 1559, the court made its way to Reims, where French kings were traditionally crowned. The weather was wet and miserable, and it rained so heavily that the ceremony, which was to take place on a Sunday, had to be postponed until the next day. My uncle Charles preached the sermon at vespers the preceding evening. While listening to his mellow voice as he spoke words of praise over the coffin of the dead king, I watched my husband, seated near the altar. He did not appear to be nervous. Rather, he seemed benumbed.

I searched for one of my other Guise uncles, François, Le Balafré. Though he wore a long face and went through the motions of mourning with impeccable style, I sensed that he and his brother were in fact jubilant. They had always tried to hide their confidence that their futures and their fortunes were tied to mine. Charles's failure to secure the pope's decree that Queen Elizabeth of England was illegitimate, which would have cleared the way for me to make my claim, had been a disappointment for the Guise family. But that was only a temporary setback. Now that I was queen of France, they had real power in their hands. They could scarcely conceal their pleasure in this sudden improvement in their fortunes.

The cathedral at Reims would have been beautiful if sunlight had been streaming through the stained-glass windows, but the skies on the day of the coronation were dark with heavy clouds. Thunder rolled as François prepared for the long hours ahead. He was still very small for his age, and he looked much younger than his fifteen years. He knew that, and it bothered him. "I do not look kingly," he complained. "I must look kingly!"

I was the one person—besides his mother—with whom he felt entirely at ease. Others found him moody, quick to anger, sometimes pompous, but with me he was none of these. He had recently taken to affecting a swagger in his walk, though I tried to convince him it was better just to be himself.

"You look every inch a king, *mon cher,*" I said, attempting to reassure him. I truly thought he looked like a small boy pretending to be king in a make-believe crown.

"I shall no doubt be bored to death," he muttered before he was led away. François needed me to bolster his confidence. He depended upon me. I knew he would be aching to talk to me during the coronation. Yet on the most important occasion of my young husband's life, by convention, I could not be with him.

We had been married for a year and a half. I called François my sweetheart and friend, and he often spent the night in my bed while we talked quietly together until one of us fell asleep. We were the best of friends, we had great affection for each other, but we were not yet lovers. That would come later, I felt certain, though without Madame de Poitiers to consult I sometimes had doubts about how our marital obligations would be met and how our duty to produce the future kings of France would be fulfilled. I refused to let that worry me, reminding myself whenever doubt crept in that Queen Catherine had been slow to fulfill her role as well.

Now I took my place near the altar in a small private alcove with Queen Catherine and Princesse Élisabeth, whose marriage celebration had been so cruelly disrupted by the accident that took her father's life. Élisabeth and her mother and the other ladies of the court were dressed in stark black in mourning for the king. Though I could have followed their example and worn black, I chose to wear my lily-white wedding gown, knowing that I stood out, that every eye would be upon me. I was now the queen of France. Why should all eyes *not* be upon me?

The ceremony continued for most of the day—anthems, prayers, the Mass, the litany. On and on it droned while rain beat against the cathedral windows, and clouds of incense stung our eyes. I knew that François was tired and restless and eager for the ceremony to end. My uncle presented François with the symbols of kingship: ring, scepter, and a gold crown so heavy that four noblemen had to hold it in place above his head.

We rose stiffly from the long hours of sitting and left immediately for the coronation feast in the great hall of the archbishop's palace. Poor King François! In keeping with an ancient ritual, the guests were seated at long tables according to their rank—all but the king, who sat alone at a table in the center of the hall, symbolizing that he, and only he, ruled France. That symbolism also reminded me that I was his consort and not, by law, his co-ruler. A poor law, I thought, for I was certain that I could supply him with the strength he sorely needed but seemed to lack.

Soon after we returned to Paris from Reims, I received two Scottish visitors who had traveled to France for the coronation. The first was Henry Stuart, master of Lennox, my handsome, fair-haired thirteen-year-old cousin. He had been sent by his parents, the earl and countess of Lennox, to bring their congratulations but also to beg a favor. Lord and Lady Lennox had been banished to England many years before over a political matter, and young Henry was asking for the restoration of his father's confiscated Scottish lands. I found the lad charming, and it pained me to turn him down, but I did so on the advice of my mother, who had warned me what he would be asking. Nevertheless, I sent him home to England with a large gift of money.

The second visitor was James Hepburn, earl of Bothwell, who had officially represented my mother at the coronation and stayed on to accompany the court when it moved to Fontainebleau. Lord Bothwell was a gruff, darkly handsome man several years older than I who had studied in France and spoke French easily. I spent considerable time with him, gathering a better understanding of the issues that faced my mother in Scotland, and we became well acquainted. I heard from him for the first time the name of John Knox, a fiery Protestant minister determined that the Reformation would end Catholic rule in Scotland. Lord Bothwell also warned me that my brother James was encouraging a rebellion of the Scottish nobility against my mother. I remembered James's glowering presence in the crowds at my wedding and his request—it was more like a demand—to be made earl of Moray.

"With all that is within my power I shall oppose Lord James and those who seek to depose the queen mother," stated Lord Bothwell. I could not have been more grateful.

In October, when Lord Bothwell took his leave to return to Scotland, he renewed his promise to me. "I have hesitated to tell you this, Madame Marie," he said, "but I fear that the health of your lady mother is declining. Not wishing to trouble you further at this difficult time, the queen mother specifically asked me not to speak of it."

I wept and thanked him for telling me, and felt confident that the earl of Bothwell would be of great service to me, now and in the future.

❧

More tears marked the leave-taking of my dear sister-in-law Élisabeth, now the queen of Spain. Her proxy marriage had been a joyous occasion, but her father's death during the celebrations plunged the court into mourning; the mood had lifted briefly for the coronation of François but then immediately darkened once more. We were still grieving when the court again began moving from one château to the next, just as it always had, but Élisabeth's departure could no longer be delayed.

Queen Catherine was so deeply stricken by King Henri's death that she could scarcely bear the thought of sending her eldest daughter off to Spain. Not until late November when the first snows lay on the ground did Catherine finally agree to let Élisabeth go. The parting was painful, for Élisabeth, certainly, and for me, her closest friend, as well. But it was agonizing for her mother. Setting aside my own sorrow, I tried to comfort my mother-in-law.

"Dear Queen Mother," I said soothingly, "you may someday travel to Spain to visit Élisabeth, just as my own dearest mother journeyed here from Scotland and spent a year among us. Surely you can do the same."

But the queen mother would not be comforted. "The journeys are long and arduous. One by one the years pass, and they will for my daughter as they have for me. I know that I shall never see my darling Élisabeth again."

IV

A Deep Stirring I Had Never Experienced

THOUGH I WAS NOT YET EIGHTEEN, I enjoyed great prestige as the queen of Scots and as the queen of France, but I recognized that I had no power. As the events of my life continued to unfold in ways I could not have predicted, my discontent grew. I desired the kind of authority my cousin Elizabeth, the queen of England, possessed and exercised. But I also yearned for something more, something deeper, something in my heart for which I did not yet have a name. My pursuit of those unnamed desires led me down the path that has brought me to this place and made me a prisoner.

CHAPTER 22

The Guise Uncles

I WAS NOW the queen of France, and I watched with growing alarm as my Guise uncles increased in stature and power. Despite the pope's ruling, they were more convinced than they had ever been that Queen Elizabeth of England was illegitimate and that I, as Elizabeth's cousin, legitimate and Catholic, was unarguably next in line.

To make sure everyone understood my claim to the English throne, my Guise uncles saw to it that it was everywhere inscribed: *François and Marie, by the grace of God, king and queen of France, Scotland, England, and Ireland.*

I did not protest. It made perfect sense to me. But no one knew just how Elizabeth would react to this new assertion that the Catholic king and queen of France and Scotland had a claim to her throne. It would not be long before I found out.

Soon after Lord Bothwell returned to Scotland, he wrote

to me that the lairds had proclaimed that they would not be ruled by any monarch. "Each laird considers himself a king of his own small piece of Scotland," Lord Bothwell wrote, signing the letter using his new rank: *Lieutenant-General, by the appointment of the Queen Regent, Marie of Guise.*

"Who are these lairds, as you call them?" asked my husband when I had read him Lord Bothwell's letter. "Are they a lesser sort of lord?"

"The lairds are the landowners—landed gentry, not noblemen," I explained. "But the noble lords, too, are being encouraged to rebel. My poor mother! I thank God that Lord Bothwell is there to help her."

"They should all be put to the sword," declared King François fiercely. "Lords, lairds, all the rebels. They must not be allowed to behave so."

That same month, as Bothwell had warned, the rebel lords entered Edinburgh and deposed the queen regent, choosing twenty-four of their number to form a council to rule in her stead. Their leader and most influential member was my brother Lord James. I could only imagine how my mother must have felt about this man who insisted that he, the bastard son of King James V, knew better than she did what was best for Scotland.

But my mother refused to give up without a struggle. She wrote urgently to my Guise uncles begging for help.

I also went to my uncles, pleading, "You must rescue the queen, my mother!" I cried. "She is your sister!"

"We will do what we can," said Charles the cardinal.

"We will see to it that your mother receives the aid she

requires," said François, duke of Guise, the military man who had not long ago been a hero of the French.

I took them at their word. They did send a handful of troops eventually, but the troops did not arrive in time to rout the rebel lords. The rebels were now in charge. My mother was not.

When I learned of this, I rushed to the king's chamber, sobbing. "You cannot let this happen, François! You hold the title of king of Scotland, and it is up to you to send enough troops to put down the rebellion, once and for all. Your father would never have allowed my mother to be abandoned, and you must not allow it either. Promise me, François! I am begging you!"

My husband stared at me, startled at this outburst. "Calm yourself, *ma chère* Marie," he said quietly. "I have never seen you so distressed. I will consult with my advisers and see just what is to be done."

Whom did he intend to consult? I wondered. His *maman*? My mother-in-law could not bear to let my husband out of her sight and kept him constantly by her side, and since he had become king, he seemed unable to breathe without Queen Catherine's consent. François had become known as *le petit roi*, "the little king," and it suited him well. In effect, his mother served as his regent, though he was of age and required no regent to rule for him.

I was furious—at my uncles, at my husband, at my brother. But I could do nothing, and my lack of power made me even angrier. I resolved that if the day ever came when I ruled, I would not hesitate to *act.*

When Queen Elizabeth learned of the rebellion in Scotland, she took full advantage of it. She dispatched English troops—not to save my mother but to keep out the French, quell the rebellion, and lay her own claim to Scotland. So this was how she reacted to my claim to her throne!

"You have betrayed me!" I cried to my uncle Charles when I learned what had happened. "Undone me, Uncle! You will be the cause of my loss of the realm!"

I began to suspect that these two men, who had been like fathers to me when I first arrived in France, were not the same people I had once revered and even loved. I began to see them in an entirely different light. They were ambitious, certainly, but they were also ruthless and could be horribly cruel. I was not simply their beloved niece whom they were bound by family ties to protect; I was actually the means—the instrument—by which they manipulated my husband to do their will. They did not care for me nearly as much as they cared for the influence they had over the young king.

The Protestant Reformation had taken hold in France as it had in Scotland. French Protestants, the Huguenots, were found in every level of society. Naturally, I considered their beliefs abhorrent, and I wanted to see the spread of their vile religion stopped. But what happened late in the winter of 1560 showed a side of the loyal Catholics that sickened me.

The court was preparing to move from Blois to Amboise.

While we were still at Blois, a Huguenot plot to seize the king and my two Guisc uncles was uncovered.

Arrangements were made for me to remain in Blois with the Four Maries while my uncles, the queen mother, and the rest of the court went on to Amboise. I was not told why we were left behind, but rumors reached my ears of what was happening a little distance away. The Huguenot conspirators were seized, their followers were rounded up, and confessions were wrung out of them by torture. Some claimed that the Huguenots did not wish to harm the king, only to speak to him, to have him listen to their concerns. The way the Huguenots felt about my uncles was a different matter; the leaders of the plot wanted to rid themselves of the Guises, whom they had come to despise.

The bloodbath had begun.

While the members of the court, my husband, and the queen mother looked on, my uncle François supervised the beheading of fifty-two Huguenot noblemen. Their heads were mounted on pikes to stare back grimly at the spectators watching from viewing stands built in the courtyard. Their bodies were drawn and quartered, and the remains were hung on the walls of the château. Over the next few days a thousand Huguenots were slaughtered or stuffed into sacks and thrown into the river to drown. The Loire ran red with the blood of the Protestant martyrs.

I tried to make sense of it. I opposed the Protestants and all they stood for, but I had no wish to have them tortured and murdered. When I tried to coax François into telling me what had happened, he first evaded my questions and then flatly refused to answer. "My mother has forbidden me to discuss it," he said.

"But I am your wife, François!" I cried. "As the queen of France, I have a right to know!"

We had never argued. I had never raised my voice to my husband. He looked at me, startled. But he shook his head and would not answer. I understood then that I would have no influence over my husband. His first allegiance was to his mother, not me. He would do what she told him, and not what I asked.

This was my first shock, but an even more horrifying one was to come. It was a month after the bloodbath; the rotting corpses and staring heads had been taken away, and the bloated bodies had been dredged out of the river and thrown into a common grave. I joined the rest of the family at Amboise only briefly, just before we left for Fontainebleau. I sought out my beloved aunt Anne d'Este and asked her to walk with me. There was an unusual chill in the air for April as we strolled by the water's edge, and we drew our cloaks tighter.

"Dear aunt," I began, "I need to know what happened here last month. My husband will not speak to me about it."

My aunt was silent for a long while, staring at the ground as we walked below the walls of the château. From time to time she sighed deeply. I wondered if she would answer or, like everyone else, remain silent.

At last she spoke. "My dear Marie, what I am about to tell you pains me more than I can say. I am the devoted wife of your uncle, and I love him deeply. But he is the man chiefly responsible for the carnage, along with his brother Charles. It was they who ordered the arrests, the torture, the savage murders. I understand that those who threatened the life of the king must be put to death, and those who took part in the planning must also be severely punished. But the hundreds of Huguenots who were rounded up and slaughtered for their beliefs? I do not understand how my husband could have participated in such a horror."

When Anne turned to face me, I saw that her tears flowed unchecked. "Now I fear that it will be our children—his and mine—who will someday pay the price for this. Revenge will surely be taken on them, and they are innocent."

What she said left me stunned. How could my uncles have been so cruel? So selfish? I felt I had lost my affectionate childhood relationship with them and could no longer trust them. I feared that Grand-Mère would take their part, and that grieved me. My friendship with my mother-in-law had also cooled, and I knew without question that my husband would side with his *maman*. My own dear mother was far away and very ill, her body swollen and in pain. I had not seen her for ten years, but though a great physical distance lay between us, in my heart I was never separated from her and clung to the hope that we would be reunited.

She could not help me now, nor could I help her.

I was powerless. And I was alone.

CHAPTER 23

Lord Bothwell

LORD BOTHWELL HAD WARNED ME that my mother was gravely ill, and I should have prepared myself for her death. Yet when the news reached me, it came as a great shock. I was sitting in a quiet little garden with Beaton, the two of us attempting to learn a new piece to play on our lutes, when my uncle Charles approached. Beaton saw him first.

"The cardinal is here," she said softly.

I was immediately on guard. Though I wished to avoid my Guise uncles whenever I could, it was not always possible. *What does he want now?* I wondered. But when he got close enough that I could see his face, I knew that he was bringing me bad news.

I set aside my lute. "What is it, Uncle?" I asked. "Tell it quickly, *s'il vous plaît.*"

"*Ma chère* Marie," he began, "I regret to tell you that your mother has died."

I had risen to greet him, but I sat down again suddenly,

my knees buckling. Beaton rushed to kneel beside me. "When?" I asked.

"On the tenth of this month," he replied.

"The tenth! This is the twenty-eighth! Have you only just learned of it?"

He grimaced. "The news reached France on the eighteenth."

I was near collapse, but I was also angry. "Why have you only now told me of the death of my mother?" I demanded.

"It was thought better to wait, Marie."

"Better to wait? Who thought so? Why did you think it better to wait ten days to tell me of the loss of the one I hold dearest?"

"Marie, you are upsetting yourself," my uncle said, trying to soothe me.

But I would not be soothed and had to be helped to my apartments. It was all too much. I fell ill, and for a month I was unable to leave my bed. I came to believe that the death of my mother was God's vengeance upon me, though I had no idea what great sins I had committed to deserve such punishment.

In August I felt strong enough to attend the funeral oration for my mother in the Cathedral of Notre Dame. I was dismayed to find that her coffin was not there. "Has the queen regent's body not been brought from Scotland?" I asked, and I was told that the Protestant preachers were opposed to the "superstitious practices" of a Catholic funeral and had refused to send it.

My hurt and rage drove me into seclusion once again, where I remained until the Four Maries succeeded in coaxing me back into the world. But this was not a world in which I felt at ease.

Treachery and betrayal loomed on every side. Just as I was regaining my strength, I learned that—without any consultation with me and certainly without my consent— the Catholic faith had been outlawed in Scotland, and the Protestant faith officially established in its place. Priests were forbidden to say Mass under penalty of death.

In another insult to my authority, the council that, under my brother James's leadership had appointed itself to rule Scotland in my stead, now entered into a treaty with England, the Treaty of Edinburgh. That treaty promised that I would give up my claim to the English throne. The agreement was presented to me in my chamber for my signature.

"I will not sign it!" I cried and pushed it away. "Not now and not ever will I give up my rightful claim!" I rose from my chair and stormed out of the chamber.

Once I was calmer, I concluded that it had been a mistake to lose my temper. I needed to find a better way to approach the problem. Perhaps it would be to my advantage to befriend Queen Elizabeth, as one queen to another, rather than challenge her.

I called in the royal portraitist and requested that he make a drawing of me in the *deuil blanc,* the long white veil that I wore in mourning for my mother. Next I summoned

Sir Nicholas Throckmorton, the English ambassador, and told him that I would send my portrait to his queen if she in turn would send me hers. I asked him to speak to Elizabeth of my desire for friendship and to deliver this message:

We are, you must remember, of one blood, of one country, and one island. As we are both descendants of King Henry VII, I am your nearest kinswoman, and it would please me if you would call me sister and cousin, in honor of this.

I was more than a little curious about my sister-queen, as I chose to think of her. I knew that I was nine years younger. I was told that I was much taller and of a better coloring. Some even said that her beauty did not compare with mine, but perhaps that was flattery. What was she *really* like? I hoped to learn that. But still I would not sign the Treaty of Edinburgh.

The death of my mother was a devastating loss for me. My husband tried to offer solace. "I understand what a great grief it is to lose one's beloved parent," François said, tenderly stroking my hand.

While my mother still lived, I had several times proposed to François that I make the journey to Scotland by myself, but he did not want me to leave him. His health, too, was delicate. He insisted upon riding to the hunt at every opportunity and then needed days to regain his strength. I agreed to postpone my trip until he felt stronger. But his health did not improve, and to my immense sorrow, I had not had the chance to see my mother one last time.

Yet in the midst of my anguish, there came a great joy. I believed that I was at last with child. As queen of France, my chief duty was to provide the king with heirs. While I worried incessantly over what was to become of Scotland, I also worried that *le petit roi* had not yet reached manhood. I prayed nightly that he would and that I could then fulfill my duty. I wished that I could go to the disgraced Diane de Poitiers for advice and counsel. The duchess had instructed us well in how to behave on our wedding night with the little vial of blood to deceive King Henri into believing that the marriage had been consummated. Perhaps she could help me now. But if the queen mother, Catherine, were to find out that I had gone to Diane, whom she had banished, she would be deeply offended and perhaps angry with me. I could not risk it.

I considered speaking to Anne d'Este, who had now borne six children of my uncle's, but I could not bring myself to raise such an intimate subject with her, and so I postponed the conversation.

I wish to say this delicately: As the king's wife, I was his dearest friend, but in fact I was still a virgin. François visited my bed often, and we lay close together and whispered to one another, but because my husband was still not a mature man, our closeness resulted in nothing. Nevertheless, we believed that it may have resulted after all in *something*, for I felt quite ill—faint and queasy—and convinced myself that these were the signs of pregnancy.

The symptoms persisted for a month. I took to wearing a long, loose tunic such as women wore as their bellies swelled. I ordered the cooks to prepare special foods for me. And I persuaded François that we must leave Fontainebleau for Saint-Germain, where the air was cooler.

François and I rejoiced privately. When we told his mother, she smiled and nodded, but I could sense that she doubted me. "It would be well for you to consult a physician," she said.

Eventually I did. The physician, after he had examined me carefully, told me what I had already begun to suspect. "Madame my queen," he said, "I regret to tell you that you are mistaken. You are not with child. It seems that you are also still a virgin." He raised a quizzical eyebrow, but he said no more, and though I thought of asking him questions, my nerve failed me.

I repeated his words to François, who was as disappointed as I. We promised each other that as soon his health improved, he would certainly reach full manhood, and our duty would be accomplished. I gave away my tunics to a servant, and I spoke of the matter to no one—not even the Four Maries, who looked at me so sympathetically that I was afraid I would burst into wrenching sobs.

I knew what was being whispered in the servants' quarters as well as in the great halls: "If the queen conceives a child, it will surely not be the king's." If I had heard these malicious comments, then François must have heard them also. But he did not say, and I did not ask.

In the autumn we had a second visit from the earl of Bothwell. James Hepburn had been devoted to my mother, loyal to a fault in spending his own funds to help her keep her regency. Now he came to ask if there might be some way to gain reimbursement for at least a portion of the money he had spent. He told us that he was betrothed to Anna Throndssen, the daughter of a wealthy Norwegian.

"Will you marry her, then?" I asked.

"Perhaps," he replied with his winning smile. "Her father has offered me a handsome dowry."

"Then perhaps you should accept it," I told him. "I am deeply grateful for all the help you gave my mother, the queen. But, I regret to say, I have no funds to repay you."

"I did it out of love for Scotland as well as admiration for the queen. I only wish I could say as much for your brother Lord James. He claims also to act out of his love for Scotland and her people, but I suspect that he acts chiefly out of love for himself."

"I wish to hear more of this, Lord Bothwell," I said. "And of other matters as well."

François, looking paler and more fatigued than usual, left us, and Bothwell and I talked on. I had many questions for the earl. "Tell me, my friend—and I do consider you my friend—tell me what you can of this Protestant minister John Knox."

"Ah, our good preacher Knox!" he remarked sarcastically. He reached again for the bottle of French brandy that stood on a table between us and poured a generous glassful.

"Knox is a former Catholic priest who became a Protestant reformer and served as chaplain to young King Edward the Sixth of England. When Edward died and Mary Tudor became queen and restored the Catholic Church, Knox fled England for the Continent. After some twists and turns, he was captured by the French and made a galley slave."

I listened, fascinated, as Lord Bothwell spun out his story. I remembered my voyage from Dumbarton a dozen years earlier and the prisoners below decks, chained to benches and forced to row hour upon hour while a ship's officer stood over them with a whip. I wondered now if Knox had been among those unfortunate men during that long, difficult journey.

Lord Bothwell paused from time to time for a fortifying swallow of brandy before he continued. "When Knox finally gained his freedom, he eventually returned to Scotland, where he was made welcome by your brother. In Edinburgh he preached openly against the Catholic Church and in favor of the Protestant Reformation. Later he moved again to the Continent, and while he was in Geneva, he wrote this."

From his leather bag Lord Bothwell pulled a pamphlet, obviously much perused. It was titled *The First Blast of the Trumpet Against the Monstrous Regiment of Women.* I could not read English yet, but Bothwell translated it for me. "Knox believes that the rule of women is unnatural."

"What women has he in mind?" I asked.

Lord Bothwell grimaced. "There are two. The first was

Queen Mary Tudor of England. It was written before Elizabeth became queen, but she would make the third, not the second."

"Who, then, is the second?"

"Marie Stuart, queen of Scotland."

I stared at Lord Bothwell, agape. "I? He finds me monstrous? This is outrageous, sir! The man has never even met me!"

"Not you in *person,* madame. No one in his right mind could find you monstrous. It is the *idea* of you that offends him. And now he is in Edinburgh and preaching against you. Your mother, the queen regent, declared him an outlaw. I regret to tell you that when he learned of the final hours of Marie of Guise, he rejoiced in her suffering and claimed it was the hand of God wreaking vengeance upon her."

"Why are you telling me this horror, Lord Bothwell?" I cried, shaking uncontrollably.

"So that you may be prepared, my lady, for what you might find when you one day return to rule Scotland."

I shuddered. "Then it is not likely that I shall return."

We had talked far into the night. Now we sat silently as the candles burned down and guttered out. I stifled a yawn. "I beg you, leave me, *s'il vous plaît,*" I said wearily. "The hour is very late, and I have a great deal on my mind."

Lord Bothwell sprang from his chair and knelt close to me. "Are you ordering me to leave, Madame Marie?" he asked, taking my hand in his. "For if you would allow it, I would spend the remainder of the night here with you and cherish every minute of it." He traced my cheek with a gentle forefinger. "A fine bonnie lass you are, Marie Stuart," he said softly.

We gazed at each other for a long moment. I was aware of a deep stirring I had never before experienced. I found myself powerfully drawn to this man, and my mouth was so dry that I could not give voice to my thoughts. When I could speak again, I said, "Aye, James Hepburn, I will not order you as my subject, but I beg you as my friend: go now."

"But first this," he said, and he took me in his arms and kissed me passionately.

It was a kiss unlike any I had ever experienced or even imagined. Stunned at first, I found myself responding to his kiss. But after a long moment I came to my senses and struggled to free myself from his embrace. "Lord Bothwell!" I gasped.

"I beg your pardon, my lady queen," he said, releasing me. "Though my behavior is unpardonable, it does reflect my deep feelings." He bowed humbly. "Adieu, my queen." Then he was gone.

With the heavy ironclad door closed firmly behind the earl of Bothwell, I sank weakly into my chair and reviewed, over and over, those startling moments in the arms of my bold countryman. I laid my head on my table and wept, overcome with rage at the abominable John Knox, sorrow for the suffering of my poor dear mother, and now this: a nameless yearning for a newly discovered feeling and the man who had briefly awakened it.

CHAPTER 24

Le Petit Roi

I TRIED WITHOUT SUCCESS to banish James Hepburn, earl of Bothwell, from my thoughts. To my shame, I even dreamed of him. But I did not see him again, though I heard that he had gone on to Denmark. I wondered when his marriage to Anna Throndssen would take place. I wondered if he truly loved her. Then events overtook me, and I had no more opportunity to allow the audacious Scot into my dreams.

The court moved to Orléans, and François began to plan a hunting expedition in the forests of Chenonceaux and Chambord, intending to be gone for at least two weeks. Hunting was the great passion in his life, despite his delicate physical state. Other young men of his age—he would soon be seventeen—were strong and hearty, but my husband was undersized and sickly. He had always been more fragile than the other children in the royal nursery. His mother still doted on him and enlisted me in her efforts to protect him.

While his servants were preparing for that long expedition, François decided to go for a brief hunt nearby at Orléans. "Do come with me, Marie," he suggested.

I did sometimes join the hunt—I especially enjoyed falconry—but I did not wish to go with him on a cold, damp Saturday in mid-November. "Another time," I promised. "I prefer to stay by the fire with the queen mother and work on my stitchery. I have some rather elaborate pieces to complete for the exchange of gifts at the new year."

"As you wish, madame." My husband brushed my hand with his lips. I noticed that he looked tired, that the skin of his face was inflamed, that he sometimes grimaced and rubbed his ear. But I thought no more of it then. He left with his gentlemen, and I joined the queen mother and her ladies for more needlework.

The queen mother's secretary read aloud a letter that had recently been received from her daughter Élisabeth. It had been a year since the princess left for Guadalajara, and I missed her. The arrival of one of her letters was always a joyous occasion.

Philip is so much older than I, she wrote, *that I feared we would have little to say to each other. But he is a most tender and attentive husband, and I count myself to be among the most fortunate to have married such a charming man.*

I was especially interested in the part of the letter in which Élisabeth confided to her *maman* that the charming Philip had found himself in such a state of delight with his new wife that he had abandoned his mistress. I managed a surreptitious glance at Queen Mother Catherine, whose own husband had never been in such a state of delight that he was inclined to abandon Madame de Poitiers.

Late in the afternoon François returned from hunting. A freezing rain had been falling for most of the day, and he was wet and shivering. The queen mother immediately began fussing over him.

"Perhaps you wish to see to your husband's comfort?" Catherine asked me pointedly.

"I believe that my husband can see to his own comfort," I replied. I too was concerned, but I felt that he was of an age to change his clothes and have a hot drink and warm himself by the fire in his quarters without help. I was his wife, not his nurse or governess.

My mother-in-law glared at me disapprovingly. "Then I shall see to it," she said, and she marched stiffly out of the chamber.

I have since regretted my words, but at the time I continued stubbornly with my work, needle in, needle out, needle in . . .

⤜•⤛

We did not realize at first how ill François was. He complained that his ear hurt. He felt dizzy. "The world is spinning," he said.

Two days later it was still spinning, and he told his physician that he heard ringing noises and buzzing. The next day, while we were kneeling side by side at Mass in the royal chapel, he suddenly slumped over in a faint. When he revived, he cried, "The pain! The pain!" as he was carried to his bed.

I did not want to accept the words of the physicians who gathered around him. They told me that he was terribly ill. "It is possible that his illness is fatal."

"You must save him!" cried his mother. "You must not let him die!"

My uncles paced, clearly agitated, but they were distressed for a different reason. They understood that if *le petit roi* were to die, they would lose the main source of their power. For a time they understated the gravity of the king's illness when members of the court asked them for reports. They claimed that he suffered from a catarrh, no more than that. But most in the court thought my uncles were lying. The rumor circulated that *le petit roi* had been poisoned.

The doctors worked desperately to save him. They bled him and purged him with enemas. His condition worsened. Watery stuff ran from his ear. At times he was unable to speak and lay motionless, staring blankly. I rarely left his side, and then only for short periods. He did not seem to recognize me.

My relations with my mother-in-law worsened. The enmity that had brewed quietly for some time had intensified after King Henri's death. Now it was out in the open. As François's condition became graver and he moved ever closer to Death's black door, Queen Mother Catherine made it plain that she, as his mother, had the right to make the decisions concerning his care. While François lay unable to tell anyone what he needed or wanted—except, perhaps, for the torment to end—Catherine took over. I was pushed aside. Suddenly I was nothing, of no consequence, and I deeply resented it.

On the fourth day of my husband's terrible illness I learned from a servant that all of the king's gentlemen had been sent away.

"By whose order?" I asked.

"The queen mother's, madame."

I believed it was my right to decide who should be dismissed from my husband's bedchamber and who might be allowed to stay, and I determined to confront her. But when I looked into Queen Catherine's eyes and saw the anguish of a mother faced with losing her beloved child, I relented.

"We must find a way to care for him together," I told her. "I love François as much as you do, Madame Queen Mother."

"*Non,* you do not," she said wearily. "But my son believes that you do, and in order to help him, I will agree to whatever you wish."

Her words wounded me, but I said no more. The two of us kept watch at François's bedside from the earliest hours of the morning. We tasted the food that was brought to him to assure ourselves that he was not being poisoned. I had a pallet made up and stayed through the night by his side so that if he was able to call my name, however weakly, I would be there to hear it, and I promised to send for his mother if he spoke even a single word. Queen Catherine then left for the night. I had asked her not to come to his bedchamber after the last visit from the physician. He was my husband, and I wanted him to myself. But so did she. I often awoke to find her, a wraith in black, hovering over his bed. No matter how much I protested, no matter how I wished she would remain in her private chapel to pray for him, the queen mother could not stay away.

When he was able to mumble a few words, I rushed to summon the priest to hear his last confession and to give him the sacrament before he lapsed into silence again. If I thought he could hear me, I lay beside him, whispering to him, sometimes singing the songs my mother used to sing to me. I endured his violent episodes, shut my ears against his screams and cries, covered my face against the terrible stench of his illness.

The days passed in what must have been utter agony for my poor *petit roi*. Increasing his suffering were the bloodlettings and purges prescribed by the physicians; they only added to his torment. When I heard them discussing the possibility of drilling a hole in his skull to allow some of the fluid, or whatever was causing the intense pain, to escape, I fled from his bedchamber. My husband's physical agony had become my heart's anguish.

Occasionally I briefly left the king's side and called upon Sinclair to bring me the oat porridge that had always been a sustaining comfort and was now the only food I could swallow. After my wedding Sinclair had asked to be allowed to return to her family in Scotland, but I begged her to stay with me: "Just for a few months, Sinclair." She had agreed, but the months had stretched into a year, and then more, and still I could not let her go. At this difficult time in my life, my old nurse remained my connection to earlier, easier days. Her fault, as well as her virtue, was that she repeated to me the rumors that always swirled through the servants' quarters.

"Sinclair, you must tell me what you hear," I said as I poured thick cream over the soothing porridge. "It is important to me."

She shook her head. "There is nothing, mistress."

I looked at her sharply. "I do not believe you," I said.

After a long silence she relented a little. "'Tis too painful, mistress. I cannot see how it would help you," she insisted stubbornly.

But I could be just as stubborn. "I order you to tell me, Sinclair. The truth, and all of it."

My old nurse sighed. "Silly tales of what evil was done to cause him his sickness," she said slowly. "That his valet is in the pay of his enemies and put a poisonous powder into his nightcap. That his hairdresser was bribed to pour a poisonous oil into his ear."

Bad enough, but not as bad as I had expected. "Is there more?"

Her hesitation told me there was indeed more. I waited.

"I've told you what I've heard from the kitchens," she continued reluctantly. "But the truly awful stories come from the peasants in the countryside. They say *le petit roi* has long suffered from leprosy, and there is but one cure for it—to bathe himself in the blood of a wee bairn."

"In the blood of a child?" I asked incredulously, and I shoved aside the bowl of porridge, unable to swallow another spoonful.

"Aye, mistress. And ignorant people so feared him that they hid their children whenever he happened to pass by."

"How awful!" I shrieked, and Sinclair folded me in her arms to console me, as she had done so often when I was a child. I closed my eyes and leaned my head against her breast. "You are right, Sinclair. I have heard enough. If there is more, I do not wish to hear it."

The hours wore on until at last my husband's agony ended, in the evening of Thursday, the fifth of December, 1560.

But my torment was only beginning.

CHAPTER 25

Mourning

NUMB WITH GRIEF, I passed the long night watching over François's lifeless body.

My husband was dead. I was a widow, three days short of eighteen. My marriage had lasted two years and not quite eight months. I was no longer the queen of France. It was a stunning blow.

The priest returned to murmur more prayers. I sent him away.

I prayed.

The queen mother was already meeting with the privy council, which was preparing to pass on the crown to François's ten-year-old brother, Charles-Maximilien. Catherine would rule as regent, I supposed. For the first time the power rested securely in her hands. I no longer had a role. I was the dowager queen, a mere figurehead.

My first duty was to return the royal jewels. Queen Catherine had already sent a sharply worded message that she expected them, along with an inventory. I summoned Seton, the most pious of the Four Maries, to help me. I trusted her to keep the silence I needed while we made a list of the beautiful jewels I had been given when I became queen. During my brief marriage I had not had a chance to wear most of these gems—lavish diamond necklaces, a huge ruby as red as blood, sleeves encrusted with pearls. Returning the jewels to the queen mother symbolized the stripping away of my rank, and also of my life. I was determined to play my role with complete correctness. The queen mother would find no fault in my behavior.

That task finished, I chose a few personal items to take with me into my mourning chamber, a room with the windows draped in black so that no natural light could enter and only a pair of candles to pierce the gloom. I had been wearing the *deuil blanc,* the white veil, in mourning for my mother; the six-month mourning period was almost over, and I soon would have given it up. Instead, I added a white gown to the veil. I had chosen to wear white at my wedding to flout the custom, having no notion that in the near future I would be wearing it as the widow of the king.

"You may leave me now, Seton," I said, and my friend nodded and silently slipped out of the chamber. I had intended to pray, but instead I lay down on the narrow bed and fell into a deep, dreamless sleep.

The long, sorrowful days passed slowly. Meals were brought to me and left on a table where I could eat them or not, as I wished.

Custom allowed visits only by people of rank, and as it

happened those were the people I least wanted to see. The ten-year-old boy who would now be King Charles IX paid his respects with a well-rehearsed speech. My Guise uncles came, their distress written plainly all over their faces. I mistrusted them but had no choice but to receive them. Let them offer their condolences, their promises of assistance! I nodded, eyes averted, silent, breathing easily only after they had gone.

Grand-Mère came. Having suffered many losses herself, she knew the value of silence. "Time will heal you," she whispered and stretched out her hand to lace her bony old fingers with mine.

On the third day after my husband's death, I reached my eighteenth birthday. No one even mentioned it.

Mostly I sat at my writing table—not writing, just turning over my thoughts one by one, like the pages of a book. Sometimes I composed poetry. The first of the verses were for my companion, my friend, my husband, my dearest François. Sometimes I was dry-eyed and empty. Sometimes I gave way to weeping and could not stop.

And though I tried to banish them, my thoughts turned unbidden to James Hepburn, earl of Bothwell. With shame I remembered his embrace, his passionate kiss, and my response—too eager, too willing.

Is this, the loss of everything, my punishment for those few moments? Am I guilty of a great sin? Was my offense so serious? Has a wildness truly taken root in me?

The body of King François, age sixteen years and ten months, was buried at the Basilica of Saint-Denis, near his father's. After the funeral, my mourning became more public. The Four Maries were now permitted to visit my mourning chamber, but they scarcely knew what to say. We gazed at one another with quivering lips. "One day soon we will laugh again," I promised them, though I was not so sure.

Henry Stuart, my handsome young cousin, made the journey from England to offer the condolences of his parents, Lord and Lady Lennox. He was fourteen and, as I could not help noticing, already even taller than my Guise uncles.

I began to receive visits from ambassadors and government officials. None dared ask, but I knew the question that was on everyone's mind: *What will she do now?*

I could not have answered the question. This was the problem with which I struggled. Once the traditional forty days of solitary mourning ended, I would go back out into a world that had changed entirely for me. I was now titled dowager queen of France. Queen Mother Catherine would surely regard me as an unpleasant nuisance as she seized the reins of power. But I still held a valuable hand. I was the queen of Scotland; my husband's death had not changed that. I needed no one to tell me that I was young and beautiful, that I was intelligent and capable of charming almost anyone. All of this would make me a highly desirable candidate for a second marriage, if that was what I wanted.

Did I? I had no idea.

My Guise uncles returned. Their demeanor was supplicating, and their words dripped with honey. I expected them to try to persuade me to marry my ten-year-old brother-in-law, the new king, Charles IX. That, of course, would not be possible for another five years and would require a special dispensation from the pope, but it would enable them to regain the control they had lost so abruptly when François died. I prepared for them to set forth this proposal and counted on Queen Catherine to be adamantly against such a marriage.

But the plan my uncles described to me was entirely different. "It is our belief, *chère* Marie, that Don Carlos of Spain would make you an excellent match," the cardinal said smoothly. "He is a devout Catholic, close enough to your age, and the heir to the Spanish throne. Highly desirable!"

Before I could react, my uncle François added, "How pleasant it would be for you to be near your good friend Élisabeth, the wife of Don Carlos's father!"

This might have been a tempting offer if I had not remembered an earlier story of the Spanish prince. Princesse Élisabeth had been pledged to Don Carlos until King Philip II decided that he wanted her for himself. My uncles surely did not know that Élisabeth's letters to me since her marriage to Philip often mentioned Don Carlos's "strangeness," though she professed to care for him nonetheless, in a sisterly way. Or perhaps they *did* know, and they dismissed this trait as unimportant, as one might dismiss crossed eyes or a crooked shoulder.

The duke and the cardinal stood before me, waiting

expectantly for me to agree to the scheme they had proposed, as I always had in the past. I understood now that they had deceived me into signing documents that, had I died while François still lived, would have made Scotland a province of France. I deeply resented their deception.

"My good uncles," I said, "I am in no mood to discuss any plans for another marriage. Surely you realize that it is much too soon for any such conversation. But I promise you, when the time is right, a second marriage will be my decision, based entirely on what is best for me and for Scotland."

My uncles exchanged dark looks, but they did not give up easily. "You are bound to receive many offers, *ma chère nièce*," said the duke of Guise. "We do not wish to see you make a serious error in your choice."

"I am unlikely to make a serious error, with your help or without it. Let me say it again: the decision, when I make it, will be mine, and mine alone."

This did not please my uncles, but I did not care. I was done with pleasing them. I dismissed them, and I wept with relief when they were gone.

As my forty days of seclusion drew to an end, I wrote to Grand-Mère asking if she knew of a small château where I could stay for a short while. *I need time away from the demands of the French court to collect my thoughts,* I explained.

The messenger returned with her reply, offering me a

simple little country house not far from Orléans. *I will have it prepared for you. You will find everything you need, including privacy.*

I immediately sent for the Four Maries, who arrived in my mourning chamber subdued but peering at me hopefully. The months since my marriage to François had been difficult for them. Though I had wanted us to enjoy one another's company as we had as children, I had had a role to play as François's wife and queen. Games and laughter, rides through the countryside, forays to the kitchens for treats— all of that had been out of the question for a long time. But now it would change.

"Pack a few simple things," I told them. "Have your mounts saddled. We leave tomorrow."

They stared at me, open-mouthed. "Where are we going, mistress?" asked La Flamin, unsurprisingly the first to find her voice.

"To the country," I said, smiling. "To enjoy ourselves."

The next morning under a bright January sky, five young women on horseback, followed by a handful of servants, a few carts piled with baggage, and a small royal escort, rode away from Orléans. I breathed deeply, glad to escape the dusky gloom of the château. The horses' hooves rang on the frozen ground, the branches of the trees glittered with hoarfrost, and yet I felt that everything around me would one day explode again in riotous bloom.

We arrived at my grandmother's country house—not as grand as the royal châteaux, but quite lovely—and as she had promised, everything was ready for us. While our horses were led off to the stables and the carts with our baggage were unloaded, we wandered through the rooms, choosing our bedchambers. Fires blazed on every hearth. Tempting smells floated up from the kitchens.

We passed the days quietly. Every morning I rode my horse, sometimes for hours at a time. Bundled in our furs, we went for long walks; later we dined well. In the evenings we played *jeux de tables* and read aloud. The verses of Ronsard were always my choice. We wrote our own poems and took turns reading them to one another. Livingston played the lute and taught us new songs, and one evening La Flamin suggested dancing. I played the virginals while the Four Maries executed the court dances we knew so well.

The subdued gaiety was a balm to my wounded spirits, and I was happier than I had been for some time. I felt as though a great weight had been lifted from my shoulders. But I also knew I was facing some important decisions. I tried to make a lighthearted joke of it with my friends.

"My Guise uncles are shopping for a new husband for me," I told them as we warmed ourselves by a fire. "It seems that half the men of royal birth in Europe are in the market for a royal bride. Both King Frederick of Denmark and King Eric of Sweden are looking for wives, as are several Italian dukes. Even Henry Stuart, that young cousin who came to my wedding, has been put forward—by his own mother! She sent him to me to personally convey the condolences of his family. He is a handsome lad with a charming manner, but he is just fourteen. My uncles believe that none of these marriages is what they have in mind for me, for none of the men is of sufficiently high rank in an important enough country. They are proposing Don Carlos of Spain."

"What your uncles have in mind for *you?*" asked Beaton, barely masking her distaste for these uncles. "What have you told them, Madame Marie?"

"I have told them nothing," I said. "They do not seem to understand *non.*"

"But surely it is something you are thinking about," Livingston commented.

"Thinking about, yes. But no more than that." I smiled at them and pushed back my chair, ending the conversation. "Now, let us dance!"

By the time the country's official mourning period for King François II ended in March, I was ready to leave my peaceful retreat near Orléans and to rejoin the court when it moved on to Fontainebleau. On our last day at Grand-Mère's house, I summoned the steward and told him to send us a group of musicians to entertain us that evening.

After my friends and I had dined well and talked of many things, I announced to the Four Maries that I had come to an important decision. In the end it had not been difficult.

"I will leave France," I told them, "and return to Scotland as the queen. And you, my dearest Maries, will accompany me."

Whatever fears I harbored about this new plan, I put

aside. I leaned forward, watching their faces. There was a moment of surprised silence and a gasp—probably from La Flamin.

"You will see your families again," I added.

Livingston managed a weak smile. "*Oui, certainement,*" she said, continuing in French, "but we are all Frenchwomen now, are we not? I scarcely remember the Scots language."

"Or indeed anything at all about my home there," Beaton put in, her voice trembling.

Seton added quickly, "*Naturellement,* we are happy to serve you in whatever you decide to do, Madame Marie."

I glanced at Marie Fleming, the only one who had not spoken. "And you, La Flamin? Are you happy to go home to Scotland?"

La Flamin bit her lip and scowled. "Scotland is not my home," she said. "France is my home. We learned the language, we learned the customs, just as you did, Madame Marie. As Livingston said, we are Frenchwomen now—and so are you!" she concluded passionately.

Her fervor spread to the others, and soon we were all weeping in one another's arms.

I was the first to recover myself. "It is my duty and God's will that I return to Scotland as her queen," I told them, dabbing at my eyes with a handkerchief. "The four of you are free to do as you wish—to accompany me to the land of your birth, or to remain in your adopted country."

I sat back, hands folded in my lap, and waited through a silence that seemed to go on too long. I had to grip my fingers to stop the trembling. But then Beaton stepped forward, followed by Seton and Livingston, and the three solemnly knelt before me. Only La Flamin held back.

"What is it, La Flamin? Why do you hesitate? What is it that holds you in France?"

"I beg your pardon, Madame Marie, but I have fallen in love!" she cried.

Her announcement seemed to surprise no one but me. "I am your cousin—how could I not know of this?" I asked. "Who is he? What is his name?"

"Jean-Luc," she said, her voice trembling. "He is a member of the king's guard. We would marry, but he has no money and no prospects." She began to weep.

"Then we shall take him to Scotland!" I declared. "We will certainly need guardsmen to accompany us there. The matter is settled."

La Flamin's cheeks dimpled in a broad smile, and she dried her tears and pledged that she too would return to Scotland and would speak to Jean-Luc the minute she saw him again. I thanked them all and clapped my hands and called for the musicians to play for us.

"Come, come, dear Maries! This is how we shall amuse ourselves in Scotland!"

CHAPTER 26

Adieu, France

I DID NOT STAY LONG at Fontainebleau but almost at once embarked upon a farewell tour of France. Everywhere I went I was warmly greeted with feasts and hunting parties and various entertainments, and I was made to feel so welcome that it was tempting to think that perhaps I might remain in France. According to my marriage contract, I was entitled to stay or go, as I wished.

I wavered: Should I take the easier path and stay in France, where I was admired, even loved, but had been stripped of any power? I understood that the opportunity to make the best use of the power that was my birthright lay in another direction: Scotland. My mother had sacrificed everything she had to preserve the Scottish throne for me; she believed it was her duty. Though I would leave France with deep regret, it was my duty to meet the challenge. I looked forward to it with growing excitement.

While I was moving from one château to another, from

one Guise aunt or uncle to the next, I received visits from two Scotsmen from opposing parties. First came a Catholic bishop representing the Scottish Catholics. Then, days later, my brother James Stuart arrived.

James was now a sober and serious man of thirty. Lord Bothwell had warned me about him: "I am pained to tell you that James Stuart did all he could to depose your lady mother." The Catholic bishop with whom I had just spoken called him "treacherous." I was prepared to stand up to my brother in every way possible. I knew that he believed he should be king of the Scots and had been prevented from this only by the accident of his birth, that he was born a bastard to my father and not the royal prince he felt himself to be. James had no doubt that he was better qualified than I to rule Scotland. But I intended to win him over and persuade him to be my chief adviser, and therefore I welcomed him with more warmth than I truly felt.

For five days we conferred intensely. The main issue was that he was now a convert to Protestantism and a follower of John Knox, while I was Catholic and would forever remain so. I made it clear to James that I would not attempt to restore the Catholic faith as the official religion of Scotland but would continue to practice my faith in private.

At last we reached an accord.

"All men should live as they please," I told him. "I believe that with all my heart."

"And you may hear Mass as many times a day as pleases you at your private chapel in Holyrood Palace," James assured me, and on this agreeable note, we parted.

My servants began packing. Two galleys would be sent for me and my retinue, and more than a dozen additional ships for my possessions, including my stable of horses. The flotilla would be under the command of the earl of Bothwell, who held the title of lord high admiral of Scotland. In July, Lord Bothwell, in France to complete arrangements for my journey, called on me. I was somewhat unnerved by his presence, unable to erase the memory of his unexpected— and uninvited—embrace some months earlier.

Nevertheless, I greeted him with what I hoped was friendly composure and inquired about not only his health but his wife's. "And Lady Bothwell?" I asked. "I assume your wife is well?"

"I have no wife as yet, Madame Marie, but I am pledged to marry Anna Throndssen, who asked me to convey to you her best wishes for a safe journey." Then he smoothly steered the course of our conversation in a new direction.

We took up the matter of Queen Elizabeth's refusal to issue me a diplomatic passport through England until I agreed to sign the Treaty of Edinburgh, promising to give up all claims to the English throne. I had dropped my superior claims to the throne, asking only that Elizabeth name me her heir if she were to die childless. But Elizabeth steadfastly refused to agree even to that, and I refused to sign the treaty unless she did.

"Where does the issue now stand, my lady queen?" asked Lord Bothwell.

"I have put off giving the English ambassador a direct answer. I told him that I must consult with my advisers in Scotland first. Meanwhile, should weather conditions or illness or some other reason require me to go ashore in England rather than Scotland, the queen would have the right to order my arrest."

Bothwell smiled winningly, leaning closer. "You need have no concerns of any kind, my lady. I give you my guarantee that you will arrive in the port of Leith safely and without incident and without the necessity of setting your royal foot on the land of the petulant queen."

We laughed together, and I thanked him for his attention to my deepest concerns. Our discussion of the particulars of the coming journey was now concluded. Once Lord Bothwell had taken his leave, I felt that the chamber in which we had been talking had grown uncomfortably warm, and I stepped out onto the terrace for a breath of cooler air.

I have no wife as yet. Though Bothwell had said he was pledged to Anna Throndssen, those few words returned to me over and over, giving me the foolish hope there might be more such intimate moments between us. But why would I wish for such a thing? Lord Bothwell was an earl, but he was not of sufficient rank or standing to deserve a place on my list of prospective second husbands. My mind raced on. *If not as husband, then as lover?* I had never considered such a possibility, though the shocking suggestion had reached me more than once while François was still alive that perhaps I *should* take a lover in order to ensure the succession.

As it happened, the terrace where I stood musing overlooked the main entrance to the château. Below me Lord Bothwell and his gentlemen were mounting their horses. As I leaned on the parapet, he turned and looked up in my direction. For a moment we gazed at each other.

I could call down to him, I thought. *"Wait just a moment," I could say. "I've thought of something." And he would race up the stone steps, two at a time, and then . . .*

And then *what?*

I raised my hand. Lord Bothwell saluted me. Then he turned, leaped onto his horse, and rode away without a backward glance.

❧

The farewells continued. At the end of July, while the court was spending the summer at Saint-Germain, I made my goodbyes to young King Charles, who had been crowned in May. His mother and a number of princes of the blood and members of the nobility were on hand to honor me. My rank as the dowager queen of France and as queen of Scotland meant that I could not be ignored. Queen Catherine behaved cordially, assured that I was indeed leaving and would not inconvenience her much longer by my presence.

My Guise family—uncles, aunts, cousins, nieces, and nephews—turned out in force for the final four-day fête. After the feasting and music and entertainments ended, I set out with a large retinue for Calais, where the Scottish flotilla awaited me. It was a slow and roundabout journey meant to confuse any English spies who might be watching for me. All went smoothly, save for a crisis with La Flamin. Jean-Luc would not accompany us, and Marie Fleming was furious.

"Perhaps he will join us later," I said, assuming that Jean-Luc had not been able to leave his commission with the royal guard.

"The devil take him!" she raved. "He has lied to me about everything! He has no royal blood, no money, and no prospects. What he *does* have is a wife and a wee bairn on the way. I am well rid of him." She tossed her head of fiery curls, and the subject was closed.

On the tenth of August we arrived in Calais, where we rested to prepare ourselves for the sea journey that the lord high admiral, the earl of Bothwell, promised me would take only a few days. We would pass through waters heavily patrolled by English ships, and though I had been refused safe passage by the queen of England, I would not be deterred. Had not the lord high admiral assured my safety?

When we boarded our galley under a hazy sun, I was pleased to see at the helm the very same Captain Villegagnon who had brought us to France all those years ago, his face weathered and his hair now streaked with gray. The anchor chain rattled, the sails were hoisted, and our galley moved slowly away from the dock. But before we had left the harbor, one of our smaller ships collided with a fishing boat, which sank quickly. Though the captain immediately dispatched rescuers and I offered generous rewards to all who could save lives, no survivors were found.

"What a terrible omen!" I cried, badly shaken by this unfortunate occurrence.

It was clear that nothing more could be done to save the victims, and Captain Villegagnon gave the order for our ships to continue. This was a deeply distressing start for my voyage. Again I had cause to wonder at the awful events that somehow seemed to follow me and to ask myself if I was somehow responsible.

As my galley sailed northward through the Strait of Dover, I stood on the deck and watched the coastline of France grow smaller and smaller. My courage suddenly deserted me. "Adieu, *ma chère* France." I sobbed, clinging to the rail. "Adieu! Adieu! I fear that I shall never again return."

V

It Would Not Be a Simple Matter

LEAVING FRANCE FOR SCOTLAND was only the beginning, the first of the tests I faced as I sought to establish my authority where it had not existed for nineteen years. In those early months my confidence grew and I accomplished a great deal. But I also made some miscalculations and committed a few errors in regard to my fellow Scots and my cousin Queen Elizabeth of England.

For those and other misjudgments, I now pay dearly with my freedom.

CHAPTER 27

Arrival in Scotland

THE CAPTAIN ORDERED the two great galleys to make all speed to avoid the English ships. The slower ships carrying my furniture and tapestries and plate, as well as my gowns and furs, plus additional vessels with more than a hundred mules and horses and their equipage were to follow as they could.

After an ominous start with the sinking of the fishing boat, the voyage could not have been more perfect. The weather presented no problems. Each day, entertainments were arranged and fine feasts prepared for me and my large retinue. Gradually my grief lessened, my optimism was renewed, and I once again believed that I had much to look forward to. A new life was about to begin!

Only five days after leaving Calais, we arrived before dawn at the coast of Scotland. I awakened early, too excited to sleep, and stepped out on deck. The sun had not yet risen, and our galley groped its way slowly up the Firth of

Forth through a thick fog. Dressed in a light summer gown and veil of purest white, the proper dress for a widowed queen of France, I shivered in the early-morning chill and asked for a black woolen cloak to be brought.

Captain Villegagnon appeared on deck out of the fog. "We shall soon reach the pier, madame," he said. "We have arrived in record time!"

The oarsmen brought the galley to the pier in the port city of Leith, and all hands leaped to their duties of docking the great ship. My ladies, their eyes still heavy with sleep, joined me on deck. The pier bustled with activity—commercial ships unloading cargo, fishing vessels fading in and out of the fog that shrouded the harbor—but there was no sign of any officials to greet me.

If I had expected the royal welcome and cheering crowds to which I was surely entitled—*Our queen has come home at last!*—I was due for a disappointment. I, who had since early childhood always been treated with the courtesy due a monarch, arrived in Scotland to discover that no one was expecting me and no preparations had been made.

"Where is everyone?" asked Beaton. "Is no one here to celebrate the arrival of the queen?"

It was a mystery, but I made light of it, and Captain Villegagnon tried to excuse it by explaining that favorable winds had brought us to our destination much earlier than anyone had anticipated. "Then let the people know, by whatever means you have, that their queen is here," I told him.

The captain bowed and gave an order. Shortly afterward

the small cannons mounted on the deck of the galley were fired, making a deafening roar. That caught the attention of the townspeople, and soon residents were flocking to the harbor, excited young boys and girls running ahead followed at a slower pace by their more sedate elders.

A ruddy-faced gentleman named Andrew Lamb appeared, shirttails untucked and cap askew, and made a little speech of welcome in the Scots language, apologizing for the absence of the officials and explaining that since his home overlooked the harbor and he personally had observed the arrival of the royal galley, he had made preparations for us. "My home is ready to receive you, my lady queen," he said, bowing deeply.

Lamb signaled to his servants to lead out a half a dozen shaggy ponies for my ladies and me, and he invited the others to follow on foot. He led the way up a winding path to a large but plain manor house, where his wife and three maidservants greeted us with shy, flustered smiles. They took us inside and soon made us comfortable in simple surroundings. To my delight, there was a pot of oat porridge bubbling on the hearth, and there was fresh cream from the cow sheltered in a nearby shed. Soon the Four Maries and I had washed and eaten and refreshed ourselves; the young daughters of the household gazed wide-eyed at their royal guest, and the sons were dispatched to inform the mayor and other officials of their queen's arrival.

It was all so ill organized that I could only laugh.

The first to appear was my brother James, accompanied by an escort of Scottish lords. My brother and I greeted each other cordially, and I heard again the explanation for the absence of the proper formal welcome I might reasonably have expected.

"No one thought you would arrive so soon!" he boomed. "Preparations are being made for you at Holyrood Palace, and you will be conveyed there before nightfall."

By midday the fog had lifted, and the northern sun worked its way through the remaining haze. A fine meal was prepared and served by Mistress Lamb and her neighbors, summoned along with their servants to assist her. The poor woman found herself with a number of unexpected visitors to feed that day, and she rose to the occasion admirably. Her simple, warm-hearted hospitality charmed me, so rather than feeling I had not been accorded the proper respect from my subjects, I was well pleased. The "auld language" was soon rolling off my tongue, haltingly at first, and then with greater ease as the day wore on.

Late in the afternoon my retinue and I were provided with mounts to ride the short distance to my residence just outside the ancient walls of Edinburgh proper. Livingston looked askance at the mount offered to her, a horse sturdy enough to serve as a draft animal. The most accomplished equestrienne of the Four Maries, she was used to a sleek, smooth-gaited palfrey.

"What sorry-looking beasts!" our Lusty muttered in French, assuming that no one would understand. "These mounts would never be allowed to carry a Frenchwoman!"

Her assumption was incorrect; James understood her perfectly. "But each has four legs and a broad back," he told her in French, "and that is all you should require, Madame Livingston." He laughed heartily as she blushed furiously.

By the time we left the hospitality of the Lambs on borrowed horses with borrowed saddles and reins, jubilant crowds had gathered all along the route my brother had chosen. My cavalcade reached the High Street, the road extending from Edinburgh Castle at the top all the way down to Holyrood Palace and the old abbey for which the palace had been named at the bottom.

Lord James rode beside me. "Mary," he said—he was the first to call me again by my Scots name—"if you look up at the house we are now passing, you may see the face of John Knox, the Protestant reformer, scowling down at you."

That dour preacher had not been able to find a single kind word for my mother at the time of her death—I had heard this from the earl of Bothwell. And when Knox learned of my intent to return to Scotland, he had said, according to the Scottish bishop who visited me in France, "She brings with her only sorrow, dolor, darkness, and impiety."

Sorrow, dolor, darkness, and impiety indeed! "If John Knox is watching me from his window, I prefer to remain unaware of it," I told my brother. "I will not give him that satisfaction."

Smiling and waving, I acknowledged the cheers of my subjects as we passed through the Netherbow Port in the ancient city walls and continued on to Holyrood Palace. At last, I was home!

CHAPTER 28

Holyrood Palace

LED BY A DOZEN SCOTTISH LORDS, we crossed the iron drawbridge and rode into the forecourt of Holyrood Palace. I leaned forward eagerly in my saddle and absorbed my first sight of it. The sun, still thinly veiled, lent the stone edifice a soft golden glow. For the first time, I would be in my own palace. This was not a château belonging to the French crown. This was mine!

The palace dated back centuries but had been remodeled in its present form by my father for his first wife, Madeleine. I could see at a glance its resemblance to the beautiful châteaux in France. It must have pleased Queen Madeleine, though she had lived here for only forty days before she died. Surrounded by a lush wilderness, Holyrood stood protected from the harsh winds and rains blowing in from the sea by a low mountain covered with greenery. "Called Arthur's Seat," James explained.

He had forgotten that I had never before been to Edinburgh. My mother, fearful of an English attack and kidnapping, had not brought me here.

The crowd shoved and jostled their way into the forecourt and would certainly have followed me into the quadrangle had Lord James not called upon his men to form a protective cordon. I turned my horse and faced the crowd. "Good people of Scotland," I cried, speaking in Scots, "I rejoice to be at home among you!"

They roared back their approval. Lord James helped me to dismount and escorted me to the central entrance. As we stepped inside the quadrangle around which the rooms of the palace were arranged, I was disturbed to see that it was entirely empty. The royal dining room had neither table nor benches. The throne room was bare. No portraits hung in the great gallery. My own furniture—beds, chests, tables, tapestries—were still on ships somewhere at sea. I looked to my brother for an explanation.

"If Queen Elizabeth has not ordered them seized, they should arrive here within a few days," Lord James assured me. "The horses and mules may take longer."

"But my mother's furniture—where is that?" I asked.

"Stored away," my brother offered with a careless shrug.

"Could it not have been removed from storage when you knew that I was coming?" I tried to keep the impatience out of my voice. Where was I to sleep tonight? And what arrangements were being made for the Four Maries, as well as for my servants and staff?

"Dear sister, you have taken us all by surprise! As soon as I had word that your galley had entered the harbor at Leith, I ordered work to begin in earnest, as you will soon see."

But why did you wait so long? I wondered. *Is it that you do not truly want me here?*

In my opinion, each room should have been adequately furnished, and I could then have replaced whatever I wished with my own things, now bobbing about somewhere in the North Sea. But I said nothing. *First, no official welcome. Now, nowhere to sit or dine or sleep.*

We climbed from the ground floor to the first floor of the tower. Here were the king's apartments, unoccupied since my father's death, nearly nineteen years earlier. Directly above them were the queen's apartments. At one time this had been my mother's, but after my father died she had seldom stayed here, preferring her other palaces. Here was where I intended to live my life. And here I now found a beehive of activity—workmen setting up a great bed and arranging benches and chests; women carrying in linens and coverlets.

I was suddenly overcome with deep feelings: grief for the loss of my mother and satisfaction that, as my father's daughter, I truly belonged here. Mingled with these strong emotions was strong apprehension. How would I fare in this land of which I truly knew so little?

"James, if it is not too much to ask, I would very much like to examine my quarters on my own," I told my brother.

He bowed and left me, taking with him the lords who

had accompanied us. A handful of servants remained, unsure what was expected of them, and I dismissed them as well.

I stood silently in the center of the queen's outer chamber. The walls were richly paneled in wood, and the coffered ceiling was beautifully carved and painted. Near the top of the circular stair, a window with a kneeling bench looked out over the old Abbey of the Holyrood. I could imagine my mother coming here to say her prayers; I would do the same. I knelt where I believed my mother once had, gave thanks to God for my safe arrival, and asked His blessing on this, the beginning of my new life.

Next to the outer chamber was the queen's bedchamber, nearly as large and just as sumptuously decorated. Adjoining were two turrets, each containing a small room. One of them, I thought, would make an intimate supper room where I could entertain my closest friends. The other would be my dressing room, where, if I wished, I could be completely alone. Through the small panes of the windows I gazed upon the gardens my mother had laid out years ago to resemble those she had known and loved in France.

I descended the stair to the great gallery. It was badly damaged; windowpanes were missing so that rain had ruined the floors, and the plaster was cracked and broken.

"The work of the English," James explained. "When King Henry the Eighth sent his troops here demanding your hand for his son Edward, my dear Mary, the palace was sacked. The great gallery suffered the most damage."

"If it was sacked on my account, then I shall have it repaired on my account," I promised.

The kitchens were not yet in order, and the cooks I had brought with me spoke only French and could not make themselves understood. But the townspeople rallied, bringing chairs and setting up boards and trestles in the great gallery and somehow contriving to put together a fine supper for my entire retinue: roast meats, vegetables grown in nearby gardens, fruits picked from the orchards. Musicians brought out their instruments, and while we passed the evening pleasantly, furniture was being hauled out from storage and set in place in my apartments. At last, wearied by the journey and the long day and the strangeness of it all, the people present went off in search of places to lay their heads.

I climbed gratefully onto a bed piled with wool-stuffed mattresses, and I would have fallen asleep immediately had it not been for a terrible racket that broke out on the palace grounds below. I stood up to see what it was. At least a hundred, or perhaps several times a hundred, musicians armed with fiddles and rebecs had gathered beneath the palace windows and now sawed away discordantly on their instruments and sang. I supposed it was intended as a sort of serenade. The Four Maries, whose shipboard beds had been set up temporarily in the king's apartments, below, rushed up the stair to find me.

"I believe they are singing," said Seton.

"It sounds like the howling of cats," La Flamin said. "Shall I go down to investigate?"

"*Oui, s'il vous plaît,*" I said. We were still more comfortable speaking French among ourselves.

Borrowing her serving maid's hooded cloak, La Flamin went out to learn what she could. The dreadful noise continued unabated, an insult to the ears of anyone who truly loved music. Presently she returned, flinging off her disguise.

"There are two explanations for what is going on, depending on the source," she reported. "Some say it is a rustic welcome. Bonfires and various celebrations are going on throughout the city, and those celebrators who own musical instruments of any kind decided to offer their queen a serenade. That is the better explanation."

"And the other?"

"Some say these are Protestants sent by the preacher John Knox to sing psalms as a way of notifying the Catholic queen of their presence. They say he has ordered them to continue for as many nights as is required until the queen gives up her idolatrous practices."

I sank onto my bed and sat there with my head in my hands. "Go now, and get what rest you can. Tomorrow I will greet them as their monarch."

The clamor continued through the night, giving me little rest. The next morning, I struggled out of bed and dressed in the best of the gowns I had available, put on a number of jewels, and had Seton arrange my hair and settle a golden coronet on my head. Then I summoned several of my own musicians to accompany me to the forecourt with trumpets and sackbuts.

I mounted one of the crude carts that had hauled goods from the ship and instructed my musicians to play a loud flourish. The local musicians stopped to stare. When they realized their queen was standing before them, they fell silent. I spoke to them, thanking them for their welcome.

"You have given me a delightful experience," I told them, "adding immeasurably to my pleasure at being here among you, my good people of Scotland. Now I bid you all return to your homes for a well-deserved rest."

They cheered, and as a chilly dawn crept over the city, the crowd drifted away. I returned to my apartments, set aside my crown and jewels, and at last fell into a deep sleep, ending my first full day and night as queen in my own kingdom.

CHAPTER 29

First Days

I HAD ARRIVED in Edinburgh on Tuesday, the nineteenth of August. For days after, I waited impatiently for the arrival of the transport ships. At last a messenger brought word from the lord high admiral that English vessels searching for pirates had detained one of our ships.

"Unfortunately, the ship has all of your majesty's horses and mules on board," the messenger reported.

"The queen of England has taken my horses prisoner?" I asked, too amazed to be angry.

"I cannot say for certain, madam. But Lord Bothwell promises that he will secure their release."

"Then I suppose I shall be pleased to use Scottish mounts," I said. "I understand that they do have fine horses here," I added wryly, for many in my stable were from Scottish stock.

Days later, my horses, mules, and their equipage were

reportedly making their way slowly from the headland where British ships had seized them. There was nothing to do but wait. Lord James did all he could to make me and my retinue as comfortable as possible.

On my first Sunday in Scotland I ordered Mass to be celebrated in the royal chapel. When word got out, an angry group of Protestants suddenly filled the forecourt, loudly condemning the "idolatry." The priest was in the sacristy preparing the bread and wine, and one of my servants crossed the forecourt with the candles to be used in the Mass. Several protesters seized him, wrested the candles from him, and trampled them in the dust.

I entered the chapel with the Four Maries. My brother, himself a Protestant but no supporter of such violence, had promised me that I would be allowed to hear Mass in my palace and now placed himself in the doorway. He was a big man with a commanding presence, and he would not allow any of the ruffians to enter the chapel. Nevertheless, those of us kneeling inside could hear the shouted threats outside. The elderly priest trembled so violently he could scarcely lift the sacred host. The service proceeded without further incident, but I was determined that no such insult should be repeated. I issued a proclamation that no one was to be prevented from privately practicing his religion, and the penalty for disobeying this edict was death.

My proclamation served only to inflame John Knox. The very next Sunday, the fiery preacher shouted from his pulpit for hours on end that a single Mass said in the royal chapel or anywhere else was more to be feared than an army of ten thousand sent to destroy the realm.

I would have to confront John Knox, and soon.

Meanwhile, the provost of Edinburgh presented himself and informed me that he had undertaken to arrange an official welcome for me on the second of September. I would host a banquet at Edinburgh Castle, the fortress that was once the home of Scottish kings. Following this, I would make my formal entry into the city, an *entrée royale* along the High Street, from Edinburgh Castle at one end to Holyrood Palace at the other. The provost assured me that all was in readiness. I needed only to be present.

The first question was what I should wear for this grand event. I was officially in mourning for my husband and still wore the *deuil blanc,* but I realized that this was not the custom here and that the Scots did not understand why I went about in a long white veil. I decided on a black velvet gown enriched with gold braid and hundreds of tiny white pearls. The Four Maries, as my chief ladies in waiting, would be gowned in gray silk.

Somewhere at sea was a ship with my gilded carriage, but even if it appeared, it would be useless on the deeply rutted track that served as the main avenue through Edinburgh. Since my horses and mules had finally arrived from their English imprisonment, I mounted my favorite palfrey, trapped to the ground in shimmering satin brocade.

We left Holyrood at midmorning on the appointed day. Surrounded by my leading noblemen, whom I was just getting to know, I rode in a stately procession up the hill to Edinburgh Castle. The rugged fortress commanded the highest ground above the city, which lay huddled in its over-bearing shadow. Smoking torches lit the blackened walls of the gloomy great hall, even at midday. A fire had been laid in the huge stone fireplace, and by the time my banquet was served, crackling flames had taken off the chill.

"Serve the richest sauces and the daintiest pastries you can conjure," I had instructed my French cooks. "My guests must be deeply impressed but not entirely overwhelmed." I wanted to make clear to the noblemen and local officials, who for years had been accustomed to acting independently, that I was their queen and must be recognized as the monarch and ruler.

It was not easy for my cooks to find the ingredients they wanted, but the dinner was, I felt, a great success. When the meal ended, we descended Castle Hill as the great guns of the castle boomed with such force that the ground shook beneath my feet.

The local townsfolk had gone to considerable effort to make a fine impression on me as well. Archways and plat-forms had been built along the High Street and pageants were performed. At each stop I made, singers and actors of all ages took part in a presentation meant to welcome their queen and to make sure I understood that this was no longer a Catholic country but a Protestant one in which the Mass was despised as an idolatrous act. The first gift presented to me was a Bible and a psalter. I recognized that I was being pressured to accept the Protestant faith, and this deeply displeased me, though I chose not to show it.

My procession passed through Lawnmarket, the neighborhood immediately below the castle, and then moved on to the High Kirk of St. Giles. The crowds there were well behaved and genuinely welcoming, but when we reached the High Cross, it became evident that the fountain was flowing with wine instead of water. The revelers were quite drunk. I signaled that we should move on. As we rode by John Knox's house, I imagined him fulminating at one of the windows above. We passed through Netherbow Port with its turrets in the ancient walls and then entered Canongate. Holyrood Palace lay only a short distance beyond. I was relieved that it was nearly over. I felt I had made the impression I desired on the townspeople and had managed to turn aside their mindless hatred of the Catholic faith.

Two days later, at my invitation, John Knox and I came face to face.

I knew about Knox's venomous sermons condemning me, and I was well acquainted with his pamphlet *The First Blast of the Trumpet*. Lord Bothwell and I had thoroughly discussed the major points of it; namely, that women were not fit to rule. The preacher found us weak, frail, feeble, and foolish creatures who were "repugnant to God," in his words. He believed in violence and the right of subjects to remove by

force a ruler who displeased them. The French had a law
that prevented a woman from ruling in her own right. Apparently Scotland had John Knox.

This would be a very interesting interview.

I disliked the man on sight and could discern neither
grace nor charm in him. He was many years my senior and
puffed up with pridefulness. The churlishness in his manner of speaking to me was irritating, and I found him outrageous in his insistence that I could be forcibly removed
from the throne because I did not worship God in a manner he approved of.

"Is that what you intend, sir?" I demanded. "That I be
removed from the throne for my religious beliefs and because I am a woman?"

"It is an act of obedience, madam, to forcibly remove
and imprison a ruler who is disobedient to the will of God
and keep that ruler confined there until the ruler comes to
his senses."

I could scarcely believe what I heard. Never before had I
been spoken to in such a way. But then, never before had
I been in a position of ruling. I had held the title of queen
of Scots since a few days after my birth, but for nearly eighteen years I had not had an opportunity to exercise the
power that was rightfully mine. Now I intended to use it.
Knox's challenge to that power astonished me.

When I found my voice, I said, "I see that you believe
my subjects should obey you, rather than me, and follow
their own wishes rather than my commands. In the end,

then, I am subject to them and to you rather than they and you being subject to me."

"It is as you say, madam," he acknowledged with a bow and a barely concealed sneer.

"Then you, sir, are dismissed!"

I could not claim any sort of victory over the rude Protestant preacher, but neither could he in all conscience declare himself the winner. Once I was alone, I gave way to tears of frustration and fury, for I had no idea how to deal with a man who held so much savagery and hatred for me in his heart.

CHAPTER 30

Royal Progress

IT HAD BEEN nearly nineteen years since my father, King James V, had occupied the Scottish throne. After his death, my mother did her duty as regent until a governing council replaced her. Now I had returned to Scotland to claim my rightful inheritance, and I needed to establish myself as ruler in the minds and hearts of my subjects in every part of the kingdom. I had to begin at once.

My first official act was to appoint a privy council. Among the councilors were my brother James, whom I now elevated to earl of Moray, as he had so long desired and pressured me to do; William Maitland, who had served my mother well as her secretary of state; James Hepburn, earl of Bothwell, with whom I felt a strong affinity; and thirteen others. Only four councilors were of the Catholic faith. In general they were an intelligent, well-educated lot; many had studied and traveled abroad. Some I trusted more than others, but they all knew the Scots people far better than I did, and many were heads of powerful clans whose co-operation I needed. I believed I could keep an eye on the one who worried me most—namely, my cousin George Gordon, earl of Huntly, about whom my mother had warned me.

I met with the privy council for the first time on the sixth of September, just two days after my distressing encounter with John Knox. When the council session ended, I left Edinburgh on a royal progress. I had two goals: to acquaint myself with my realm, and to allow my subjects to become acquainted with their new queen. My cortège, with a large retinue of servants and friends, followed a semi-circular route to the north of Edinburgh. We stopped first at Linlithgow Castle, where I was born, and then moved on to Stirling, where I had spent my early years with my mother; after this we went to Perth and Dundee, and finally we traveled by ferry across the River Tay to Fife. At every stop I made a triumphal entry and received a hearty welcome and fine gifts. The greatest gift was a new appreciation of Scotland's rugged beauty, so different from the more refined landscape of France. If my elegant gilded carriage ever arrived, it was destined to remain unused on the land's deeply rutted roads, which were by turns rocky or muddy and were often impassable.

As we made our way through the country shires, I met the wealthy nobles and the prosperous lairds, those proud, powerful men who ruled their landholdings as though they were small kingdoms. These men and their wives greeted me with the same warm hospitality that Andrew Lamb's family had shown me in my first hours in Scotland. I enjoyed meat roasted on spits and every kind of delicacy from the sea, prepared simply. They presented me with lengths of woolen cloth marvelously woven in plaid patterns and assured me that I would appreciate the warmth of these woolens as the weather turned cold and damp and winter sank its teeth into every corner of the kingdom, not to let go for many a long month.

While the lairds and nobles lived in luxury in their turreted castles surrounded by walls and moats, the poor huddled in squalid hovels with neither gates nor fences, their few animals wandering freely among the hedgerows. I was deeply moved when country folk in their mended clothes rushed out of their humble dwellings and crowded around us, not to beg for alms, as I had seen so often in the towns and cities of France, but to offer their greetings and their blessings. They seemed to ask nothing in return but my goodwill, and I promised myself that as their queen I would do all in my power to improve their lot in life.

After a stay at St. Andrews, where the views from the castle were magnificent but the bloody works of the Protestant reformers a few years earlier were still fresh in everyone's memory, we moved on to Falkland Palace. I was shown the chamber where my father, lying on his deathbed, had heard the news that Marie of Guise had borne him a daughter—"a lass." Deeply disappointed, he had turned his face to the wall and breathed his last. I sent away my escorts and remained alone in the chamber. "I was the cause of your death, Father," I murmured, still unable to rid myself of that conviction. "What would you think of me now? What would you say to me? How would you advise me?"

The walls gave back no answer, and I had no wish to linger. My entourage was waiting for me in the antechamber, exchanging worried looks. "Shall we go on?" I asked with false cheer.

We resumed the progress, still within a long day's journey of Edinburgh. When I reached Holyrood Palace at the end of September, Scotland was, as promised, already in the firm grip of winter.

I was elated to find that while I had been away, the transport ships that had set out from Calais weeks earlier had finally arrived in Leith. Carts from all over the city were commandeered to unload my possessions as well as the baggage of the staff of French servants who had accompanied me. The gilded carriage was sent off directly to storage to await the day when the Scottish roads might become passable.

The chests of furnishings and trunks containing most of my finery were carried to my apartments. For the next few weeks, when I was not meeting with my advisers regarding matters of governance, I was having a delightful time decorating my new home.

Tapestries were hung in every hall and chamber, and

Turkish carpets that were both beautiful and warm underfoot were rolled out on the stone floors. Special stools, carved and painted, were set out for my Four Maries, with folding stools available for visitors. My gilded throne, covered in crimson velvet and cloth of gold, was placed in the throne room with a splendid cloth of estate mounted above it. The dining hall was now properly furnished with banqueting tables and benches, and cupboards displayed enough gold and silver plate and goblets and ewers and salvers to supply the grandest banquet.

The Four Maries helped me decide where to keep my collection of gowns, furs, and jewels. "Perhaps much of it could be kept below, in the king's apartments," Livingston suggested.

"Until you have installed in those chambers a king of the realm," La Flamin added archly, a remark I chose to ignore.

"A good thing that you will not be required to wear mourning for much longer," observed Livingston as servants carried away armloads of silks and velvets.

She had observed correctly; I could scarcely wait to lay aside the somber clothes that I had worn for nearly a year and dress once again in my elegant gowns. On the fifth of December, the anniversary of my husband's death, I called for two half days of mourning at Holyrood, out of respect for King François. Almost no one other than the Four Maries attended the memorial Mass with me. It seemed that *le petit roi* was nearly forgotten—and it was true that I rarely thought of him. My life had taken me in a direction we had not considered, and I had no choice but to get on with it.

When the two half days of mourning were over—on the eighth of December, and my nineteenth birthday—I put away my mourning clothes and eagerly selected a dark green damask trimmed with gold braid and the proper jewels to go with it. People were arriving in the city from the surrounding countryside for the coming Yuletide.

Beginning that day, I ordered banquets and entertainments and masques, music and dancing and feasting every night through Twelfth Night, the sixth of January. I wanted this to be a brilliant season—an entire month of celebration! Song and poetry were part of it, and I hired a number of musicians as permanent members of my staff and appointed a court poet to provide the celebrators with verses as needed. Three of my *valets de chambre* formed a singing group to perform regularly at my banquets, but they needed a fourth to sing the low part in the quartet. A member of the Italian diplomatic delegation, David Rizzio, was said to have a fine bass voice. I summoned Rizzio to my chamber.

"The quartet requires a bass," I told him. "Do me the favor of joining them."

Rizzio agreed, and when the ambassador returned to Italy at the end of the Yuletide season, Signor Rizzio stayed on in Edinburgh.

There was much to celebrate at the beginning of 1562. A monarch again occupied the throne of Scotland. Holyrood as well as the other royal palaces had been restored to a magnificence not seen in a long time—I had paid for it from my own funds. I was confident that all would go well in my kingdom, my "auld country."

The climax of the season was Twelfth Night. The cooks produced an enormous black bun cake, rich with dried fruits and spices. Somewhere inside the cake was a bean; whoever found the bean was crowned king or queen for the night. As it happened, Mary Fleming triumphantly produced the precious bean and claimed the golden crown. La Flamin took her place on my throne, and I knelt humbly before her and swore my fealty to the new queen. The "joyousity" that the Scots nobility expected and had made clear to me they wanted had returned, to the delight of everyone—except John Knox.

Just after Twelfth Night, my companions and I and members of the court made a long day's journey south of Edinburgh to James Hepburn's Crichton Castle for the wedding of Hepburn's sister Lady Janet to my half brother John Stuart. I had a fondness for weddings, and I could now indulge my taste for fine gowns and jewels, though I still often dressed in widow's black, which I found flattering. After three days of banquets and masques and other entertainments so welcome during the long nights and short days of the Scottish winter, we returned to Edinburgh to prepare for the next big wedding: my eldest brother, James, who now enjoyed the title of earl of Moray, was to marry Lady Agnes Keith. The wedding took place in February at the High Kirk of St. Giles, only a short distance from Holyrood. John Knox himself preached the sermon, and then we all withdrew to Holyrood Palace for three more days of brilliant celebration.

The preacher complained that the banquets and masques and dancing offended many godly people. It was hardly a surprise, then, when the following Sunday John Knox thundered from his pulpit in a sermon lasting some two hours condemning the "wanton skipping" by women who could not have been "honest" or they would never have indulged in such wicked behavior. The women skipping wantonly included *me*.

Among the celebrations and the joyousity, an instance of poor judgment on my part led to disastrous consequences. A young page, Pierre de Boscotel de Chastelard, had been among those who accompanied me to Scotland from France. Chastelard was a poet and musician of considerable skill as well as an exceptionally graceful dancer. When he sent me flattering verses, I invited him to court, delighted by his talent and pleased by his presence. I gave him generous gifts of money to buy himself new clothes, as I often did to those whom I particularly liked. But I did not realize that Chastelard thought he was in love with me. Worse, he misinterpreted my friendship and convinced himself that the welcome I offered him and the compliments I paid him proved that I returned his love.

Soon after the weddings of my two brothers I danced with Chastelard until a late hour. That night, apparently carried away by his romantic delusions, he crept into my bedchamber before I arrived and hid beneath my bedstead. My grooms discovered him there and dragged him out by his ankles. When I heard the tumult, I rushed in, and, horrified at the liberties he had taken, I ordered him to leave Scotland and never return. He wept and apologized many times over, but I refused his apologies. I considered the matter finished.

I was wrong. In a matter of weeks Chastelard returned to Scotland—it is possible that he never left—and insinuated himself once again into my court. As I did not see fit to send him off to serve a term in prison, as I should have and as he deserved, he apparently believed he had been forgiven and restored to my good graces. For a second time he dared to invade the privacy of my bedchamber, this time as my ladies were preparing to undress me. My brother James heard my screams and ran in with his men-at-arms.

"He came here to ravish me!" I cried, truly terrified. "For this he must die!"

Chastelard was carried off and thrown into a dungeon to await a public trial. I worried that he would somehow convince the judge that I was at fault and had encouraged him, toyed with his deep feelings. But he was found guilty of treason and condemned to death. He begged for clemency, which I refused to grant.

My brother Lord Moray made me an unwilling witness to Chastelard's beheading. "If you order a man's execution, madam, you must be prepared to see it through," said my brother coldly.

I took my place on a parapet overlooking the market square at St. Andrews, where a scaffold stood ready. My hands were shaking, and my legs were so weak that I had to sit down as the poet was led to his doom. Chastelard gazed steadily at me as his last moments drew near and called out, "Adieu, you who are so beautiful and so cruel, you whom I cannot stop loving!" And then the ax fell.

It was terrible. I screamed and fell to the floor in a faint. Afterward I could not rid myself of the sense that I was responsible and had brought about his end, though my friends assured me Chastelard was quite mad to have behaved as he did.

Not everyone agreed that I was blameless. John Knox did not miss the opportunity to lay the culpability on my shoulders, insinuating that I must have been the young man's mistress all along, which I most assuredly was not. Even Lord Moray stated bluntly that I had acted unwisely.

"You enticed him," James said. "He would not have behaved so badly had you not encouraged him."

But later it was proven that Chastelard had been hired by French Protestants who wished to sully my honor and my reputation, and who had very nearly succeeded. I vowed that I would never again open myself to such criticism.

"From this day forward," I told Mary Fleming, "you must sleep in my bedchamber to preserve my reputation as an honest woman."

For some time she did, though weeks passed before I

could shake off my mood of melancholy that came with the realization that it *was* my fault. I had made a serious mis-step. Perhaps there was a wildness in me, and I was not as firmly in command of it as I wished to be.

CHAPTER 31

The Gordons

SCOTLAND WAS NOT FRANCE, and the Scots were not like the French. Yet I believed that I had won the goodwill of most of my subjects—nobles, lairds, commoners. One exception was John Knox. He and the rabid Protestant reformers pressed me relentlessly to abolish the Catholic faith in all its forms. Knox was conniving with Queen Elizabeth's chief adviser, William Cecil, to undermine my authority any way he could.

I refused to sign the Treaty of Edinburgh. I had no intention of renouncing my claim to the English throne until Queen Elizabeth agreed to name me her heir if she died without leaving any legitimate children. Elizabeth was twenty-eight, only nine years older than I, but one could never predict how many years a gracious God might grant each of us. My brother François de Longueville had died just before his sixteenth birthday, my husband his seventeenth, while my grandmother, nearly seventy, continued to enjoy good health. Thus far Elizabeth had not married. Perhaps she had no intention of marrying. She had even said that she would die a virgin. If she truly meant that and did not change her mind, as I had heard she so often did, I had no concern that Elizabeth would produce an heir and move me further down the line of succession. Even if she *did* change her mind and marry, she might not produce an heir, and then I should still rightfully inherit the English crown. So I firmly believed—but I had to persuade Elizabeth of that.

I set out to gain her trust and her friendship. I wrote to her assuring her of my amity and appealing for hers. I reminded her that months earlier, I had arranged to have my portrait made and sent to her and had requested that she do the same for me. She had not responded to that request, but she had sent me a handsome diamond in the shape of a heart, which I treasured.

Still she refused to name me her heir, stating frankly that once an heir was named, plots to displace her would inevitably begin.

Elizabeth and I began writing back and forth, sending gifts, even composing verses for each other. We discussed an eventual meeting, a thrilling prospect for me. I had begun to feel a deep kinship with her, almost as though she were my sister, a kinship that would be sealed once we actually met. I was certain that, face to face, I could persuade her of my suitability as her heir, even though the major sticking point remained that she was Protestant and I a devout Catholic.

In the summer of 1562 I sent William Maitland to England to arrange the details of a meeting. But Elizabeth had changed her mind yet again. The meeting would be postponed. I wept with disappointment

Very well, I thought, *I will follow a different path. I can be as stubbornly elusive as the English queen. She will not hear of my shedding tears on her account.*

Late in August I set out on a second royal progress, this time journeying to the Scottish Highlands, going as far north as Inverness. I had arranged for my priest to say Mass at the royal chapel when we arrived at Stirling Castle, but he was prevented from doing so—by my own brother Lord Moray!

"James," I cried, upset and incensed, "you promised that I could hear Mass in my own chapel. You have broken your promise!"

"I guaranteed that you could continue to hear Mass at the royal chapel in Holyrood," he said, his jaw set stubbornly. "But that guarantee does not extend to Stirling, or to any other place."

It was pointless to argue, and on this occasion we compromised. The priest set up a small altar in my apartments for me and the Four Maries and a few others. I had made up my mind to walk a careful line in dealing with the religious issues that plagued my country. I would adhere to a policy of tolerance, and I would not allow this strategy to be undermined.

My brother's highhandedness angered me, though I knew that he was trying to mollify Knox and the others. I had not yet forgiven him for making me feel guilty about the Chastelard incident. A gulf had opened between us. A confrontation was coming.

After leaving Stirling we rode for days in a constant drizzle of rain and fog, and by the time we reached Aberdeen, everyone was wet and miserable. It had also become difficult to find enough supplies along our route to feed my large entourage.

On our way from Aberdeen to Inverness we passed near the castle belonging to my cousin George Gordon, earl of Huntly. Inverness Castle was said to be one of the finest in all of Scotland. Lord Huntly was a member of my privy council, and though we were constantly in disagreement over several matters, we were related by blood—King James IV was our common grandfather—so I was prepared to ignore our disagreements and accept Gordon's famous hospitality.

"We will be treated well here," I assured my companions. "Fires will blaze on every grate, the beds will be soft, and food and wine will be plentiful."

But I was walking into a hornets' nest.

Huntly was lord chancellor of Scotland and the most powerful of the Catholic noblemen. He vigorously opposed my intended meeting with Queen Elizabeth and any sort of agreement with Protestant England. He also made no secret of his resentment of me for making my brother the earl of Moray, giving James control over lands that Lord Huntly felt belonged to *him.*

At the castle gates, the keeper of the castle—one of Huntly's sons—stood with hands on hips, flanked by guards armed with swords.

"What sort of welcome is this for your sovereign queen?" I called out.

"No welcome at all, madam!" came the reply. "On the orders of my father, George Gordon, earl of Huntly and master of this castle, entry is denied."

His reply stunned me. This was treason. I was not about to tolerate defiance of my royal authority. "My greetings to my cousin and countryman," I called back. "Open the gates."

"Entry denied!"

I called upon my guards to withdraw, heard them muttering, and glanced up to see the archers on the battlements. My decision came swiftly. I ordered the captain of the guards to dispatch messengers across the neighboring shires, summoning the leaders of clans I knew were hostile to the Gordons. Most of my retinue were sent off to the nearby town to find what lodgings they could. The Four Maries refused to leave me. We waited, wet and mud spattered, but determined. Within hours several hundred clansmen had assembled, armed with pikes and cudgels and ready to fight.

"Storm the castle," I ordered the men. "Seize the young Gordon who has refused to open the gates to his queen and sovereign and hang him from the battlements."

The captain looked surprised. "Hang him, my lady?"

It was harsh, but I knew that I had to establish my authority quickly and without wavering. "Hang him," I repeated.

We watched from a low rise as the men stormed the castle. It was over quickly.

"There is still time to change your mind," Seton whispered. "About young Gordon."

"I will not change it," I said, but I hid my trembling hands.

⚜

The next day my spies informed me that another of Huntly's sons, John Gordon, planned to have me kidnapped and then force me to marry him. Here was a Scot who must have been as mad as the French poet Chastelard! The battle was joined at Corrichie, near Aberdeen. My brother commanded an army of three thousand men; the earl of Huntly had only a third of that number. John Gordon was captured, and I ordered him beheaded the next day. This was not the same as my order for the execution of Chastelard. John Gordon was clearly guilty of treason. That same day, the old earl died of a stroke on the battlefield. His embalmed body was later taken to Edinburgh, where in its coffin the corpse was found guilty of treason and Lord Huntly's lands forfeited to the Crown. His eldest son and heir, George Gordon the younger, was spared and put under house arrest.

None of this was what I had intended when I set out on my progress. I had demonstrated by my actions that I was not to be trifled with or intimidated, but I had blood on my hands, and the deaths of two more men troubled my conscience. Despite this, my show of strength and fortitude had not brought me a single step closer to a meeting with the queen of England and the result I sorely desired: to be named Elizabeth's heir. Now as I rode back toward Edinburgh, I thought I knew what might hasten that end. By the time I reached Holyrood Palace I had come to a decision, as important as my decision to return to Scotland.

I must search for a man who will aid me in my goal to inherit the English throne, and marry him.

I must have a husband.

CHAPTER 32

A Suitable Match

THE QUEST FOR A HUSBAND would not be a simple matter. As a queen, I desired to marry a king; failing that, a prince who was next in line to be king. I understood that it did not have to be a love match—my marriage to François was not, though we shared a deep affection that began in childhood. Love was a luxury I could not allow myself, but of course I hoped for a marriage that would be mutually gratifying.

The list of such candidates was short.

My Guise uncles, who had begun searching for a suitable match within weeks of my husband's death, now pressed me to consider the twelve-year-old King Charles IX of France, my brother-in-law. I had expected this. But I had finally recognized my uncles' aim for what it was: an entirely selfish attempt to restore themselves to power through me. No doubt they would again try to persuade me to sign away Scotland to France! But I was no longer so naive or so easily manipulated, as they must have realized. Queen

Catherine rejected their proposal. For my part, I was nearly twenty and not interested in marrying someone eight years younger, no matter how high his rank.

Since I would not marry King Charles, my uncles again proposed Don Carlos, prince of Asturias and son of King Philip II of Spain. He had been recognized as heir to the Castilian throne and would soon be made heir to the crown of Aragon as well. My uncles ignored the unpleasant reports that Don Carlos was arrogant and spiteful, behaved strangely, and was furiously jealous that Élisabeth had married his father.

Queen Catherine opposed the match, and so did King Philip II, an ally of Queen Elizabeth. I suspected they believed it would give Scotland too much power. Then a dark secret was revealed: in the vague language favored by diplomats, the Spanish ambassador informed me that a recent fall down a stone staircase had damaged the prince's brain. He did not say precisely that Don Carlos had descended into madness, but I drew that conclusion myself and wrote to my uncles that they must put away any idea they entertained of such a match.

Then, to my utter astonishment, Queen Elizabeth decided that *she* would choose the appropriate husband for me! It fell to Elizabeth's ambassador to Scotland, Thomas Randolph, to inform me of her decision. "It is the belief of Her Majesty the queen that the interests of Her Majesty and Your Majesty"—here he made a graceful bow—"would best be served if you were to marry a man of her choosing, and an Englishman."

I liked Sir Thomas. He had accompanied my retinue on my progress to the Highlands, and though he was a man of nearly forty years, he had joined eagerly in the fighting against Lord Huntly's forces. I knew him well enough at this point, early in the new year of 1563, to judge that he was not happy that he had to deliver this message from his queen.

The ambassador explained that no Spaniard or Frenchman, or indeed any king or prince or earl or duke from the Continent whom I might consider marrying, would please her. I did not need to untangle his diplomatic sentences to understand that since my marriage to a foreign nobleman would strengthen my hand, Elizabeth would not allow it.

I offered a careful answer. "Most of the time I, like any other monarch, have not to follow my own will but must do the will of others. But my heart is my own, and cannot be controlled by another."

"Shall I carry this message to Her Majesty?" Randolph asked.

"I beg you, Sir Thomas, tell Her Majesty that Queen Mary of Scotland wishes for nothing more than her sister-queen's enduring affection and goodwill," I said, mustering a pleasant tone. I was frankly infuriated, but I was also curious to learn whom she wanted me to marry, limiting my authority while still dangling the promise of making me her heir. I could not resist asking, "Does Her Majesty the queen have a particular Englishman in mind?"

"She has not so informed me," said the ambassador.

"When she does, I pray that you will then so inform *me*."

Sometime later Randolph returned to Scotland and gathered the courage to deliver his queen's decision. Her candidate was Lord Robert Dudley, with whom Elizabeth had allegedly been carrying on an affair for several years. Queen Elizabeth of England wished me to marry her lover! Furthermore, she expected me and my new husband to live at her court. How cozy that would be! The suggestion was outrageous, scarcely deserving a reply.

"Does your queen truly wish me to marry Lord Dudley?" I asked, managing to keep my temper. It was not a private conversation. Many others were present, including the Four Maries and my brother James. They listened, open-mouthed.

"She does."

James broke in. "Why do you not persuade your own queen to marry and not try to marry off our queen? She has no more need to marry than she does to call for supper when she is hungry!"

I laughed, breaking the tension, Randolph turned quite red in the face, and I sent everyone except my Four Maries away. It was not a laughing matter, but we could not help ourselves.

My pleasure was often to spend an hour or two or three amusing myself at intimate meals in my pretty little supper room with my ladies. Now, with the English ambassador gone, I invited my friends to sup with me and turned my problem over to them.

"Ladies," I began, "we are all at an age when our thoughts turn naturally to the appealing subject of love, or to the more practical matter of marriage." With their full attention, I continued, "The time has come for me to think seriously of marrying again. It is your duty as my oldest and best friends to propose a candidate. Only the figures in the tapestries on these walls are to know of our discussion."

La Flamin was first to put forth a name. "I propose James Hepburn, earl of Bothwell," she said with a wicked smile. "I seem to remember that he turned your head once after he visited you, long before we even contemplated leaving France. Observing his behavior when he is in your presence, most recently at Crichton Castle for the marriage of his sister, I would say that he is strongly drawn to you."

I felt the blood rushing to my face. "Bothwell is a knave!" I said, laughing.

"A most attractive knave, I should say," put in Beaton, straight-faced.

"Then perhaps you should set your cap for him, Beaton!" I suggested, though I suspected her heart already belonged to none other than Thomas Randolph, the English ambassador.

"Did you not know," Beaton asked, "that my aunt was Bothwell's mistress for some years?"

I did *not* know, and neither did the other Maries. "Tell, tell!" cried Livingston, and we leaned closer to hear her story.

"James Hepburn was just twenty-four when they became lovers," Beaton explained, "and my father's sister, Janet, was nineteen years older. She had already married three times and borne seven children, but she was still quite beautiful. Men were always falling in love with her. Her affair with Lord Bothwell lasted for some time, and even after it ended they remained friends, and other men were already eager to succeed him."

"I have heard that she practiced witchcraft," Mary Fleming said. "To preserve her beauty and to attract men."

Beaton turned to La Flamin. "Much as your mother does," she said flippantly.

"My mother does not practice witchcraft!" La Flamin protested.

"I meant she does attract men with her charm and beauty—just as you do, Mary. Even men much older than yourself, I hear."

The gossip had spread through my court like wildfire that my secretary of state, William Maitland, had fallen madly in love with Mary Fleming. Maitland was about thirty-seven and a widower; La Flamin was just a year older than I, twenty-one, and as I now recalled quite vividly, had enjoyed a young lover in France, the faithless Jean-Luc. After little more than a year in Scotland, she was being assiduously courted by one of the most influential men in the kingdom.

La Flamin blushed furiously. "I have no idea what you heard, Beaton," she said. "But speaking of older men, I believe your friend the English ambassador is nearly forty, is he not?"

The conversation was not taking the direction I wanted.

I tapped on my wine goblet with a silver spoon. "Ladies!" I called out. "We are gathered here this evening to talk about a very particular kind of husband—mine! Be good enough to put aside your own private desires for the moment, interesting as they are, and give me your best advice. Your list must preclude our immensely appealing Lord Bothwell, who—as you are surely aware—seems to have a talent for finding trouble when it does not find *him*. He has been imprisoned in Edinburgh Castle, escaped from the dungeon there, made his way to England by chance or by design, and is now shut up in the Tower of London on the orders of my cousin Queen Elizabeth."

Livingston—Lusty—removed a pair of jeweled combs from her hair and laid them on the table. "I shall wager this set of combs and the diamonds on them that the knavish Bothwell will somehow get himself out of the Tower and set himself to wed the richest and most beautiful lady in all of Scotland."

"And who might that be?" Beaton asked, not innocently.

"But will she have him? That is the even greater question," La Flamin exclaimed.

"In answer to your first question, our lady mistress, Mary, queen of Scots." Livingston glanced at me. "In answer to the second, my reply is aye, many times over."

This was greeted with amusement by everyone but me. "I do not deign to reply to such a ridiculous assertion, Mistress Livingston. Let me guide you back to my original question. The aforementioned candidate being unavailable due to his present incarceration in our neighboring country, kindly nominate someone else."

I turned to Seton, who had sat quietly through all of this raillery. "Mistress Seton, have you something to contribute to the conversation?"

"I do," she said. "I hereby nominate Henry Stuart, master of Lennox."

"I remember him!" Livingston exclaimed. "He was just a young lad of thirteen when he came to France to the coronation, but he made a fine impression."

Seton continued in her usual thoughtful manner. "He is old enough—seventeen, I believe—he was well made and fine-looking when we last saw him, he is of good family and noble background, he is Catholic, and—of great importance, I think—he is *tall*. He was tall even at thirteen, and if he continued to grow may now be even taller than you, and that is a rare thing."

All of this was true. And that is how Henry Stuart came into my thoughts and consideration. As it turned out, Seton was not the only one with this notion. Henry's mother, Lady Lennox, had been promoting the idea since the earliest days of my widowhood. And she had not given up.

VI

I Could Not Afford a Foolish Mistake

HE WAS THE HANDSOMEST MAN I had ever met, an Englishman, though not the Englishman Queen Elizabeth would have had me marry. I defied her; I would marry whomever I chose. But I knew that I had to choose carefully; if my judgment was wrong, I likely would not recognize it until it was too late. Nevertheless, I missed the warning signs and confidently pressed ahead, not guessing that my decision would bring me misery and deliver me into the hands of my enemies.

CHAPTER 33

Henry Stuart

I UNDERSTOOD THAT Elizabeth's offer to find me a husband was a clever trap, but I pretended to consider it. She held the advantage. She would promise to name me her successor only if I married her favorite, Lord Robert Dudley, and was living in her court, but there was nothing to prevent her changing her mind once I had done so. Since Dudley did not hold a rank anywhere equal to mine, she raised him to earl of Leicester to make her offer less insulting to me. Dudley himself did not bother to pretend he was interested in marrying *me*.

I had never met Robert Dudley, but I knew that his reputation was tainted by scandal. A few years earlier his wife, Amy Robsart, had fallen down a flight of stairs and died of a broken neck. Some said it was not an accident, that it was murder, arranged with the queen's complicity so that Dudley would be free to marry her. Still she did not marry him—or anyone else—though nearly everyone believed she and

Dudley were lovers. I could only assume that their *very close* relationship would continue, even if I married him.

Queen Catherine, too, engaged in matchmaking for me in an attempt to cement relations with her neighbors. She proposed that Queen Elizabeth, who was thirty, should marry my former brother-in-law King Charles IX, age thirteen. I could well imagine Elizabeth's reaction to that! Then, said the queen mother, I had her permission to marry the duke of Anjou, Charles's younger brother.

The Four Maries scoffed at the notion. "You will soon be twenty-two! Anjou is twelve!" La Flamin said.

"You can do better," the others agreed. "Much better!"

"Henry Stuart," Seton reminded me quietly. "The master of Lennox."

In fact, all the while, without speaking of it, I had been thinking of that very tall, beautiful young man I had met twice before. There was much to recommend him besides his height; our blood ties would greatly strengthen my claim to the English throne. The Lennoxes were obviously pleased at the prospect, and they plied me with gifts, including the magnificent Lennox Jewel, which was not actually a single jewel but a locket set with rubies and emeralds and a huge sapphire. They lavished all sorts of pretty trifles on the Four Maries for good measure. Henry's father, the earl of Lennox, was my guest at Holyrood and made a favorable impression. But it was Henry I was most eager to see again.

In February of 1565 Henry Stuart left England to join his father in Scotland. He arrived in Edinburgh in midmonth and stayed with the English ambassador, Thomas Randolph. A Catholic, though not a devout one, he ingratiated himself with John Knox by attending Protestant services at St. Giles on his first Sunday in Edinburgh. A few days later, I formally received the master of Lennox—he was styled Lord Darnley in England, but the Scots did not recognize his English title. I was on a progress in Fife, on the northern coast of the Firth of Forth. Henry joined my retinue as we returned by ferry to Edinburgh. From then on he was constantly with my court.

From the very first Henry charmed me. He was surely the handsomest man I had ever met, with fair curly hair, finely chiseled features, a winning smile, and shapely long legs shown off by his black hose. But his best attribute was his height; for the first time in my life, my dancing partner was taller than I, and by at least a hand span. He was skillful and graceful, and I was quite aware of the elegant picture we made as we danced a galliard.

Mary Fleming did not hesitate to announce boldly what others apparently thought: "You make an outstandingly handsome couple, madam. This is the man you must marry!"

It was not just his dancing and his height. Henry Stuart was intelligent, witty, and a talented lute player with a sweet tenor voice. I was quite enchanted by him. But did I want to marry him? I did not know. It seemed the prize eluded me. As it stood, only if I married Dudley, now the earl of Leicester, would Elizabeth name me as her successor. But if I chose the master of Lennox instead, might she eventually change her mind? I needed some final word from her so that I could know how to proceed, and I asked her ambassador to bring me her reply with all possible haste.

The most severe winter in memory brought Scotland to a standstill. Icicles hung from the battlements in glittering curtains, and snow fell day after day. Travel through the Lowlands came to a halt. No messengers could get through from the south. On Shrove Tuesday we celebrated the marriage of Mary Livingston—our Lusty—to John Sempill in a ceremony performed by John Knox. I paid for the bride's wedding gown and gave her a handsome dowry, and when the ice and snow prevented the guests from going home, I ordered the festivities continued for several days afterward, with banquets and masques suitable to the Lenten season.

Lusty was the first of my Maries to marry, and that gave me a pang. Surely more would soon follow—La Flamin was still being courted by Thomas Maitland, though I thought the pair ill suited; Beaton was being avidly pursued by Randolph, Elizabeth's ambassador, though they tried to keep it secret. Only Seton remained unattached. How I wished myself a part of that happy band!

And there was still no word from England's queen.

In mid-March when the roads were again passable, Randolph reluctantly delivered Elizabeth's reply. Eagerly I broke the seal and read the spidery writing. *We cannot grant our cousin's wish to be named our heir until we ourselves choose to marry*

or, on the other hand, definitely decide NOT to marry. We cannot say when we shall make that decision.

I read the message twice more, each time hoping vainly to find some glimmer of hope, but there was none. I dismissed Sir Thomas before venting my rage and ripping the parchment to pieces. The queen would not deal with me fairly. Her behavior angered me, and the impossibility of the situation saddened me. I wept with disappointment and frustration.

I continued to see a great deal of the beautiful young Englishman. My emotions were in turmoil. My heart was my own, but I knew that I had to make the right decision for my subjects as well as myself. My mother had invested her whole life in preserving the kingdom of the Scots that I would one day rule as queen. I could not afford a foolish mistake.

Not everyone approved of Henry Stuart. They would not have approved of any foreigner. My brother James was cool to him and always referred to him as Lord Darnley to remind me that Henry was an Englishman and not a Scot.

But Henry had won the favor of David Rizzio, the Italian who had joined my court as a musician. Rizzio was an excellent singer and a fine lute player. I found nothing attractive about his physical person—he was short and swarthy and ill formed—but he was an educated and intelligent man, amusing and clever. As our friendship grew, I came to rely upon him for advice and assistance. When my private secretary was sent away for taking bribes, I asked Rizzio to replace him. Rizzio championed Henry, dismissing those few who disapproved of Henry and called him foppish and lacking in substance.

But not everyone approved of David Rizzio, either.

Admittedly, there were problems with him. He was not as skillful a secretary as he was a musician; he wrote French poorly; and I sometimes found his advice wanting. His presence soon caused jealousy in members of my inner circle—particularly my brother James, as well as William Maitland, my secretary of state. Both men distrusted David, but I had come to depend on him and his loyalty, and I accepted his favorable judgment of Henry.

The weather warmed, the snow melted, and in April my court moved to Stirling Castle, with its magnificent great hall and the elegant decorations of the palace rooms that showed my mother's influence. For the first day or two we spent most of our time playing billiards, but I could not bear to stay indoors. The gardens in April were still winter brown and far from their bloom, but I was eager to go hawking.

As my party rode out with our birds on our wrists, Henry was suddenly taken with a high fever. He left us and returned to his room in the castle. Concerned for his health, I soon followed. His catarrh quickly yielded to a heavy rash; the fever raged, and he suffered from pains in his stomach and head. Physicians were summoned, but I was not satisfied to leave Henry in their care. He was in such misery that I had him moved from his quarters to my own royal apartments and determined to nurse him myself.

I had a pallet made up beside his bed, and I rested there

when I was not placing wet cloths on his head or spooning broth into his mouth. When he was feeling up to it, we talked, covering a great many subjects. I told him about my life in France, and he described his youth in Yorkshire and his deep feelings for his parents. Sometimes I read to him or played my lute and sang to him in French. I hardly noticed as the days passed. Much of the time he slept, and I sat, a piece of needlework forgotten in my lap, gazing upon his sleeping face, his closed eyes, his perfect nose, his elegant brow, his golden curls damp with feverish sweat, his glowing skin, his well-formed lips.

He sighed in his sleep, murmuring, "Mary . . . Mary . . ." I laid aside my embroidery and leaned close to him to better hear what he was saying. Without thinking, I pressed my lips gently, very gently, upon his. His eyes fluttered open. He looked at me for a long moment, lifted his arms from the coverlet, and embraced me, pulling me close and returning my gentle kiss with passion.

I had only once experienced such a kiss, from Lord Bothwell. Never had I known such a depth of feeling that now welled up in my breast, a feeling of intense physical desire. My head told me that I must break away from him immediately, before a physician or a servant or anyone at all should enter the chamber and find us locked in an embrace. I had already created a scandal by staying the entire night in Henry's chamber with the intent of caring for his needs as tenderly as only I could. I had cared not at all what the dourly disapproving old men around me had to say, and I had ignored their raised eyebrows.

"Mary, dearest," Henry whispered, his finger lightly tracing the curve of my ear. "Let us marry, and soon!"

"My love," I murmured, "to marry you is my fondest wish and my deepest desire!"

Held so snug against his chest that I could feel each breath he took, I believed that I was in love—madly, deeply, passionately. My fate was sealed, my future inescapable. I was the prisoner of my own wildly beating heart.

CHAPTER 34

Royal Wedding

I WAS IN LOVE, and I wanted everyone to share my joy. Henry and I were constantly together. I could hardly bear to be separated from him. We exchanged tokens of our love: bracelets, rings, letters, and nosegays of flowers. Sometimes we disguised ourselves as ordinary townsfolk—a shopkeeper and a ladies' maid, for example—in order to stroll unrecognized through the streets of Edinburgh, holding hands, stopping on street corners to exchange a kiss or a caress.

"Everyone knows it is you," Beaton told me, laughing. "The two tallest, best-looking people in the city—perhaps in the whole country—can scarcely avoid being recognized." She added, more soberly, "My lord Thomas Randolph tells me that some say you must be bewitched, doting as much as you do on Master Henry."

"Bewitched? Indeed, Beaton, you may tell Sir Thomas

that I *am* bewitched. Bewitched by love! Surely he knows about love—as you do as well, do you not?"

Beaton colored deeply and lowered her eyes. "Aye, I do, though perhaps not so much as does he," she confessed.

My brother James refused to pledge his support. "Your decision comes with too much haste, dear sister," he said sternly. Thereafter Lord Moray joined with those opposed to my plans to marry Henry.

I was not just disappointed but angry, too. I thought I knew the reason for Moray's opposition: My brother wanted to set the crown on his own head. Now there was less of a chance of that happening.

Fortunately, not everyone opposed my choice. The Four Maries appeared to be deliriously happy for me, none more so than Mary Fleming, and through her, I discovered an unlikely ally: William Maitland. My grave, conservative secretary of state had ridden endless distances and passed numberless hours in the pursuit of a match for me that would satisfy Elizabeth. This one did not satisfy the queen, but La Flamin bade him to support me, and out of love for her, Maitland did as she asked.

I proposed to marry within three months. That would give ample time for Queen Elizabeth to come around and approve my decision, if she chose to, and for the pope to grant the dispensation for cousins to marry; Henry and I shared a grandmother in common, Margaret Tudor, sister of Henry VIII. In mid-May the nobles gathered and gave their approval. Lord Moray claimed to be too ill to attend, though everyone knew he was unyielding in his opposition.

Plans for the wedding moved along quickly. To ensure that Henry had the proper ranking as the bridegroom of a reigning queen, I raised him to knighthood, made him a baron, and then created him the earl of Ross—all on a single day.

"And I shall make you the duke of Albany in due time," I promised my beloved, thinking how much this would please him.

"Then why delay?" he asked irritably.

The sharpness in his tone surprised me, but I blamed the display of irritation on his illness, from which he was still feeling the effects. "The title belongs only to Scottish royalty," I explained. "For that we must wait a little longer, until I have Queen Elizabeth's approval for our marriage."

But Henry continued to insist. His temper became short, and it was rumored that he often vented his anger on any who came near him, threatening to knock heads and once even drawing his dagger on a gentleman who had crossed him. I had other, deeper concerns than Henry's occasional outbursts of rage, which were not directed at me. Queen Elizabeth had ordered Lord Darnley and his father, Lord Lennox, to return to England.

"What are we to do, my love?" I asked, on the edge of tears.

"Defy her," Henry said with a careless shrug. "My whole loyalty and allegiance is pledged to you, my queen," he said, smiling in the way that always set my heart racing.

"But that is treasonous," I reminded him. "You are her subject."

"Treason must surrender to love" was his reply. His insolence shocked me, but I also found it thrilling.

These were the moments I treasured, when I was assured
of Henry's love and devotion. But sometimes I did wonder
if he was truly being honest with me. There were times
when I felt that he did not love me so much as he loved the
idea of marrying a queen and being a king. He insisted that
he be given the Crown Matrimonial, which was not an actual crown but the legal right to reign equally with me. And
he wanted it immediately—not later, but *now*.

"You must wait until you are of age, my darling," I told
him. "And Parliament must approve it."

"Parliament be hanged!" he shouted. "I deserve it now,
and I shall have it now!"

I promised to do what I could to persuade Parliament,
but I was beginning to resent my soon-to-be husband's
constant demands. I did everything possible to please him,
but it was never enough. And he seemed less and less interested in pleasing me.

I was certain that once we were married, all that would
change. He was young, three years younger than I, and
could be tutored in ways to make him more amenable to
our subjects—more of a king and less of a boy inclined to
unwise speech and actions. I blamed his tempers on the
strain we were under as I devoted myself to preparing for
our wedding.

But as the days went on, it seemed I was losing support

for the marriage rather than gaining it. Many of the most powerful lords spoke out against the match. And to my great disappointment, so did the Four Maries. They had undergone a complete change of heart and had switched sides. For a time I refused to speak to any of them. Their desertion wounded me deeply. Only Livingston—outspoken Lusty—had the courage to tell me honestly what others were saying privately.

"Not everyone understands how you can love Master Henry as you do," she blurted out, "for he is arrogant and willful and is known all around for his drunkenness and his consorting with vile and unwholesome people. They say that he will bring you to disaster. Dear madam, I beg you—we all beg you, out of our great love for you—please reconsider!"

"And I beg you, though I know you speak out of friendship, to remember and to respect that I have the right, every right in the world, to choose my own husband, and I have chosen Henry Stuart."

I had spoken boldly, but in truth I was shaken. I did have the right to choose, but had I chosen wisely? In a way, I did not care. The wildness in me that had been safely restrained for so long seemed to have broken loose, and I allowed it to run free.

The day of my wedding drew closer. I received word from several reliable sources that my brother was plotting to kidnap me and Henry and the earl of Lennox as we traveled to a christening. One informant reported that Lord Moray intended to deliver us to Queen Elizabeth, but others had heard that he had more dire plans: he wanted to have us killed. The plot was foiled when we traveled under heavy guard and at a different hour than my brother's henchmen anticipated, and we escaped unscathed. Had my own brother really planned to do such an evil thing? How could I ever trust him again?

The one person—besides Henry's father, the earl of Lennox—who remained steadfastly in favor of my marriage was my private secretary, David Rizzio. Of all the men in Scotland, only homely, misshapen, loyal Davy said, "Aye, my queen, he is the best man for you!"

On Sunday, the twenty-second of July, 1565, the banns of matrimony were read out in the High Kirk of St. Giles as well as in the royal chapel at Holyrood, though I had not yet received the papal dispensation required. I assumed that it would arrive shortly, and I simply decided to take the risk rather than delay any longer. That afternoon I created Henry the duke of Albany, as he had insisted. Again I acted without waiting for the approval I needed, this time from the lords.

I also promised him, on the evening before the wedding, that as soon as we were wed, Henry would be proclaimed king of Scotland.

"Good," he said.

It was one more promise made without approval—that of Parliament.

The sun rose at five o'clock on the morning of the

twenty-ninth of July, but I was awake long before that. This was my wedding day, and as I prepared I could not help but remember another wedding day, seven years earlier. How different it all was! I was young then, not much more than a child, an innocent and a virgin, naive in the ways of the world and certainly in the ways of men! All my decisions had been made for me. Now I was a mature woman and responsible for making my own choices. And I had chosen to marry this man, Henry Stuart.

One thing had *not* changed: I was still a virgin. I knew that many people doubted that. There had even been a rumor racing through the court that Henry and I had been handfasted in early May, soon after I had definitely decided to marry him. Handfasting was a simple betrothal ceremony, and in fact Henry had pressed me to agree to it for one reason: the promise to wed allowed us to lie together.

"Come, my darling," he coaxed, "what can be the harm in it? Why waste a single day in which to express our love for each other while the rest of the world scrabbles about with agreements and debates and approvals and delays?"

I was as eager as Henry, for the flame of desire burned hotly whether he was present or absent. But I was also afraid. "Suppose I were to become with child as a result of our love?" I asked. "It is my greatest wish, but not until we are pronounced man and wife by a priest. I cannot risk the scandal of a pregnancy in advance of that."

Henry pouted and argued, in vain, to convince me to lie with him. The temptation was strong, and whenever we were alone he would try to undo my laces and touch the tender, secret places of my body. As much as I yearned for that touch, I did keep him from it.

Now, as the first rays of the sun reached the stone tower of Holyrood Palace, I knew that my day had come, and my night would soon follow. My Four Maries, whom I had now forgiven for their opposition to the match, finally gave their approval, out of their affection for me. After spending the night with me, they helped me put on a magnificent mourning gown of black. I was a widow, and this was the tradition. I chose not to break with it as I had when I had shocked everyone by wearing white at my wedding to François. Seton arranged my hair, as she had for my first wedding, and all four helped to arrange the *deuil blanc,* the white veil of widowhood that would soon be discarded.

Before six o'clock, I was ready. The Four Maries walked down the stair with me to the royal chapel. Henry's father, earl of Lennox, and a second high-ranking nobleman, the earl of Atholl, waited for me. A short time later they escorted in Henry, who was so magnificently attired and looked so handsome that tears sprang to my eyes. He glanced at me briefly as the ceremony began, a mysterious little smile playing on his sensuous lips. I was so transported that I was only dimly aware of the ladies and gentlemen who had crowded into the chapel. The words were spoken, the vows exchanged, and Henry placed three rings, including one with a magnificent diamond, on my finger.

Henry kissed me lightly then and left, as we had agreed, to wait for me in my chamber while I heard Mass. His reason was good enough: he did not want to give Knox and his

Protestant band any chance to say that Henry did not support their cause. After he had gone, all those remaining helped me to cast off my *deuil blanc,* each of them removing one pin, marking my passage from widow to wife.

The mood much brightened, my ladies led me off to change out of black and into an elegant gown of ivory satin encrusted with gems. Beaming, I greeted my husband, and as trumpets blew a fanfare, we led our guests into the great hall for the finest dinner my cooks could design: sixteen dishes, consisting of chicken, lamb, and various kinds of fish and fowl. Several times we stepped out into the forecourt of the palace to acknowledge the cheers of the crowds gathered there to wish us well and to toss them handfuls of gold and silver coins.

"Such a fine-looking pair!" we heard over and over when we returned to the great hall to lead the dancing. There were masques performed that had been written for the occasion by the court poet, George Buchanan; singing done by a chorus that included my secretary, David Rizzio; and still more dancing.

Late in the afternoon we all retired to our chambers to rest while the servants and cooks prepared a supper to be served later to a second group of guests. It was my expectation that Henry would join me in my chamber, perhaps just to lie by my side and sleep a little, though I was much too excited for sleep.

But Henry did not appear in my bedchamber. He had, it seemed, gone off to gamble with his friends, Rizzio among them. Not wishing the Four Maries to witness my disappointment, I stayed alone until it was time for my ladies to begin dressing me for the evening.

The supper was just as sumptuous as the dinner. The pastry cooks had outdone themselves. The masques were more elaborately staged, the music even livelier, and my husband accompanied himself on the lute when he sang a song he himself had composed for me. There were sour notes of a different sort: my brother Lord Moray had refused to attend my wedding. Another who refused the invitation was Thomas Randolph; as Elizabeth's ambassador, he could do nothing to show support for my marriage to Henry Stuart. The one who suffered most from Randolph's absence was Beaton, who would have been happy to have her admirer for a dancing partner.

When the revelry ended, long after midnight, my husband and I withdrew to my bedchamber. As we left the hall, the Four Maries and I exchanged our special signal—left hand to right eyebrow—and smiled. I was not nervous. I was no longer a naive girl of sixteen, and though I had not experienced the raptures of the marriage bed during my twenty months as the wife of François, my body had told me during Henry's passionate kisses and intimate caresses what I might expect. There would be no witnesses to the consummation, no requirements for proof of my virginity. And when Henry came to my bed that night and took me in his arms, I knew at last the transports of love.

CHAPTER 35

Discord

MY HUSBAND AND I retreated to Seton Palace, where
George Seton, brother of my devout Mary, kept a beautiful
suite in readiness for us. There we abandoned ourselves to
the delights of our new marriage. My passion for Henry,
imprisoned for so long by the demands of my great status as
queen, was suddenly released. I was like a starving man before a banqueting table, determined to have my fill; a woman
craving water whose thirst would now be slaked.

"You are like a wild thing!" Henry laughed, his long,
elegant limbs entangled with mine. "My wild queen." He
pinned my arms to my sides and kissed me. "And it is my
duty to tame you."

Far from being tamed, I was inflamed.

After only two days, we had to leave; we could indulge
ourselves no longer. Too many duties awaited me. Reluctantly, we returned to Holyrood.

In our absence John Knox had delivered another of his

hateful sermons, calling me "the harlot Jezebel" and denouncing the sumptuous style in which we had celebrated our wedding. "Three days of nothing but balls and banquets," he had railed, perhaps angry that he had not been among those invited.

We heard of Elizabeth's fury when she had learned that our marriage had actually taken place. She seized all the properties of the Lennox family and ordered Henry's mother to be held prisoner in the Tower of London and made as miserable as possible. When the angry queen dispatched a representative to chastise me, I sent him back with a sharp rejoinder:

"Stop meddling in affairs that do not concern you."

My biggest problem was not the preacher or the queen of England but my brother James, earl of Moray. While I had been young and unmarried and dependent on my brother's counsel, the jealous monster lying dormant in his heart had slumbered. Since the hour of my birth, my illegitimate half brother had known that I, and not he, would inherit the Scottish throne. But James wanted more than anything in the world to be king. Now my marriage to a man he did not like had awakened the beast. My growing confidence to make my own decisions merely fed his jealousy. He was preparing to lead a rebellion against me.

Informed that my brother was a traitor, I ordered Lord Moray—I would no longer call him familiarly James—to appear before me within six days and explain himself.

I feared for my safety and for Henry's if Lord Moray gathered enough support to conquer my army and seize us both. His rebellion had to be put down swiftly. I knew that I had the loyalty of the common people, and I was confident they would rally around me and would not aid the rebel lords. But I needed help.

First I wrote to James Hepburn, Lord Bothwell, who had been living in Paris since his escape from the Tower of London. (Livingston had won the first part of her wager, that he would somehow get himself out of the Tower, and had kept her diamond combs.) I forgave him whatever misdeeds he had committed that had landed him in prison and then in exile. I sent for him now.

At the same time I freed George Gordon the younger, son of the earl of Huntly whom I had defeated in battle two years earlier. I restored to Gordon his lands and his title as well as his freedom, and in gratitude he promised to aid my efforts to stop my brother and the rebels.

Six days had passed since my ultimatum to my brother, with no response. I summoned the messenger-at-arms and gave him the order: "Go now and put Lord Moray to the horn." The messenger obeyed, proceeding to the High Cross near the fountain on the High Street. After blowing the royal horn, he loudly declared, "Hear ye, hear ye! Know ye that James Stuart, earl of Moray, is hereby declared an outlaw by order of Her Majesty Mary, queen of Scots!" He repeated this horn blast and declaration three times.

A month after the magnificence of my wedding day and the splendid nights of indulging my passion for my husband, I assumed another role. Donning a metal helmet and placing a loaded pistol in my saddlebag, I mounted my strongest horse, and with Henry, king of Scots, beside me—how he loved that title!—I rode at the head of an army of eight thousand. I led my men out of Edinburgh and west, toward Glasgow, where I intended to confront my brother and his rebel troops. Heavy downpours sent every stream surging over its banks, hindering our advance but not stopping us.

Lord Moray and his rebel followers managed to elude my forces, riding east and slipping past me to Edinburgh, where they attempted to take the castle. My loyal troops drove them out. We had successfully held off the rebels, but I was nevertheless immensely relieved when Lord Bothwell reached Scotland.

"Thank God you are here!" I cried when my old friend was ushered into the outer chamber at Holyrood. "Are you all right, Lord Bothwell?" I asked anxiously, for he looked exhausted, his beard in need of trimming, his clothes of fine quality but ill-fitting.

"As well as can be expected, my lady queen," he replied with the crooked smile I found so charming. "Queen Elizabeth did her best to capture me when she learned that I was on my way here. Her warships were plying the North Sea in search of me, and she even sent a notorious pirate to seize me! But as the pirate and his minions boarded my ship, I let myself down the other side with several of my men, and we escaped undetected in rowboats. We came ashore south of here with a few pistols and little else. I set out immediately for Edinburgh, stopping for the night at Dunbar Castle with Lord Huntly, lately restored to your good graces. He made me a gift of clothing, but I regret, madam, that we are of a somewhat different size."

I applauded his outrageous tale of escape, ordered quarters readied for him, suits of clothes found, and a fine meal prepared. I reinstated Lord Bothwell to his position on my privy council and announced my intention to put him in command of my royal army. Then we set to work on our strategy to put my brother Lord Moray in his place.

When Henry found out, he was angry. "I mean my father to command," he said. "Revoke your order at once, Mary."

"It is my army and my choice, not yours, Henry. Lord Bothwell stays."

Henry erupted in a rage. "And I say that he goes! You will obey me, for I am your husband and your king!"

My anger rose up to match his. "You are the king because I made you the king," I snapped. "Before me, you were nothing. Nothing!"

That reminder was like a match to tinder. More harsh words were exchanged. I pounded the table. Henry hurled a candlestick across the room. Servants witnessed it all, pretending to avert their eyes.

The argument raged, died down, and flared again. In the end tempers cooled, and we reached a grudging compromise. Lord Lennox would lead the advance troops, and Lord Bothwell and Henry would ride together at the head of the main forces.

Early in October we were ready. Nearly twelve thousand men had answered my call! I gave the order, and the army marched southward, toward the border with England. I understood very well what Moray and the rebel lords intended: they wished to depose me and make Scotland a Protestant country. I could not allow that to happen. I wanted the rebels crushed and James Stuart, Lord Moray, taken alive.

My brother, counting on Queen Elizabeth's support, retreated across the border with the rebel lords, only to find that Elizabeth was unwilling to help him. I put out the order requiring him and his friends to appear in Parliament in March to learn of the forfeiture of all their property. I believed that the earl of Moray was unlikely to trouble me further. After a splendid banquet at Dumfries to celebrate our victory over my brother and the rebels, Henry and I made our way back to Holyrood, leaving Lord Bothwell with troops to guard the border.

I should have been happy, deliriously so. I was enormously popular with the common people of Scotland. I had shown Queen Elizabeth that she could not interfere in Scottish affairs. I had routed the rebel lords without a drop of blood being shed. I grew increasingly confident in my ability to rule. And best of all, I suspected that I was with child.

What made a mockery of my triumph was this: I had begun to recognize that my husband was not the man I had thought he was. We argued about nearly everything, and I often ended in tears. In the first flush of new love and passionate fulfillment, I was so eager to please him that I agreed to almost anything he wanted. Now I balked at some of his demands.

Henry insisted that on every document we signed together as king and queen, his name should be on the left, the position of honor. Mine, he said, should come second, on the right.

I resisted. "As queen, it is my privilege to place my name first, on the left."

"I am your lord and master!" he cried. "And I shall sign on the left!"

That was just one issue. We were headed for trouble, and I knew it.

CHAPTER 36

Unhappiness

I PRAYED TO HAVE A SON, and as the new life quickened inside me, I was convinced that it would be a boy. This was a great joy and consolation to me, for I understood more with every passing day that my husband would provide neither joy nor consolation. I had hoped that as Henry got older—he would turn twenty the day before I turned twenty-three—and with the guidance of some of my most able and trusted ministers, he would grow into his role as king of Scots. But what grew instead were his arrogance and insolence. There was no way to reason with him, to make him understand that I had been a queen practically from birth, the daughter and granddaughter of kings, and he was king only because I had made him one. I was willing to share power; I was not willing to surrender it. But Henry truly seemed to believe that I would hand over to him all my authority as sovereign simply because he was a male and my husband! It was disgraceful. For the first time I understood the reluctance of Queen Elizabeth of England to marry.

There was one important policy in which Henry stubbornly opposed me. In the face of the growing legions of Protestant followers of John Knox, I had always insisted that all men had the right to worship as they chose. While I demanded my right to hear Mass in my own chapel, I would not try to deprive the Protestants of their right to follow a different way—even those rebel lords who opposed me. Henry had grown up Catholic, as I had, but he had attended Knox's services and sat through the tirades against me and the Catholic Church. Now Henry decided that he would make his mark by forcing the Protestants into submission and returning Scotland to the one true church.

"It is my desire to be recognized as the greatest king in all of Europe!" he announced; I cringed and said nothing. Restoring the country to Catholicism was the means by which he intended to accomplish his goal.

By Christmas of 1565, barely five months after our spectacular wedding, it was clear to me and surely becoming evident to everyone else that whatever love Henry and I had borne each other—if indeed he had ever truly loved me, and if the desire I had felt for him had really been love—had vanished like the early-morning mists on the firth.

The ones who knew best were the Four Maries, often witnesses to what happened between us. I had decided to pardon a nobleman and his whole large family who had been enemies of Lord Lennox for a long time. When Henry heard of the pardon, he stormed into my outer chamber, where I sat with my ladies, stitching a little garment for the bairn. He did not bother to greet me or my ladies civilly but merely announced loudly, "You have pardoned people without asking my permission. I forbid any further pardons, madam!"

Startled, I looked up from my needlework. How dare he speak to me in such a manner! My ladies, who had been chatting amiably among themselves, fell silent and gaped at Henry.

"You forget yourself, my lord," I retorted. I was trembling, but I tried to keep my voice steady. "You have no authority to forbid me to do anything."

"I am your husband!" Henry shouted. "I am your superior!"

There was a gasp from my ladies as Henry and I glared at each other.

"You may believe yourself superior to the man who cleans your boots," I said coldly, "but you are certainly not superior to me."

Bellowing incoherently, my husband turned and stormed out even more angrily than he had entered.

There were a few moments of uncomfortable silence. "We have our differences," I said and picked up the tiny gown. But I was too upset to take another stitch and burst into tears.

The Maries rushed to comfort me. "How dare he speak to you in that manner!" they cried.

Most of them were not strangers to unhappy love affairs. Mary Fleming was still deeply involved with William Maitland, who had long enjoyed my confidence as my secretary of state. But I had come to rely more heavily on David Rizzio; Maitland resented Davy, and that had driven a painful wedge between La Flamin and me. Beaton had broken off her affair with Randolph, Elizabeth's ambassador to England and generally no friend to me, and was in love with a man named Alexander Ogilvie. But Ogilvie was possibly about to marry another woman, a situation that kept Beaton in a state of misery. Livingston, married for three years to John Sempill, did her share of complaining about men in general and her husband in particular. Only Seton, deeply pious and claiming to have no interest in marriage, had little to say on the subject but was always quietly sympathetic. None of them could bear Henry Stuart.

Henry received the symbols of kingship at a ceremony of investiture on the Feast of Candlemas, the second of February. I had informed him that he would be denied the right to use the royal arms of Scotland on his coat of arms. This infuriated him, as I had expected it would, but I was not done. He still signed his name *Henry R,* the *R* for *Rex,* or king, and he always succeeded in getting his signature on the document first, in the place of honor on the left, but I was determined he would not receive the Crown Matrimonial, which had to be approved by Parliament. Without that, he could never be crowned, would never rule as king, and had no right to succeed me if I should die before him. I would have him where I now wanted him: not in my bed, but under my control. Henry would have to wait until he was worthy of the responsibility and the honor.

So far he was not. I heard far too many tales of his drunken carousing and of his dalliances with low women and even, though I scarcely believed it, with men.

The investiture ceremony was followed by a banquet for the foreign ambassadors who had come from all over the Continent to attend. I took this occasion, with so many dignitaries present, to remind them that I, and none other, was the true queen of England as well as Scotland. Nothing more was said about it, but the look of shock on all those aristocratic faces was something to behold.

If I could not enjoy a happy marriage to a loving husband, then I was more determined than ever to have the English throne.

On the twenty-fourth of February in 1566, I attended the wedding of James Hepburn, earl of Bothwell, to Lady Jean Gordon, sister of the recently forgiven George Gordon, earl of Huntly. Lord Bothwell was a close friend of Lord Huntly, and I knew that he had demonstrated much interest in Lady Jean. But his suit had been rejected until a broken heart changed the picture dramatically.

Lady Jean was deeply in love with Alexander Ogilvie, but he had broken off with her and married Mary Beaton. This was the very same man Beaton had been weeping over just weeks earlier. Now it was Lady Jean who came to me weeping over the perfidy of her beloved Lord Ogilvie.

"Why has he done this to me?" she wailed, bursting into fresh tears.

"It is, I think, the way of men," I said, remembering that Madame de Poitiers, for all her charms, had not been able to keep King Henri from Lady Fleming's bed. "Now it must be your way to make the best of your life," I counseled. I comforted her and recommended Lord Bothwell to her.

Lady Jean seemed to take my advice to heart, and soon she came to tell me that plans were being made for the wedding, though she still wore black to show that she was like a widow in mourning for her lost love.

I sent immediately to my wardrobe mistress and ordered suitable lengths of cloth of silver and white taffeta, and then called upon my seamstresses to make Lady Jean a wedding gown. The banns were read out for their wedding; I was present at the signing of their marriage contract, and after the ceremony at St. Giles I entertained the bridal couple at a banquet at Holyrood. Bothwell seemed content—he had acquired a large dowry from his bride—but the new Lady Jean Hepburn looked glum.

After a few days with her husband at Seton Palace, the bride was wearing black again and had gone alone to Bothwell's Crichton Castle while Bothwell returned to Edinburgh on his own. In fact, he asked my permission to stay at Holyrood Palace. I granted it, promising that we would sup together soon.

I sighed and wondered aloud to Seton when he had gone, "Do you not think it possible for two people to be happy together?"

"Our sole happiness is in God," she assured me, and I wondered if she was right.

CHAPTER 37

Murder

FROM THE END of February and into early March, much was going on without my knowledge. William Maitland, La Flamin's lover, had dropped broad hints to Henry that I was having an affair with David Rizzio, my private secretary, whom Maitland despised. This was a complete fabrication and Sir William knew it, but he was not above making mischief. Henry, jealous of many people for many things, swallowed this lie. It had been easy to convince my dissolute husband that he had been betrayed by a man who had once been his close friend.

On a winter night in 1566, when I was six months' pregnant with child, I was witness to an unspeakable event. I was in the small tower room hung with crimson and green just off my bedchamber, enjoying a late meal with several friends. Among them was David Rizzio. Henry appeared unexpectedly. We seldom dined together, he having no interest in my supper parties and card games and much preferring to go drinking in the town with his disreputable friends.

While we spoke briefly, in a not unfriendly way, a half dozen of Henry's so-called gentlemen burst into the tower room from a secret circular stairway that connected my bedchamber to Henry's directly below. The men, all heavily armed, boldly ordered David Rizzio to accompany them to answer to some unspecified charge.

"What is this about, my lord?" I asked Henry sharply. "Why are these men here? Who let them in?"

"I know not, my lady," he said, laying his hand on my shoulder in a way meant to soothe me. I did not believe him. Henry surely knew what it was about and had a role in it.

When the intruders continued to insist, more rudely now, I rose, angrily demanding, "What is Signor Rizzio's offense?"

"A grievous one," growled one of the men.

I shook off Henry's hand and ordered the men to leave. "Under pain of death for treason!" I shouted.

But one of the men drew a dagger and lunged at David Rizzio. Davy tried to evade the knife, crying out to me to save him. My guests moved to defend him, and in the melee that followed, the table and stools were overturned. Silver plate, goblets, and platters of food crashed to the floor. Ewers of wine spilled everywhere. Candles were extinguished, save for one, by whose flickering light the horrific scene unfolded.

The main stairway to my outer chamber had been locked; I was certain of that, for I had locked it myself, but someone—possibly even Henry—had unlocked it. That door now burst open and a much larger crowd of men surged through the outer chamber and into my bed-chamber. They were armed with swords and daggers; one carried a pistol. My guests were quickly overpowered and watched helplessly as the assassins seized the terrified David Rizzio and dragged him into my bedchamber.

When I cried out and tried to protect my secretary with my own body—surely they would not kill their pregnant queen!—the one with the pistol held it to my belly and my unborn child. They stabbed Davy over and over until he stopped screaming. Finally, I did too.

Henry held a dagger but could not bring himself to use it. Someone snatched it away from him and thrust it into Davy's throat, the final savage blow, leaving the king's dagger in the victim's body like the signature on a royal decree: *Henry R.*

"It was your wish that he die," the murderer growled at Henry. "This proves that you were a part of it, and you cannot deny it and lay the fault on others."

"You?" I cried. "You ordered this?" I stared at my husband, unable to say anything more. As I grasped that this was all his doing, that he was behind the plot to assassinate my secretary and friend, I seethed with hatred.

The assassins left, and Henry opened his mouth and closed it again, shaking his head, as though he could not believe it himself. He was plainly not accustomed to such violence and bloodshed.

"Why have you done this, Henry?" I asked in a low voice,

stifling the revulsion I felt for him. "What has David Rizzio done to you to deserve this fate? What have I done, that you use me so ill?" When still he said nothing, I raised my voice. "Answer me!"

Henry was pale, trembling with a mixture of fear and rage. "I am your husband, and on the day of our marriage you promised to obey me. But you betrayed me with him," he said, his voice breaking. "Everyone takes me for a cuckold, and they laugh at me and hold me up to ridicule."

"I have not betrayed you, you fool!" I cried. But I realized that my life was still in danger. One shout from Henry, and the assassins would return for me. I must use some other approach with him, and I repeated my words in a placating tone. "Henry, I have never betrayed you. I am a loyal wife. What is it you want of me?"

"You pay me no attention," he complained, pouting like a petulant child. "You preferred to play cards and make music with that foreigner rather than come to my bed."

"It is not for me to come to your bed, my lord, but for you to come to mine," I reminded him, for that was the way of husband and wife, no matter what their ranks. "Now I beg you, leave me in peace."

I sat in my bedchamber, weak and speechless from shock. Blood was everywhere. In the outer chamber David Rizzio lay dead, his furred damask gown and blue satin doublet slashed to shreds. There were, I learned later, fifty-six stab wounds in his poor body. Shortly, several of the assassins returned. I nearly fainted, for I thought they had come for me. Instead, they dragged the body away and flung it down the staircase.

I did not yet realize that guards had been posted all around; I could not leave, nor could any of my friends come to help me or offer comfort. I was a prisoner.

No more tears now, I decided. *I must think upon revenge. But first—escape!*

The assassins allowed only Lady Huntly, George Gordon's elderly mother, into my apartment, along with two servants. I was surprised to see her there, for we had once been adversaries. Lady Huntly was the widow of old George Gordon, who had denied me entrance to Inverness Castle, and in the confrontation that followed I had ordered the execution of two of her sons. In an odd twist of fate, Lady Huntly and her son George had later become my supporters. But now, unnerved by what had just happened, I wondered if she might have changed her allegiance once again, and I was on guard.

When the servants cautiously entered the supper room to clean up the disarray caused when the table was overturned, Lady Huntly quietly delivered a message sent by her son and Lord Bothwell.

"Earlier this evening in another part of the palace, they heard the shouts and screams coming from the tower," she whispered. "They had no idea of what was happening, but they believed they too might be in danger and made their escape by a rope let down from a window. They are on their way to Dunbar Castle, but they asked me to assure you that they have vowed to rescue you. We must speak no more of this now." In a voice intended for the ears of any eavesdroppers, Lady Huntly announced, "Time for you to rest, madam, for the sake of the child as well as yourself!"

Sleep was surely out of the question. While Lady Huntly dozed, I passed the long night pacing through my chambers, sometimes weeping in sorrow, sometimes barely suppressing my fury.

In the small hours just before dawn, I heard a timid knock at the door to the secret stair. "Mary, unlock the door." It was Henry! *How dare he come here now!* "I have something to say regarding your safety—yours and mine," he said softly. "We must talk. Let me in."

I considered for a moment. I despised this man for his cowardice, his arrogance, his treachery. He had used me. Now, I thought, I had best use him. I needed to win him over, at least until he publicly recognized the child I carried to be his own. If he insisted it was David Rizzio's, and he was certainly cruel enough to do so, then my child would be born a bastard.

I swallowed my loathing, pushed aside the tapestry that concealed the door, and opened it for my husband.

I had never seen a man appear so frightened and so sorry for what he had done. I believed the fear—his eyes were filled with it. But I was less convinced that he was truly contrite, no matter how much regret he professed. I vented my anger at him without mincing words.

"Do you have any idea of the wrong you have done me?" I demanded. "Do you really think I can ever forgive you, let alone forget? I find it difficult to believe that you are sincere in your apologies or in the affection you claim to feel."

Henry whimpered and repeated again how much he repented of all the harm he had caused. "Perhaps if you were to pretend that you are in labor and about to give birth prematurely, they will take away the guards," he suggested. "They refuse to listen to me."

I was reluctant to trust him, but I did grant that since he claimed to recognize the evil he had done, it was up to him to find a way to get us both out of it.

I agreed that later I would cry out with pain and we would summon the physician and the midwife. I would send messages to my loyal friends to help me escape. After we settled on a plan, Henry left, and I was about to take some nourishment when my brother the traitorous earl of Moray shoved past the guards and into my outer chamber.

"Sister!" he exclaimed. "Has any harm come to you?"

I still harbored a great deal of anger toward him, and I had no reason to trust him any more than I did my husband, but my strength suddenly deserted me. I collapsed, sobbing, into his arms. "Oh, my brother, if only you had been here! I have never been so heartlessly treated!"

Taking my hand in both of his, Lord Moray knelt before me. "If I had only known, I would have come to you sooner," he said. "I would have done all in my power to prevent this horror."

I did wonder at this, for with so many people engaged in the conspiracy to murder my poor friend Davy, it seemed unlikely that my brother had known nothing about it, and it

seemed even more unlikely that he would have done anything to prevent it. Yet I badly needed his support, and it
seemed better to leave some things unsaid, at least for now.

꧁꧂

Later that day I put Henry's plan into action. I cried out
and called for a physician to attend me. After a cursory ex-
amination, the physician informed the lords that I would
surely miscarry if I did not leave Holyrood. The lords
promised to remove the guards if I agreed to sign papers
pardoning them. I knew that to reestablish my authority in
my kingdom, I would have to forgive many whom I would
have much preferred to punish—including those who had
plotted the murder of David Rizzio. But first I had to escape from Holyrood. Henry passed along the word that I
had signed the necessary papers—a lie; I had not—and the
lords, believing him, removed the guards and withdrew for
supper.

As soon as the guards were gone, I smuggled a message
through Huntly's mother to Bothwell and Huntly telling
them to wait for me at Seton Palace, ten miles east of
Edinburgh. Then I sent word to Arthur Erskine, my chief
equerry; Thomas Stewart, my captain of the guard; and a
page named Anthony—three men I trusted.

We will meet at midnight in the Canongate cemetery, the messages informed them, referring to the cemetery in the shadow
of the old abbey of Holyrood. *Have four strong horses saddled,
and be ready to ride.*

Chapter 38

Escape

Two days after the terrible murder of David Rizzio, I was ready to make my escape. I prayed that no guards still lurked; that somewhere the rebel lords slept soundly, assured that I had pardoned them; that Erskine and Stewart and my page were waiting with horses and had not been detected; that the messenger had gotten through to Lord Bothwell and Lord Huntly; that my husband would not suddenly turn on me treacherously, as he had in the past. I prayed that all would go well.

At times I had been betrayed by my own weakness, bursting into tears just at the moment I needed to show strength and resolve. But now I was calm and resolute, confident that I was doing this for my unborn child as well as for myself and for the loyal Scots who revered me as their queen. Still, as the midnight hour drew near, my nerves were taut, and I started when the tapestry concealing the door to the secret stair was pushed aside. Henry and the page Anthony entered my supper room, lately the scene of so much bloodshed.

They signaled that all was well and it was safe to follow. In silence we made our way first down the secret stair and then down a narrow stair used by servants to reach the palace wine cellar. Anthony lit a single candle to guide us through a musty underground passage. I brushed past spiderwebs, drew in my breath at the scurrying of mice, and emerged at length into the fresh, cold air of the church-yard. By the light of a mist-shrouded moon I made out a fresh grave.

"Who lies here?" I whispered to the page.

"Signor Rizzio, madam," he replied.

I halted. "I must stop here and offer a prayer for him."

"There is no time for that, Mary!" Henry snapped.

"Then I shall *make* time," I said, and dropped to my knees in the damp earth and prayed while Henry paced in a torment of fear.

The equerry and the captain of the guard were waiting just outside the cemetery with horses, and I was flooded with relief that this first critical piece of the plan had fallen into place. Scarcely speaking a word, we mounted—I rode pillion behind Erskine—and urged the horses into a trot, their hooves echoing much too loudly on the cobblestones of the sleeping city. But no one stirred.

Once outside the walls, the horses settled into an easy canter toward Seton Palace. Still, I was not truly at ease until we were met on the road by Bothwell and Huntly, accompanied by a number of loyal gentlemen called by

Bothwell. We all embraced, jubilant that the second piece of the plan had succeeded, changed to fresh horses, and pressed on to Dunbar. It was another three hours' ride, and we arrived just as dawn was breaking.

To say that I was exhausted when we reached the royal castle hardly begins to describe my condition. Exhausted, yes, but also exhilarated! In fact, once I had refreshed myself and changed my clothing, seeing that the kitchen staff was not yet on duty, I dispatched several of the noble gentlemen to the henhouse to gather eggs, which I then cooked for them. We sat down to breakfast and ate heartily, congratulating ourselves on our escape.

Everyone treated King Henry with respect that not a single one of us felt he deserved.

That night my loyal servant of many years Sir James Melville came to sup with me. In a fit of sadness and gloom, I complained of Henry's disloyalty and lack of gratitude for all I had done for him. Before I had finished my list of grievances, Melville responded, "It is because of his youth, madam. He is easily misled by those who wish to do evil." Then he added, "I beg you, Your Majesty, to remember that you yourself chose him, though many were against your choice."

It was the wrong thing to say to me. I angrily dismissed my old friend, knowing in my heart that he was right.

For several days I rested at Dunbar, a fortress looming high on a cliff above the North Sea. There I felt safe. My loyal supporters, noblemen and lairds alike, began to gather. I issued a proclamation calling for the lairds to muster their troops at Haddington, on the banks of the River Tyne. When I reached Haddington, which someone pointed out was the birthplace of my nemesis John Knox, nearly eight thousand men had assembled there, pledging their support.

The next day I rode out at the head of my troops. Henry rode beside me. Lord Bothwell, Lord Huntly, and several others accompanied us as we entered Edinburgh and were welcomed with cheers from the common people. No one challenged me. No lives had been lost. I had successfully demonstrated my authority.

But I could not bring myself to return to Holyrood Palace. The memories of what had happened there, the terror and the bloodshed in my own apartments, were too vivid in my mind. For several nights I stayed with friends inside the city walls until quarters could be prepared for me at Edinburgh Castle, with Turkish carpets on the floors, damask hangings on the walls, and elegant furnishings throughout the queen's apartments. It had been a long time since any Scottish sovereign had lived in this great fortress; most had chosen Holyrood Palace instead. Holyrood was indeed beautiful, surrounded by lush parks and gardens, but Edinburgh Castle on its high volcanic outcropping was impregnable. Once I was comfortably—and safely—settled there, I turned my attention to punishing those responsible for the murder of David Rizzio.

First, I had to decide how to deal with my brother Lord Moray. On the one hand I needed his wisdom and support, but on the other hand I did not trust him, and for good reason. He was as treacherous as Henry. Each man believed he, and he alone, should rule Scotland.

Then I had to deal with my husband. I learned that Henry had written a statement acknowledging his primary responsibility for the plot to murder Rizzio and promising to protect the others whom he had involved in the plot. There was his signature, *Henry R,* and the date, the seventh of March, two days before Davy had been set upon and stabbed to death. My husband was not innocent, despite his insistence that he was. He had not been led astray by evil men, as others had tried to persuade me. He was guilty, guilty, guilty! I would never trust him again, no matter what promises he made. I would not forget what he had done. And I would never forgive him.

Everyone knew that my marriage was a shambles, but I had to take care not to make matters worse. I would have been within my rights to have my husband condemned to death for treason, but had I taken that drastic step, Henry might have countered by charging me with adultery—there were still those ready to believe that Davy was the true father of my unborn infant. Until my child was born and Henry had publicly acknowledged it as his own, I could not risk having him declare, in a fit of temper or vengeance, that the child was not his.

As angry as I was at Henry, I did sometimes remember how I had adored this beautiful young man in the weeks before I had married him, how I had craved him, and—aye, the truth—lusted for him in a shameful way. So doting I was, so wildly in love! But the passion had melted away like a late-spring snowfall. Once, I could scarcely bear to be apart from him. Now, I could hardly bear to be in his presence.

But I could do nothing to get rid of him.

The one good thing to come of my passion was the infant growing inside me. No matter what was happening, I kept up the pretense that all was well as the time of my confinement drew near. In early June I made the ceremonial withdrawal from all public life, drew up my will should I die in childbirth, arranged for the presence of a midwife, had the infant's cradle prepared, and settled down to wait.

Late one night I knew the waiting had ended. My child was about to be born.

VII

All That Could Have Been and All That Was Lost

THE EVENTS I DESCRIBE HERE took place long ago. I have been judged guilty of a murder I did not commit, the evidence against me fabricated by those who had everything to gain by depriving me of my rightful place on the throne. Throughout my lonely months of imprisonment I have had ample time to contemplate the joy of motherhood, the wretchedness of an unhappy marriage, the exhilaration of victory, the despair of defeat. And though I confess that I am guilty of many sins, I will maintain until my death that I am innocent of any crime.

CHAPTER 39

Prince James

ON THE NINETEENTH OF JUNE, 1566, I bore a son and duly named him James. My ladies had faithfully attended me throughout my ordeal, my good midwife had assisted, and the infant was pronounced both healthy and handsome. The big guns of Edinburgh Castle were fired and hundreds of bonfires lit throughout the city and beyond the ancient walls to announce the birth. Everyone rejoiced—from the nobles, who quickly gathered in my state bedchamber, to the humblest peasants pausing in their labors. A prince had been born to Scotland!

Later that afternoon Henry came to visit me and to inspect his son. I desperately wanted to sleep, but I was most anxious that he acknowledge the boy as his own.

"My lord," I said, "God has given us a son."

Henry kissed the infant, and I felt immense relief. Perhaps now all would be well. But then, to my disappointment and disbelief, we began to argue about some trifling matter, an argument that quickly escalated. I reminded him that at the time of Rizzio's murder, one of Henry's accomplices had held a pistol to my belly. "If the gun had fired," I cried, "both your son and I would be long dead!"

It was a sour note on what should have been a happy day, and as soon as my husband left my chamber, I wept.

The next day the High Kirk of St. Giles was crowded with worshipers from every walk of life, come to give thanks to God for sending the kingdom an heir. Within an hour of the infant's birth, my friend Sir James Melville was on his way to England to deliver the news to Queen Elizabeth. I wondered how the queen would feel when she learned that I had done what she had not and perhaps never would.

Meanwhile, Henry continued to roister about the city, keeping company with lowlifes, drinking companions and women of ill repute, and then returning so late, drunken and loudly reveling, that guards had to unlock the castle gates for him, try to quiet him, and escort him to his quarters, which were at some distance from my own in the castle.

I was fearful. My relationship with my husband had broken down to such a point that I was afraid he might conceive a plot to seize Prince James, make off with him, and force the privy council to allow Henry to rule as regent. The very thought of this struck terror in my heart, and rather than establish a separate household for tiny Prince James, as was customary, I decided to keep the infant by my side. I ordered his cradle placed next to my bed, and his wet nurse and the women hired to rock him and change his napkins moved into my bedchamber.

I was still not fully recovered from my confinement, but I could not ignore the demands of governing. I called upon the two men I knew I could trust, Lord Huntly and Lord Bothwell. Bothwell was Huntly's brother-in-law, having married his sister, Lady Jean. There was no suggestion that this was a love match. When Lady Jean married Lord Bothwell and turned much of her fortune over to him, it had been no secret that she still loved Alexander Ogilvie.

Nor, apparently, did Lord Bothwell have much affection for Lady Jean. If he did, it was not enough to keep him from the pursuit of other women. The entire court was gossiping about Lady Jean's pretty, dark-eyed serving maid Bessie Crawford and Lord Bothwell's adulterous trysts with her in the tower at Haddington Abbey and in other unseemly places. Lady Jean dismissed her maid, and Lord Bothwell presented one of his castles to his unhappy wife as a peace offering.

The two gentlemen continued to be my stalwart friends and advisers. Though many did not trust Bothwell, and for good reason, I knew that he was completely loyal to me. I relied heavily on his advice and counsel at a time when my nobles were continually feuding among themselves. Many more were suspicious of my brother, believing he was complicit in Rizzio's murder. Guilty or not, Lord Moray always seemed to be stirring up trouble somewhere. At this critical time after the birth of my child, I needed to turn a blind eye and a deaf ear to the rumors and find a way to bring about some sort of reconciliation among the various parties. I hoped Lord Bothwell could help me.

⧫

The twenty-ninth of July was the first anniversary of my marriage to Henry. But Henry was not to be found, and I spent most of the day caring for my month-old son. Exactly a year earlier, I had been the blissful bride in a magnificent and joyful wedding, confident that great happiness lay ahead. And that night I had experienced the fulfillment of my passion for my beloved husband. Now I held the sleeping bairn and wondered sadly, *What happened to that joy, that passion?* I was left with only the dregs of disappointment and bitterness.

Believing that a change of air might improve my melancholy mood, I boarded a boat early one morning for a brief trip up the River Forth to the quiet village of Alloa. Lord Bothwell arranged for the boat but stayed in Edinburgh as the newly appointed captain of the prince's royal bodyguard. "Have no worries for the well-being of the bonnie wee prince," Lord Bothwell assured me.

"You have surely heard the rumors," I reminded him. "Beware of King Henry. He may be dreaming up a plan to kidnap his own son."

"He can dream all he wants, madam," Bothwell said with barely concealed scorn.

The time on the river refreshed me, and the welcome at Alloa Tower by my hosts, John Erskine, earl of Mar, and

Lady Mar, was a warm one. I was preparing to enjoy the entertainments they had arranged for me when without warning my husband appeared. The peace and contentment I had begun to feel were instantly dispelled.

"What are you doing here, Henry?" I asked wearily.

"You left without informing me," he complained. "When I learned where you had gone, I saddled my fastest horse and rode hard to join you here. You are my wife, Mary—you seem to have forgotten that. You refuse to allow me to visit your bed as is my right. Your behavior as a wife is shameful."

"You call *my* behavior shameful, sir?" I demanded, my temper rising. "I have not plotted the murder of a loyal servant nor subjected my unborn child to the threat of death! And you dare call my behavior shameful?"

Our argument went on, loudly, until I ended it with this: "Since we cannot agree even on a definition of what is shameful and what is not, then I bid you good day."

Henry stormed out of the chamber, and I put my head in my hands and shed more bitter tears. When I had finally somewhat restored my calm, I was relieved to learn that Henry had leaped on his horse and galloped away. No one knew where he had gone—or cared.

I paced the grounds of the palace, muttering. I had to find a way to end this mockery of a marriage. There were no acceptable paths open to me. An annulment was out of the question—only the pope could grant that, and I knew well that he would not. I could attempt some sort of reconciliation, but how could I reconcile with a man for whom I had not a shred of trust? Who treated me with such disdain? Who had behaved brutally when I was great with child? Whose one driving goal was to be king of Scotland?

These questions bubbled continually in my thoughts, and when I prepared to return to Edinburgh a few days later, I was no closer to a solution to the problem of my marriage than ever I had been. I was certain, though, that I had to do whatever was necessary to protect my son. Given his father's overweening ambition and untrustworthiness, I had come to believe Prince James might be safer with his own separate household and a governor responsible for his care.

At the end of August, Prince James was carried from Edinburgh Castle and taken in a grand procession with an escort of five hundred musketeers to Stirling, the castle where my mother had once kept me safe from the forces of Henry VIII. We were welcomed by Lord and Lady Erskine. A beautiful nursery awaited James, the same nursery that I occupied in my childhood with Lord Erskine's father as one of my governors. Henry rode with me in our son's procession, though we were not together in any sense other than that which public ceremony required. He was bad-tempered throughout my stay there.

I had one bit of diplomatic business to attend to while at Stirling. My former secretary of state Sir William Maitland wanted to be restored to my good graces, and I was moved to grant that, for many reasons. Though Maitland believed he had been pushed aside in favor of David Rizzio, he had worked tirelessly to help me persuade Queen Elizabeth to name me as her successor. Though our efforts had so far been unsuccessful, I needed him now to negotiate on behalf of little Prince James.

I invited Maitland to dine with me. "You are again officially a part of my court, Sir William," I told him.

This would not please Lord Bothwell, nor would it please my brother Lord Moray. What a nuisance, to have the three men I depended upon dislike one another so heartily! I persuaded all three to make a show of friendship, and they agreed, though I doubted they would succeed even in that.

When I left Stirling, Henry refused to accompany me. We were not speaking. If I had had my way, I would never have spoken to him again.

~~~

The Borderlands south of Edinburgh were often troubled with lawless bands of brigands and warring clans. In early October I arranged a progress through that region to attend to some important judicial matters. With my brother, a number of the most powerful lords, and a large entourage including several judges and lawyers, I rode south from Edinburgh and in half a day reached Borthwick Castle.

While I was there, I learned that Lord Bothwell had been involved in a violent attack and now lay gravely, perhaps fatally, wounded.

He was lodged at Hermitage Castle some thirty miles distant, and despite heavy rain, muddy roads, and warnings of hostile parties, I made the long, hard ride to visit him.

The journey took about five hours. I found Bothwell in great pain and weak from loss of blood, but he was able to talk. "I have every intention of surviving, madam," he said, gripping my hand.

Reassured, I set out again for Borthwick. On the way my horse lost its footing in a muddy bog and went down, throwing me into the mire. I was drenched and covered with mud, in such a sorry state that my companions insisted we stop at a farmhouse to have my clothing dried and mended. Later I discovered that I had lost my watch.

At the time I made light of the incident—I had spent much of my life on horseback, and it was certainly not my first tumble—but a few days after my return to Borthwick, I fell ill, desperately so, with a fever and pain and vomiting. In my delirium, I asked repeatedly if my watch had been found. My friends were alarmed, and when I did not improve but grew steadily worse, they feared I might die. Lord Bothwell, receiving news of my illness, had himself carried from Hermitage Castle on a horse litter. I was barely conscious when he was brought to my chamber and allowed to speak to me.

"Dear madam," he said, "is it because of your exertions in coming to my bedside that I must now come to yours?"

I was barely able to whisper. "No, my friend." I struggled to form the words. "It is some other cause, but I know not what."

"And your husband? Where is King Henry while you lie here suffering?"

"In Glasgow," my brother answered for me. Glasgow was

the Lennox family's traditional center of power. "He talks of going abroad. We do not know for what purpose."

Nothing good, I thought. Or perhaps that is what I heard Lord Bothwell say as I drifted off again.

Over the next few days I endured great pain; I was told later that I fell into such deep unconsciousness that I was taken for dead. My servants, to allow my soul to fly from my body, opened the windows. My grieving ladies sent for mourning garments. My privy councilors, including Lord Bothwell, began to arrange for my funeral.

And then, nothing short of a miracle! My French physician thought he saw me make some slight movement. Immediately he set to work, bandaging my limbs, massaging my body, pouring wine down my throat, and dosing me with clysters and herbs. To everyone's wonderment, I opened my eyes and spoke. Slowly I came back to life. There was a further sign of hope: my watch was found and returned to me, still in working order.

Early in November I was well enough to travel and was determined to finish my progress through the Borderlands. After stops at Kelso, Hume, Langton, and other towns to complete the judicial work that remained, I returned to Edinburgh to prepare for the christening of Prince James.

I could not yet bear the thought of staying in Holyrood Palace—not after the terrible night of murder and my fearful escape. Though the events had occurred six months earlier, the memories were still as fresh as yesterday. Craigmillar Castle, only a few miles south of Edinburgh, was an elegant place and large enough to accommodate everyone in my court. John Knox had denounced the owner, Sir Simon Preston, as "a wicked man of no religion," and that alone would have served as the highest recommendation. I accepted Sir Simon's invitation to lodge there.

I planned to stay for a fortnight. Craigmillar proved to be the most critical stop of all.

CHAPTER 40

Christening

THE CHRISTENING OF MY SON was not just a celebration of the birth of the prince but also a demonstration to the great powers of Europe—Spain, France, England, Austria—that Scotland was not the rough and backward nation many supposed but a grand and cultured kingdom. Therefore I gave it my full attention, drawing up guest lists and arranging the events. I invited Queen Elizabeth to be his godmother, thinking it would establish a bond between us, and King Charles IX of France to be his godfather.

A week after I arrived with my court at Craigmillar, Henry appeared, uninvited and unannounced. "I wish to speak with you, madam," he said, adding, "in private."

I was uneasy about being with my husband, whose behavior toward me had been so threatening. "Whatever you wish to say must be said in the presence of my ladies, my servants, and my guards," I told him.

Henry scowled and made as though to leave, but he

finally decided to speak his piece before a full audience. "As your lawful husband and the father of our child, I wish to resume conjugal relations."

"But *I* do not," I responded with scarcely a moment's hesitation. It had been some months since I had welcomed Henry to my bed, and I was not about to do so now. "I have been unwell," I explained, though this was not the real reason and he surely knew it. "My physicians have forbidden it," I added.

The real reason was that I loathed this arrogant, selfish, heartless man who now stood before me. *I would rather sleep with the devil,* I thought.

Henry and I stared at each other. I refused to give an inch. "Then I shall trouble you no more, madam. I shall go abroad, do my work there, and leave you to—" He stopped, and I caught my breath, wondering, *Go abroad? What work do you intend to do there?*

He did not finish the sentence. He bowed, turned on his heel, and marched out. As always, I was relieved to see the back of him.

Later, as I was walking alone with William Maitland, he confided to me that he wished to marry Mary Fleming. "Nothing will make me happier than to have her as my wife," he said. "I have been a bachelor all my life, and I did not think I would ever be swept away by the forces of love, but Mary Fleming captured my heart almost from the first day I met her, and she still holds it prisoner."

On and on went my secretary of state, a man of at least thirty-six years, and I listened patiently until I could bear it no longer. Then I did something I rarely permitted myself to do: I let down my guard. "I remember when I felt much the same as you, Sir William," I said, sinking into melancholy. "I wish you much happiness. Whatever once captured my heart has long since let it fly away, never to return." I turned to Maitland and caught at his sleeve. "Oh, sir, I am so utterly miserable! I am desperate to escape, to free myself from this intolerable marriage in which I have not one day, one hour of happiness! I allowed myself to be swayed from the exercise of good sense by a passion I had not known in my first marriage. The only good to have come of it—and I do not discount it—is my lovely son. The little prince is now the center of my life."

Maitland nodded sympathetically and patted my hand. Once I had begun to speak of my misery, I seemed unable to stop. "I was warned. There were many who knew I was on a disastrous path, but I would not listen. And now I can see no way out."

"Divorce, madam? Is that not the best way?"

I shook my head. "There is too much risk of having my son then declared illegitimate, as has happened to others. He would lose his right to the throne. And I cannot do that to my child." I sighed, filled with self-pity.

"And if we can find a way that would not work against the best interests of your son?"

"Then I would most willingly agree."

The cold November mist in which we had begun our walk through the orchards of Craigmillar had turned to a fine drizzle that seemed to be made of ice crystals. Wrapped in our thick woolen cloaks, we ignored the stinging cold and kept on, deep in our conversation.

"Suppose," Maitland went on, thoughtfully stroking his beard, "that King Henry were to be arrested and charged with treason. He is certainly guilty of that offense."

"I myself once considered it but abandoned the notion lest he then deny that Prince James is his son. Lately it has come to mind again, but as you know I am going to great trouble and expense for the christening of the prince in order to raise Scotland's reputation among the great nations of the world. Imagine the scandal if the king were accused of treason on the eve of his son's christening when all the world was watching!"

"That is a dilemma," Maitland agreed, "but let me think on it. There must be a way to release this beautiful bird from her iron cage without damaging a single feather of her good name or her honor."

<hr/>

For the first time since David Rizzio's murder, more than nine months earlier, I returned to Holyrood Palace. In my absence, everything had been made new—tapestries, carpets, bed hangings. I wanted nothing to remind me of the horrific events, though they still haunted my dreams.

On the eighth of December I observed my twenty-fourth birthday. Henry's twenty-first birthday had fallen the day before mine. In better times I would have arranged a great feast for a joint celebration, but I was in no mood for that. Henry was not even in Edinburgh, having left for Dunbar after another of our loud arguments. We had fought, as always, about two principal subjects: the Crown Matrimonial and conjugal relations, both of which I withheld.

"I have every right to the crown, and I demand it!" he fumed.

"You can demand all you want, Henry, but only Parliament can grant you the right to reign equally with me," I reminded him. I did not remind him that the lords were unlikely to do such a thing without my full approval.

"Parliament granted the Crown Matrimonial to François before he even became king of France!" Henry said, his voice rising. "You cannot deny me any longer!"

From there it was only a short leap to the second subject: my refusal to share his bed. He demanded, and I demurred. Had he not considered wooing me with acceptable behavior and kind words?

The conversation ended, as always, with his furious exit. The situation was going from bad to worse. I was thoroughly sick of this man, and I was also becoming more afraid of him, fearful of what harm he might do. There was no celebration of the king's birthday, and my own observance was muted: a procession through Edinburgh and gifts distributed to the poor in my name.

The next day I left for Stirling for the christening of Prince James.

I was surprised, and not at all pleased, to find that Henry had already arrived at Stirling. Soon the foreign ambassadors would begin to gather, and I wanted to keep Henry away from them, as I did not know what schemes he might be brewing. I was told that he was brooding in his apartments and still threatening to leave. I made no effort to see him, nor did he try to see me. I thought it best to leave things as they were.

Gifts poured in, including a solid gold baptismal font, enameled and bejeweled, sent by Queen Elizabeth. The queen wrote that she hoped to meet with me soon to confer about my claim to the succession. She had apparently reconsidered, and it seemed we were approaching some sort of agreement. I was overjoyed to receive this message. My world would have been nearly perfect were it not for my detestable husband, whose behavior threatened to spoil everything.

On December 17, 1566, the little prince was christened in the royal chapel at Stirling with all the pomp and ceremony and majesty that a prince deserved and the Catholic Church could offer. The countess of Argyll stood as Queen Elizabeth's proxy. My son was named Charles, in honor of the king of France, his godfather, and James, in honor of my father and grandfather.

I spared no expense for three days of celebration. My chief nobles wore splendid new suits of clothes that I paid for. There were banquets, dances, masques, and fireworks. Though it had required raising taxes and borrowing money to finance the festivities, everyone agreed it was worth it; Scotland had never seen the like.

But my husband, the father of the smiling and gurgling little prince, chose not to appear.

CHAPTER 41

Another Murder

CHRISTMAS EVE is a time for forgiveness and reconciliation. Believing this, I decided to pardon all those who had been involved in the plot to murder David Rizzio—even the assassin who had held a gun to my belly and threatened to shoot my unborn child. Henry now feared that his life was in danger, that the men I had pardoned would return from exile and seek their revenge for his refusal to take responsibility for his part in the murder. He went skulking off to Glasgow to his father, dropping hints that he would sail shortly for the Continent. I did not know if he was telling me the truth or plotting something else.

I put aside my worries and determined to enjoy one of the most rewarding hours of my life. The wedding of the chief of my Four Maries, Mary Fleming, to Sir William Maitland took place in the royal chapel of Stirling on Twelfth Night. The other Maries were present; Mary was radiant in a gown of my own that I had given her—there was no time to have a new one made—and all of us tearfully shared in their happiness. We recalled many previous Twelfth Night celebrations in which La Flamin had contrived to find the bean in her slice of cake, entitling her to rule the festivities as queen and to choose the king to rule with her. On this occasion she found the bean and pretended to debate her choice, at last throwing her arms around the neck of my blushing secretary of state.

Several days into the new year of 1567, I heard fresh rumors of Henry's plot to kidnap Prince James, make himself regent, and imprison me. I was deeply worried. I decided to return to Edinburgh and take little Prince James with me. Stirling Castle was too close to Glasgow for my peace of mind. I knew that Henry's spies watched me at all times and everywhere, but I had no spies to supply me with information about his whereabouts and doings. I felt that my son would be safer at Holyrood.

Then word reached me that on his way to Glasgow Henry had fallen dangerously ill. At first his illness was thought to be from poison. I sent my own physician to see to him, then prepared to journey to Glasgow myself to convince Henry to return with me to Edinburgh, where he would be better cared for.

Lord Bothwell and Lord Huntly tried to dissuade me. "What you have in mind is foolhardy and dangerous, madam," Bothwell argued.

"What can you gain by going to Glasgow and bringing King Henry to Edinburgh?" asked Huntly.

"To have him close at hand where I can keep him under

my watch and be prepared if he puts in motion a plot to overthrow me. And if he plans to sail off to the Continent and engage in who-knows-what mischief against me, then to thwart those plans as well."

I did not tell them that I also wanted to prevent him from causing any scandal that would interfere with my negotiations with Queen Elizabeth for my succession to the English throne.

"If you insist on doing this, we shall accompany you," said Bothwell.

"Along with a large party of musketeers on horseback," added Huntly.

I gratefully accepted their offer and we set out, but once in Glasgow, I felt myself in the midst of so much danger that even my musketeers were not enough protection. I took refuge at the nearby home of Lord Livingston, father of Mary, the same Lord Livingston who had made the journey with me to France almost twenty years earlier. He welcomed me like a daughter.

I sent word to Henry that I had come to visit him. Surrounded by my bodyguard, I arrived at the Lennox family castle. My physician, who had been attending Henry for the past weeks, came out to meet me.

"How does my lord the king?" I asked.

"Not well, madam." The physician grimaced. "He suffers from the pox."

"The pox!" I exclaimed, though I should not have been surprised. It was a terrible illness common among the low women with whom he consorted.

"His appearance is shocking. You must not touch him. It can be passed from person to person by way of the pustules that cover his body."

There is no danger of my getting close enough for that, I thought as I climbed the stair to his bedchamber.

A taffeta mask covered Henry's face. I greeted him and inquired about his sickness. It was not easy to keep a civil tongue when he replied, "It is you who are the cause of it."

I did not argue but used my most persuasive powers to convince him that I truly wished him well. At times he seemed genuinely sorry for his failings, though I did not believe his repentance would last. He finally agreed to travel back to Edinburgh to receive the treatments he hoped would cure him.

"You are too sick to ride a horse," I explained, "so we will provide you with a horse litter to ease your travel."

He first protested, and then yielded, insisting upon certain conditions. "You must promise me, Mary, that when I am cured, you and I will lie together again as husband and wife, and that you will not leave me."

I felt nothing but revulsion for him, but I promised that I would do as he asked. "First you must be purged and cleansed of your sickness so that you are not a danger to me."

Toward the end of January, when we were fairly certain the winter weather would not endanger him further, we began the slow journey to Edinburgh. Ominously, a raven accompanied us every mile of the way, circling overhead, stopping when we stopped, flying on as we moved forward.

I noticed it but chose not to comment, though others did, and I brooded upon its meaning. When we reached Holyrood, the raven was still hovering.

My original plan had been to lodge Henry at Craigmillar Castle, where the owner could be counted on to keep him under control. Certainly he could not stay at Holyrood, for I believed there was grave danger he might infect the infant prince. But at the last minute Henry refused apartments at Craigmillar, eventually agreeing to lodgings near an old church known as Kirk o'Field, a quiet, pleasant house surrounded by orchards and gardens just inside the city walls.

"It is a place of good air where King Henry can best recover his health," promised Lord Bothwell, who had procured the house. Henry's physician concurred. There Henry would receive the curative baths he hoped would erase the pockmarks from his face and body.

Everything possible was done to ensure his comfort. Furniture was hastily hauled the short distance from Holyrood, and within a day there were hangings on the walls, carpets on the floor, a velvet-draped bed that had once belonged to my mother, and other luxurious furnishings to satisfy a man who was never easily satisfied. On Saturday, the first of February, my husband took up his temporary residence in the dwelling known as the Old Provost's Lodge.

Relieved to have him settled, I returned to my apartments at Holyrood, though I promised Henry I would come often to visit and even to sleep there in a bedroom on the ground floor. He spoke of his love for me and assured everyone we were about to be reconciled, boasting that he would soon be enjoying the pleasures of the marriage bed.

That unnerved me, but I realized that perhaps the only solution to my disastrous marriage was no solution at all: If I had any hope of Elizabeth's naming me as her successor, I would simply have to endure it as best I could. Divorce or annulment would create a scandal and put an end to all my hopes; I would never rule England and, more important, neither would Prince James. Securing my son's future was worth everything I would have to bear.

The next few days passed quietly. A welcome calm settled over us. *Perhaps,* I thought, *Henry really is trying to be conciliatory. There may be no plot to overthrow me, imprison me, crown our son, and make himself the regent of Scotland until James is of age.*

Henry began planning his return to Holyrood. "I shall spend Sunday here, and on Monday I shall move to my apartments at the palace to be with you again, my Mary," he said fondly.

I forced a smile, for though the past days had been completely amicable, I dreaded having him again in the apartments connected to mine by the secret stair.

The ninth of February was the last Sunday before Ash Wednesday and the beginning of Lent. In the morning I attended the wedding of my valet Bastian to one of my gentlewomen, Christina, in the royal chapel at Holyrood. The bridal gown was my gift, a lovely creation of silver tissue and rich embroidery. I left in midafternoon after the wedding dinner, promising to return later for the masque and dancing. The celebration could be expected to go on past midnight.

I changed one gown for another to attend the formal dinner given by a bishop for a departing ambassador. Lord Huntly and Lord Bothwell accompanied me, but when I looked for my brother, he was not to be found.

"Where is Lord Moray?" I asked.

"At home in Fife. He went this morning to tend to his wife's illness," Bothwell said. "She has suffered a miscarriage."

I thought it odd that Lord Bothwell knew of the loss she had suffered but I did not.

And where were Sir William Maitland and his new wife, Mary Fleming? No one had seen them.

Once my official duties were done, I made another change of dress into carnival costume, and with the ladies and gentlemen of my court I rode to Henry's lodgings at Kirk o'Field to visit him on his last night there. He no longer wore a taffeta mask, and he looked completely recovered, his face smooth and unscarred. The gentlemen congratulated him on his return to health, and Henry himself had a compliment for our carnival dress, particularly Lord Bothwell's elegant black velvet and satin with trimmings of silver, even down to his hose.

The evening passed pleasantly enough until Henry, who had been drinking heavily, began to pet and fondle me and to make suggestive remarks that some thought amusing and others, including me, found embarrassing.

"Tomorrow I shall be mounting our stairs once more!"

he roared. "But we do not need to wait for tomorrow, do we, my Mary? You intend to stay here tonight, do you not, good wife? And I shall come down the stair to find you!" He clutched at my bodice, making as if to unlace it or rip it from me, but I contrived to slip away.

On and on he ranted and made boisterous jokes while I tried to think how I might quiet him and put him off for tonight and then deal with him tomorrow. Many eyes were upon us, Lord Bothwell's in particular; he was observing the scene with his usual keenness.

I pulled a ring from my finger and presented it to Henry. "A token!" I cried gaily. "Tomorrow, my lord! But now I must leave you, for I have given my word to my valet Bastian and my lady of the bedchamber Christina to attend their wedding masque. Bastian wrote it himself, and you know how clever he is."

"You promised to stay here tonight!" Henry whined, as he did when he did not get his way.

"That was before Lord Bothwell reminded me of my previous promise to Bastian!" I explained. Henry continued to pout. He slid my ring onto his little finger and lunged for me again.

Laughingly eluding him, I called for my furred cloak. "Good night, dear Henry!" I trilled, wrapping the cloak tightly around me. "Until tomorrow!"

I hated the position in which Henry had put me. I was not naturally flirtatious, nor had I ever needed to be, though I had seen plenty of such games played regularly at the French court. Diane de Poitiers had known every ploy to keep King Henri close to her, and now I needed a ploy of my own to keep my husband at bay.

Down the stair I ran and out into the black night. A sliver of new moon hung low in the sky, and a light sprinkling of fresh snow lay on the ground. My horse was waiting, nostrils steaming, and as my groom prepared to help me mount, I recognized my servant Paris standing off to the side. By the light of a torch I noticed that his face was very dirty.

"How begrimed you are, Paris!" I exclaimed.

He nodded and murmured a reply I could not make out. I rode away with my train of courtiers. The horses' hooves rang loudly on the cobblestones, and my thoughts were no longer on my servant's blackened face but on the festive event I was about to attend.

It was not yet midnight when I entered the great hall where Bastian's wedding masque waited for the queen's arrival in order to begin. I regretted having missed the dancing, but when the masque ended I joined the merry custom of escorting the couple to their marriage bed before retiring to my own apartments.

The day had been long and, on the whole, pleasant. In the morning I would have to deal with the return of my newly amorous husband, for whom I had neither passion nor even affection. I was certain I could find a way to live in some sort of accord with him. There was a chance that he could be taught the refinement he sadly lacked.

My maidservant blew out the candle, and I fell asleep at once.

A violent noise, an explosion as loud as twenty or thirty cannon being fired, startled me awake. I leaped up, calling "Guards! Guards!" and dispatched several into the streets to find out what had happened. Surrounded by my frightened maidservants, I waited impatiently for the guards to return. They rushed back, stunned nearly speechless by what they had to report. The Old Provost's Lodge at Kirk o'Field had been blown up.

"The entire dwelling, walls and all else, is destroyed, nothing remains, not a single s-stone," stammered their lieutenant. "Not one person was found alive."

Kirk o'Field! "No one?" I cried. "You say that all are dead?"

"Aye, my lady, all. Not a single soul lives to explain it."

So there it was: My husband was dead. And I knew without a doubt that whoever murdered King Henry had intended to murder me as well.

CHAPTER 42

Aftermath

FEELING FAINT, I lay down. The room whirled and would not stop. I could not think clearly. The same thoughts raced through my mind: *Henry is dead. My husband. Murdered. Who is the murderer? Am I next?*

The one thing of which I was certain was that Divine Providence had me change my mind about staying the night at Kirk o'Field. I was put off by Henry's behavior and used Bastian's wedding masque as an excuse to leave. Had I slept at Kirk o'Field, as I had planned and as Henry had tried to insist on, I would have been blown up as well. I had been delivered from certain death, an assassin's plot, by an act of God.

I fell on my knees and prayed, thanking God for His mercy, praying for the soul of my dead husband, and asking for guidance in the difficult days that lay ahead.

I would withdraw into mourning for forty days, as I had after the death of François. Certain things must be done. I called in my mistress of the wardrobe and ordered black mourning gowns, the *deuil blanc*—the white veil, worn for the death of a king—and several ells of black taffeta with which to drape a mourning chamber at Edinburgh Castle.

I felt safer at the castle than I did at Holyrood, but still I was terrified. I could only think of the plot that had been formulated against David Rizzio; I believed that the same devious planning had gone into a plot against Henry and me. The villains had succeeded in destroying my husband, and I felt sure they would not stop until they killed me.

Naturally, I called upon those I believed were closest to me for support at this time of crisis. Foremost among them was Lord Bothwell. He arrived, offering his most profound condolences, and told me something I did not know: "Your husband, the king, did not die in the explosion," he said. "King Henry's body and his valet's were found in the south garden, at some distance from the lodging."

"God save us!" I cried, shocked at this revelation. "How then did he die?"

"Suffocation, according to a physician who has seen the bodies. Henry must have become suspicious, some alarming noise perhaps, and lowered himself from the window before the explosion. He would have gotten away, but the murderous villains seized him and the valet and killed them in such a way as to leave no visible marks."

"Those responsible must be found and punished," I said, my voice unsteady. "There must be a thorough investigation into the murder."

"I will assist you in every way possible, my lady queen," Bothwell promised.

I thanked him. "And there must be a funeral too."

"The simpler the better, I believe," Lord Bothwell suggested. "A large state funeral may not be appropriate, under the circumstances."

"See to it," I said, trusting that he would.

I passed Monday as though I were in a dream. I retired that night but slept little, an hour here, a few minutes there, my rest troubled by frightening images. My thinking remained clouded. My head pounded, and my stomach gave me no peace.

Tuesday morning I sat in my bed trying to recall what it was I was supposed to do that day. Then I remembered: a wedding. I was expected at the wedding feast of Margaret Carwood, a favorite lady of the bedchamber. I had bought her dress and arranged for the banquet. Perhaps I should order it canceled? Put the court into mourning immediately? I tried to think. But the day was Shrove Tuesday, the last day before Lent began and the last day Lady Margaret could be married until after Easter. Seeing nothing to be gained by a delay, I would allow the wedding to go forward.

I called for maidservants to help me dress, but I could not decide what to wear. The maids fluttered about in confusion when I asked them to choose for me, but finally settled on a plain black gown. "Perhaps with only a few jewels, madam," they suggested, and I nodded and let them choose the jewels as well.

When they had dressed me, I descended to the royal chapel. Everyone stared at me when I entered, and then all of them dropped to their knees, as was customary. After that, no one knew what to do. The bride rushed up and, in tears, embraced me. I did not understand why she was weeping. She loathed King Henry. So did her intended husband, John, my distant cousin.

"We shall all weep later," I told the bridal couple, and I signaled that the ceremony should begin.

When it ended and the couple had been blessed, everyone was to join a happy procession to the great hall, but the mood felt anything but joyous. The musicians waited for a cue. Perhaps if I left, I thought, there would be some good cheer. I returned to my apartments and sat alone, staring at the wall. Later in the day I moved to a darkened chamber at Edinburgh Castle to begin the forty days of mourning. Outside the castle, the wind howled like a wounded animal.

⚬━⊱⊰━⚬

On the evening of Friday, the fourteenth of February, King Henry was laid to rest next to my father in the royal tomb at the old abbey. There was little ceremony. Only a few mourners gathered in the early darkness of a winter night—few, because most of the noblemen were Protestant, and this was a Catholic sacrament.

It had not yet occurred to me that I might be blamed for his death.

But soon I was dismayed to find that I had become a target of criticism. People began to suspect, and then to convince one another, that if I had not actually ordered the murder, I was at least complicit in it. Queen Catherine wrote to me that Henry's death was the subject of much discussion in France; many there felt my intentions were sinister. In fact, she sent me a strongly worded challenge: *Avenge the killing, or suffer dishonor and disgrace.*

My uncle Charles, the cardinal of Lorraine, sent me no message of sympathy or support. He pretended that I did not even exist. Instead, he chose this moment to write to my brother and tell him that they must cooperate in restoring order to Scotland! The pain of my uncle's action hurt me almost beyond words.

Worst of all was the letter from Elizabeth. I received the diplomat who delivered it in the mourning chamber at Edinburgh Castle and strained to read it by the light of the single wavering candle. It was written in her own hand. *Many people here are saying that you will look through your fingers at this deed instead of avenging it, and that you will take no action against those who have done this in your name or at your order.* I forced myself to continue reading. *I exhort you and beg you to take this to heart and will not fear to touch even him you have nearest to you if he was involved.*

Even him you have nearest to you. Whom did she mean? She went on to spell it out exactly: *Bothwell, if the father of King Henry accuses him.*

Why Bothwell? What rumors had reached her? Did she despise him because he had managed to escape from the Tower of London? Why would she choose to believe the accusations of the old earl of Lennox, who had long ago fallen into her disfavor and whose wife Elizabeth still held prisoner? There were several men close to me—Lord Bothwell, certainly; Lord Huntly was another; my brother Lord Moray; Sir William Maitland; others. Elizabeth must have had her own personal reasons for pointing a finger at Bothwell.

The queen ended her letter by stating that there was no longer any question of naming me her successor, and I must agree to sign the Treaty of Edinburgh as it had originally been drawn up. Everything I had dreamed of, longed for, worked for, artfully argued for was gone now, erased in one brief sentence. The murder of the king of Scotland was too shocking, too scandalous, to allow the agreement to go forward.

The diplomat expressed the hope that he would have a reply to carry back to his queen within the week. I made some little movement of my head, neither aye nor nay. The gentleman withdrew, and I gave myself over to sobs that went on for a very long time.

Sitting alone in my darkened chamber day after day, I tried to think through what was likely to happen now, not only to me but to little Prince James. Whatever befell me, I was determined to preserve my son's present safety and future reign. But I had no idea what to do or where to turn. My suspicions fell on first one nobleman and then another. I had begun to believe that my brother had organized the plot. I had never been certain of Lord Moray's loyalty, and now I felt more strongly than ever that though I had often turned to him for advice and wise counsel, he was mostly interested in securing the crown of Scotland for himself. That conviction grew when he went into exile in France, sending me only the briefest message of his departure.

I, who had always felt secure in my role as queen, now felt defenseless; it seemed my power had been swept away by rebellious lords who wanted the authority for themselves. My thoughts turned to my former mother-in-law the queen mother of France. Catherine had no trouble exerting her power. I might learn a valuable lesson from her: *Avenge the killing, or suffer dishonor and disgrace.*

I had to find someone whom I could trust completely. The only person left in whom I had total confidence was James Hepburn, earl of Bothwell. He had been unwavering in his loyalty. He had shown himself to be intelligent and courageous. If in the past he had sometimes come down on the wrong side of the law, he now represented it as high sheriff of Edinburgh with a number of armed men under his command.

There were other qualities I admired in the earl. My husband was just twenty-one at his death and in most ways still a boy, an unformed youth. Lord Bothwell was thirty-two, eight years older than I, mature in judgment and seasoned in experience. I knew that he was disliked by many

people, but I took that as a sign of jealousy of the high regard in which I held him. Had it not been for him, I would
have been completely alone, totally isolated.

I called for him, and he appeared immediately, as though
he had been expecting my summons. "My lord Bothwell,
you have long been a friend to me, as you were to my dear
mother. I am asking you now to pledge me your help in all
things, to place your loyalty to me above all others."

Lord Bothwell dropped to one knee and placed his hand
on his heart. "My lady queen, you need not ask it, for you
already have it," he said. "I am your faithful servant in all
things, as I have been in the past, am now, and shall be
evermore."

I was so moved that to demonstrate my complete faith
in him, I promised him some fine gifts—Henry's splendid
stable of horses as well as his most luxurious suits of clothes.
Lord Bothwell raised my hand to his lips and kissed it tenderly. He left my presence chamber, both of us feeling
pleased by our conversation.

Watching his confident swagger as he departed, I had a
moment of self-doubt. *Have I made a mistake in giving him those
things?*

But I brushed away the thought and prepared to meet
with my secretary.

CHAPTER 43

Abduction

ON THE SUNDAY before Easter I ended the forty days of mourning by ordering a solemn requiem Mass for the soul of King Henry. As the choir chanted a mournful dirge, I was overcome by emotion and collapsed. For three days I lay in bed, my mind in a turmoil. Then I collected myself with difficulty and moved from Edinburgh Castle back to Holyrood to observe the great feast of Easter.

Lent was over, the official mourning period for King Henry had ended, and by custom it was time again for feasting and music and dancing. Slowly my deep melancholy faded. Gradually I began to feel brighter about my future. I sent nine-month-old Prince James off to Stirling, where I believed he would be safe, under the governorship of Lord and Lady Erskine. But I was stunned when I realized I could no longer count on the love of the common people of Scotland. Placards accusing Lord Bothwell of plotting the assassination of the king began to appear around Edinburgh. Women in the streets jeered at me as I passed by. The first time it happened I was so shocked by their rude shouts that I swooned. I would have to work hard, do everything correctly, to win back their trust and their support, but I felt sure I could accomplish that in time.

Henry's father, the earl of Lennox, was relentless in his determination to name those responsible for Henry's death and to see them punished. On the day after my mourning period ended, Lord Lennox demanded the right to accuse Lord Bothwell in front of Parliament of the murder of King Henry—just as Elizabeth had warned. I had no choice but to allow it.

Lord Bothwell himself seemed little disturbed by this accusation. "Have no worry over this matter, my queen," he assured me. "I can easily put the matter to rest."

The trial would take place in a fortnight. Lord Bothwell continued to be unperturbed—Lord Huntly was in charge of the court proceedings—and I marveled at his self-assurance. I was convinced of his innocence, but I was not as certain as he was of his acquittal. That the man in whom I had put my complete trust now had to face such a trial strained my nerves. I fell again into a state of despondency and was given to fainting fits.

If Lord Bothwell had enemies, he also had many supporters, and they began to arrive in Edinburgh by the hundreds until they numbered nearly four thousand. I watched from my window at Holyrood as he rode off to his trial. Mary Fleming stood beside me. "Never have I seen a man so confident of the outcome of his own murder trial!" she remarked.

"Of course he is confident," I said. "He is innocent."

"He rides the favorite horse of the man he is accused of killing. And is that not one of the king's suits, adjusted to Lord Bothwell's size?"

I did not reply, but I realized that even my closest friend was showing some misgivings. I glanced at her. Was it not possible that her husband, William Maitland, had been in some way involved with the murder?

James Hepburn, earl of Bothwell, was formally charged with regicide, the murder of a king. His accuser, the dead man's father, did not appear after he was informed by Lord Huntly that he could bring only a half dozen of his three thousand men with him into the city. No doubt Lennox feared reprisals at the hands of Bothwell's men.

Hours later, the jury acquitted the accused of the charges.

Bothwell was jubilant. I felt great relief, though the jury's verdict did not answer the question of who actually was the guilty party. When he swept into the courtyard of Holyrood, I went out to greet him. He leaped off his horse, and as he approached I held out my hand for him to kiss, which he did. Moments later he was gone. "Off to celebrate!" he shouted.

The change in Lord Bothwell's attitude was immediate and abrupt. He had always had a certain swagger; it suited his personality. He had also always been self-assured and something of a braggart; now that assurance took on a noticeable arrogance. He was notorious for his displays of temper, though I myself had never witnessed one. After the trial, that changed; he no longer tried to mask his true nature. He barked at servants in my presence and treated beggars and supplicants harshly.

He had begun to act as though he were in charge.

I saw it happen, and I was helpless to prevent it, but I also saw Lord Bothwell as my one reliable champion. He might turn on others, but I had persuaded myself he would not betray *me*.

The memory of King Henry took on an almost holy aura among the Scots. He was becoming beloved in death as he had never been in life; he was now remembered—falsely— as a charming and beautiful boy whose days had been cut short by his terrible end. Most troubling, an ever-growing number of ordinary people believed that I was the one ultimately responsible for the king's murder. More scurrilous placards began to appear, these portraying me as a half-naked mermaid, the symbol of a prostitute. I, who until then had enjoyed the people's love and respect, had become an object of derision.

The stresses of the past weeks were taking their toll on me. I could not organize my thoughts. My eyes were red and swollen from the fits of weeping that occasionally swept over me, leaving me exhausted but unable to rest. I felt ill. I decided that a few days at Seton Palace, where Henry and I had spent our wedding night, would give me a healthful change of air. On Saturday, the nineteenth of April, as Parliament ended its session, I left for Seton, little more than an hour's ride from Holyrood. From there I intended to proceed secretly to Stirling to visit my darling son.

The next day I was walking about in the fresh spring air at Seton with several of my ladies after hearing Mass when horses clattered into the courtyard. Lord Bothwell, Maitland, and their accompanying gentlemen greeted us genially, waving their caps.

"Great news, my lady queen!" Bothwell called out.

"Then tell it, good sir," I called back. "We are always eager for great news!"

"In good time, madam, in good time! My friends and I are famished and parched, and it would be better if we were first refreshed."

It was certainly not in order for a visitor, even an earl, to demand that the queen provide him food and drink. Nevertheless, I called for refreshments, and we retired together into the hall.

When the men had eaten and drunk their fill, Lord Bothwell asked that all others be excused from the hall, a request I granted, though I felt this, too, was out of place. Bothwell and I sat alone at the long table.

"You have all you have asked for," I said, growing impatient as he continued to work his way through a large roast fowl. "If you please, what is this great news you bring me?"

Lord Bothwell pushed aside the remains of the fowl.

The previous day, he told me, he had invited the lords of Parliament to a banquet at Ainslee Tavern. "A favorite dining establishment of all those gentlemen," he needlessly reminded me. They had enjoyed a fine meal, he said, "and nearly drained the wine cellar with all the good cheer that was in abundance." Reaching for his tankard of ale now, he continued, "There followed a long and interesting discussion on the well-being of our sovereign lady—you, my queen."

I frowned, waiting for him to go on.

"It was noted that our queen is now without a husband, a solitary state in which it is not wise for her to remain if she is to control the rebel lords, and it was proposed that she should take a new husband without undue delay." My mouth dropped open at this, and I would have spoken, but Bothwell hurried on, not permitting me to say a word. "I offered my hearty and affectionate service and said it might be very likely that our queen, dear madam, might see fit to choose me, a native Scot, to be her lawful husband." He sat back, watching me as a hawk watches a mouse.

I was stunned. I took a moment to recover my wits. "Do I understand you correctly, sir? You and the lords of Parliament have decided that I should marry *you?*"

"Aye, in sum, that is what was decided. And as I had already drawn up a bond to that effect, twenty-eight of your loyal subjects, nearly all of those present, signed it then and there."

Lord Bothwell drew out a document—a bond, he had called it—and laid it in front of me. I read through it quickly. It set forth exactly what he had just described, and there were all the signatures. I pushed the bond away, too shocked to speak.

"My lady queen," he said, leaving the document where it lay. "Marry me. It is the right thing for you to do. The *only* thing for you to do. You know that I am the one man in this kingdom who can control these fractious lords. Without me, they will trample you into the dust."

"My lord Bothwell," I replied as firmly as I could, though I trembled with indignation, "my answer is unequivocally no. My husband was murdered less than two months ago. I have not yet found those responsible, and frankly I do not think I ever will. You have been acquitted, for which I am heartily glad, but too much scandal is still attached to his death. And may I remind you of one thing more? You are a married man!"

"Lady Jean has agreed to a divorce," he told me hastily. "On grounds of adultery with Bessie Crawford."

How dare he! What effrontery! I closed my eyes for a moment and took a deep breath. "The answer is still no. You are dismissed, Lord Bothwell."

"As you wish, madam. Perhaps you will reconsider." He rolled up the parchment and brandished it. "When you realize how much you cannot do without me."

The earl of Bothwell bowed and strode out, his swagger not in the least diminished.

Before dawn on Monday I left for my secret visit to Stirling Castle with only Lord Huntly and Maitland and some thirty horsemen to accompany me. In the best of times I could have made the journey easily in one day. But I had slept little the night before, and I therefore was weary when we left Seton and exhausted when my party reached Stirling late that evening. Lord Bothwell's marriage scheme whirled in my head and left me no peace. "What am I to do?" I muttered, over and over. "What am I to do?" Surely he could not be serious! Yet I knew he was, and I feared he would mount a campaign to wear me down.

My wee bairn was asleep when I arrived, but I stole into the royal nursery to look at him. He slept sweetly, tiny fists waving in a little dream. *What a beautiful lad he is, and what a handsome man he will be someday!* I thought, gazing down at him in his cradle. He was growing to resemble his father— already he had a full head of golden curls—and that was a knife twisting in my heart. That our marriage, begun in such ripeness of passion, had ended in such violence saddened me deeply, for all that could have been and all that was lost. My tears dropped on the babe's coverlet until I turned away.

The next morning I rose early, not wishing to miss an hour of my precious time with Prince James. I watched the changing of his napkins, his bathing and dressing, his suckling at the breast of his wet nurse. I rocked him and sang to him and played with him, little games I made up as I went along, just to see him smile. It was a perfect day. That night my sleep was disturbed by uneasy dreams of France and poor François—it was the ninth anniversary of our marriage—and on Wednesday morning I kissed my babe before he was yet fully awake and rode off toward Edinburgh.

We stayed the night at Linlithgow, continued on the next day, and were within a few miles of Edinburgh and about to cross the River Almond when a large contingent of horsemen appeared suddenly out of the surrounding forest. There were hundreds of men, all with their swords drawn. My small escort of thirty was surely no match for them.

The earl of Bothwell stepped boldly forward and laid his hand on the bridle of my horse. *What does he think he is doing?* I wondered, horrified by this unseemly behavior.

"What do you mean by this, sir?" I demanded. "Do you intend to take me prisoner? What you are attempting is treason!"

"I mean only to protect the life of my queen," Lord Bothwell replied easily, as though he were joking. Then he continued seriously. "Madam, you are in danger of an armed insurrection in the capital. As the high sheriff of Edinburgh, I have a duty to remove you to a place of safety."

Was it true, that an armed insurrection was brewing in Edinburgh? "And where do you believe I will be safe?"

"Dunbar Castle. We shall go there directly."

"Dunbar! A long day's ride, Lord Bothwell."

"But necessary, madam." He made to lead my horse away.

My mind was racing. Bothwell had once helped me to

escape from David Rizzio's murderers. But I did not now feel that the high sheriff was my savior—quite the contrary. I stalled, wondering if I could bargain my way out of this situation. "Do allow me a word with my men, and I will come willingly."

Bowing slightly, Lord Bothwell let go of the bridle, and I rode back to where my escort waited uneasily, aghast at what was happening. "This is nothing short of abduction, my lady! We are ready to defend you to the death," declared the captain, plainly frightened at the prospect of his thirty men against Bothwell's hundreds. Huntly and Maitland were ashen-faced, their expressions unreadable. *Are their signatures on the bond?* I wondered. *Are they complicit in this abduction?*

"There is no need for bloodshed," I told them. "I will go with Lord Bothwell as he wishes. I do not know his intentions, but one of you must ride hard to Edinburgh and tell the citizens what has happened to their queen."

I turned and rejoined Bothwell and rode off with him, having no notion of what lay in store.

CHAPTER 44

Possession

HAD LORD BOTHWELL used the black arts to bend me so easily to his will?

I pondered this as we moved swiftly from the bridge at the River Almond and then skirted Edinburgh to the south. The guns from the castle boomed out—the message of my abduction had reached the commander—but the cannonballs fell far short of Lord Bothwell's men and did not deter them.

"Did you order that, Mary?" Lord Bothwell asked rudely. I was startled to hear him call me by my Christian name, and not at all pleased. Only my Four Maries and my two husbands had shared that degree of intimacy, and then only by my invitation. He shook his finger at me as though I were a naughty child. "And I suppose you asked the men of the city to take up arms to rescue their queen? Did you? But we are on horseback, and they are not. Small chance of their catching up with us, I will wager!"

I shook my head, too frightened and distraught to say a word. Of course he was right. I would not be rescued. I would have to try to understand my situation and use my wits to survive it as well as I could. On we rode, mile after mile. It was an unusually clear night, and we made our way by moonlight. I was so wearied that I could scarcely keep my seat.

We arrived at Dunbar Castle after midnight. The great iron gates clanged shut behind us and the bolts were thrown, loud as gunshots. Servants of the castle were ordered to escort me to my bedchamber in the royal apartments, and I understood that Lord Bothwell's own chamber was close by. My maidservants, who had been forced to accompany us, were brought to me, carrying my belongings. They were as exhausted and terrified as I was. I threw myself on my bed, too weary even to allow my maids to undress me.

There was a knock on the door, which swung open before I could say aye or nay. Lord Bothwell strode in, smiling broadly. "Will you be comfortable here, madam?" he asked. "Is there anything you need?"

I said there was not. *What will happen now?* I wondered fearfully. *Has he gone mad?*

"Then I bid you a good night's rest," he said, and closed the door as he left. I fell into a troubled sleep, still in my clothes, forgetting even to recite my evening prayers.

❧◆☙

The next morning Lord Bothwell again knocked on my door. I was awake but little refreshed and I had not yet changed my gown. "Shall we go walking?" he asked, as though I were a guest here for a brief visit and not a virtual prisoner.

I agreed, feeling I had little choice. We strolled near the cliff's edge, overlooking a dark sea laced with whitecaps. The sun floated in a gauzy mist. The path was uneven and strewn with rocks, and I stumbled, turning my ankle, and nearly lost my balance. Lord Bothwell, who had kept a respectful distance, moved quickly to steady me. He drew me to him, not roughly but with unexpected gentleness.

"Mary," he said, "I am asking again that you marry me."

I shook my head and tried to pull away, but he held me close—again not roughly but certainly firmly, so that I could not free myself. He kissed me passionately, though I resisted. It was awkward, for I was a very tall woman and he was a man of only middling height.

"I am again telling you that I will not," I said with a gasp when he released me.

"Then I will keep you here until you change your mind and consent to be my wife," he said, as gaily as though he had just suggested we dance a galliard.

I tried to think of someone to summon for help but knew of no one. Maitland and Huntly had reached Edinburgh and sounded the alarm, and the castle guns had been fired, to no effect. Would help arrive? Lord Bothwell invited me to dine with him; I refused, and then I realized I would not dine at all if I did not accept his invitation. Reluctantly I joined him, and we dined graciously. Afterward he played the lute and then passed it to me. I played poorly, finding no pleasure in the music.

"Have you changed your mind, my lady?" he asked.

"I have not," I said. "And I will not."

That night I again slept restlessly, fearing intrusion, though I was allowed to sleep undisturbed. The next day we again went walking, this time on a different path, and again we had the same conversation, with the same outcome. How long would this continue?

On the third day Lord Bothwell left with several of his horsemen. I had no idea where he had gone or when he would return. In his absence I searched for a way to leave the castle, but the gates were firmly locked and heavily guarded. That evening as I supped alone, I heard noises and a loud voice in the courtyard. Lord Bothwell had returned, but he did not come to the hall. When I had finished my supper, I returned to my bedchamber. I found an unfinished piece of embroidery among my belongings, and I decided to work on it to calm myself. I was quietly stitching when the door opened—there was no knock this time—and Lord Bothwell entered. He dismissed my maidservants, who scurried away like frightened mice.

"Well, Mary," he said, removing his jerkin and doublet and tossing them aside, "are you ready to accept my proposal to wed?"

"No, James, I am not." Did he hear the irony in the way I spoke his name?

"Then I shall have to find another way to persuade you."

Against my will he lifted me and carried me to my bed, ignoring my protests. I fought hard against him, but he was strong as a young bull, and my struggles were useless. "You are a wild one, Mary Stuart," he muttered, and then his mouth was hard on mine, his hands found their way beneath my petticoats, and his body joined mine.

"There," he said when he had finished, "now you belong to me. I have possessed you, and you have no choice but to marry me."

He arranged his clothes and left quickly, and I lay weeping and wishing for death.

The next morning I lay abed until late, too wretched and broken in spirit to rise. When at last I did, I found a servant and made a timid inquiry as to Lord Bothwell's whereabouts. "Gone to Edinburgh on his fastest horse, madam."

I would have given much to have the Four Maries with me, especially devout Seton, the only one of the four not married and still vowing she would not. I wondered if the others had found satisfaction in marriage, as I surely had not in my first two. Now it seemed I would be coerced into a third. My friends' presence would have comforted and strengthened me.

The iron gates were again locked and guarded. I considered ordering the guards to open them for me. I was their queen. They could not refuse me. I could order the stable master to saddle a horse for me, command several guards to accompany me, and set out for Edinburgh alone. It was already late in the day; it would be long after midnight before we reached Holyrood. I was ill, with a weary and aching body—could I withstand such a long, hard ride? And what was in store for me in Edinburgh? Lord Bothwell had said there was an uprising against me. What if those who had plotted the murder of the king were now planning my death as well?

I managed a weak smile and a greeting for the guards at the gate, and then I returned to my bedchamber to await the return of Lord Bothwell.

VIII

A Woman Who Fights Is As Likely to Lose As She Is to Win

WHEN DID MY LIFE BEGIN to spiral dangerously out of control? Was it when I married Henry? Or later, after he was murdered? I wonder now what accommodations I might have made had he lived to bring us some peace and concord. I had already begun to lose the love and loyalty of my people. Perhaps, given the proper guidance, Henry would have grown into his role as king of Scotland. If he had not, would I have been strong enough, wise enough, to rule effectively in spite of him? And what of my brother? What role would he play? As it is, I made a disastrous decision that has brought me to ruin.

CHAPTER 45

Another Union

LORD BOTHWELL KEPT ME at Dunbar Castle for twelve days. Each day he asked the same question: "Are you ready to marry me, Mary?" And each day he received the same answer. "No, James. Not now. Not later. Never."

He did not pretend to love me. That was not the issue. He did not offer me love, nor did I ask for it. He offered me protection. He offered me his loyalty. Not the loyalty of the marriage bed—he was incapable of that. Gradually, during those days at Dunbar, I came to see that I needed his strong hand to keep the rebellious Scottish lords in check and help me regain control of my realm. I could not do it alone. These men would run roughshod over any woman who tried to rule without a man at her side.

We talked at length about what steps needed to be taken to restore order. We talked as we rode together near Dunbar, as we walked along the lonely path overlooking the sea, and as we supped together in the evenings. At night he came to my bed, though I pleaded with him not to. When I resisted, it seemed only to inflame his ardor.

"I like a woman who fights," he said approvingly as I wept and struggled. "You are indeed my wild queen!"

"You will get me with child," I cried. "My reputation will be ruined. And I am committing a grievous sin by lying with a married man."

"Aha!" he crowed triumphantly. "I can absolve you of that sin, for I am no longer a married man! Lady Jean has accepted my terms, and the judge has issued a divorce decree. I am a free man again! You have no more excuses for refusing my suit, Mary, and many reasons for accepting it. You have no choice but to make me your husband."

And so, God help me, I agreed to marry him.

Early in the morning of the sixth of May, we left Dunbar Castle accompanied by a large contingent of musketeers and rode straight to Edinburgh, keeping up a hard pace. Bothwell sent a messenger on ahead to the castle to order the great guns fired in salute as we arrived. Late in the day we entered the city by the West Port.

He dismounted and took the reins from me. "I will lead your horse," he said.

Up the hill we went toward the castle. The boom of the cannon summoned huge crowds—crowds that in the past had always turned out to cheer for their queen. But this time there was no cheering. Only silence and grim stares greeted us.

"These fools will pay for their insolence," Bothwell muttered angrily.

His first item of business was to order the preacher at the High Kirk of St. Giles to proclaim the marriage banns on the next Sunday, the eleventh of May. The minister, an assistant to John Knox, refused. James threatened to have him hanged. When I stepped in and ordered the minister to read the banns, he obeyed but delivered a long harangue from the pulpit condemning the marriage.

I felt as though I were wading upstream through waist-deep, rapidly flowing water, moving slowly against the current while everything else sped past me in a blur. If someone asked a question, I was hard put to answer. Bothwell made all the decisions for me. Once again I suspected him of using the black arts to control me, but I had not the strength to stop him.

On Monday, May twelfth, I officially pardoned him for my abduction, and later that day I created him duke of Orkney and lord of Shetland, ranks that made him suitable to marry a queen. But even as we were enacting this ritual, with the newly proclaimed duke swirling his ermine-trimmed robes while I sat on my gilded throne, I was much aware of growing opposition to my coming marriage. All those men who had signed the bond at Ainslee Tavern urging me to marry the earl of Bothwell were now changing their position. Not just the lords of Scotland opposed it but the foreign emissaries who learned of it. And my dearest friends, the Four Maries, each in turn had warned me in the strongest terms: *Do not marry this man.*

Livingston—Lusty, the outspoken one—added, "I once wagered a set of combs that this would come about. I said he would get himself out of the Tower of London and set himself to wed the richest and most beautiful lady in all of Scotland. Do you remember? My lady Mary, if you marry him, you will surely live to regret it."

I would hear none of this. "But I recognize his good qualities, and they are many," I protested. "I have truly come to care for him and to trust that he will be my protector!" I could not bring myself to confess the shame I felt at having lain with him.

The Four Maries had stared at me in disbelief.

I stopped my ears to it all as I lifted the golden coronet of a duke and placed it on his brow. It seemed I could hear only his voice and no others, and I saw in him only what I wished to see.

I married James Hepburn in the great hall of Holyrood Palace on the fifteenth of May. At ten o'clock in the morning I entered the hall wearing the long white *deuil* of a widow. There was not time to have a new gown made for the occasion, but my seamstresses stitched gold braid to a black gown of cut velvet, and underneath it I wore a black taffeta petticoat that had been given a new lining of red silk. The bridegroom strutted about in a handsome suit of silk and velvet, a suit that had been one of Henry's favorites. The ceremony was the Protestant rite, which pained me, but James was Protestant and would not hear of a Catholic sacrament.

Following the ceremony, I removed my widow's veil and changed into a yellow silk gown for the wedding dinner, to which many had been invited but which few had chosen to attend. My husband had decided to forgo the masques and dancing that I so enjoyed.

"A dinner is enough," he said. "No need for more than that."

I acquiesced silently.

We sat at a long table in the great hall, I at one end and James at the other, far enough apart that he could not see the tears that rolled slowly down my cheeks and dropped, one by one, onto my uneaten food.

Later that night a placard appeared outside the palace with a quote from the Roman poet Ovid. *This is what the people say: Harlots marry in the month of May.*

My people held that I was a fallen woman. King Henry had been dead only three months, and I had just married the man they were convinced had murdered him.

I was miserable. I had begun to believe that I loved my new husband. Despite his sometimes rough behavior, his words to me had been kind, and I thought that gentle manner signified his growing affection for me. But within a single day of our wedding we had begun to argue, sometimes bitterly. He had me in tears almost constantly with his suspicions and accusations. I tried hard to please him, but nothing I did satisfied him. I felt I could not endure more.

"If someone will only bring me a knife, I shall kill myself!" I cried, and I truly meant it.

In public I did my best to give the impression that I had made a wise and considered decision to marry James. In his turn, he behaved courteously and showed me great respect as a queen, though in private he treated me with little respect as a woman. I was his to be used as he wished. I could not hide that from my friends, who witnessed much of his abuse and could do nothing to help.

But James and I faced a problem more serious than our own personal turmoil. Three days after my abduction at the River Almond a number of powerful lords had gathered at Stirling. For four days they debated what to do. Calling themselves the Confederate Lords, they set three goals: to free me from captivity; to kill the earl of Bothwell, whom they termed a barbarous tyrant and the cruel murderer of the king; and to protect Prince James, all for the good of Scotland. As I was creating Lord Bothwell the duke of Orkney and preparing for our wedding in Edinburgh, these rebel lords had set up a court at Stirling in my son's name. They performed a masque that showed Lord Bothwell being condemned and hanged. When James inevitably learned about it, he went nearly mad with rage. The oaths that spewed from his mouth were the foulest I had yet heard.

"I shall be revenged on these so-called Confederate

Lords!" he shouted, and continued with a stream of profanities.

I was angry too, but most of all I was deeply hurt that men I had once trusted had turned against me. Then came the worst desertion of all: James and Sir William Maitland got into a heated argument that became very ugly. Sir William declared that he had had enough and was joining the rebel lords.

Sir William, my secretary of state and close adviser for so long, could not bring himself to bid me farewell. His wife, my oldest and dearest friend, Mary Fleming—La Flamin, the chief of the Four Maries—came to me later that day when she thought I would be alone. Both of us burst into tears.

"There are no words for what I feel," she said, choking on her sobs.

"Nay," I said, "there are not."

We held each other in silence, except for the sounds of our weeping.

"Adieu, *ma chère* Marie," I said at last and hid my eyes as she tiptoed from my chamber.

"Adieu! Adieu!"

CHAPTER 46

Rebellion

"THE CONFEDERATE LORDS are preparing to attack," James said gruffly. "Take what you need, Mary. We are leaving."

"Where are we to go, my lord?" I asked.

"Borthwick," he answered shortly, and strode out of my presence chamber.

I called for my maidservants to begin gathering clothing and whatever else might be needed. James was shouting "Hurry! Hurry!" and I was forced to leave almost empty-handed.

We rode hard for Borthwick, south of Edinburgh. I had not been to the castle for several years, but I knew it was well fortified, one great tower with walls several feet thick. We had been there for four days when the rebel lords surrounded the castle and prepared to launch an attack. It was an hour before midnight and still light.

"You will be all right here," James assured me. "It is me

they want. Meet me at Dunbar when you think it is safe for you to get away."

With those words, James flung himself on his fastest horse and escaped through the postern, a small concealed gate in the rear of the castle. When the rebels realized their quarry had eluded them, they entertained themselves by shouting insults at me. A strange way to treat a queen they had sworn to free from captivity! I tried to ignore them while I made my own preparations to leave. When they tired of taunting me, they withdrew.

I rested for a few hours. Then, just before dawn, I made my escape. Dressed in men's clothes borrowed from a servant, I had myself lowered from a window by a rope and chair to the ground. A horse waited, saddled and ready, and then I, too, was away through that same postern. Not far from Borthwick several of my husband's men met me and escorted me to Dunbar, where James was waiting.

His greeting on that occasion was so warm that I was reassured of the affection he had for me. Our reunion was brief. Within an hour he was on his horse again, this time to round up his troops. The Confederate Lords had seized Edinburgh Castle, and three thousand armed men were ready to fight for the rebels in the name of my son, Prince James, for the benefit of Lord Moray.

We were at war.

And I knew with certainty that I was with child.

I could not afford now to sit and weep and yield to melancholy. I had to act. It was imperative to take possession of Edinburgh and put down the rebels at once. Summoning what troops I had, I set out from Dunbar with a scant handful but gathered more on the way. By the time I reached Haddington, six hundred men followed my command, not nearly as many as I had thought would answer my call, but I did have with me three cannon from the munitions store at Dunbar.

James met me with his force of two thousand. He laughed when he saw me. "What is that you are wearing, my queen?"

With no time to pack more than a handful of hairpins before I left Holyrood, I had assembled an outfit belonging to a local woman—a short red petticoat and skirt, a pair of sleeves, a partlet covering my neck and shoulders, and a jaunty velvet hat.

"My military garb," I replied gaily. "Practical for riding and visible to my troops."

That night while our soldiers rested and prepared for battle, James and I stayed at Seton Palace. We were both weary but also tensely exhilarated, anticipating the battle that was sure to take place the next day when our forces met those of the rebel lords. It was in this setting that I chose to tell James the news that affected us most personally.

I stated the situation simply. "James, I am with child."

He gazed at me, nervously smoothing the ends of his mustache. "You are sure?"

"I am, my lord."

"Yet one more reason, then, that we must achieve victory. For my son!"

"Aye, James. For *our* son."

❦

The morning sky was light at five o'clock when we rode out together. We stopped a few miles east of Edinburgh and drew up our army on the crest of Carberry Hill. The rebel lords and their superior forces took a position farther down the hillside. The summer sun rose, the day grew hotter, and our men began to suffer from thirst. Though they were loyal to us, they did not want to fight this battle, and as the day wore on, I watched our army quietly melt away.

"We are outmanned," I told James. "It will be a bloodbath."

"Then I have a solution," he said, leaping to his feet. "I will issue a challenge of man-to-man combat, and that will determine the outcome with the loss of only one life—mine or a rebel lord's."

I opposed the idea, for I did not want him killed. But he was defiant.

When the challenge was issued, it seemed that first one rebel lord and then another would answer it. Finally, believing that such a fight would resolve nothing, I stepped forward and intervened.

"What is it you require of me?" I asked the leader of the rebels.

"Your surrender, madam" came the reply.

"Then I am ready to surrender, in the best interests of the people of Scotland."

After some discussion it was decided that I would give myself up peacefully to the lords and that I could do so safely and without fear of treachery. James Hepburn, duke of Orkney, would go free.

James and I looked at each other. Hastily he drew from his leather bag a tightly rolled document and pressed it into my hand. "Mary, take this and keep it safe. 'Tis a copy of the bond agreeing to the murder of King Henry and bearing the signatures of those who plotted his death. There are a number, all of whom you know well. You will find mine there too."

I drew in my breath sharply. "Yours, James? You are telling me now that you took part in the murder?"

"I did, madam. I did it for what I believed was the good of Scotland. But I hasten to add that the other signers are among those lords who now stand waiting for me to go so they may kill me later, and they fear that if they keep me here I will point the finger exactly where it should be pointed. And now I do humbly ask your forgiveness."

James dropped to his knees and gazed up at me.

It was a bitter blow. So I had indeed married my husband's murderer! And yet . . . and yet . . . My heart was in turmoil. I felt as though I were falling through a vast empty void.

"Aye, James Hepburn. I do forgive you." I took his two hands in both of mine and raised him up.

"I thank you for that, my queen. Mary, my wild queen!

This is not the end of our story. I swear to you that I will do all in my power to rescue you. Until then, take care for our son! Farewell!"

We embraced one last time. I watched my husband mount his horse and ride away with a dozen horsemen. "Farewell, dear James!" I called after him, but he did not look back.

Then I turned, bowed my head, and offered my hand to the rebel lord who came to take me prisoner.

CHAPTER 47

Imprisoned Again

WHAT A SIGHT I must have been! My hair had come loose from its pins and flew wildly about my face. The short red petticoat and partlet I had borrowed days earlier were caked with dust and mud. But the rebel lords helped me mount my horse as though I were dressed in my most regal robes and then led me away.

Such royal treatment disappeared in an instant when the rebel soldiers began to shout terrible things at me. "Burn the whore!" "Kill the murderess!" As though I were the one responsible for Henry's death, when in fact the murderers were among these men who had made me their prisoner!

I was taken to Edinburgh by a pack of ruffians. The streets were so crowded, my horse could scarcely pick its way through the screaming, cursing mob. Their shouts followed me all the way to the house on the High Street where I was to stay, the home of the provost who had first welcomed me to Edinburgh. I had no idea how long I would be kept there. Half dragged by my guards, I climbed the stair to an upper chamber and collapsed on the bed, numb to any feeling but the deepest despair.

There were no servants to help me undress, bring me warm water for washing, see to my comfort. Instead there were guards outside my chamber, and two more were stationed inside, men who would not leave even when I wished to use the chamber pot. Would there be no end to my humiliation?

"Is this the honorable treatment I was promised?" I demanded. I got no reply, only the sneers of my guards.

I lurched to the window. Across the way, where I could not fail to see it, hung a white banner depicting King Henry's body lying beneath a green tree with a small figure representing Prince James kneeling close by. It bore the motto *Judge and avenge my cause, O Lord.*

In the street below, the jeers and curses raged throughout the long night. "Kill her!" "Drown her!" "She is not fit to live!"

Were the guards there to protect me or to prevent my escape? Suppose those who wished for my death overcame them, or were actually helped by them! I was so terrified that I could not close my eyes, and dawn arrived with the furious voices still echoing throughout the city.

⸎

Hours later I was led on foot down the High Street to Holyrood Palace, insulted by rude shouts from angry crowds as I made my way. Faithful Mary Seton and Mary Livingston waited for me, and I fell into their arms, weeping gratefully at the sight of their loving, if deeply worried, faces. I had not eaten for some time and was weak with hunger, and when supper was brought I ate greedily. One of the rebel lords stood behind my stool. When I was only half finished, he announced that the meal was over and I must prepare for a hard ride.

"Where are you taking me, sir?" I demanded.

He replied insolently that the destination was not my concern.

"Are my ladies to come with me?" I asked.

They were not. Only two maidservants, sisters Maggie and Maud, could accompany me.

Nor was I permitted to take any clothing but a sleeping shift and a cloak. Among the things I left behind was the bond James had placed in my hands, the document bearing the signatures of the lords who had agreed to the murder of King Henry.

The two Maries and I began weeping and protesting until the lord ordered us to "be quiet and cease your wailing." After another hasty embrace, I followed my captor, my lips trembling and my tears still flowing.

It was dark when I was taken from Holyrood Palace, and the crowds had mostly dispersed, save for a few drunken louts shouting profanities. A boat waited at Leith to take us across the Firth of Forth. We then rode north, traveling fast. I was feeling quite ill, but when I pleaded to slow down, the guards whipped my horse and drove it on.

Around midnight we reached Loch Leven, an enormous lake with a forbidding castle on a bleak island far from the shore. One of the guards pulled me roughly from my horse and thrust me into a boat. No one spoke; the only sound was the creak of the oars. The boat reached the pier, and I was hauled, stumbling, into a round tower and up several flights of stairs to a chamber no better than a cell for a common criminal: two or three rude pallets on the floor, a bucket and a basin, and little else for comfort. I threw myself onto one of the pallets and sank into a state resembling death.

I knew about Lochleven Castle. The laird to whom it belonged was William Douglas, a half brother of my own half brother Lord Moray. Their mother, Lady Margaret Douglas, had always resented me, believing that her son Moray deserved the Scottish throne, not I. The old lady was certainly no friend to me.

After a fortnight in the tower, my strength slowly returned, as did my will, and I began to plot how I could escape from this vile prison. I would need friends to help me. I began to converse warmly with those responsible for guarding me. One was Lord Ruthven, who had always been among those opposed to me; now he brought me news from Edinburgh. I longed for word of my husband, but I held my tongue and merely smiled and nodded and listened to whatever Lord Ruthven wished to tell me. None of it was good.

"The duke's friends are being pursued with the goal of punishing them for the murder of the king," Lord

Ruthven told me. He meant the duke of Orkney, my husband, James.

"And the duke himself?" I asked.

"Summoned to the court to answer for his crimes, or he will be put to the horn and declared an outlaw."

As the days passed, Lord Ruthven was my sole visitor. I observed that he seemed to be growing overly fond of his prisoner, and I looked for ways to use this to my advantage.

"Are you well, my lady queen?" he asked solicitously.

"Not well, Lord Ruthven, but better," I replied. My maidservants, Maggie and Maud, had brought me some fine linen and needle and thread, and I was working on a set of tiny garments for the child I was expecting in a few months.

Lord Ruthven began to walk about, inspecting the small chamber, which had recently been much improved with the addition of a proper bed and other furnishings, even a tapestry on the rough stone wall and a threadbare carpet on the floor.

"Are you comfortable then?"

I looked at him incredulously. "Is a prisoner ever comfortable?"

"Perhaps I could bring you something that would give you pleasure," he suggested.

"My freedom, Lord Ruthven!" I exclaimed. "That is what I am most lacking!"

Abruptly, Lord Ruthven dropped to his knees. "My lady

queen, you have bewitched me! If only you will love me, I will see to it that you are freed."

I was appalled by his proposition. What I had perceived to be his affection for me had gone much further than I had expected, and much more was expected from me in return. Here was a man offering me my liberty, but at what cost? I did not trust him, and I cut him off before he could say more. "Lord Ruthven, I find your offer insulting. I bid you leave me and not return."

I had been imprisoned at Lochleven for more than a month when I experienced severe pain and realized that I would miscarry my child. A physician was brought from the town of Kinross, on the western shore of the loch, but he could do nothing to save the infants—I learned that I had been carrying twins—and little to stanch the flow of blood.

As I lay there in utter desolation, Lord Ruthven, ignoring my order not to return, clattered into my chamber without so much as a by-your-leave, accompanied by several lords.

"Good day to you, my lady," one of them said brusquely. "We have here three documents, a pen, and an inkpot, and we ask that you sign them straightaway."

"Documents?" I asked, too weak even to lift my head. "What documents are these?"

Lord Ruthven cleared his throat. "By the first, you agree to abdicate in favor of your son, Prince James. By the second, you appoint your brother Lord Moray as regent until the prince is of age to rule. And by the third, you nominate the lords to serve until Moray returns from France, which he is expected to do shortly."

I could scarcely believe what I was hearing. I had been right not to trust Lord Ruthven, who had now turned against me. Had I not still been bleeding heavily, I would have risen from my bed and railed at them, giving them every reason at my command why I would not sign, and then I would have ordered them from my chamber and sent them to the devil. But I could do no more than shake my head and whisper, "I will not sign."

"Yes, Mary Stuart, you will sign, and you will do it now!"

"I will not sign," I repeated, my voice a little stronger.

One of the lords bellowed, "Then you had best get up now and dress, because I swear that if you do not sign, we will throw you into the loch and let you drown!"

I gathered what little strength I had and said, slowly but clearly, "You dare to speak that way to your queen and sovereign? I will not sign!"

"Sign, damnable harlot, or I will cut your throat myself!" he roared.

Believing he would do exactly as he threatened, I seized the pen, scribbled a signature on the three documents, and sank back weakly on my pillow. "When I am by the grace of God free again, I shall not honor these, for you know as well as I do that I have signed against my will."

The lords snatched up their documents and stormed out. I heard their footsteps on the stair, receding into silence. A door slammed. A bolt was thrown. *Perhaps,* I thought, *it would have been better to let them throw me in the loch and drown me, for what is my life worth now? Nothing! My country is torn apart by warring factions. I have lost everything I ever valued.*

In the silence that followed the departure of the hateful lords, and in the agony of my soul, I prayed that I might die.

CHAPTER 48

Escape

I DID NOT DIE. Impoverished in body and mind, lacking health and strength, bereft of all I cared for, still I did not die!

Therefore, I decided to live. I had been compelled against my will to sign a document of abdication, and I knew well that a coerced abdication had no force of law. I resolved to build up my endurance, find a way to escape, make my way to England, and ask Queen Elizabeth's help to regain my throne. Only then could I begin to heal my sorely wounded country. That was my plan, and I was determined to see it through.

My two maidservants, Maggie and Maud, were always the best conduits for gossip gathered in the kitchens. They brought me the news that my fourteen-month-old son had been crowned King James VI of Scotland in the parish church at Stirling on the twenty-ninth of July, just five days after I had been forced to sign away my crown.

"Not many attended, my lady queen," Maud told me. "Those that did had to listen to John Knox preach the sermon that went on until your wee bairn screamed so loud it shut the preacher up and he could not go on."

"Knox!" I cried. "So he is back in Edinburgh?"

"Aye, madam, and speaking out most vigorously against you and your husband," reported Maggie, always more inclined to tell me the truth than was her sister, Maud.

"*Wheesht!*" cried Maud, trying to silence Maggie, who enjoyed her role as bearer of ill tidings.

But Maggie would not be silenced. "Called you 'that whore of Babylon,'" she reported smugly. "Said you was a scarlet adventuress and ought to be hanged for murdering the king."

Then Maud could not resist adding, "The preacher said God will send a great plague to Scotland, worse than locusts, worse than fire, if you're not punished."

"And do the people believe him?" I asked.

"Aye, they do, madam. They do."

I wondered if my maids believed him too, but I feared asking, lest they tell me the truth.

In mid-August my brother, having returned from France, came to see me. I had expected the visit for some time, half dreading it, half desiring it. We did not embrace. I did not offer him my hand.

"A fine mess you are in, dear sister!" Lord Moray said coldly. "Were you not warned about where a marriage to a man like Lord Bothwell would lead you—or do we call him Lord Orkney now? It seems you have reaped what you sowed!"

"Surely I do not deserve all of this!" I cried. I was eager to tell him how I had been misused by the rebel lords but found him unsympathetic and began to wish that he would leave, for he was no solace to me at all.

Then he softened his tone and begged me to promise I would not try to escape or ask for help from my Guise relatives or from Queen Elizabeth. When I balked at making such promises, he hardened against me again, and so it went for the rest of his visit—back and forth, back and forth. At times he comforted me, and at other times he threatened, gradually wearing me down, and when he promised he would do what he could to help me, I was persuaded that it was perhaps best for him to assume the regency for the infant king of Scotland.

My brother and I did embrace when he left, and a few days later Maggie and Maud reported that he had been proclaimed regent to act for little James until he came of age.

Too late, I realized that I had been duped. My brother had no intention of helping me. He had the power he wanted and believed by rights was his.

In early autumn, as cruel winds howled around Lochleven and cold rains lashed the windows of my prison, I made a vow that I would reclaim my throne and restore my honor no matter what it took, or how long. I had not yet given up hope that my husband would somehow find a way to rescue me, though garbled rumors had reached me that he had made an escape by ship with the lords in pursuit, had been arrested on his way to France to secure help for me, and was now imprisoned in Norway on charges of piracy. I wondered if I would ever see him again, but I clung to the slender thread that he would keep his promise to me.

I found ways to improve my spirits. Though I had lost the twins who were to have worn the tiny garments I was sewing, I finished a set and gave it to one of the ladies of the castle. I persuaded Lord Douglas to allow me to have my own cook as well as several other domestic servants, including one who was French and enjoyed speaking with me.

Seton was permitted to come to stay with me. We often walked together in the garden when the weather was fit, and since fine weather was a rarity on the loch, we walked there even when it was foul. On long winter evenings we read to each other and played cards by a small peat fire. We never tired of each other's company.

On the eighth of December I observed my twenty-fifth birthday. I asked for and received a lute and invited some of the servants and residents of gloomy Lochleven Castle to my chambers in the tower for music. We even danced! At Christmas I joined the Douglas family at a Yuletide feast. There I found the companionship of Lord Douglas's handsome and charming younger brother, George, who was fondly called Pretty Geordie by his family. We talked together several times, and I began to see that Geordie might very well be my way out of Lochleven.

During the long, harsh winter I cultivated the friendship, and then the love, of Geordie. He was younger than
I—just twenty—and obviously smitten. We began to meet
secretly, and though he pledged his love to me I cautioned
him that there was really nothing he could gain from this.

"I am a married woman," I reminded him, though I was
under continual pressure to divorce Lord Orkney. "And I
am a queen. I can offer you nothing but my heartfelt thanks
and sisterly affection for the help you give me."

"Then that shall be enough for me," he said, his wide
young eyes shining with adoration.

Geordie arranged for a boat to take a certain "laundress"
from the castle to the village on the mainland shore. He
helped me with the disguise, wrapping a muffler around my
face and lacing heavy boots on my feet. On a blustery morning in March, after an imprisonment of more than nine
months and carrying a basket heaped with linens from my
own bed, I made my way to the jetty where the boat was
moored and scrambled awkwardly aboard. I had never
done anything like this in my life, accustomed as I was to
being assisted whether I needed it or not. I nodded to the
boatman, who untied the boat and began to row while
keeping up a steady stream of conversation. I replied with
nods and murmurs.

We were halfway across the loch, the wind kicking up
little whitecaps, when suddenly the boatman stopped rowing and stared at me. I, in turn, stared at my boots and

prayed that he had not recognized me. But he lunged at me, trying to pluck off my muffler. My hands flew up to stop him, and he began to laugh.

"The hands of a lady!" he cried. "I'll say it plainly: the fair white hands of a queen! 'Tis true, isn't it?"

"Aye," I said, "it is true, indeed, but I beg you to keep rowing to the shore, and I will pay you all I have."

He paused, considering my offer. "'Tis not that I lack sympathy for you, madam, but 'twould sure be the end of me if Sir William found out I had helped his best and most famous prisoner escape."

"Then do with me as you will," I said, thoroughly dispirited. "Though it may mean my death."

"Nay, my lady, I won't let that happen. I will take you back, and you must slip into the castle the same way you came out, and none will be the wiser."

That was the end of that, though I fretted that the boatman would not keep his word. My lovelorn friend Geordie despaired at least as much as did I that our plan had failed.

"We shall try again," he said firmly. "But the next time we will plan more carefully, and I promise you that we shall succeed."

Several weeks later I made a second escape attempt. This time Geordie enlisted the help of Willie Douglas, a young page, not yet sixteen, and rumored to be Sir William's illegitimate son, though he was officially described as an orphan. Little Willie, as he was called, would row me in a boat to the village on the mainland shore, where Geordie would meet us and lead us to the town of Kinross. Lord Seton, Mary's brother, would be waiting at Kinross with a small group of armed men.

There were many pieces to this plan that had to fit together perfectly if it was to succeed. The first challenge was to escape the constant companionship of the laird's wife, who was expecting a child but who often—too often, in fact—liked to sleep in my bedchamber; his mother, old Lady Douglas, who talked ceaselessly; and his young daughter, Fiona, and her cousin Kirsten, who followed me around worshipfully, begging me to tell them stories about my life in France. Somehow I was going to have to elude this gaggle of chattering females.

The laird's wife unwittingly cooperated by giving birth late in April, an event that served to distract the others for several days. Therefore, on a rare sunny Sunday afternoon, the second of May, while most members of the laird's family were enjoying themselves at May Day celebrations on the eastern end of the island, Little Willie stowed some clothing and other items in one of the boats tied up at the jetty near the castle's main gate, which faced west. He took this opportunity to allow all the other boats to fill partway with water—not enough to sink them but enough so that bailing would be necessary. He still needed to get the key to unlock the main gate.

Later, the family went in to supper, inviting me to join them. I declined, pleading a headache. Seton and I exchanged our clothes; I put on her red kirtle, she took my blue one, and I covered myself with her long mantle, pulling the hood up over my hair.

"You must not worry about me, dear Mary," Seton counseled. "If an alarm is raised and they come looking for you, I will be sitting in your chair and stitching on your embroidery, and that will gain you a little time. And I shall not worry about you, for I know that my brother will keep you safe."

I waited by the window of my tower chamber, watching for Willie's signal. When it came—he pulled a red kerchief from a pocket—I kissed Seton and crept down the winding stair to the courtyard. Servants were bustling about, but none paid me the slightest attention. I was not concerned about them; it was Fiona and Kirsten who worried me. And indeed, there they were. I held my breath, but they mistook me for Mary Seton; I was holding a prayer book, and they passed by without interrupting my devotions.

I continued to murmur prayers until I joined Willie near the main gate.

"I have it," he said, grinning and brandishing a big iron key. "Sir William always hangs it on a hook near the door."

The lock resisted at first. Willie cursed softly. My nerves, already stretched taut, grew even tighter. At last the lock yielded, and Willie pushed open the heavy gate just enough for us to slip through and then closed and locked it again. He tossed the key into the mouth of a squat black cannon as we ran past. "That should slow them down for a while," he said.

We hurried out onto the jetty, and Willie pointed out

the half-submerged boats. We jumped into the only dry one and cast off the ropes, and he began to row as hard as he could across the loch. It was about a mile to Kinross. I marked the point at which the boatman had seen through my disguise as a laundress.

"Do you think Sir William has discovered our absence by now?" I asked Willie.

"Not yet," he said. "They are entertaining guests from the other islands, and there is plenty of wine." Then he added, "And when they do, they will discover that all the boats are filled with water."

"The guests' boats as well?"

"Of course!" he said, pleased with himself.

Geordie, the laird's brother, was holding several fine horses, saddled and ready, as we came ashore. "From the laird's stables," he explained. "He keeps them here on the mainland, rather than ferry them back and forth to the island. Fortunate for us."

"He will be beside himself when he learns what has happened!" I exclaimed. "His prisoner gone and his horses too!"

"Aye, he will," Geordie agreed dryly.

I mounted the gelding Geordie recommended. "Willie, will you go back now to Lochleven? How will you explain what has happened?"

He shook his head. "Nay, my queen. I'll not go back. I have pledged myself to serve you."

"As have I," added Geordie.

I began to make a little speech of gratitude, thanking them both for their support, but Geordie was eager to be off. "You may thank us later, madam. Now we must find Lord Seton and his horsemen and put as many miles as possible between us and Sir William."

And off we rode. For the first time in nearly a year, I was free!

Chapter 49

Freedom

WE RODE HARD through the soft spring evening, heading directly south from the loch. I was jubilant. My strength had returned, as had my confidence. I was at liberty. How glorious! A pale light still remained in the sky as we made for the ferry where the Firth of Forth narrowed and found boatmen willing to take us across.

When my companions met again on the south shore, we speculated on what might be happening back at Lochleven Castle.

"Sir William is in a fury," said Geordie. "He has found himself locked in from the outside. His key is gone. He cannot remember where he keeps the duplicate. He calls everyone to look for it."

Willie continued, "His face is red with rage. He sends servants clambering over the wall. They report that the boats are all filled with water and must be bailed. He searches for Geordie and me, first one, then the other. He cannot find either."

"Suddenly he remembers his royal prisoner," I added, laughing. "She is gone!"

I had not laughed so heartily in a very long time, but beneath the laughter I was uneasy. What no one said was that Sir William had certainly reached the mainland by now. He would have found his stables raided and sounded the alarm. We were surely being hunted. What was more, he would have sent word to my brother Lord Moray, now in Glasgow. We could not afford to stop or even slow down.

Lord Seton rode in the lead, taking us to Niddry Castle, another of the fortresses that belonged to his family. "Accommodations will be simple," he warned me. "Nothing luxurious has been prepared for us, for I did not want rumors to get out concerning our royal guest."

"Does your sister know your plan?" I asked, suddenly fearful that the laird in his rage might pry the information out of Mary Seton, my stand-in for the past several hours.

"She would not think of Niddry. It has never been her favorite place. Too bleak, she claims."

"Bleaker than Lochleven?"

Geordie and Willie laughed. "There is naught bleaker than Lochleven!"

We reached Niddry around midnight. It was as Lord Seton described: starkly simple. Waiting for me were two loyal men. One was my husband's cousin Sir Alexander Hepburn, whom I dispatched to secure Dunbar Castle for me. He agreed to leave at once and ride through the night. The other was Sir James Hamilton.

After a few hours of sleep—I slept more soundly than I had in some time—we were ready to move on to Craigne-than Castle, belonging to Hamilton. Within a day or two I had established a small court at the laird's castle. This gave me a base to rally support and make necessary decisions. I did not want to go into battle again—I had had quite enough of that at Carberry Hill, where our army had been so badly outnumbered.

"It may be your only opportunity to seize the throne that is rightfully yours," Geordie reminded me. He had no love for his half brother Lord Moray—who of course was my half brother as well. I had come to loathe Moray as much as I loathed anyone, understanding finally that any kindness he had ever shown me had been with an eye toward one goal: to rule Scotland as its king.

"You must fight," insisted Lord Seton and Geordie, as well as the others.

In the end I agreed, as it became clearer each day that I was still much loved by the Scots who lived here in the countryside, far from Edinburgh. Many of the lords who had at first joined the rebels were now deserting their ranks and coming to side with me. I knew that I had superior numbers. My troops would triumph, my army would win the day, and my brother would be vanquished once and for all. I would put him on trial for treason, as he deserved. I would not forgive him for the way he had treated me. Our numbers continued to swell.

On Thursday, the thirteenth of May, I knelt and prayed with my troops and then mounted one of Sir William's finest chargers. I planned to ride at the head of my newly formed army toward Dumbarton, the huge and nearly impregnable fortress from which I had sailed for France twenty years earlier. At Dumbarton, to the northwest on the far side of Glasgow, I would be able to unite my allies to fight against Lord Moray's rebel troops.

Though I felt sure my troops would carry the day, my heart was pounding as the battle began. Alas, from the very beginning, it went badly! The lord set to lead the main army failed completely in his command, and in less than an hour more than a hundred of my men lay dead, and three hundred more were taken prisoner—including my dear friend Lord Seton, who had been dangerously wounded. Lord Moray had won. I tasted again the bitterness of defeat.

"Flee," urged Geordie. "You must, madam. Flee for your very life."

Young Willie stood with me, tears in his eyes. "Aye, my lady queen. I will go with you and share whatever fate befalls you."

I nodded. "To my stronghold at Dumbarton."

Geordie stopped his anxious pacing and stepped forward. "Too dangerous, madam. You will be cut off. You must flee southward."

I considered. I could not abide the thought of being seized by Lord Moray and imprisoned again after less than a fortnight of freedom. Dumbarton was too far, and too big a risk. Grimly, I agreed. "Southward, then."

Lord Herries, one of the most loyal of Catholics from the wild western part of Scotland, came to my assistance and offered himself as our guide through this rough and unforgiving country. We set out, winding around and sometimes doubling back to avoid being in the neighborhood of those who would be allied with my enemies. Search parties had been sent out in all directions with the intent of capturing me. We paused long enough to destroy an ancient wooden bridge to further impede those who might be following close behind.

The weather turned hot and then cold, and we were so hungry and thirsty I did not see how we could keep going. But we did—more than ninety miles without knowing exactly where I was headed, or where I would end. I slept for a time on the hard, rocky ground of a poor-looking farm, shivering with cold, though young Willie gave me his jerkin for a pillow and Geordie covered me with his doublet.

When I awoke, an old crone brought out a basin of oatmeal and a spoon and offered it to me, along with a pitcher of soured milk. That was my supper, and I was glad to have it and thanked her for it. She smiled broadly—she was missing several teeth—and replied in the Gaelic language that I could scarcely understand, though I thought she addressed me as "my sovereign queen."

"How do you know who I am?" I asked, surprised, for I was mud spattered and uncombed and looked anything but regal.

Still smiling she reached out and touched a lock of my

auburn hair, which had gone without dressing for several days. I understood: she recognized me by my hair.

My companions insisted that we could not afford to rest any longer. We rode through the night and stopped in the hour just before dawn at the home of the laird of Lochinvar, where I borrowed clean linens and a mantle and hood.

"Have you a knife, Willie?" I asked. The boy hovered nearby, ready to be of assistance whenever I let him.

He hesitated, no doubt fearing that I intended to do harm to someone, perhaps even myself. "Aye, my lady," he replied tentatively.

"Then do me the favor of cutting off my hair. I do not wish to be recognized by it."

Willie did as I asked, working quickly, until hanks of long reddish hair lay on the ground. I saw Willie twist a lock of hair into a circlet and put it away in the bosom of his shirt, and Geordie did the same.

We were on our way again, stopping briefly at Lord Herries's castle for fresh horses and then pressing on to a castle belonging to Lord Maxwell, a friend of Herries and a man faithful to my cause. It was the opinion of these two lords that I would be safe there while I decided on my next move.

"You can surely hold out here for at least forty days," said Lord Maxwell. "That will give us time to rally our forces and to conquer the regent Moray once and for all."

"Or to arrange to have help sent by your family in France, troops to assist you or a boat to take you there," said Lord Herries.

I heard them out, listening carefully to the arguments advanced by each of my devoted friends. Then I interrupted them. "Gentlemen," I began, "I do value your advice, but I have already made my decision. I will go to England and place myself in the hands of my dear cousin and friend Queen Elizabeth. I have no doubt that the good lady will make me welcome, and when the time is right, she will do whatever is necessary to help me regain the throne of Scotland."

My friends objected vehemently to my plan. "I will say it bluntly, madam," declared Lord Herries, "you must not trust Queen Elizabeth. The English have a reputation for clapping Scottish sovereigns in prison. What persuades you that she will not do the same to you?"

The more they tried to convince me otherwise, the more stubbornly I held to my belief that my sister-queen could not refuse to help me. Though I had lost or had taken from me most items of value—including the bond James had given to me before he rode off, and a silver casket containing a number of important letters—I had somehow kept hold of the diamond ring that Elizabeth had sent me as a token of her friendship. I produced it now from the chain I wore around my neck and proposed to send it to the queen along with a letter begging for her help.

"Permit me to have my own way," I told the sad-faced men gathered around me.

The two lords and the rest of my disconsolate friends stared at me. I did not want to wait for Elizabeth's reply. She would not refuse me.

"My mind is made up," I said. "Who will come with me?"

I sent the letter and the diamond ring off to Elizabeth. Then, my head shorn and my clothing disguised, I made my way from Lord Maxwell's castle to Glenluce, a Cistercian abbey on the coast of Solway Firth, opposite the shores of England, which were barely visible in the distance.

The next day, the sixteenth of May in the year 1568, after hearing Mass at the abbey chapel, I prepared to leave Scotland, not quite seven years after I had returned there from France. At three o'clock in the afternoon, with a handful of friends, Little Willie and Geordie Douglas among them, I boarded a small fishing boat.

The boat cast off from the jetty, and the sails bellied and snapped as the winds filled them, carrying us into turbulent waters. I did not bid a tearful farewell to Scotland as I left its shores. Soon Elizabeth would receive my letter and the ring enclosed as a token. She would surely respond with an invitation to come to London. I would have to procure a periwig to cover my shorn head, and I had no proper gowns in which to be received by the queen, but these were small problems, easily solved!

For now, I kept my face turned bravely toward England, certain that I would return one day to my kingdom as the triumphant queen of Scots.

I could not have been more terribly wrong.

CHAPTER 50

Fotheringhay

AS THE FISHING BOAT made its way across Solway Firth
toward England, there came a moment when I was seized
by the certainty that I was making a great mistake by putting my life in the hands of Queen Elizabeth. Better, I
thought, if I had elected to go to France, as Lord Herries
had tried to persuade me.

I hurried to the captain of the little vessel and told him
I wished to change course. "Take me to France," I pleaded,
though I knew the fishing boat was ill-equipped for such a
voyage.

He looked at me as though I were mad. "Cannot do it,
my lady," he replied gruffly. "Tide is against us. Wind too."
He squinted up at a leaden sky. "Storm coming. Take shelter
in the cabin. Save France for another day."

I had no choice but to acquiesce. I had to tell myself that
it would have been difficult, perhaps impossible, to sum-

mon French ships. Calling upon Elizabeth for aid was the better course.

After four hours, the fishing boat reached the small and undistinguished village of Workington. When the lord of Workington Manor recognized who had just disembarked—my shorn head fooled no one—he took us all to his home and offered food and rest and hospitality. The next day, every local person having learned of my arrival, I was greeted by an honor guard and a band of gentlemen and conveyed to Carlisle Castle, where I was installed in pleasant quarters. My needs were well attended, and I was treated with dignity and respect, but I soon realized that I was being kept under heavy guard. I had once again been made a prisoner, but of whom?

As the days went by, one by one by one, I understood that I was imprisoned by order of the queen of England. Elizabeth seemed to have no intention of inviting me to London.

I learned that I was to stand accused of the murder of King Henry.

Through all the years I had tried so earnestly to seal my friendship with Queen Elizabeth and at the same time to assert my God-given right to succession to the English throne, the queen's chief adviser, William Cecil, had implacably opposed me. Cecil wanted to be rid of me by one means or another. If I had never before recognized how dangerous William Cecil was to my very existence, I had to acknowledge it now.

Cecil called for an investigation. He hoped to prove my guilt and keep me shut up forever. My brother Lord Moray was only too willing to help him in order to maintain his position as regent.

I did what I could. Over and over I wrote to my sister-queen begging to see her, but to no avail. Queen Elizabeth refused to meet with me in private or receive me at her court until I had been cleared of the charges of murdering my husband.

In July, after two months at Carlisle, I was removed to Bolton Castle, a high-walled fortress remote from London and equally remote from the Scottish border, so as to preclude any chance of rescue. Many of my servants—cooks, seamstresses, and others—made their way from Scotland to attend me, but the most welcome addition to my modest household was Mary Seton.

We fell into each other's arms, weeping and laughing a little. But when she saw my hair, and the scraps of it that were now growing back to cover my naked skull, Seton, who had been fixing my hair since we were both little more than children, threw up her hands and cried, "Now I know that God has truly sent me to you."

My trial commenced in October. I was not allowed to speak on my own behalf. I will not detail here the events of the trial, but as a result of the machinations of my hated brother and Elizabeth's adviser Cecil, I was found neither guilty nor not guilty. Still I was not allowed to go free.

At the end of January of 1569 I was removed from Bolton Castle to a place even more remote and with even less of a possibility of rescue. From there I was moved again, and yet again. Some of my servants and friends remained with me through it all—Mary Seton was one, Geordie Douglas another. Willie was sent away, a sad parting for us both. There were schemes for my escape, all foiled. So it went, month after month.

❧

My greatest heartache has been the loss of my son. After Lord Moray persuaded me to abdicate, James was crowned king of Scotland when he was still a wee lad of little more than a year; Moray ruled as regent until he was cut down by an assassin's bullet a year and a half later. I wasted not a single tear when I learned of it. James's grandfather the earl of Lennox succeeded as regent, and at Lennox's death, another took his place. I was not permitted to write to James, and if he or his guardians wrote to me at any time during those years, I did not receive their letters. I had very little news of my son, though I was told he was being brought up in the Protestant faith. I longed to see him, to speak with him, to at least have some word of him. All of this was denied me.

The years passed, and I clung to the hope that my son would one day help me to leave my prison and return to Scotland to rule jointly with him. Then in July of 1586, as King James VI of Scotland, my twenty-year-old son signed a treaty with England. Finally I grasped that my son would do nothing for me. He would, he said, honor me with the title of queen mother. I was crushed and furious, in equal measure.

Do not further insult me with the title of Queen Mother, I wrote. *There is neither king nor queen in Scotland but me,* and I signed it *Marie R,* as I always had and still do. I do not know if the letter was ever delivered to him, for I have heard nothing from him since.

That same year, letters were found implicating me in a plot to assassinate Queen Elizabeth, and I was again brought to trial but denied access to the papers and to legal counsel. On the twenty-sixth of October, 1586, I was found guilty and sentenced to death.

Here I have waited, Elizabeth's prisoner for nineteen years. I was twenty-five when I fled Scotland for England, begging for the queen's mercy. I pass the hours with embroidery, remembering how I was tutored in this womanly art by Queen Catherine. I often dream of my early days in France and weep when I awaken to the reality of my life. Sometimes I think of James Hepburn, Lord Bothwell. Years ago, I learned that after a desperate attempt to elude his enemies resulted in his capture, he endured years of solitary confinement, chained to a wall in a Danish prison, and died miserably there in 1578.

For nineteen years I had not given up the hope of meeting face to face the queen whom I call sister and cousin. I learned yesterday that this is now impossible. Six days ago Elizabeth signed the warrant for my execution. The warden has told me to prepare to die today on the scaffold. The hammering in the great hall has stopped. All is silent.

In a few hours, my imprisonment will end, and so will my life.

I write these words from my chamber at Fotheringhay, the last of several English castles where I have been kept prisoner. I have had more than enough time to contemplate the course of my life. From my earliest days I have too often found myself at the center of disastrous events. Many I could not have prevented—the death of my father, for example. The death of François, surely not. But what of the others? David Rizzio? My second husband, Henry? Am I guilty of their deaths? Sometimes I blame the wildness in me; other times I believe it was God's will.

One weakness I surely acknowledge: I have given my trust too easily and to the wrong people. Those closest to me have betrayed me, turned against me, or let me down: my uncles; my brother; my second husband, Henry; my third husband, James Hepburn.

It no longer matters.

In a few hours I will mount the steps to the scaffold to meet the executioner and his bloody ax. I will try to remember my mother's advice given to me many years ago, when I was a child: *It is your duty as queen to appear calm and steadfast, no matter what you may feel.*

That will be the end of it. In a few hours I will die.

Perhaps someone will take note of a motto I once

embroidered—*In my end is my beginning*—and remember the life of Mary, queen of Scots.

MARY CR

Fotheringhay Castle, England

February 8, 1587

Epilogue

AT NINE O'CLOCK on the morning of Wednesday, February 8, 1587, Mary, queen of Scots, dressed in a black satin gown trimmed in velvet and carrying a crucifix and a prayer book, walked calmly to the scaffold in the great hall of Fotheringhay. She was accompanied by the sheriff and other officials and six of the women closest to her. A large crowd of spectators watched in silence. With great dignity she mounted the steps to the scaffold, knelt, and began to pray.

When her prayers were finished, the executioners asked her forgiveness. "I do forgive you," Mary told them, "with my whole heart, for you are about to bring an end to all my troubles." Mary stood, and her weeping women removed her black gown, revealing a red petticoat and bodice, the color of martyrs. One of the women covered Mary's eyes with a blindfold. Mary knelt on the white satin cushion, placed her head on the block, and began to pray in Latin. The executioner raised his ax.

It took three blows to do the deed. Afterward, the executioner seized a handful of auburn hair and raised the severed head, crying, "God save the queen!" But suddenly the hair separated from the skull, and the head fell to the scaffold floor and rolled away while the executioner stared at the wig he was left holding. The crowd gasped. Mary's own hair had turned quite gray during her long captivity. She had chosen to wear a wig to her beheading.

Sixteen years later, Queen Elizabeth died, on March 24, 1603. Although Elizabeth had never officially named him her successor, Mary's son, King James VI of Scotland, was immediately proclaimed King James of England and Ireland. It is said that he eventually regretted his hardhearted treatment of his mother. To atone for it, he arranged for her entombment in Westminster Abbey and honored her with a memorial effigy, larger and more magnificent than the one he also commissioned for Elizabeth.

It is interesting to note that every British monarch from King James's son Charles I to the present-day ruler is descended in a direct line from Mary, queen of Scots. Biographers and historians still debate the innocence or guilt of Mary in the death of her second husband, Henry Stuart. A few still hold that the so-called Casket Letters, offered as evidence against her, are damning. Others insist that the letters are out-and-out forgeries. Nearly everyone agrees that much of the Scottish queen's wildness remains shrouded in mystery.

Bibliography

Fraser, Antonia. *Mary Queen of Scots* (New York: Random House, 1969)

Guy, John. *Queen of Scots: The True Life of Mary Stuart* (New York: Houghton Mifflin, 2004)

Weir, Allison. *Mary, Queen of Scots, and the Murder of Lord Darnley* (New York: Ballantine, 2003)

www.marie-stuart.co.uk The official site of the Marie Stuart Society based in Scotland

Plus innumerable additional websites for details of dress, food, customs, language, etc.

CAROLYN MEYER is the award-winning author of more than fifty books for young people. *The Wild Queen* is the seventh installment in her acclaimed Young Royals series. Carolyn Meyer lives in Albuquerque, New Mexico. Visit her website at **www.readcarolyn.com**.

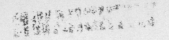